I0655300

IN A GREEN DRESS, SURROUNDED BY EXPLODING CLOWNS

AND OTHER STORIES

ROBERT JESCHONEK

BLASTOFF
BOOKS

IN A GREEN DRESS, SURROUNDED BY EXPLODING CLOWNS
AND OTHER STORIES

Published by Blastoff Books
An Imprint of Pie Press
411 Chancellor Street
Johnstown, Pennsylvania 15904

Subscribe to the Blastoff Books Newsletter:
http://newsletter.blastoffbooks.net

PRAISE FOR IN A GREEN DRESS AND OTHER STORIES

On *In A Green Dress, Surrounded by Exploding Clowns:* "Set a hundred years after Facebook, social networks 'ruled the world,' at least according to the story, and as in reality TV shows, people 'voted to determine others' fates right down to the smallest detail.' The idea of people's lives being controlled by the sort of people who get a thrill out of making their lives a misery seems to be the norm in this story, but Agent Grice wants to change all the negativity, and the possibility that there could be a hacker in (the social network) Crowdlife gives him further concern."
— Sandra Scholes, *SF Site*

On *Piggyback:* "*Piggyback* is narrated by a parasitic creature, undetectable by humans, which controls the actions of a homeless alcoholic. As frightening as this is, the creature itself is terrified of the god-like being it serves. This story is likely to raise a few goosebumps with its notion that there are many unseen entities among us."
—— Victoria Silverwolf, *Tangent Online*

On *As If My Every Word Has Turned to Glass:* "I have been very lucky to have a story of (Jeschonek's) in every issue (of *Pulphouse Fiction Magazine*) I have edited so far. Actually, readers have been lucky. And this amazingly original story of looking at Alzheimer's and a writer's muse will prove the point. And to writers, this might be the most frightening story ever written."
— Dean Wesley Smith, Editor, *Pulphouse Fiction Magazine*

ALSO BY ROBERT JESCHONEK

IN A GREEN DRESS, SURROUNDED BY EXPLODING CLOWNS

Heaving for breath, I spin in a circle, looking for a way out. But I see the same thing in every direction.

Nothing but clowns. Dozens of clowns.

Every one of them laughs, giggles, or guffaws at the same time. They bobble their heads, slap huge clown shoes on the parking lot pavement, and toot horns. All face-paint and bulbous red noses and baggy costumes in all the wild colors of the rainbow, they look like they'd be right at home at a circus or a carnival or a kid's birthday party.

Except for the malevolent sneers etched into every one of their faces. Not to mention the jagged, shark-like teeth lining their red-lipped maws.

As the clowns close in, my heart hammers in my chest. I'm a big guy, I'll fight them--but I'm exhausted after what I've been through. The past two days of nonstop madness have wrecked me, I admit it. And I wasn't feeling up to snuff to begin with; the pain in my gut was bad at the start and has only been getting worse.

Plus which, I'm wearing a bright green knee-length dress and spiked heels.

Not exactly the ideal outfit for a five-eleven, two-hundred-twenty-five-pound guy to wear while fighting a mob of savage clowns.

"Back off!" Even as I shout it over the crazed laughter, I see it does no good. The clowns are still moving toward me.

Swallowing hard, I prepare to make my stand. I crouch and turn slowly, arms extended from my sides.

Suddenly, I hear a wild scream behind me. I whip around just in time to see a clown with a big plastic daisy on its pink derby hat charging toward me.

As I stumble back a step, the unexpected happens. The charging clown gets to within six feet of me and explodes, blowing apart in a burst of orange flame.

I throw up my arms to shield myself. Lumps of dead clown splatter all over me, smelling like burnt bacon.

Then, I hear another shriek and spin to see a second clown charging. Trying to dodge him, I trip on my spiked heels and go down hard.

This time, the clown gets closer, within five feet, before exploding.

And then I hear another scream, and another, and another. I hear three pairs of floppy clown shoes paddling toward me. I wonder how close this new batch will get before blowing up. I wonder if they'll get close enough to take me with them.

And I wish to God that I'd never gotten on the lifehacker radar in Crowdlife.

THREE DAYS AGO, I could not have imagined how things would turn out for me. I was busy just doing my job as an agent of Crowdlife Outcomes Enforcement--the C.O.E.

My last case, the one that changed my life, led me to a rundown tenement apartment on Skid Row. A family of five was living in this three-room dump, dressed in rags, immersed in squalor.

Make that a family of five plus a screeching chimpanzee in a purple turban and glittering gold diaper.

"Look at this place!" said the man of the house, Mr. Byron Chellingham. "There's been a mistake, I tell you!"

"Sorry, sir," I said, looking around the dilapidated apartment. "Crowdlife has spoken."

"Like hell!" Byron swatted at what was either a passing bug or a gnat-cam--one of the multitude of tiny airborne camera-bots zipping through modern humanity's environment at all times. Gnat-cams constantly beamed video and audio signals to augmented reality devices like my contact lenses and aural implants, enabling them to enhance what I and others saw and heard. Gnat-cams also streamed data back to the social network providers; without them, Crowdlife, Yapstream, and the like wouldn't have a window on the world.

"Calm down, Mr. Chellingham." I raised my voice, trying to snap him out of it...doing my best to hide the fact that I felt sorry for him. "You need to get a grip, sir."

"But someone gamed the system! Don't you see?" Byron flapped his arms like he was trying to take flight. His bright green eyes were bugged out, his wife-beater tank top t-shirt soaked with sweat. "We don't *deserve* this!"

As if to punctuate his comment, the diapered chimp screamed its lungs out on the far side of the room, in the filthy makeshift kitchen.

"You signed the T.O.S." With practiced flicks of my eyes, I played the controls of my A.R. contact lenses. The image of a terms of service agreement appeared in midair between us, visualized as a sheet of paper filled with print and adorned with Bryon's signature at the bottom. Long ago, he had signed over his destiny to Crowdlife, the ultimate crowdsourcing social network, just like all the rest of us.

A century after Facebook and company, social networks truly ran the world. Everyone's fate was in the hands of everyone else; people voted to determine each other's fates, right down to the smallest detail.

The system ran pretty well, truth be told. Hard work and kindness were often rewarded by majority vote; cruelty and criminality were often punished the same way. People pretty much got what they deserved...usually.

Though I'd be lying if I said that the outcomes always made sense, or that everyone was always happy with their own personal outcome.

"I agreed to accept the will of the Crowd, yes," snapped Byron. "But that *can't* be what *this* is, Agent Grice."

As he glared at me, brief notes appeared in midair around him, visible to my A.R. lenses--social messages from the Yapstream posted by the multitudes watching Byron's story unfold:

69Bill69: *Yes it CAN be!*

FrtInspktr: *The Crowd says U SUK*

SuzieQ4U: *But what if he's 4 real?*

Just then, Byron's wife, Sylvia, emerged from a doorway, armed with a broken broom handle. Waving it at the chimp, she drove the animal back three screeching steps. "Our like-ability index is sky-high!" She scrubbed dirty fingers through her willy-nilly bird's nest of tangled brown hair. "We get *millions* of smiles on Crowdlife every *day*!"

Something swam past me--gnat-cam or insect, I couldn't tell--and I swatted it away. "You know that isn't how it works, ma'am. Likeability doesn't always correlate with fate-voting."

BoogaBooga99: *Damn right!!!*

FrtInspktr: *Forget smiles, I'd give em puke faces all the time.*

NoItAll3000: *But I like em! Giving em 100 smiles right now in fact!*

"I'm telling you, something's *wrong* this time!" Sylvia lunged with the broom handle, driving the chimp back further. "We're too *well-loved* for the Crowd to drop us this *low*!" She jabbed the handle again, and the chimp whirled and darted through a doorway. As Sylvia raced after it, the animal's screeches were joined by the screams of the Chellinghams' three young children.

All that noise made my stomach churn, setting off the ongoing pain in my gut. "Look." I turned to Byron. "I get it. You don't like this outcome."

SweetHawk7: *You tell im, COE boy!*

CowwSezMoo: *Spoiled rich piece of crap*

"Being transformed from billionaire to pauper? Terrorized by a chimp in a diaper?" Byron laughed like he was ready to jump off a building. "What makes you say that?"

"These things have a way of working themselves out," I told him. "If you play your cards right, the Crowd could send you straight back to the top overnight."

SuzieQ4U: *Thats right we could do that.*

Gr8Wite: *I'll vote for em in a heart beat!*

ExpltvDletd: *Me too*

FrtInspktr: *I say vote em another monkey!!*

"But what if this *isn't* the will of the Crowd?" said Byron. "What if a single embittered individual is behind all this?"

I scowled. "A lifehacker?"

"I've heard of it happening before!" As Byron said it, the screeching chimp barreled out of the kids' room and hurtled across the apartment. "Trolls hacking the fatevote to get what they want."

"Fairy tales," I said. "Crowdlife's unhackable."

69Bill69: *I heard theres a guy who*

FrtInspktr: *Nothings unhackable you boob.*

Jabbawokky75: *#lifehackers. No such thing bitches.*

"Will you at least look into it?" Byron stepped forward and raised a hand as if to touch my arm, then withdrew it. "Please?" His eyes practically throbbed with desperation. Behind him, his wife charged after the chimp, howling with rage. "Because I don't know how much more of this I can take."

CowwSezMoo: *That's what they all say*

Too true, that note from the Yapstream. I'd never met a gracefaller who didn't say the same thing. Words to that effect, at least. And I'd never met one who said they deserved what the fatevote stuck them with.

FrtInspktr: *Tellim eff off LOL!*

HackensteinXXX: *Looooser!*

Still, something kept nagging at me. Even as my brain and the Yapstream told me to turn my back on these people, my gut said something different. In all my years with the C.O.E., I'd never seen a fall from grace so precipitous or bizarre.

What if lifehacking wasn't a fairy tale, after all?

As I stood there, thinking about it, someone knocked hard on the apartment door. Byron brushed past me and opened it wide.

KangaCult101: *Oboy I cant wait to see this!*

SinrHatr: *Latest fatevote's in, I just saw whats comin.*

CowwSezMoo: *Holy eff eff eff!!!*

"Mr. Chellingham?" A man in a white Crowdlife Fatemaker uniform looked in from the hallway. He didn't wait for Byron to answer before pushing a wheelbarrow loaded with snakes through the doorway. "Special delivery, sir."

The Fatemaker dumped the snakes in the middle of the floor, sending them squirming in all directions.

CallMeGodd: *OMG! Look at em all!*

Jabbawokky75: *Dance, bitches, dance!*

"See what I mean?" Byron stared at me. "Do you really think I deserve all this? Why would the *Crowd* vote to do something this *insane?*"

But the Fatemaker wasn't done yet. "Bring in the next load!"

A second white-uniformed man rolled in a rusty gray steel drum on a dolly and set it down near the snakes. With help from the first man, he pushed the drum over, sending putrid brown sludge oozing over the floor.

It was raw sewage. The smell was so strong, it made me gag.

"Excuse me, Mr. Chellingham." The first Fatemaker held out a tablet computer and a stylus toward Byron. "Wouldja put your John Hancock right there, sir?"

FrtInspktr: *Suh-weet!*

JudyJudyJulie: *Talk about adding insult to injury!*

Byron just glared at him.

The Fatemaker cleared his throat. "Just, uh, need you to sign for this, sir. Please."

Byron turned to me. I could hardly hear his next words over the chimp's screeching as it swung fistfuls of snakes against the wall, bashing their heads in. "Will you at least look into it?"

I told him I would.

AFTER THE CHELLINGHAMS', I went straight home and jacked into the Crowdlife Backlot--the vast virtual workspace linking employees like me with Crowdlife's behind-the-scenes infrastructure.

As interpreted by my A.R. contact lenses, the Backlot looked like an enormous crystalline city sprawling over a sun-soaked plain. My point of view was high above it, gazing down from a gold-tinted sky. The view was uniquely private, free of all social network connections.

I blinked hard, and a drop-down text menu of city sectors appeared in the upper right corner of my field of vision. Flicking my eyes, I chose the last option and began my approach, drifting down through streamers of cloud toward a tall tower.

When I found the right office, on the tower's 85th floor, I flew straight in; there were no walls or windows to block my way in this virtual environment.

As I landed, a young woman looked up from inside a conical well of holographic computer screens, dozens of them flashing with rivers of data.

"Cage!" She perked up instantly when she saw me and tucked strands of glossy black hair behind her ears. She was beautiful, and not just because that's how she chose to look in the Backlot. "What's the occasion?"

"Just paying a visit to my favorite Outcomes Analyst." I couldn't help smiling when I said it. "And let me just say you're looking lovelier than ever, Liz."

"Flatterer." Liz brushed a hand along the well in front of

her, opening a gap, then got up from her chair and walked through it. "But I like what I'm hearing."

"There's more." I shrugged. "I'm looking for something."

Liz grinned and moved closer. "Aren't we all? I'm sure we can find it together."

"I wouldn't be so sure," I said. "Do lifehackers even exist?"

Liz looked at me like I was crazy. "Lifehackers? That's what you're looking for?"

The ever-present pain in my gut spiked, then receded. "There's this family of gracefallers. They've been handed an unusually extreme outcome."

The fire drained right out of Liz as she leaned back away from me. "Crowdlife has spoken. They signed the T.O.S., didn't they?"

"Yeah, but..." I shook my head. "This outcome. It's so extreme, it's *insane*. We're talking a billionaire reduced to poverty, forced to live on Skid Row with a crazed chimpanzee."

Liz shrugged. "It happens, Cage. Sometimes a crazy outcome goes viral and sweeps the fatevote."

"It gets crazier," I said. "There's a wheelbarrow full of snakes and a drum of raw sewage dumped in the apartment."

Liz sighed and turned away, heading back to her data well. "Lifehackers are a myth. Crowdlife is unhackable."

"So I've heard." I followed her to the well. "Could you do some digging anyway?"

Throwing herself down on her chair, she closed the gap in the well as if she were drawing a curtain across it. "Let me see what I can do."

WHILE LIZ DUG deep on the data side of things, I punched out to take some personal time. I had to step away for an appointment I'd been dreading.

Because as much as I wished it were otherwise, not everything was controlled by Crowdlife.

As I sat in Dr. Duncan's office and waited to hear his verdict, Yapstream posts popped up around him via my A.R. contacts.

SuzieQ4U: *Praying for him so hard.*

JudyJudyJulie: *Fingers and toes all crossed*

TouchyFeely50: *I can't stand the suspense!*

I read a few, but they were coming thick and fast. Moments like this brought the rubberneckers out in force.

"Mr. Grice," said Dr. Duncan. "I'm afraid the news isn't good." His eyes were locked on the tablet computer in his hands. "Not good at all."

"Sorry to hear that." I sat back in my chair.

"Gene therapy has failed to prevent additional metastatic activity," said Dr. Duncan. "Future remission of your cancer is unlikely."

"Right." I nodded. "Okay then."

DogssBreakfasst: *Poor son of a bitch*

TouchyFeely50: *I swear Im gonna cry!*

SweetHawk7: *OMG!*

"What this means," said Dr. Duncan, "is a dramatically reduced life expectancy."

I cleared my throat. "How much time do I have left?"

"Based on your latest test results, I'd say not much." Dr. Duncan looked up from his tablet. "Two months, minimum. Four at the outside."

"I understand." Swallowing hard, I tried to ignore the swarm of popups filling the A.R. field all around Dr. Duncan.

SweetHawk7: *I AM CRYING SO HARD RIGHT NOW!!!*

PrestoKarmaKid: *Poor guys got NO ONE, does he?*

FrtInspktr: *Not since we voted for his wife to divorce him.*

"Now, it's possible," said Dr. Duncan, "that we might prolong your life a bit with targeted nanotherapy. Millions of guided nanomechs would deliver microburst neochemotherapy to cancerous sites." He paused. "Though as you know, that brings with it certain undesirable side effects."

"How much more time would that buy me?"

"One to two months," said Dr. Duncan.

ZpprBrkr33: *Do it!!!!*

Tinatastic: *Take the nano, man, take the nano!*

CowwSezMoo2: *Dont be stoopid man!*

Closing my eyes, I shut out the tide of Yapstream posts. "So in a best case scenario, I've got six months left."

"Yes," said Dr. Duncan. "So what do you want to do?"

I TOLD him I needed to think about it, and then I left. I decided to take the rest of the day off and headed straight for my favorite bar, where I ordered up the hard stuff as soon as I walked in the door.

As I sat and drank, gnat-cams or gnats buzzed around me, drawing the occasional swat. Yapstream posts popped up around me, too, telling me to do one thing or another.

Then, the message I'd been expecting arrived: the announcement of a Crowdlife-wide fatevote to decide if I should have nanotherapy.

Just then, another message got my attention...an incoming call. Flicking my eyes over the contact lens controls, I answered it. Instantly, the appearance of my surroundings shifted, reshaped by the A.R. lenses to look like the interior of Liz's office in the Backlot.

"Hey, Cage." Her voice was clear in my head, beamed in through the aural implants behind my ears. Her image was right in front of me, seated as always within the holographic control well. "You owe me a steak dinner, hon, plus top-shelf cocktails."

"Oh yeah?" I straightened on my barstool.

"I thought your whole lifehacker theory was pure baloney," said Liz. "But then I analyzed recent protests among grace-fallers and noticed a pattern. Seems there've been other cases of inexplicably insane outcomes in Crowdlife lately."

"How many?"

"Fifty-seven worldwide over the past two weeks," said Liz.

I whistled softly. "Any connection between the victims?"

"None." Liz ran her fingers over the glowing controls in the well. "But I did turn up a link between the fatevotes that led to their outcomes." She tapped a finger on one of the screens in the well. "What I found is an elaborate system of vote trading conducted by an army of kamikaze A.I. proxy drones.

"The proxy drones commandeer Crowdlife lobbyists--A.I.s dispatched by system users to convince other users to vote certain ways. The proxies use the lobbyists to assemble blocs of carefully aligned votes, and then *boom*. They trigger a chain reaction of fatevotes setting off a web of outcomes.

"Then the drones self-destruct," continued Liz. "The only traces they leave are the recorded movements of the enslaved lobbyists, which are buried under layers of obscure vote trades."

I shook my head in amazement. "Who could be capable of implementing a strategy that sophisticated?"

"Someone who doesn't want to be found," said Liz. "But I

found 'em, anyway." She pointed at the name on the screen facing me.

"Dada Wyrm, Inc." I felt a jab of pain in my gut and winced. "Got a physical address for this outfit?"

WITHIN THE HOUR, I was standing in front of a door in an uptown apartment building--number 23. Gut aching, I took a deep breath and raised my fist to knock. At least I wasn't distracted by any Yapstream popups; as a C.O.E. agent, I was able to block Yapstream during moments of imminent danger.

As I knocked on the door with my left hand, I kept my right wrapped around the grip and trigger of my gun. No one answered my knock. I leaned closer but could hear nothing from the other side of the door.

"Crowdlife Outcomes Enforcement," I shouted. "Open up. We need to ask you a few questions."

Next time, I knocked with the butt of the gun. Again, there was no reply.

Reaching down, I tried the doorknob...and was surprised when it turned in my hand. Pushing the door open, I stepped over the threshold. Sweat trickled down my back as I peered into the darkness, keeping my gun raised in case of attack.

As I took another step forward, a holographic panel leaped to life in front of me, an online screen as tall as I was and twice as wide. Blinking at the sudden flare of light, I saw the familiar orange and green homepage of Crowdlife zoom out of the center and fill the screen from edge to edge.

Gut burning, I tried to walk around the screen for a closer look at the rest of the room...but the image of the screen stayed in front of me no matter which way I turned.

Suddenly, the screen changed from the Crowdlife home-page to the familiar box-and-column layout of a fatevote in progress. The question being voted on appeared at the top of the screen in bold black letters: *Should Agent Grice hop on his left or right foot while battling the three killers walking down the hall?*

The tally was in the hundreds of millions for either option, and the leader was "Right Foot" with 67% of the vote.

I spun to face the doorway with my gun at the ready, and the screen stayed square in front of me. I heard three sets of footsteps in the hall, not far away, but it was hard to focus with the fatevote tally flashing in my face.

Just then, the numbers stopped changing, and the winning choice turned bright red and expanded to five times its original size. "Right Foot" had won by a landslide.

An audio message played in my aural implants. "Agent Grice must now comply with the outcome of this fatevote, according to the Crowdlife terms of service that he signed on October 21, 2192."

The screen finally dissolved...just as a tall man dressed in a red uniform pushed through the doorway, brandishing a rifle.

Without hesitation, I fired my pistol, throwing two shots into the intruder's forehead. The impact spun him to the floor with a heavy thud, clearing a path for the next guy to push through.

I was getting ready to fire again when the Crowdlife screen reappeared smack in front of me with a familiar message: *Agent Grice must now comply with the outcome of this fatevote, according to the Crowdlife terms of service that he signed on October 21, 2192.*

"Damnit!" I gave in and hopped on my right foot, and the screen vanished. With a clear shot at the bad guy, I let loose three slugs--one to the forehead, one to the throat, one to the chest in quick succession.

As soon as the second shooter dropped, number three barged in and started firing. Taking aim while hopping wasn't easy, but I managed to tag him in the temple and shoulder, dropping him beside the other two attackers.

With all three down, I stopped hopping and bolted into the hallway. Looking one way and then the other, I saw no additional intruders.

But a heartbeat later, the Crowdlife screen leaped up in front of me without warning, displaying the tabulation of another fatevote in progress. This time, the Crowd was voting on a new question: *Agent Grice: Off limits or open season?*

So far, there were zero votes in favor of me being off limits.

Heart bashing my ribs like a boxer's fist, I charged down the hall. The whole time, the Crowdlife screen stayed in front of me, making it tough to see where I was going.

Just as I reached the elevator, it dinged, and the Crowdlife screen hopped aside. The doors sprang open, revealing a pack of howling maniacs wearing hockey goalie masks and brandishing machetes.

The screen slid back in front of me, revealing the fatevote results. It came as no surprise that the winner was "Open Season."

The Crowdlife screen vanished. Bolting past the elevator, I ran for the stairs. Every step of the way, the howls and footfalls of the machete-bearing maniacs were close behind.

Throwing open the door, I barreled down two flights of stairs like my feet were on fire. When I got to the bottom, I crashed through the exit door without slowing down.

And I found myself facing a mob armed with cream pies and fire hoses.

As soon as I emerged from the stairwell, the cream pies

came flying in my direction. One after another, they bombarded me, covering me with gooey cream.

When that fusillade stopped, I wiped enough goop from my eyes to see that the Crowdlife screen had reappeared. This time, the text was a direct message to me: *No more advance warnings, Agent Grice. Our fatevotes will be invisible to you from now on. You will pay the price for sticking your nose in our business.*

As soon as the screen blinked out, the mob cut loose with the fire hoses.

I was blasted back by what I thought at first were jets of water...but I quickly realized the liquid was something else. Something with a noxious smell I knew all too well.

Gasoline.

Pinned against the stairwell door by the force of the jets, I shut my eyes and mouth. Gathering my strength, I staggered right, letting the current push me until I rounded the corner of the building.

Then, I charged down the street away from the mob. I ran as hard as I could into the night, praying no one would flick a lit cigarette in my direction.

DRENCHED IN GASOLINE, spattered with pie cream, I ran for blocks, winding my way through the heart of the city. When I finally thought I was clear, I ducked into an alley and threw myself against the wall, heaving for breath.

I was in over my head this time; the only help I could turn to was Liz in the Backlot. Without further delay, I flashed her an emergency ping. There wasn't time to traverse the virtual environment of the Backlot in the usual way, soaring down into the crystalline city and alighting in her office.

She responded immediately. Through my A.R. contacts, I saw her image pop into the alley, standing three feet away from me.

"Cage!" She looked instantly worried. "What happened?"

"Lifehackers," I told her. "They ambushed me at the Dada Wyrm address."

"You look terrible!"

"I barely got away." My stomach twisted, and I doubled over...then sucked in my breath and straightened. "They're spinning rogue fatevotes, siccing the Crowd on me. They want me dead, Liz."

She nodded grimly. "I'm on it, Cage. I'll do what I can."

I heard voices in the distance and looked at the mouth of the alley. "I don't think we've got much time for it, either." I swatted at the ubiquitous swarm of tiny bugs swirling around me. "They can track my feed from the gnat-cams through Crowdlife."

"I'll do everything I can." Liz stopped working unseen controls and met my gaze with her warm brown eyes. "Just try to hang on, Cage."

Because I've got so much to live for? The cancer would take me in a matter of months, anyway. I shouldn't care, should I?

But I did. "I'll do my best, Liz."

Just then, the voices rushed up, and people poured into the alley. They washed over me in an angry tide, snatching away my gun and hauling me off my feet.

As they dragged me away, I heard Liz's voice over the frenzied roar, calling to me from the Backlot. "Hang on, Cage!"

Then, she was gone, and I was on my way to whatever madness awaited in unknown quarters.

THE MOB STRIPPED me naked in the street, then wrapped me in Christmas paper and pelted me with eggs. When that was done, they stripped off the wrapping paper, rolled me in a red carpet, and peed on me while singing cartoon theme songs from the 70s.

My treatment went downhill from there. Each abuse, each outcome of a Crowdlife fatevote engineered by the Dada Wyrm lifehackers, was more bizarre than the last.

They dragged me through an art museum in a little red wagon and smashed famous paintings over my head, one after another. When they were done with that, they shoved me into a koala costume, poured grease down my back, and spun me in circles until I vomited. Next, they stuffed me into a knee-length green dress and spiked heels and made me bungee jump off the Crosstown Bridge.

All the while, the pain in my gut intensified. By the time they plunked me on the dance floor in a nightclub and beat me with frozen legs of lamb to the tune of "The Chicken Dance," I felt myself losing ground. I hadn't been at my best to begin with; I wasn't sure how much more insane torture I could take.

Not that the mob ever seemed to run out of new ideas. They blindfolded me, threw me in a dumpster full of loaded diapers, and let me dig my way out with one arm tied behind my back. They put on stork masks and pecked the hell out of me while reciting the preamble to the Constitution. They tried to force-feed me live tarantulas and crumpled-up pages of old comic books.

Then, finally, there was a break in the action. They led me into an empty school gymnasium and left me there.

Heaving for breath, I stood at center court and looked around. The place was peaceful and dark, lit only by the dim red Exit signs over the doors.

For a moment, I dared to hope that my ordeal was over. Maybe the lifehackers were finally done with me; maybe they figured I'd gotten the message.

I wiped blood off my face with the back of my arm, then wiped my arm on the front of the green dress. I was about to kick off the damn spiked heels and head for the nearest door, just in case I had a chance to get away.

That's when the lights blazed to life and the clowns rushed in.

They poured through the doors and surrounded me, cutting off all escape routes. Laughing, howling, giggling, they closed in around me, jagged teeth glistening.

Then, one at a time, they charged toward me and exploded. I dodged once, then twice, barely avoiding being blown to bits along with the clowns.

The next time, three come at me at once.

THE THREE CLOWNS charge toward me from three different directions, shrieking like berserk Vikings. As beat as I am, I can't imagine that one of them won't get me. Maybe I'll be better off that way, going out with a bang instead of fading painfully as the cancer takes me.

But something deep inside clicks into place, and I refuse to give up. Maybe it's just that I'd rather go down fighting, or maybe it's plain stubbornness. Maybe it's sheer anger after what I've been through. Does it even matter?

Sucking in a deep breath between shattered teeth, I gather

what strength I've got left--which isn't much--and leap into action.

Just as the clowns are nearly upon me, I dart out of the way. They collide and explode with shuddering force, spraying clown bits in all directions...but no Cage Grice bits. Though the blast knocks me down hard, I'm still alive.

But for how long? Even as I hurry to get back on my feet, I hear more floppy shoes smacking toward me. Looking around, I see three clowns...four...*five* this time, shrieking and charging in my direction all at once.

Looking around frantically, I wonder what my next move should be. Running and dodging seems to be the only choice. If I try to fight the clowns hand-to-hand, I'm guessing they'll blow up on contact.

Wait! Maybe that's the key.

On the floor a few feet away, I see the blown-off arm of one of the dead clowns. I bolt toward it, grab it up, and keep running, heading straight for the nearest of the five attackers.

I haul the severed arm back like a baseball bat, gripping the wrist and hand, and swing it hard at the clown's chest. As soon as the arm makes contact, the shrieking clown explodes.

The blast knocks me off my feet, and I roll twice with the impact. When I come to a stop, I see another clown almost upon me with arms outstretched.

Kicking off the shoes, I scoop one up and whip it at the clown with all my might. He explodes in mid-shriek, sending chunks in all directions; some are big enough that they set off other clowns, which in turn trigger others and so on.

I keep my head down until the blasts subside. When I look up again, the ranks of the explosive clowns have thinned out noticeably. Maybe now, I have a fighting chance.

Grabbing the other shoe, I scramble to my feet and take a

quick look around. From what I can see, a dozen clowns remain. The odds are much improved.

Picking the spot where the fewest clowns remain, I get ready to make a run for it. Adrenaline burns through my bloodstream, setting my heart spinning like a dervish. The pain in my gut peaks and refuses to subside, but I'll push past it.

Every muscle in my body tenses as I prepare to sprint. If I die trying to escape this surreal trap, so be it; at least I'll have given it everything I've got left.

Brandishing the shoe, I start running. I expected the clowns to close ranks in my path, and they do...but they also take me by surprise. Wheels sprout from their floppy shoes, enabling them to move much faster than before.

The clowns swoop toward me like angry bees, and I keep running. As I go, I realize this is likely the end for me, but it doesn't freak me out at all. I feel like I'm watching it from a distance, from outside my body, and all I can think is how this isn't the way I'd ever thought I'd die. If someone had told me even a year ago that this would be my death scene, I would've laughed in his face.

Yet here I am. Running in a green dress, wielding a high-heeled shoe against a pack of clowns in roller shoes.

Then, suddenly, the doors slam wide open all around the gym. Men dressed in loincloths and bunny slippers barge in, armed with blowguns--hollow tubes held up to their mouths, jungle weapons loaded and ready.

They all fire the blowguns at once, sending a barrage of darts into the cavernous gym. But none of the darts comes anywhere near me.

It quickly becomes clear that the blowgunners are shooting at the clowns. Again and again, as the darts hit their floppy-shoed targets, the gym booms with thunderous explosions.

All the clowns go up in short order, surrounding me with fiery blasts that make my ears ring. Clown bits rain down everywhere, splattering the floor and covering me with shards of bone and tissue.

Somehow, I stay on my feet through the series of blasts. I'm shaking my head hard, trying to clear the ringing in my ears, when something zips toward me--not a dart, thankfully.

It's a Crowdlife screen, as tall as I am and twice as wide. It zooms up from a pinpoint to full size in a heartbeat, displaying a message in big, bold letters.

All current fatevotes impacting Agent Cage Grice are hereby nullified in accordance with the Mercy Provision of the Crowdlife Terms of Service.

"What the hell?" It's too good to be true; the start of another twisted torture, perhaps?

Or maybe it's just as advertised. As I read the message, the blowgunners turn and leave the doorways...and the doors don't close behind them. All the ways out are wide open and apparently unguarded.

Just then, Liz's image appears alongside the screen, grinning. "All better now," she says. "Sorry I'm late, but you wouldn't believe how long it takes to round up a tribe of blowgunners at this hour."

Seeing her puts me instantly at ease. "So it's over?" My body untenses, and the spiked-heeled shoe falls from my grip. "It's really over?"

Liz nods. "I didn't think I could pull it off at first. The defensive bots and A.I. countermeasures were useless against the lifehackers. Everything we sent after them ended up compromised and turned back against us."

"But you still did it." I smile, broken teeth and all. "You still saved me. I owe you big time."

"Actually," says Liz, "you owe your cancer."

I scowl at her, wondering what the hell she's talking about.

"There's a Mercy Provision in the Crowdlife Terms of Service." Liz gestures at the Crowdlife screen beside her. "*A fatevote necessitated by terminal illness supersedes and nullifies all others.*" She points a finger at me. "And it so happens there's just such a vote in progress for you, my friend."

I have to think for a moment before it comes to me. "Oh, right." In all the madness, I forgot. The Crowd was voting on whether I should undergo nanotherapy for my cancer. The treatment could buy me 1-2 months of life, accompanied by undesirable side effects. But the vote started hours ago; why is it still in progress? "There's a Crowdlife provision for this?"

Liz nods. "Typical Crowdlifer. Sign your fate away without reading the T.O.S." She sighs loudly. "The provision's meant to restore a person's dignity if they're dying. It gives them one last bit of control over their lives at the end."

I frown. "How? If the person's still subject to the will of the Crowd on that fatevote 'necessitated by terminal illness,' how do they have any control?"

"Because the one who's dying always gets the last vote. The *deciding* vote, that overrules all others." Liz walks up to me and places her phantom hand upon my shoulder. "*You* get to cast the deciding vote."

So that's why the vote is still in progress after all this time. "They're waiting for me to vote."

"Good thing you put it off when you did." Liz's voice softens as she stares into my eyes. "Good thing it happened in the first place."

"Yeah." I smirk. "Thank God for cancer."

We laugh, and then we stand there for a moment in silence. The mob hasn't come back, and Yapstream remains offline; I haven't removed the imminent danger block since entering Dada Wyrm's apartment.

The only intrusion is the Crowdlife screen, with the all-important fatevote announcement emblazoned across the top: *Should Agent Cage Grice undergo nanotherapy to treat his cancer?*

Pain shoots through my belly, and I wince. I haven't had much time to think about this, what with the lifehackers and exploding clowns and all.

"So?" Liz looks at the screen, then back at me. "What'll it be? Nanotherapy or no nanotherapy?"

I gaze at the results as they now stand: 93% of the vote in favor of nanotherapy, 17% against. It's a landslide.

Should I take those results as a sign? Would a slightly longer, less pleasant life be preferable to a shorter one without so many side effects?

It's all up to me. After a lifetime of putting my destiny in the hands of other people, I finally have the power to set my own course. The cancer gave me that much, at least. The one thing that could not be controlled by social networks has liberated me from them in the end.

Maybe it's time to take that liberation to the limit.

"What's it going to be, Cage?" Liz's brown eyes lock expectantly with mine. "How are you going to vote on Crowdlife?"

I look once more at the screen with its question and results...the fulcrum upon which the rest of my life will turn. And then I grin.

"None of their business." I pop the A.R. contact lenses out of my eyes, and the Crowdlife screen disappears. So does Liz. "Every vote's a secret ballot from here on out."

Then, I flick the contacts over my shoulder and wander off through the gym, the remains of exploded clowns squishing between my bare toes.

MONKEY SEA, MONKEY DO

Have you heard the one about the woman who turned into a water-breathing Sea Munky creature just as the world's bodies of water mostly dried up? Hilarious, right? Unless *you're* the woman, in which case...

"How many times do I have to *tell* you idiots? Quit *pissing* in one of the last pools of water on *Earth*. Some of us have to *breathe* in here, y'know?"

In which case, you guessed it--*major suckage*.

And yes, I *am* that woman slash Sea Munky, she of the poorly-timed wish. My name is Ida, and I was a teacher in my human days...a teacher with a desperate need to get away and a lifelong fascination with Sea Munkies.

Yes, *those* Sea Munkies--the ones sold via misleading ads in the pages of comic books back in the day. Some people collect knick-knacks with frogs or pigs or cows on them; me, I *became* the object of my freakish obsession.

And look where it's gotten me. Sure, I'm five foot five with neon pink scales, webbed flippers, a ridged back, and a long, prehensile tail. Sure, my skull is topped with four stiff spikes...a kind of crown accented by a bright red bow and an upswept fan of blonde hair. Sure, my gills enable me to stay underwater indefinitely.

But what good does all that do if I'm stuck in the same shitty oasis pool in a dried-up world with a bunch of other water-wish misfits?

The answer is, no good at all. I *hate* my life.

Oscar the Merman floats a few feet away, looking sheepish. "Sorry, Ida. I had to pee so bad, I couldn't get ashore in time."

I smack my hands flat on the surface. "It's a *thirty-foot diameter pool*, Oscar! It's not that *far* to the *edge*."

Oscar shrugs. "Does it *matter*? The pool is *mostly* piss at this point, isn't it?" With that, he combs his bony fingers through his long brown hair and submerges.

"That *doesn't* mean we should stop *trying!*" Angrily, I whip my tail, spraying precious piss/water onto the sandy shore. Immediately, I regret the move; given the worldwide über-drought conditions, there's no replacement moisture on the horizon.

Any stray water gets instantly soaked up by the palm trees that ring our desert oasis. I'm grateful they keep the worst of the blazing sun off us, but I also hate that their roots drink up the liquid we so desperately need.

Just then, a long green neck sways up out of the pool, supporting a head like a football with a blunt nose and big, dark eyes. This is Vanessa, another wisher like me--though *she* wished to become a Loch Ness Monster type instead of a humble Sea Munky. (Lucky for her, the pool is much deeper than it is wide, since she's a good bit bigger than I am.)

"Why *shouldn't* we stop trying?" Vanessa swings her head

over and stares, inches from my face. "It's only a matter of time for us, Ida Mae."

"I refuse to accept that," I snap.

"Sooner or later, this pool will dry up," Vanessa says in her sing-song voice. "Or the surviving humans--as few as they are--will come for it. Thirsty people will finally figure out it's here and will come for it."

"They'll have a fight on their hands." I nod defiantly. "But in the meantime, we have to make sure it's *worth* fighting for. Not just a puddle of piss in the desert!"

"*That* ship has sailed," says a male voice from the far side of the pool. "Don't you think?"

I don't answer. I have nothing to say to him, though technically he's one of my kind--the *last* male Sea Munky in the world.

And he's part of the *family*, too. He's my *husband*, the one I haven't said a word to in the past nine years of the Drypocalypse.

THE ONLY OTHER Sea Munky in the world, my long-estranged husband Lee, leans back on his elbows on the shore like he's having a soak in a hot tub. A shaft of bright sunlight streams down between the fronds of the palm trees, making his neon pink scales glitter and gleam.

"If you could have one wish granted, I wonder what it would be?" Lee knows I won't answer, but he keeps talking anyway. "Bet you can't guess what *mine* is."

Vanessa won't talk to him, either, though she *has* been known to *bite* him on occasion. She's my best friend, after all.

"It *might* involve being the *last* Sea Munky on Earth," says

Lee. "Or the last *anything*. At least *then* I wouldn't have to over-hear your incessant *whining*."

Sometimes it's hard to remember that I used to feel guilty about Lee. After all, when we caught that magic whelk twelve years ago, I was the one who wished it would turn us into Sea Munkies.

Since the change made me happier than I'd ever been, things between us were fine for a while. But once the Drypoca-lypse kicked into high gear, and the oceans, lakes, and rivers started evaporating, our relationship soured. Staying in human form would have been stressful enough, as humans were dying of thirst in droves and killing each other over what water was left...but being aquatic creatures was even harder. Though we were magically attuned, able to find and swim through secret portals between the remaining bodies of water we needed to sustain us, those bodies were quickly disappearing in the most terrible drought of all time.

As we went from one watery refuge to another, only to have them all go up in steam, Lee got progressively grouchier, and I got sick of his attitude. Life in the vast ocean turned into life in a tiny pool in a desert oasis, and I finally broke it off.

Trapped in such close confines, it isn't easy to ignore him, but I do. "Vanessa, I'm going to clean this cesspool up some." Reaching out, I pat her Loch Ness Monster neck. "I respect your opinion, but you're welcome to..."

Suddenly, there's a splash, and Lee pops up between us so there's no longer any way we can ignore him. "What would you say..." He clears his throat and speaks louder. "What would you *say* if I told you..."

Vanessa swats him away with a flex of her neck, tossing him head over flippers across the pool. He barely misses colliding with Tina the Nymph, who has just surfaced over there with a couple of pals.

Lee splashes down but quickly comes back up between us. "What if I told you there's an *unused wish* floating around in this pissy little pond?"

LEE GRINS. "The possessor of said wish assures me it has most definitely not been cashed in yet, magically speaking."

Vanessa decides the time has come to break her silence. "How is that even *possible?* We're all on the verge of *extinction* here. If someone *had* a wish, they sure as hell would've *used* it by now."

Lee shrugs. "Saving it for a *rainy day,* so to speak. Or a *not-so-rainy* day, is more like it."

"That makes no sense whatsoever," says Vanessa. "If this supposed wish-keeper had just wished us and the world back to normal, he, she, or it wouldn't *need* to save the wish for a rainy or not-so-rainy day."

"What's the hurry?" Lee's long pink tail emerges from the water and twitches slowly. "This wish is like a get-out-of-jail-free card. The bearer can wait till the last minute to use it, if he or she so desires. Meanwhile, this individual can see if a better purpose comes to mind."

"*Better purpose?*" sputters Vanessa. "What *better purpose* could there be than reversing the *Drypocalypse* and saving *everyone?*"

"Yeah, but why be hasty?" Lee spreads his scaly pink arms. "Especially if we're talking about what might be *the last wish in the world.* There aren't too many *wishers* left, so I can't imagine there are too many *wishes.*"

Suddenly, a single word emerges from my lips, the first word I've said to him in a full nine years. *"Who?"*

His eyes widen with delighted surprise, as if he can't believe his luck and doesn't know just what to do about it. "Who what?"

"This supposedly unused wish," I say coldly. "Who has it?"

"I can't believe you don't know already!" says Lee. "It's..."

Before he can finish, a white-skinned creature leaps from the sandy bank and engulfs him in its huge maw. Lee's fizzy pink Sea Munky blood sprays everywhere as the creature's jagged teeth clamp down on his shoulder and throat.

Thank God Vanessa takes swift action. Stunned by the attack, I just gape as her vinelike neck snaps around, and she sinks her own razor-sharp fangs into the creature's pale hide.

The beast roars and thrashes, heaving Vanessa aside. As it lurches around to face me, I get my first clear view of the thing.

Though the creature launched itself from the bank, it is nearly identical to a fierce oceangoing predator (from the days when there *were* oceans): the great white shark. If not for its gnarled, needle-tipped claws, it could *be* such a shark, from its oblong nose to its triangular back fin.

The shark-thing roars, about to pounce on me--until Vanessa charges across the pool and slams her bulk into it. Belly up, the beast skids toward the shore, claws clacking helplessly.

That's when I finally snap out of my state of shock. Lowering my head like a bull, I brace myself and bolt toward the invader as fast as I can. Just as the shark-thing flops against the bank but before it can right itself, I drive the four spikes atop my skull into the meat of its belly as hard as I can.

This time, the blood spilling into the pool is the shark-thing's. It rushes out and slicks the surface of the water, and there's more to come.

Howling with rage, I tear my spikes free, then drive them in again. And again.

I'm furious, a Sea Munky possessed. Lee was an asshole, the two of us were over, but seeing him slaughtered right in front of me was too much to bear.

Again I wrench out my spikes, and again I drive them in. I manage one more strike, then another, before the glistening gray tentacles of Scott the Mer-Squid slither up from below to wrap around the shark-thing's corpse and drag it down into the depths of the pool.

"WHAT THE HELL *WAS* THAT THING?" Milky white shark-thing blood runs from my crown spikes down over my face. "Since when are there *land-sharks?*"

"Maybe a *shark* wished it could survive without an *ocean?*" Vanessa boosts her body onto the bank and stretches her neck high like a periscope, gazing out at the desert. "Oh, dear." Bracing her back against a palm tree, she stretches higher still. "It isn't *alone,* Ida Mae. I see triangular fins cutting through the sand at a high rate of speed...and they're coming *this way.*"

My heart's still hammering from the fight. "How many of them?"

"Six," says Vanessa. "Make that *seven.* They'll be here in *minutes.* The first one must have been a *scout* or something."

Just then, several pool inhabitants poke their heads above the water's blood-slicked surface.

"What's *happening* up here?" Jenny the Nymph looks scared. Her long blonde hair picks up a little red from the blood. "We just saw Scott hauling some *shark* with *claws* down to his burrow."

"Oh my God!" Rick the Sea Horse catches sight of Lee's carcass floating nearby. "Did you finally *kill* him, Ida?"

"It was the *land-shark*, and there are more on the way!" Vanessa slides back into the pool. "We all need to *go deep*, right *now,* or we'll end up like *him.*"

"Don't have to tell *me* twice!" Jenny climbs on Rick's back, and the two of them plunge out of sight into the depths. So do the others--Philosophical Water Bear and Jilly the Mer-Jellyfish.

Vanessa and I are the only ones left above water.

"Are you all right, hon?" she asks.

I take a deep breath and let it out slowly. Lee deserves a decent burial, but there's no time for that now. Though maybe there *is* a way to save more than his remains.

"I *will* be," I tell Vanessa. "Just as soon as I find out who has that last *wish* Lee told us about. Assuming he wasn't just being full of shit like he was ninety-nine percent of the time."

SPEAKING underwater is very different from talking above the surface. It requires extreme mastery of airflow, vocalization, scent, movement, and even taste. To a human, it wouldn't make any sense...though after twelve years as a Sea Munky, I understand it perfectly.

Which, in this case, is unfortunate, because my interrogations in search of an unused wish are getting me nowhere fast.

"I know you were a good friend of Lee's." That, more or less, is what I say to Oscar the Merman. *"You spent a lot of time together, didn't you?"*

Oscar shrugs, looking jumpy...but I can't hold that against him, because we're *all* jumpy right now. The land sharks are still up above us in force, hungrily circling the shore around the pool.

At least they haven't dived in after us, yet. They might be able to race through sand as if were water, but they don't seem too inclined to jump into *actual* water.

"Did Lee ever mention an unused wish to you before?" I ask Oscar, watching for any twitch that might suggest I've struck a nerve.

Oscar shakes his head and swishes his scaly green tail, which doesn't sparkle much here in the deeper, dimmer water.

"Oscar, please." I try to sound sympathetic. *"This wish, if there is one, might be the only way any of us survives this."*

"We're already on borrowed time," says Oscar. *"The whole world is."*

"What if it doesn't have to be?" I reach over and lower a flipper-hand onto his shoulder. *"Think about it, Oscar. If there's a wish, and we use it right, who's to say we won't be able to fix all that?"*

Oscar looks more and more skittish. *"The only wish I ever had was the one I used to become a merman."*

This interview is so much like the other three I've done so far, I want to scream. No one can (or will) help me with Lee's secret.

"Are you sure, Oscar? He never said anything about an errant wish that someone in here was holding onto?"

33

"All we did was hunt bugs and minnows together, says Oscar. *Most of the time, he was off with his girlfriend, Jilly."*

Finally, someone tells me something I don't *know...*as hard as it to *believe it. "Jilly the Mer-Jellyfish? They were..."*

Just then, a fat bug with gleaming, silvery wings drops down between us. We both fall silent, mesmerized as the bug gently weaves through the water.

I know we're both having the same thought. We're starving, and that bug looks delicious.

But before either us can make a play for it, Chuckie Tuna lunges up from below and snaps it up. It's only then, as Chuckie drags the bug away past a fish with a glowing lantern hung from its head, that I see the danger.

The light reveals a line stretched through the water, attached to the bug in Chuckie's mouth.

"Chuckie, no! Spit it out! Spit it out!"

Even as I shout the words, I know it's too late. His mouth opens wide, but nothing comes out. The line tightens, dragging Chuckie up toward the light.

He's been *hooked.*

He struggles with all of his might, but it's for nothing. The line keeps pulling him higher, ever higher.

"Oh my God," says Oscar. *"They got him, they got him!"*

Other denizens of the pool crowd around us, watching Chuckie rise. When he reaches the surface, his body is hauled out of the water by seven pairs of scrabbling pale claws.

"It's the land sharks!" says Jenny the Nymph. *"They're* fishing *for us!"*

AT FIRST, there is panic in the pool. Water folk swim this way and that as the fishing continues, dodging hooks and lines with the speed that terror brings.

But after a while, when no one else takes the bait, the number of lines decreases. When we water-breathers start tying lines together, the novelty wears off even more quickly. The land sharks reel in everything, leaving us to mourn our lost Chuckie.

Or, in my case, to see a jellyfish about a wish.

I find Jilly drifting ten feet below the surface--a little too close for comfort to the shark gang, but still out of their reach. Her glistening bubble of a body floats near the middle of the pool, frilly tentacles hanging languidly as hair or Spanish moss.

"A wish?" says Jilly. "Lee never mentioned a stray wish to me."

Can I expect honest answers from Lee's girlfriend? If I were her, I'd probably hate me for not saving him or dying instead of him. I'd probably hate me just because I was once part of his romantic life.

"He never talked about someone saving a wish for a rainy day?"

Jilly bobs silently for a moment, considering. "Never."

Not getting any traction, I try a different approach. "Was there anything that made you curious? Anything he did that seemed mysterious or off?"

Jilly's tentacles undulate with growing agitation. "Why do you care? Aren't you happy you finally got rid of him?"

I don't dignify her question with an answer. "Jilly, if there's a loose wish around here, it could save us all. Maybe it could even bring back Lee."

She swims closer, interested. Maybe I'm finally getting through to her.

Then, suddenly, a huge rock crashes into the water right on

top of her, plunging her into the depths with all the speed of a lightning strike.

"Jilly!" Looking up, I see more rocks drop into the water, thrown into the pool one after another. Apparently, the land sharks have abandoned fishing and taken up a new mode of attack.

It's a simple approach, yet brutally effective. The rocks shoot through the water like depth charges, colliding with anything in their paths--like Jilly...

Or *me*. Just as I'm diving to seek refuge, one of the rocks smashes into me, catching my ridged spine and hurling me down into the darkness like the anchor of a ship.

WHEN WAS the last time I hit bottom?

It's been a while, but the silt still feels as soft as I remember. I come in fast, weighed down by the heavy rock, but the downy silt cushions the impact, protecting me from injury.

I lie there for a moment after I hit, gazing upward. In the brighter water above, I see dark shapes plunging downward--more rocks pitched into the pool by the land sharks, all plummeting in my direction.

Galvanized by the sight, I heave aside the rock that brought me down and scramble upright. A big rock splashes down right where I was just lying, sending up clouds of brown and green silt.

Propelled by my webbed feet and tail, I race for the stone wall of the pool in a flurry of bubbles. Rocks fall behind and to either side of me, blasting into the bottom with far more force than I did when I landed.

One grazes me, striking my hip, which sends me tumbling.

Head over shoulders I go, coming to rest on my back at the base of the wall.

When I look up, I see another rock barreling toward me, too close to evade. I realize the moment of my death is upon me, and there's nothing I can do to escape it.

I snap my eyes shut, bracing for the collision...but it never comes.

Instead, someone grabs me from behind and drags me out of the way through a hole in the stone wall. As the rock crashes down, and the hole fills with swirling silt, I get dragged further down a tunnel by someone I still can't see.

THE NEXT THING I KNOW, I'm being hauled out of the water into an air-filled cave, then lowered onto a wet slate floor.

Whoever brought me here speaks with a high-pitched voice, like that of a female child. "Are you all right?"

Coughing, I brace my webbed hands on the floor and push myself up to a seated position. I can see my surroundings, as the place is lit with glowing white moss clinging in patches to the rock walls.

Before saying a word, I turn for a look at my rescuer--or captor, depending on my luck.

And I do a double-take.

Standing not three feet away is a kid with scaly pink skin, webbed hands and feet, a long tail, and five head spikes that look like a crown.

I never knew. "What the...?" I never knew.

I never *knew* there was a *third* Sea Munky living in a cave at the bottom of the pool.

IT TAKES a long moment for the shock to wear off and the words to start coming. "Who *are* you?"

The Sea Munky child frowns. She doesn't look older than nine or ten years old. "Who do you *think* I am?"

I get to my knees, mystified by this secret made flesh. "You're like *me*. A Sea Munky."

The child touches the black bow between her two front head spikes, then adjusts her hair. It's upswept like mine, but it's bright red instead of blonde.

"You're not supposed to be here," she says. "But you were in trouble. I had to bring you in."

"What's your name?" How long has she been here, I wonder, hidden away? How many times have I swum overhead, never guessing she lived down below?

"My name is Mira," says the child. "And you should leave. I don't want him to be mad."

"Him who?"

"Daddy," says Mira. "He lives here with me."

A thought occurs to me. "Your Daddy. He looks like *we* do, doesn't he?"

"Like a Sea Munky, you mean?" Mira nods briskly. "Of course! He's my Daddy, isn't he?"

I hesitate to ask the next question. "Mira." But I know I need to hear the answer. "Who's your mommy?"

"It doesn't matter," she tells me. "Don't you know Sea Munky *daddies* are the ones who have the babies?"

I didn't, but I don't want to admit it. "There has to be a mommy *somewhere* along the way, doesn't there?"

Mira narrows her eyes. "Where's Daddy? You know where he is, don't you?"

Given who her father *has* to be, I hate to answer. I hold back.

But Mira tunes in to the truth anyway. "Something *bad* happened to him, *didn't* it?" Her voice rises with anger and fear. "He always said that was the only way *you'd* ever get in here."

"Mira..." I'm having trouble finding the right words. The truth is, I'm struggling just to wrap my head around all this.

Because it's clear to me now. Her. Him. Me.

Us. I know what we are.

As hard to believe as it is, I *know*.

"He's *gone*," says Mira. "*Isn't* he?"

Though I only met her moments ago, I want to reach for her. I can't stand to see the pain on her little face, hear the sadness in her voice.

I want to take her in my arms and comfort her, help her get through this. Because as strange as it seems, the only logical explanation here...

Is that we are *family*.

SUDDENLY, there's a tremendous *boom* from the direction of the pool, and the cave trembles around us.

"What was that?" asks Mira.

"Let's go see," I suggest.

The two of us dive into the water and swim back out the way we came. Quickly, we reach the end of the tunnel and peek out of the hole into the depths of the pool.

Just in time to see a hand grenade drop on the far side of the pool and explode.

Everything shakes violently as Mira and I duck back into the passage. Our wide eyes meet, and we retreat, darting into the air-filled cave.

"Now they're *bombing* us." I shake my head in disgust. "Where they got the *explosives*, I'll never know, but they're *using* them."

"Who are *they?*" asks Mira.

"Land sharks. They're trying to kill everyone in the pool."

Mira nods thoughtfully. "Did they used to be people, too? Like the other people in the pool? People who wished they could be something else?"

"Or sharks, maybe. I don't know." I shrug. "They're not natural, that's for sure."

Mira paces to the wall, to a niche in the rock. "Where do people get these wishes?" Her back is turned to me as she talks.

"Different places, I guess. Genies, magical creatures, falling stars, magic spells..."

She glances over her shoulder at me. "Is that where you got yours?"

"From a creature, yes. A magic *whelk*, if you can believe it. Like a snail."

Mira reaches for something in the niche. I can't see what it is.

"What happened to the magic whelk?" she asks quietly. "After she made your wish come true?"

"I don't know."

"I do." Mira turns so I see what's in her hands...and I gasp.

She's holding what looks like a conical snail shell, pale yellow, banded with gray and brown speckles. A black-mottled foot extends from the shell's opening, and a pair of fleshy white hornlike appendages slowly twitch in my direction.

"I have her right here." Mira smiles. "*This* is the magic whelk."

THERE'S a blast outside the cave, and our refuge shakes around us.

"Is this possible?" I walk over and crouch in front of Mira, gazing at the whelk in her hands. "I think...I must have just let go of it when the wish took hold."

"*Her*, not *it*." Mira sounds indignant. "And you *did* let go, but *he* caught her. *Daddy* held onto her."

"He did?" Wonderingly, I reach out one index finger, and the whelk's horns gently graze it. When they do, I feel the slightest zap, like static electricity jumping between us. "But why?"

"Just in case." Mira raises the whelk to her eye level and stares at it. "He said he had his doubts about the wish. About becoming a Sea Munky. It was never *his* wish, was it?"

"No." How many times did he remind me of that? Even now, beyond the grave, his words haunt me.

"It was a good thing he *did* save Ethel here," says Mira. "It turns out, if she grants a wish, and a person who wasn't the wisher gets dragged into it, that person gets a wish of their own. It's only fair, isn't it?"

Now I get it. I understand what Lee was hinting around about before the land shark got him. *He* was the one with the unused wish all along.

But if that's the case... "Then the wish is useless." The hope I've been clinging to fizzles out.

"I knew it." Mira's eyes narrow. "Something bad *did* happen to Daddy. He *is* gone."

My heart goes out to her. This world the two of them shared is quickly fading away. Nothing will be the same after what I say next...but I feel like I owe her the truth anyway. "Yes. Your father is gone."

When Sea Munkies cry, their tears turn to bubbles swirling with color and float away. That's why little bubbles drift from Mira's eyes now.

"I'm sorry." Is it because I'm her mother that I want to rush over and comfort her? Or is it just because she's a child, and I've taken someone from her forever with a handful of words?

"It was the land sharks, wasn't it?" Just as she asks the question, there's another explosion outside the cave.

"Yes," I tell Mira. "It was the land sharks."

More tears bubble up from her, gently wafting on the still air of the cave. Sniffling, she wipes them away with the back of her arm. "That's all right," she says softly.

"Why is that?"

"Because." She nods firmly. "I inherited his wish."

THERE'S ANOTHER EXPLOSION, but its shockwaves don't reverberate nearly as long as the implications of what Mira just told me.

"You mean..." My mind is racing. "You mean, *you* can use your Daddy's wish since he's gone?"

"Mm-hm." Mira holds the whelk closer and strokes the curve of her shell. "Because I'm *special*. That's what Ethel says. I wouldn't be the way I am without *your* wish, just like Daddy. I didn't have any *say* in the matter...so now I *do*."

Another grenade explodes, continuing the countdown to

the end of our watery little world. It might be mostly piss, but I still hate to see it go.

"Do you know what you're going to do with the wish?" I ask Mira. "Have you given it any thought?"

She shrugs. "What do *you* think I should do?"

The answer has been taking shape since Lee first told me about the unused wish. "I think you should fix the world. Put it back the way it was."

"Wet and green, you mean?" says Mira. "Like Daddy told me?"

"Yes." I walk over and lay my hand on her shoulder. "Before it all dried up."

"Before Daddy died, too?"

"Before that, yes. And before I made the wish that changed us." I gently flick my tail. "Can Ethel do all that? Can your wish make everything right again?"

Mira stares hard at the whelk. The little creature's horns flex as if they're beaming a message to her mind, or communicating their own delicate sign language.

"Y-yes," Mira says finally. "But you have to do your part. You have to make up for the suffering you caused with your selfishness."

"Is that so?" I don't like hearing it.

"Will you?" asks Mira. "Will you do your part?"

I want to resist, but whatever that sea snail asks, it's a small price to pay. "Yes, of course."

"Okay." As another grenade booms beyond the cave, Mira closes her eyes tight and bows her head. Her lips move, but I don't hear whatever it is she's saying.

Meanwhile, the whelk pulses with amber light in her hands. The pulsing quickens, and the light expands outward-- then shoots off in all directions in a shower of blazing sparks.

"It's done." Mira opens her eyes and looks up at me. "There's just one thing you have to do for me before it happens."

"What's that?"

Multicolored bubbles fizz from her eyes. Reaching out, she takes my hand.

"Show me," she says. "Mommy, I want you to show me."

I TELL Mira to close her eyes before we swim out of the cave, and I'm glad I do. The water is full of bits and pieces of friends and neighbors, blown apart by the bombardment.

I hold her close with one arm, and she clings to me. With my other arm, I guide us through the debris, dodging familiar faces and body parts.

Propelled by my tail and webbed feet, we spiral up from the depths, rising toward the light. A long, green neck I know all too well twists in our path, and my heart catches with hope...but it is no longer connected to the monster who was once my best friend and defender.

I push past it, and still we rise.

Building momentum with powerful kicks and thrashes, I cruise ever upward. I see the stubby snouts of the land sharks ringing the view, and I grit my teeth, climbing harder.

When we break the surface, they all roar and reach for us. We're past them in an instant, carried by our momentum, shooting skyward.

I squeeze Mira, and she opens her eyes, looking around at everything--our sad little oasis, the sadder desert of pale sand all around it. She's never seen the world above the surface, never glimpsed daylight or blue skies undistorted by rippling water. It's something she wanted to see more than anything, especially now.

Because she knows what will happen after the wish takes effect. Ethel told her.

Ten feet up, twenty, we go...and hit the apex of our flight. Our momentum fades, and we're a breath away from falling.

Mira knows what that means. It's time to keep up her end of the bargain.

"I love you, Mommy." She gasps out the words, then closes her eyes tight.

"I love you, too," I tell her, as her lips move and Ethel glows brighter on her shoulder.

Then, her last wish, maybe the last wish in all the world, comes true.

I blink, and everything is different.

THE WARM SALT water parts before me, yielding to my enormous bulk in vast, foamy swells. The size of a major city, I plow onward through the skin of the ocean, through sun and storm alike, never flinching.

My giant tail swoops behind me, churning the sea like a hurricane's gust. My massive flippers steer me, turning me like a carrier along the curls of the tidal flows and streams.

Call me a whale at your peril. The biggest whales are dwarfed by my enormity, splashing like sunfish alongside an atoll. I am more like a *place* than a *thing*, dominating the briny kingdom such that nothing natural or otherwise can come close to matching me.

Except him. Roaring up beside me, he is my equal in *every* way, and my *love*. Like me, his emerald bulk is colossal, the force of his passage powerful to the point of godlike. Ships and creatures give him a berth so wide, it is like he is in a sea by himself.

Like me, he inhales immense clouds of polluted air and purifies them, devouring the excess greenhouse gases pumped out by human life. Like me, he cleanses the atmosphere, devours the waste, and breathes out epic draughts in perfect balance, staving off the apocalyptic transformation of the weather of the world.

Like me, his sole purpose and greatest joy is plying these glittering blue seas, making music with each fresh billow from the monumental emerald chimneys that tower on his back like giant organ pipes.

But unlike me, he does not remember the *other* world, the one that was drying up around us. The one that was drawing to a desiccated, whimpering close until someone made that one last wish that changed everything.

To him, this is the only world that ever was. These are the only selves that ever were, the only "us" we've ever known.

He does not remember that he was once Lee, or I was once Ida. He does not know the significance of the pink spines jutting from our titanic skulls, that they are the remnants of the fragile Munky forms we once wore in that pitiful pissy pool in the desert oasis.

And he does not remember the name or face or voice of the one who wished this glorious new world into being in the first place. He has no recollection of that person.

But to me, it is as if I last saw her only moments ago. And though I knew her only briefly, the memory of her good, sweet soul lingers in every tear that rises as a multicolored bubble from my eyes the size of mountains.

THE FIRST HOLLYWOOD COWBOY OF THE BROPOCALYPSE

W hat's it like having a brother who's the end of the world?

Not so hot sometimes, to be honest. But, full disclosure, I know it's not always a picnic being *my* brother, either.

When I show up on the doorstep of his apartment this morning, for example, I'm not there for a friendly visit. The truth is, I drop by out of the blue to try to get him to *kill himself*. Plain and simple.

And he *knows* it. I've done it before. *Lots* of times.

Call me persistent. Because when my brother, John Glass, dies, he will take the world with him. All *humanity* will end when he finally does himself in.

And that's something I've been craving for a very long time.

WHEN THE DOOR creeps open after my seventh knock, I'm hit by the smell first. Body odor, beer, cigarette smoke, burnt popcorn, and some kind of incense or patchouli. Plus an overlay of feces?

Then I see his wretched face peering out of the shadows, somehow bloated and sagging at the same time. Hair the color of straw hangs in greasy flops from a pocked, gray scalp. Blood-shot eyes squint into the bright Los Angeles sunlight, shielded by one scrawny, upraised arm.

When he talks, his voice is as hoarse as any wino's after a hard night's hacking it up in alleyways between screaming cats. "Loogie? 'Zat you?"

I have to admit, he does resemble the end of the world in human form. He looks like seven shades of shit, like death warmed over.

None of which changes the fact that he's my brother.

"Hey there, John." I smile and snap off my overpriced Oakley sunglasses--one of the status symbols that comes with my lifestyle as an ultra-successful media mogul. "How's it hangin'?"

John's attire is the polar opposite of mine. He scratches his chest through his yellowed wife-beater t-shirt, stuffs his hands in the pockets of his tattered bluejeans, and frowns at me like I just started using a foreign language. His lips move a little, though I can't tell if he's trying to form words or just trembling from the aftereffects of substance abuse.

"May I come in?" I shrug and keep smiling. "Or do you have company?" I shoot him a salty wink.

John shakes his head, but I think he's trying to clear the cobwebs instead of telling me no. "I gotta pee." He pulls the door further open and drifts off into the shadows inside the apartment.

When I cross the threshold, I nearly trip over an effing guinea pig scampering past. It's running loose, dribbling turds on the filthy beige carpet. The mystery of the feces smell is solved.

As I walk the rest of the way inside, I want to leave the door open to let in some fresh air, but I guess I can't do that in case the guinea pig gets out. Might not be the best way to get off on the right foot...though John looks so far gone, I wonder if he even knows that the animal's there.

"Make yourself at home." John shouts the words over the sound of buckets of urine blasting into a toilet bowl in the other room.

Not a chance. Even with blackout blinds keeping out most of the daylight, I can see by the TV's glow that the place is squalid as a rat's nest. There's garbage everywhere--mostly pizza boxes, Chinese takeout cartons, beer cans, and liquor bottles. The battered gray sectional sofa's covered with dirty clothes, some of which I could *swear* are moving. Then there's the big crimson stain on the carpet across the room, which could be anything from red wine to blood.

What with the smell, which is so much stronger inside with the door shut, it's enough to make me gag. And you wanna know the tragic part?

It isn't even the worst place I've found him in over the years. Not even close.

"Want a drink?" I notice the toilet doesn't flush before he walks back into the living room. No hand-washing water runs in the sink, either. "You see a half-empty bottle of Mad Dog laying around in here, Loogie?"

I don't correct him for the billionth time that my name's not *Loogie*, it's *Doug*. What difference would it make? "I've got a better idea. Put some shoes on, and I'll buy you breakfast."

The guinea pig runs over and stops between his feet. John leans down for a look, and his shredded blue jeans drop around his ankles.

He's *that* skinny at this point. He's that ragged. Looks like he's not long for this world. Like he'll die soon enough without any encouragement.

But he won't. Trust me, I know. He's not going anywhere unless he damn well wants to.

For a long moment, he just stands there like he doesn't realize his pants are down and his baggy gray briefs are hanging out. A blank, lost look hovers over his face, like maybe he doesn't even realize where he *is* anymore...and my heart goes out to him.

He may be many things, but he's still my brother.

"Hey, John. Pants." I point at his jeans. "I think they need a lift."

John nods slowly and bends over. As soon as his jeans clear the floor, the guinea pig shoots out from under them and disappears under the sofa.

"Any chance you have a belt in here somewhere?" I ask him.

"A belt?" He says it like it's something he's never heard of or imagined.

Which is why I trot out the one thing I know will reach him. "What about your Tom Mix anniversary belt? The one with the commemorative buckle?" As I say it, I step over and touch his arm, giving him a little zap of my rejuvenating power--one of the perks of being who I am instead of the end of the world like him.

It's just enough to blow away some of his fog. He blinks his eyes hard, and they come back into focus. "Tom Mix?" His slack jaw tightens in a smile. "Yes, I know I've got that around here somewhere."

And just like that, he's my old brother John again, the way he should be. I knew he was in there somewhere.

AT FIRST, I think I'm going to have to spoon-feed him his breakfast. He stares at the tray of McDonald's hotcakes and sausage like it's changing colors and doesn't make a move to pick up his plastic cutlery and dig in. Then, he nods off and slumps toward it.

"Hey, John!" When my voice fails to wake him, I jump up from my orange plastic bench and lean over to give him a shake. "Breakfast time, remember?"

His eyes flicker open and find the food. "You can have mine, Loogie."

"I can't eat my Egg McMuffin *and* your hotcakes and sausage, bro." I jam the black plastic knife and fork in his hands and sit down at my side of the table again. "You gotta help me out here."

He pokes a yellow hotcake with the fork and scowls. "I didn't ask for this, Loogie."

I smirk and unwrap my Egg McMuffin. "So you don't think Tom Mix would eat a breakfast like that if someone put it in front of him?"

Even without a zap of my power, he perks up at the mention of that name. He always does.

Reluctantly, John cuts off a sliver of hotcake with the plastic knife. "He did believe in a healthy breakfast, Loogie."

Does McDonald's qualify? I admit, I didn't want to take him somewhere nicer until I could get him cleaned up. "Most important meal of the day, they say."

John forks the sliver into his mouth and chews it slowly.

When he swallows, his Adam's apple lurches like he's gulping down half a porterhouse. "I just wish I could find that belt."

He's talking about his Tom Mix belt with the commemorative buckle. He looked everywhere in his shithole apartment before he gave up and let me cinch his jeans with duct tape. "It'll turn up," I tell him.

"I love that belt." Tears mist his veiny green eyes. "Almost as much as I loved that hat." He wipes his mouth with the back of a shivering hand. "Remember the hat?"

How could I forget? "Sure I do." It was a white ten-gallon hat, a replica of the one Tom Mix wore in the movies. John wore it everywhere as a kid, though it was a few sizes too big for him and often fell down over his eyes.

John pinches the tears from his eyes with a thumb and forefinger. "God, I miss that hat." He chokes out a sob.

I've heard it all before. I just eat my Egg McMuffin and let him cry it out, mourning for his beloved Tom Mix.

Now, you might think it's odd for a middle-aged guy like John in the early 21st century to be obsessed with Tom Mix. To look at him, you might not think he's old enough to remember an old-fashioned movie star cowboy like Mix, let alone to have seen his movies when they first debuted in the 1920s.

And guess what? You'd be so effing wrong, it's not even funny.

Not only that, but *I* was there, too. Saw the same movies when they premiered on the big screen, in fact.

But enough of the Tom Mix crybaby crap. I've got to get my big brother on track or I'm never going to get him to kill himself on schedule.

"John, hey." I reach over and pat his arm. "Eat up. It's gonna be a busy day."

One last sob, and he lowers his fork and knife to the Styrofoam platter again. It seems like it takes a major effort to cut more slivers from the hotcake and push them into his mouth, but he forces himself to keep eating.

As for me, I polish off the Egg McMuffin and sip black coffee while I watch him at work. "It's like old times, isn't it? You and me having breakfast together?"

He nods and narrows his eyes at me. Suddenly, I feel like the fog has completely burned off, and his focus is back to laser intensity.

"So what do you want, Doug?" He cocks his head. "Why the fuck are you here, instead of tending your fucking media empire?"

He's right about the empire, though I make it a point never to rub his nose in it. I own three cable networks, TV stations in five of the top ten markets, and a video streaming service that's number seven with a bullet on the interwebs. Let's just say I haven't been resting on my laurels during all those decades of waiting for this Godot wannabe. "Oh, you know." I smile cryptically over my black coffee.

"The usual?" His eyes get narrower.

I shake my head as I blow on my coffee. "Can't I just spend some quality time with my big brother?"

"So you're *not* here to get me to kill myself?"

I let out a chuckle. "That ship has sailed, John. You need to get over it."

"Bullshit." He stares at me some more. "You'll *never* give up. You *can't*." He spears his whole sausage patty with the fork and shakes it at me. "It's your *nature*."

I shrug. "People change, John."

"Sure." He nods knowingly. "But we aren't *people*."

He's got me there. We might *look* like the other customers

at the tables around us, but we're as far from ordinary people as they come.

And he's right about my never giving up. My core purpose in life depends on him. I can't truly come into my own until he finally lets go.

Because just as he's the end of one era, I'm the start of the next. I'm fated to bring to life what comes *after* the end...which I can't do while he's still kicking. He needs to perish, and I've got a plan to make sure he does.

But keeping all that to myself is part of the gambit. So is lying through my teeth.

"I've changed, John," I tell him. "So has everything else. I can't help it if you were too far up your own ass to notice."

"Changed how?"

"Changed so we both get what we always wanted." I toast him with my coffee. "Here's to the happy ending to end all happy endings, my brother."

AFTER BREAKFAST, I take him shopping at a discount store, picking up clothes and toiletries and a razor--a cleanup kit. He fades out on me a little, lost inside his own head, maybe considering the hints I dropped at McDonald's about the way things have changed.

By the time I get him to the local YMCA, he's back to shuffling like a hung-over zombie. Makes me wonder if he's on hard drugs again, but I guess that's irrelevant.

I send him into the showers with a bar of soap and a tube of shampoo, and then I wait. He's in there a while, but I don't mind.

The son of a bitch has already kept me waiting for decades. What difference will another couple of minutes make?

It might not look like it, what with the media empire and all, but I've kept my life on hold because of him for longer than most people have been alive. I've put off fulfilling my true destiny, becoming who and what I was always meant to be, because of that selfish prick dragging his feet.

But not for much longer, if things go according to plan.

Suddenly, I feel a wave of impatience. "Doing okay in there?"

He says something I can't make out over the running water, but I'll take it for a "yes."

Turning, I catch sight of my reflection in a full-length mirror on the locker room wall. Tall, trim, sober, well-groomed, good-looking--the opposite of him. My tailored Italian suit-- close-fitting, black with razor-thin red pinstripes and a crimson designer necktie--has nothing in common with his wife beater t-shirt and shredded jeans. With my jet black hair, brown eyes, and high cheekbones, I don't even look like I had the same mother.

But it makes sense, doesn't it? Considering who he is and who I am, it makes perfect sense.

As he waddles out of the shower naked, grabbing a towel off a hook on the wall, he doesn't look at all like the end of the world. But that's what he is.

Though, to be specific, I guess I should say he's the end of the part of the world that matters to people. The end of all the *people*, that is.

As for me, I'm also a world-changing force in human form, but my essence--and the footprint it's fated to leave on the face of the Earth--are very different indeed.

"Ready for a shave, John?" I gesture at the razor and travel-size can of shaving cream on the edge of the sink.

John finishes buffing the water from his chest and belly with the towel and gives me a funny look. "What's the catch, Loogie? You're not planning on taking me to a *funeral*, are you?"

"It's a surprise." I smack him on the back on his way to the sink. "You'll thank me later."

He scowls over his shoulder, suspicious. I can practically see the gears turning...but he won't guess what I have in store for him. He's my brother, we've known each other forever, but there's always been a gulf between us that can't be crossed. Because there's always a distance between an ending, like the end of the world...

...and a *beginning*, like me.

WHEN THE FIRST Dodger batter steps up to the plate in Dodger Stadium in the bottom of the first inning, I catch John grinning with unabashed delight. The suspicion he's been oozing at my every word and action blows right out of him. He's just glad to be here in an awesome front row seat along the first base line, watching a Major League baseball game in person for the first time in God only knows how long.

"Holy shit, holy shit, holy shit." He's sitting on the edge of his seat, drinking in everything except the ballpark beer he begged for (which I wouldn't let him get). Seeing him like that, all cleaned up and clean-shaven, wearing a new black polo shirt, tan khakis, and black Oxford shoes, I can hardly believe he's the same dirty, dead-eyed guy who answered the door at that rat's nest apartment a few hours ago.

He cheers when the Dodger batter hits a single, smack

between the shortstop and third base. The runner rounds first but gives up on second when the left fielder snags the ball in time to scare him off.

"Nice hit!" John claps and grins. For a moment, it's like old times. I remember the two of us watching the original Dodgers, the Brooklyn Dodgers, playing at Ebbets Field in Flatbush. John and I side by side, laughing in the sunshine, cheering and pumping our fists in the battered baseball gloves we'd brought to catch any foul balls that came our way.

Did we know by then what we were? Did we realize where our preordained destinies would take us? Honestly, I forget. When you live as many years as we have, the details tend to blur. It's like riding in a fast-moving car; you get a sense of the landscape passing by, but you don't always know where you've been.

Days like this stand out, though. The ones where the surprises happen. The ones with the drama.

The ones where your heart beats faster because you're in the stands at what's probably the last ballgame you'll ever see with your brother. What's probably one of the last ballgames in the history of humankind, in fact.

And as much as you welcome that ending, as much as you've effing *longed* for it, you still feel a stab of dread and nostalgia because of the change about to come.

Another batter smacks a grounder and lands on first, and John and I cheer and stomp. We *really* get in the spirit when the next guy loads the bases, and the Dodgers' best hitter comes to bat.

He whiffs twice, and we hold our breath. Then, with one mighty stroke, he blasts the ball out of the park. *Grand slam.* Just like that, it's a four-to-nothing ballgame.

Everyone's on their feet, including us, as the runners trot

home. John elbows me excitedly, whooping and flailing as the grand slam hitter circles the infield.

"Oh my God, this is great!" He shakes my shoulder, his face glowing with pure, perfect joy. "I'm so lucky I was here to see it!"

"The tickets *were* hard to get," I tell him. "The Dodgers are having a hell of a season."

"I'm not talking about the *tickets*." John shakes me again. "I mean I would've *missed* all this if I'd *killed* myself! I would've missed *so much,* Loogie. So many of the little *surprises* that the world has in store! We *all* would have missed them, because the world as we know it would be gone!"

I smile, but we're not on the same page here. His not killing himself isn't such a blessing in my book. Letting humanity continue to overrun and poison the planet isn't much of a plus, if you ask me.

The stubborn bastard hasn't done me any favors by sticking around. I guess the thousands of people in the stadium would feel differently about it if they knew. None of them would be here right now if not for him refusing to accept his responsibility and step aside.

But I'll bet the *next* ones, the creatures who are supposed to inherit the Earth and finally get it *right* this time, would have another take on things. They might not appreciate that this asshole brother of mine has kept me from ushering in their brave new world--especially if they knew just how long he's kept them waiting.

I see them clear as day in my mind, all squirming tentacles and suckers and inside-out, quivering organs. Their multifaceted eyes stare back at me accusingly, aching for their time in the sun. Pressing me to do the one thing I was made for, to usher in the golden age that will be the culmination of all Earth's millions of years of time out of mind.

Humans want to believe they're the end result, the apex of evolution. They'd never accept that they're nothing but a stepping stone, a transitional lifeform laying the groundwork for the planet's true success story.

John won't accept it, either. He never has, though both of us were given full knowledge of its inevitability long ago.

And I'm the only one who ever calls him on it. "You're happy to be alive. I get that." Now it's my turn to give *his* shoulder a shake. "So why do you spend so much time getting *wasted*? Why do you insist on living the way you do?"

John shrugs as his eyes wander to the field, where a walked batter is taking his base. "Because why not? This world is so *fragile* and *finite,* as we both know. Why not do what makes us *happy* while we can? Why bother putting on appearances and living the way other people think we should live?"

"Good point," I tell him. "It's all going to end sooner than expected, anyway."

"No it's not," says John. "I'm not planning on dying anytime soon."

"You still think it *matters* what you do?" I smirk and shake my head. "Then you're more out of touch than I *thought* you were."

Just then, there's the solid crack of another hit on the field, but John doesn't follow it. He's too busy squinting at me with a confused look on his face.

"What the fuck are you talking about?" he asks me.

"The end of humanity is already in progress." I nod knowingly. "Even as we speak."

John's confused look turns into an angry scowl. "You're full of shit, Loogie."

"Can't you hear it?" I cup my left hand behind my ear. "The fat lady's singing up a storm, Johnny boy."

"Pretty sure *I* would have noticed," snaps John. "Seeing as how *I'm* the one who's supposed to set it in motion."

"Better check your job description, bro. I think it might have changed."

"You're not making any *sense*," says John. "You and I are *constants*. The *end* of one world and the *beginning* of the next."

"Which was all supposed to happen *when*, John? When was the Great Transition originally set to occur?"

That subject takes some of the wind out of his sails. "The Missile Crisis." He mumbles the words. "The one in Cuba."

"In 1962?" I shake my head. "That wasn't the *original* scheduled end of the world."

Something makes the crowd cheer, but John's too busy glaring at me to look at the field. "1942, then. The Second World War."

Again, I shake my head. "You know that's not it, John."

He rubs his freshly-shaven chin. "1915." He says it grudgingly, as if he hates to admit it.

"Ding ding ding." I give him a little round of applause. "Give the man a cigar."

"World War I." He stares in the direction of the field but seems to look right through the players.

"Well, guess what happens when you delay the apocalypse a century?" I spread my arms and smile. "It happens anyway!"

John's frown deepens. "You don't know what you're talking about."

"Sure I do. I can *feel* it happening. I can *feel* humanity's replacements rising out of the muck." I shoot him a wink. "The wait is over, John."

His eyes narrow. "I'm supposed to believe this is all

happening without me? That it's just happening *spontaneously?"*

"I didn't say *that.*" I gesture at the crowd in the stands around us. "It's happening because of *them.* You can't hold them *back* anymore! They *want* it to be over."

His eyes narrow even more. "You're talking about global warming? Climate change?"

"It isn't *always* about climate change, John." I snort out a laugh. "I'm talking about extinction level shit you've never even *heard of* yet. These dumb fucks are circling the drain, and there's no turning back."

Just then, as if on cue, the whole crowd moans and boos. Looking at the field, I see that the Giants are at bat and have just brought in three runners on a homer to left field.

Meanwhile, John's oblivious to the game. I can practically feel the heat radiating from his overclocked brain as he processes what I've told him.

"So how long do we have, Doug?" His voice is even, impossible for me to read. "How long till the end?"

I close my eyes, pretending to tap into my mystic link with the end times and the reboot that will follow them. "Very soon, John. A matter of weeks." I open my eyes. "The final stage is already underway."

"Weeks." Eyes still narrowed, he nods at me, measuring my words. "Then what? What happens to *me,* if humanity ends without me flipping the switch?"

"Live on as a remnant of the old world, maybe?" I frown. "Help guide the new kings of the Earth? Assuming you find a way to communicate with them, that is. They won't be much like humans, I'm afraid."

"Sounds like a blast," says John. "What if I just fade away, instead?"

"I guess that's a possibility, too."

"So what's the use, am I right?" John leans toward me. "Why not get out while the getting's good?"

Sarcasm. The jig is up. Whatever substance-induced haze was clouding his mind, it's burned off, now. So has any chance that this lame-ass reverse psychology of mine might convince him to off himself.

C'est la vie. It was only ever an opening gambit, anyway. The biggest trick is still up my sleeve.

"Want me to do it *right now?"* John raises his hands, palms forward, and closes his eyes. "Just release myself in the top of the third inning and be done with it?"

"Up to you." I shrug. "Or it might make for an interesting seventh inning stretch."

He opens his eyes and sneers at me. "I *knew* it. You *never* change, Loogie."

"How so?"

"Did you really think this would work? Did you think you could talk me into it that easily?"

"Nope." I shake my head and get out my phone. "I thought *this* might work, though." I open an app and hold up the phone for him to see.

He scowls at the image of himself on the screen and the text underneath it. "What the *fuck?"*

"I was right, wasn't I?" I can see it in his eyes. "Gotcha, bro!"

John grabs for the phone, but I jerk it away, then take a look at my handiwork on the screen. The word "TERRORIST" is emblazoned across his photo. The text under it tells the story of his plot to destroy Los Angeles. His *fake* plot, dreamed up by yours truly.

"What kind of joke *is* this?" Aware of the people around us, John lowers his voice. "I'm no *terrorist*."

"And I suppose you're not a *serial pedophile*, either?"

"Of course not!"

I touch a button on the screen, and a countdown appears in red digital numbers above his photo. "Five minutes from now, you *will* be." I raise my eyebrows and nod. "This story, complete with the locations of damning evidence, will go out to every news organization and law enforcement agency in the country."

John's eyes pop as reality sets in. "*What?*"

"And did I mention the Jumbotron?" I point the phone at the giant video screen across the ballpark. "It goes up there *first*. So maybe fix your hair a little, there's a cowlick right..." I reach toward his head.

He swats my hand away. "No!" Panic spreads over his features like a wine stain on a wedding dress. "You can't *do* this!"

"That's one theory." I waggle the phone in my grip. "But what if I *can?* What if I *do?*"

His mouth falls open, but no words come out.

"*I'll* tell you what. Life as you know it is *over*, that's what. So much for enjoying all the little surprises that the future has in store. Starting in..." I check the countdown. "Starting in three minutes, you'll be captured, ruined, imprisoned, and made to suffer for the rest of your existence. Your life will become a fucking *nightmare*. Everything you *love* will be out of reach *forever*."

"But I'm *innocent.*"

"Not for long." I shake my head decisively. "Stick a fork in yourself, Johnny boy. You're *done*."

"You *can't*..."

"I *can*. Media empire, remember?" I waggle the phone in his face. "*One minute.*"

"Oh God, oh God." Doors are slamming behind him. All he can see is the darkness ahead.

When he woke up in his usual stupor this morning, he never imagined today would work out this way. Now here he is, and the clock's running out. There's only one thing left to say.

"All right." He slumps in his seat, the picture of absolute defeat. "You win."

I touch a button on the phone, and the countdown pauses at ten seconds. I shake the screen at him. "Back out, and I take it off pause. Capische?"

He nods brokenly, staring into space.

"It's for the best, you know," I tell him. "You put it off as long as you could."

He turns his head, then, and meets my gaze. "I could have put if off longer. I *would* have."

If not for me. "Whatever."

He sits up straighter. "There's just one thing."

I frown. "What's that?"

"I have one condition," says John. "A last request." Somehow, he manages a small smile, and then he tells me what he has in mind.

John and I stand in the middle of Ventura Boulevard in the low late afternoon sun, facing East, and wait as the human race dies out around us.

Screams and sirens and gunshots fill the air from all directions. Flames lap at the blue sky above us as Studio City burns to the ground.

Thanks to John, who has flipped the inner switch that will soon end his life, the final chapter of humanity's sordid story is being written at last. No more wars, no more poverty, no more endless murder and torture and violation.

We have brought down the curtain on a failed experiment, paving the way for something kinder and wiser and more viable by far. We've traded up for the kind of rulers the Earth deserves, the kind it should have had all along.

Now it's time for me to live up to my end of the bargain. Time to grant the final request John made me promise to fulfill back at the ballpark.

"Where is he?" John sounds nervous, like he's wondering if I'll go back on my promise.

But I won't. "He'll be here." It's the least I can do, now that Armageddon is finally unfolding. Now that I've gotten what I want.

More than that, it's the least I can do for my brother. It's the least I can do for the one person I've known and cared about all my life, even as he drove me crazy and held me back from coming into my own.

When the action dies down, and the world of humans breathes its last, he'll fade away. Soon enough, I'll never see him again.

So I'm glad, this one last time, that I can make him happy again. That I can give him something he's longed for as much as I've longed for an end and new beginning of the world.

"Is that him?" Excitedly, John points at a distant figure that appears down the street. "Is it?"

Low, roiling smoke clouds the view. "Don't know." The figure is unclear at first, bobbing and swaying in the murk. But a distinctive sound precedes it, high-pitched enough to penetrate the apocalyptic cacophony of dying L.A.

Whistling. The figure is whistling something...a song. The closer it gets, the more clear it becomes, until I recognize it for what it is: "Don't Fence Me In."

John steps forward, peering into the smoke. "Wait...wait..."

The figure resolves itself, pushing through the worst of the smoke, but I leave it to John to announce who it is. I let him be the one to say the incredible words he must never have imagined he would say or hear again.

"That *is* him." John's voice shakes with gleeful anticipation. "That *is* Tom Mix!"

Fuckin'-A right it is.

As the man on the horse rides closer, I have to admit they both look great. They both look like they're in their primes in the 1920s or '30s.

Not bad for a pair of corpses that've been moldering in the grave for ages.

When Tom gets within thirty yards of us, he smiles and waves. He's dressed in white Western garb--white shirt, white trousers, white chaps, white ten-gallon hat...and a white belt with a pair of pearl-handled six-shooter revolvers in white holsters, one hung from either hip.

Tom's famous horse, Tony, is mostly brown, with a blaze of white extending along his face and muzzle. He tosses his head in the same jaunty way that Tom just waved, as if to say hello.

John's eyes are huge. I can tell it takes everything he has to keep from racing over to greet his idol.

"Howdy!" says Tom when he gets a little closer. "Good to see you fellers!"

As soon as the words leave Tom's mouth, Tony whinnies in agreement.

John raises a hand and waves. For a moment, he is dumbstruck by the miracle riding toward him.

I have to admit, I'm damn proud of my work. As a force of creation, of the beginning of a new species, I have the power to reenergize hungover brothers--or reanimate dead legends for at least a little while. It's not a trick; that's the real Tom and Tony over there. But it did cost me dearly.

Bringing them back took so much juice that the debut of humanity's successor species will be delayed. A wait that has already felt like an eternity will be prolonged many months more. Mother Earth's reboot will be put on hold until my weakened power recharges enough to kick-start evolution.

But it's worth it. Worth every minute of additional waiting.

"What're your names, pardners?" asks Tom as he rides up and stops a few feet from John and me.

John stays tongue-tied, so I speak on his behalf. "I'm Doug, but this man here is your biggest fan. His name's John Glass."

"Is that right?" Tom grins and tips his hat to John. "Well, good to meetcha, Glass. You half-empty or half-full?"

"Half-full." John says it softly, like a shy little boy meeting Santa Claus.

I laugh. "Ain't that the truth!"

John is beaming. He finally finds the words he's been searching for. "I can't tell you how wonderful it is to meet you, Mr. Mix. I've been a fan of yours forever."

"Very kind of you, John," says Tom. "And please, call me 'Tom.'"

"You were always my hero, Tom," says John. "I thought of you when I felt the most lost, and you helped me find my way."

"Funny you should say that." Tom tips his hat back with one white-gloved hand. "I'm feelin' pretty lost about now myself." He looks around at the blazing city, which continues to ring with screams and sirens.

"Could you use someone to ride with, Tom?" I ask. "Someone to show you around a bit?"

"Sure could." Tom winks and pats his horse's neck. "Got anybody in mind?"

Tony winks, too.

I look at my brother, as if there's ever any doubt. "What do you say, John?"

John's eyes fill with tears, and he wipes them away. His lips form a tight line as he clenches them against the sobs fighting to get out.

Grinning, I bob my head toward the man on the horse. "Burning daylight here, Johnny boy. What do you say?"

Suddenly, John lunges forward and throws his arms around me. *"Thank you."* He whispers the words in my ear as he holds on for dear life.

I pat his back. "*De nada*, pardner." I think I've got a few tears of my own on the way.

"Sorry for keeping you waiting, brother," whispers John. "I just couldn't let go."

"I know the feeling." I'm having trouble letting go myself. Now that I'm faced with the thought of losing him, I hate to break the hug.

Fortunately, Tom intervenes. "Maybe I better hit the dusty trail on my own, fellers."

John gives me one last squeeze and pushes away. "Not a chance, Mr. Mix. I'd love to be your guide."

Tom narrows his eyes. "You sure about that?"

"I wouldn't miss it in a million years," says John.

"Then saddle up, pardner." Tom pats the horse's back behind him. "Time's a-wastin'."

John hurries over, and Tom reaches down to give him a

hand up. Light as a feather, John swings a leg over Tony and lands in the saddle behind Tom.

"Seeya, bro." I smile and wave.

John looks perfectly comfortable riding with Tom, as if he's always belonged there. It's hard to believe he was ever a hopeless addict and an obstacle to planetary evolution.

It's also hard to believe that I'm never going to see him again.

"Aydios, pardner," says John with a goodbye gesture--a salute of his index and middle fingers glancing off his left temple.

Tom tugs on the reins. Tony whinnies and tosses his head, then turns and trots off down the street.

"Hasta la vista!" Tom waves without looking back, then whistles "Back in the Saddle" as he and my brother ride west. A warm wind blows toward them, clearing a path through the smoke as if on cue in a Hollywood movie.

They are silhouetted by the setting sun as they sway off down Ventura Boulevard, outlines blurring against the bright golden disk as it melts like butter into the rippling horizon.

IN ALL YOUR SPARKLING
RAIMENT SOAR

Though all of existence, to us, is a poem, certain verses are not exactly joyful. *Mmm-bzzz.*

In those days, for example, our first days on this world among humans, our tasks were not happy ones. We took no pleasure in what we did to them, though we did it for good reasons. Though we sought to find

The beauty of the burning dawn,

A spectrum woven out of eyeblinks

And tears, the heatless flickering

Of featherless wings rising

Mmm-bzzz

Rising from the darkling pool colliding

With the swirling curtain of an opalescent

Luminescence.

But the truth is, in the *mmm-bzzz* in the beginning, we did not know if we would ever reach it. If the horrible things we were doing to these creatures, primitive yet every bit as sentient as we, would ever yield up the prize we were determined to set free.

SUBJECT 1. That was her official designation. I called her *Clarity*, because that was what I saw in her eyes the first time we met; that was what impressed me about her the most. We didn't know what she called herself, if anything. We didn't understand her language, if there was one. Not that it mattered.

At least that's what we'd thought in the beginning. That the details didn't matter.

But oh how they mattered. Like the downy black fur that covered her body. The long, dark mane

So soft, so flowing,

A beautiful veil cascading over shoulders

Over chest like a waterfall at

Night, a solar wind wrapping

Around the silver skin of a

Caressing the skin of a

Dreaming the form in the formless

Deep.

As if words could ever *mmm-bzzz* could ever express her radiance. As if scientific measurements could ever convey the dimensions of her

Magnificence.

As if any attempt to recreate the memory of her could somehow excuse what I did to her.

But back in those days, four million years ago as you measure *mmm-bzzz* reckon time, Clarity filled my thoughts. *Our* thoughts, I should say. The collective thoughts of ten thousand of us, bound in the harmony of the hive mind.

It didn't matter that she was so different from us. That, on the surface, she had so little in common with insects like us.

In a way, we were made for each other. Our ship, hibernating underground for many months after landing, built us from the genetic building blocks most prevalent on your world. The automated systems constructed us in a way that best suited the local environment, our mission, and our biological software. Our *soulware*.

We'd been built and rebuilt thusly many times, on many different worlds. Always maintaining *mmm-bzzz* preserving what kept us special. What kept us the most efficient and productive pollinators and gatherers in the galaxy.

Clarity was one of the first humans we saw when our ship finally burrowed out of the ground and the hatches irised open. As we tasted the air of this world for the first time, she stepped fearlessly out from behind a boulder.

The rest of her tribe cowered in the shadows, but not her. *Mmm-bzzz.* I can still see her, meeting us clear-eyed and square-shouldered when even the brawny males wouldn't come forth. She was unafraid, confident, graceful. A born leader.

Clarity gazed at us with wonder in her bright green eyes. And I gazed back at her with more of the same, transfixed. I knew there was something unique *mmm-bzzz* special about her right away.

Which, of course, was one of the reasons we chose her on the spot as the first subject retrieved for our operations on this world.

IN OUR SWARMS, we are ten thousand strong. Each member of the swarm is no bigger than a human fingertip, but together we have

Power.

Working together, perfectly synchronized, we can arrange ourselves in the shape of a human body and execute a wide range of tasks. For example, we can guide a human female into a shipboard lab.

Which is where we can restrain her *mmm-bzzz* strap her to a metal table and drive a spike at her forehead.

Clarity didn't scream when the spike shot toward her. She didn't even watch it approach. Her eyes were fixed on me the entire time.

Was she defective for not expressing fear? Did she lack the proper response mechanism to potentially fatal stimuli?

Not if there was no possibility of *fatality.* Not if the tempered metal spike shattered like ice when it hit her forehead, leaving not a mark of damage on her.

WHEN WE APPLIED the same test to other human subjects in our shipboard labs, the results were identical.

Clarity and her species were nearly indestructible. As we confirmed through our experiments, no external physical attack could harm them. Through some miracle of evolution, humanity had become perfected *mmm-bzzz* immortal.

And that was why we'd come here. Not to become attached to these primitive creatures, so abysmally low on every scale of development of which we could conceive. We'd come to find a way to kill them...and ensure salvation for the human race and our own species besides.

How could we possibly *save* humanity by *killing* it? Because only in death can a human being, or any sentient lifeform, evolve to the next level.

My people specialize in making that possible. We free intelligent beings from their physical bonds like a shoot from a seed.

Have you ever wondered why you hear nothing from the skies *mmm-bzzz* from space? No intelligible signals from the impossible vastness?

Surely, in all that everything, there must be someone like you on another world. Someone to talk to. Someone to connect with. What are they waiting for? Why won't they call?

The answer is this: It is because
they have all become
Light.

This was the destiny we had come to help humanity attain *mmm-bzzz* realize. Enabling humans to die would free the inner light from their corporeal shells and allow it to escape into space. Allow it to join the light of countless other lifeforms in the infinite reaches.

And my people, as we ushered humankind on its way, would experience *mmm-bzzz* undergo our own transformation.

One that would save us from ruin.

Our souls were ancient. Our soulware had become degraded. When it collapsed, our sentience would dissolve; we would lose our sense of self and be unable to perform our mission. Time was running out for us.

But when humanity died and moved to the next level, the resulting surge of inner light would allow us to save ourselves. We would channel enough of humanity's light through our ship's instrumentation to burn away the impurities and reboot our degraded souls.

In a way, humanity's souls would pollinate our own, bringing new life to us. In that one tremendous release, my people would be reborn.

We would regain our immortality in the corporeal world just as humanity lost its own.

ALL THIS WAS RIDING on the shoulders of beautiful Clarity, though I'm sure she knew it not. To her, each day was an ordeal without explanation. Though I did what I could to leaven the ordeal with moments of kindness.

I would wake her in the morning by brushing *mmm-bzzz* dabbing honey on her lips. Her eyes would flutter open

Like the wings of butterflies,
soft as velvet, damp with dew,
diaphanous, intangible,
closer to whispers or
thoughts,
closer to intentions,

The feelings of lingering love from a
dream,
All that's left when you can't remember
the lover.

And then her tongue would slide out and touch the glistening honey on each lip. It would glide languidly along the top and then the bottom, licking up the sweetness as I watched *mmm-bzzz* gazed through ten thousand pairs of eyes, ten thousand facets in each eye, each facet soaking up a different part of the visible and invisible spectrums.

And then I would go to work on her. I would try to kill her again and again, day after day.

AT FIRST, I went through the same techniques my people were employing on other specimens. I had to confirm they would lead to *mmm-bzzz* produce the same effect, that her baseline was identical to the rest.

So I gathered my ten thousand buzzing selves in one body and attacked her. I tried to cut her throat and split her head open. I tried to choke her, drown her, set her on fire. I tried to break her in every way possible.

Through all of this, she remained unharmed and no more alarmed than when the spike had shattered against her forehead. Like the rest of her people *mmm-bzzz* species, she was indestructible.

She didn't seem to experience any discomfort, either. Stimuli applied externally were as ineffective at causing her pain as they were at damaging her body.

So we moved on to stage two. The introduction of pain by other methods.

T<small>HOUGH WE HADN'T SUCCEEDED</small> in killing a human, we *did* manage to stimulate pain. This, we thought, could be the gateway to death for these creatures.

The strongest results came from electrocution or intense irradiation. Strong natural forces channeled *mmm-bzzz* focused internally were able to provoke the nervous system, evoking a pain response.

I can still hear her first screams piercing the air of the lab. I'll never forget the way she thrashed on the metal table, fighting her restraints, convulsing. Eyes rolled up in their sockets or pinched shut against the waves of agony.

But her eyes were not always rolled up or pinched shut. Often, they were fixed in my direction, wide and bloodshot with suffering and desperation.

H<small>OW MANY OTHER</small> humans did I torture on any given day? Clarity was not my only subject, after all.

Yet who among them possessed the grace to set aside the suffering when it ended? To face the torturer with a measure of tranquility?

Only Clarity. Only this singular angel could muster a smile in my presence.

Between sessions, I fed her honey and wheat germ. I poured purified water between her parched red lips.

Others of her kind accepted nothing from me, perhaps expecting *mmm-bzzz* fearing it would bring them more pain. But as much as I abused her, Clarity trusted me. She still seemed on some level to sense my good intentions.

I wonder sometimes how this was ever possible, given the gulf between our species. The lack of common language between us. The sheer differences in physiology. I must have looked fearsome to her, a cloud of insects roughly shaped like a man. Thousands of unblinking eyes

Like chips of polished
Ebony, thousands of black and yellow
Stingers, known only to her by the
Screaming in her own throat,
The thoughts in her own mind,
The new, suffering thing she had become because of
Me.
Her divinity, I suspect, made this miracle real.

I COULD NOT ALLOW her to leave the ship, could not even let her off the table for fear of corrupting the experiment.

But between sessions, I brought the world to her. Projectors in the lab recreated her habitat in three dimensions around us.

So though she *mmm-bzzz* though she still lay strapped to the table, destined for more torture, she could see at least for a few moments the familiar grasslands outside the hull of the ship. The amber plains rippling

In the wind, in the blazing sunlight,
Shadows of clouds gliding over the sea of grain,
Twinned in the mirror-skins of watering holes,
Slipping over creatures bristling with horns and
Tusks and teeth and claws and beaks of every angle,
Long necks parting the treetops,
Spear tips bobbing in the lazy current.

She sighed when the image of a brightly colored bird swooped overhead, silhouetted against the sun. She smiled when a lithe gazelle sprinted past, followed by a hail of spears and a team of human hunters who'd thrown them.

When she smiled at me, too, the fascination *mmm-bzzz* adoration I felt multiplied a thousand-fold. I felt redeemed, at least a little, for the work I had to do.

And therefore able to continue to do it.

THE INFECTIONS TOOK weeks to administer. One after another, I pumped her system full of bacteria, viruses, phages, fungi, and exotic microorganisms from other worlds. I administered them one and two and ten and twenty and a hundred at a time, carefully watching *mmm-bzzz* recording the effects.

This microbiological warfare had an impact. By attacking her internally, they triggered powerful shocks to her system. Like electrocution and irradiation, they caused intense pain.

But not death. Her immune system rose up always and wiped away the invaders as if they'd never existed.

NEXT, it was time for stage three. It was time for innovation.

Following protocols, I had charted the baseline and covered the same ground we'd been over with other subjects. Now that I'd established *mmm-bzzz* determined she was biologically identical to other humans, I could explore new approaches. Any success would likely extend universally to the rest of her species.

If I could kill *her*, I could kill *all* of them.

I'LL NEVER FORGET the first time I heard Clarity laugh.

I was embarking on a promising new direction in the lab--genetic manipulation. To begin testing, I needed to obtain a sample of genetic material, what you know as DNA.

I planned to collect the sample by swabbing the inside *mmm-bzzz* the lining of her mouth. I sent one of my ten thousand selves to accomplish *mmm-bzzz* perform this task.

But Clarity wouldn't open her mouth. My tiny single self hovered in front of her lips, bobbing in the breeze from her nostrils, and she wouldn't let me in.

She looked at my larger self looming over her, and I saw the worry in her eyes. This was new to her. Maybe she was afraid *mmm-bzzz* scared I was going to hurt her again.

Whatever her thinking, I sent my lone self closer to her mouth. I used his feelers and wings to tickle her soft lips.

Suddenly, Clarity's lips parted. She let out a flurry of noises from the back of her throat, a string of quick, chiming tones resonating through her sinuses, ringing from the top of her head. They were high-pitched as the song of a bird,

The tinkling of icicles snapping from a tree branch,
The whistling of wind through a hollow stone,
The singing of flowers with pollen-heavy pistils,
The cries of the stars in the night, forever
Sighing x-rays gamma rays radio waves neutrinos
On solar breezes swirling with glittering powder.

It was the first time I'd heard a human laugh. For an instant, I thought I'd hurt her somehow...but then I realized she was smiling. The fear was gone *mmm-bzzz* vanished from her eyes.

Seizing the opportunity, I tickled her more. Her mouth opened wider, and I

flew

inside.

My whole perspective changed in there. It was one thing to see her every day, to understand the functions of her body. To communicate in a rudimentary way.

It was quite another to be *part* of her, if only for a moment. To be intimately connected *mmm-bzzz* joined together.

Afloat in the warm red vault of her, I drifted over the moist mound of her tongue. I hovered between her flat yellow teeth, hoping she wouldn't bite down, and extended my own hollow tongue toward the inside of her cheek. Rubbing the slick flesh, I drew in a sample of her buccal cells, rich with genetic material, and stored it in my second stomach.

I wished I could have lingered, but I must have tickled her again. Her laugh sounded ten thousand times louder from inside her mouth. The expulsion of air threw my tiny self tumbling from her lips.

WHILE CLARITY SLEPT, I tampered with her DNA. My component selves zipped this way and that through the lab, mapping her genome and feeding the data into the computers.

Digital simulations predicted the likely *mmm-bzzz* probable outcome of each change. I could see the affected traits and the nature, degree, and viability of their altered expressions. Sophisticated algorithms calculated the likelihood that the changes would flip the right switch.

The switch that would bring down the wall that protected humanity.

I HAD DONE this kind of work before on many *mmm-bzzz* countless worlds, with other species. Such is my people's purpose in life: to help those who cannot help themselves. To rectify the flaws *mmm-bzzz* solve the problems that hold certain species back from their rightful destinies.

This work always follows certain patterns. I've learned to recognize key moments--the breakthrough, for example--and quickly grasp their significance.

How many times had such a breakthrough led me to a solution? How many times at such a moment had I felt the certainty of rightness in all my thousand thousand stomachs? It had always been a cause for celebration.

But not this time.

In fact, when the latest simulation suggested a new direction, and I knew in my thousands of guts that I'd found the key, I set it aside. I avoided it.

Instead, I went to Clarity and fed her. I watched her smile as she licked the honey from her lips. I made her laugh with a new trick I'd invented, tickling her by fluttering *mmm-bzzz* flickering the wings of my ten thousand selves all over her body at once.

But all along, the knowledge grew in the back of my hive-mind. Dread expanded like a storm cloud above us.

EACH TIME I went back to my work, I knew I was making progress. Each time I took it a step further, the certainty in my bellies became stronger.

Resequencing her DNA according to the template I'd designed would make her susceptible. If applied to other members of her species, the effect would be the same.

Here is the genius of it. Her body was perfected, indestructible. How then to pull away *mmm-bzzz* remove the shield?

The same way you scratch a diamond. Turn the indestructible against itself.

If, that is, you can stand *mmm-bzzz* bear to do it.

As weeks passed, I realized I might be the only one to design *mmm-bzzz* find a solution. In our daily meetings, the other swarms claimed not to be anywhere near a remotely viable approach.

Maybe, if I said nothing, I could still save Clarity. If I kept my solution to myself, and no one else came up with the same idea or an equally effective alternative, perhaps Clarity and her species would be spared.

But it was a slim hope, and I knew it. Other swarms were also researching *mmm-bzzz* exploring genetic modalities, and we were all working from the same baseline data. They could find the solution as easily as I had.

Unless I started submitting falsified reports. Unless I intentionally misdirected every other swarm by steering them away from what I knew was the answer.

In which case, I would be violating *mmm-bzzz* breaking sacrosanct rules of my species. I would be undermining the purpose of our holy *mmm-bzzz* sacred mission to this world. I would be jeopardizing the future of my own species.

But the one creature I'd found precious in all the galaxy, the one being whom I adored with all ten thousand of my hearts, would *live*.

ONE NIGHT, I was called *mmm-bzzz* summoned to join the others for The Rite.

All the swarms flowed out of the great silver ship at once, shimmering dark ribbons rippling into the night sky. We merged together into one giant cloud, one great swarm of all our multitudes on this planet. We formed concentric circles and began to turn, each ring rotating in a different direction, alternating clockwise and counter-clockwise.

The bright stars cast their flickering light upon us,
Glittering from our wings
and the polished cobalt facets of our eyes.
A billion trillion streams of starlight
Rushed out of the limitless heavens
and washed down over us.
So much light everywhere,
Direct, reflected, refracted, visible, invisible.
The universe a filigree of criss-crossed streamers,
The planet tumbling through a coruscating mesh.

And as I flew with the others through the tailings of that illuminated fall, I was reminded of our purpose, of our faith in that purpose. The sheer scope and importance of that purpose.

I'd come to think of it as something I could set aside just this once. As if denying an entire species its destiny was something I could live with.

The feeling of companionship with Clarity had been so profoundly *mmm-bzzz* powerfully alluring. It was so unlike the unity I felt with my hive-mind brothers, which was always inflexibly predictable. The pressure of the swarms in all their thousands upon thousands was ever-present, intrusive, demanding. Emotionless.

Lonely.

But did that absolve me of my responsibilities? Did it negate the sacred trust that had given my existence meaning for eons upon eons?

HERE IS how The Rite ends. How it ended that night.

Each of us carries a photoelectric wafer, tiny but highly sensitive. As we fly in glittering circles in the sky, the wafers absorb starlight and store it.

Then, at the right moment, we disperse, carrying our tiny burdens. All the millions of us, laden with our blue-glowing wafers, filter into the night. We seek out

the darkest shadows,

pitch black lightless

holes, hollows, burrows,

under roots, under rocks, in caves,

and we converge there, releasing our cargoes. The shadows blossom with tiny constellations of azure light.

It is a sacrament. *Mmm-bzzz*. It is a symbol.

We are pollinating the darkness

with starlight.

AFTER THE RITE, all our swarms came back together and mixed under the stars, merging our hive-minds into one mega-consciousness.

It was then, in that one colossal union, that the collective reasserted itself. I lost myself for a while in the mega-hive, surrendering *mmm-bzzz* submerging my own swarm's identity in the crushing embrace of the all-encompassing overmind.

Smothered by consensus, I felt the drive of species preservation in its fullest extreme. The urgency of our mission overshadowed *mmm-bzzz* choked out all other considerations. Surviving and helping humanity reach the stars were the only things that mattered.

When thoughts of my love for Clarity filtered into the gestalt, they were instantly extinguished. The mega-hive-mind tingled with disapproval

and disgust.

And they didn't give her a second thought. *We* didn't give her a second thought.

We had no desire for Clarity.

I EMERGED from the mega-consciousness like a drowning creature gasping for breath. As the collective disengaged *mmm-bzzz* released my swarm, I scrambled to pull myself back together, to retrieve the uniqueness that had been squeezed out of me.

When I did, I realized I was different from before. Merging with the overmind had reaffirmed my attachment to my people. Saving them felt more imperative than ever.

But as my individual thoughts and feelings came back to the fore, my love and commitment to Clarity remained strong *mmm-bzzz* undimmed. I could no more bear to lose her than I could bear to betray my people.

Two conflicting and powerful demands warred for dominance within my swarm. If Clarity and humanity lived, my people would devolve into non-sentient drones. If I saved my people, Clarity and her species would perish.

Then, suddenly, new insight blossomed within me. I saw the path to a new solution, flawed *mmm-bzzz* imperfect

but maybe one I could live with.

THE MORNING AFTER THE RITE, I awakened her as always, dabbing honey on her lips. Her clear green eyes flickered open, no less beautiful than the day before or the first time I'd seen them.

I worked hard all day, checking *mmm-bzzz* and rechecking my calculations, running and rerunning the simulations. Growing and programming legions of surgical nanobots to follow my instructions precisely.

I fed them to her that evening, with her wheat germ. And then I waited and watched.

THE NEXT DAY, there was no visible change. Clarity smiled and laughed like always. Her radiance was undiminished.

But when I scanned her, the equipment told a different story. Her DNA had changed. Overnight, it had radically altered *mmm-bzzz* transformed her metabolism.

The tests I performed confirmed the success of my treatment. Clarity had begun to deteriorate.

She no longer had the capability to live forever in her physical form.

BEFORE LONG, Clarity's condition was not unique among humans.

After she received the treatment, and tests confirmed its effectiveness, the swarms decided to administer it to all humans in the labs.

Of course, no one knew the full truth behind it. No one knew the way it would *really* work.

No one had found the secret coding I'd hidden away within my intricate genetic construct. They saw the surface changes, analyzed the modifications they would cause, but they didn't detect the catch I'd built into my solution.

WHEN THE RESULTS of the treatment were the same on the other humans in the labs, the swarms wasted no time going forth to treat every human being in the world.

But the swarms didn't realize there was no need to hurry. Humankind wouldn't die any time soon.

It was true that we'd brought down *mmm-bzzz* toppled the protective wall around Clarity's species. But what only *I* knew was that the process would be a *slow* one. It would take *years* for individual humans to die.

And it would take even *longer* for the human species to perish in its entirety.

I'D MADE life last as long as it could. Not just weeks and months, but dozens of years.

The human body would turn against itself over time, breaking down *mmm-bzzz* eroding on a long, slow slide to oblivion. I'd chosen prolonged aging and decline as humanity's lot instead of sudden, jarring extinction.

I'd given Clarity time to fully appreciate the joys of corporeal life before leaving it. I'd given her time to adjust to her mortality.

I'd given *myself* time to adjust to her mortality, too.

I'D ALSO ARRANGED for my people's salvation...though that, too, would take a while.

Humanity would not die all at once as originally planned *mmm-bzzz* anticipated, releasing a burst of inner light massive enough to reboot our soulware. In fact, it would take ages for enough human light to become available.

Thanks to my concealed genetic tampering, the altered trait I'd devised would be passed down to every generation of humanity with absolute fidelity all down the long ages.

As humans died, our ship would collect *mmm-bzzz* gather portions of their inner light, just enough that their escape to the stars would not be impeded. Someday, many generations later, the ship would have enough light to conduct the reboot, and my people would return to their mission.

In the interim, though, we would devolve *mmm-bzzz* revert to a primitive state. Until the Great Restoration, we would exist as common insects *mmm-bzzz* honeybees, lacking sentience. We would pollinate flowers, gather nectar, and build hives, but we would not remember who we were, where we'd come from, or what our mission had been.

It was a steep price to pay, but I decided it was better than the alternative. Better, I thought, to give Clarity a long life and delay my people's restoration rather than hastening it by killing her and the rest of humanity outright.

So THE FATES of humans and bees were intertwined and set in motion.

We bees would tend the fields and flowers of Earth as once we'd tended infinitely strange species of sentient lifeforms on distant worlds. Meanwhile, generation after generation of humans would inhabit the world and depart into space upon death as pure light.

In space, humans would find glittering multitudes of species from other worlds lighting the darkest night like glowing beacons,

Shooting through starfields,

Swimming through nebulae,

Criss-cross

ing flares flash

ing past a trillion wonders,

Weaving a tapestry of light

ning, a restless paint

ing of shimmering threads, rush

ing rivers all in photons of gold,

Never limited

Never alone.

And *Clarity* had made it all possible.

THERE CAME a day when I freed her from her bonds and opened the door of the ship to the outside world. She left...but to my surprise *mmm-bzzz* delight, she came back.

She always came back to me. Through all the weeks and months
and years
mmm-bzzz and decades that followed,
She always came back.

ONE DAY, a lifetime later, as the sun set over distant, snowcapped mountains, Clarity returned to me once more.

By then, my handiwork was plain to see; thankfully, I still had enough of a mind to comprehend it. Though other swarms' soulware was almost completely degraded by then, mine was just starting to lose ground to the Great Breakdown.

Clarity's fur had turned gray, and her flesh was sagging and wrinkled. She moved slowly, plodding *mmm-bzzz* hobbling through the tall grass, choosing each step with great care. Stooped and withered, she had changed so much since the first time I'd seen her, over fifty years earlier.

Her green eyes were sunken and filmy. Tears flowed from them
into the gray down
on her cheeks.

I think she knew what was coming. I think that was why she was there. She was weak and fragile beyond belief.

She almost fell to the floor, but I caught her and helped her to the silver exam table. She sat on the familiar metal surface, head bobbing, then slowly lay back.

Her eyes closed *mmm-bzzz* drifted shut, and she lost consciousness. As she slept there, curled up on the table, I examined her with my instrumentation. The joy I'd felt at seeing her turned to grief.

According to the tests, Clarity had reached the inevitable moment. The one I'd programmed into her DNA and delayed as long as I could.

When I realized what was happening to her, my ten thousand selves flew apart, swarming the lab in denial and confusion. I was dizzy with the whirlwind of impending loss, though I'd known this moment was approaching for decades. Though I was the one who'd invented it.

I could not bear the thought of existence
without her.
The knowledge that my work would lead to
Endless days
A procession
A weight
A space
A longing
All the worse
For having once
Been quelled.

It was then I realized, as much as I'd changed her, she had changed me more. As I hovered over her, gazing at her from every angle with my twenty thousand eyes, I knew how different I was because of her.

My hive-mind had realigned in fundamental, ineffable ways. I had reached beyond the swarm and shown personal compassion to another creature of another species. Not as part of an altruistic mission programmed into my genes, but because of the

yearning

of my ten thousand beating hearts.

In changing me, she had changed everything for herself and her people. Unlocked potentials that had yet to express *mmm-bzzz* manifest themselves.

And now, for her, for us,

there could be no going back.

Gathering my scattered selves together, I pushed back the grief as best I could and prepared for the final stage of our project.

CLARITY SLEPT SOUNDLY for hours on the hard metal table. As much suffering as she had found there, I think it still felt like home to her.

The monitors told me she was failing, but I didn't pay much attention to them. I was too busy watching Clarity's face as her allotted corporeal lifespan ran out *mmm-bzzz* expired.

I watched her toothless mouth as ragged, staggered breaths flowed in and out of it. I watched her nose wrinkle and flare as it caught some scent or the memory of one. I watched as her closed eyes flickered behind the lids, following the course of a dream.

Eventually, her eyes fluttered open

Like the wings of butterflies,

Soft as velvet, damp with dew.

By then, everything was in place. What she saw when she looked around were the grasslands of her home,

The amber plains rippling

In the wind, in the blazing sunlight.

Spear tips bobbing in the lazy current.

I tilted the table so she could see what lay ahead. A silver ship burrowing up out of the ground. Doors opening along the length of it, letting out ribbons of tiny, glittering creatures.

Suddenly, a woman emerged *mmm-bzzz* stepped out from behind a boulder. She walked unafraid with shoulders squared as her fellow humans cowered and ran. Her long, dark mane rippled in the morning breeze,

So soft, so flowing,

A beautiful veil cascading over shoulders

Over chest like a waterfall at night.

Clear eyes wide with fearless wonder, she gazed at the swarm, and the swarm *mmm-bzzz* and we *mmm-bzzz*

And *I* gazed back at *her*. Thousands of unblinking eyes

Like chips of polished ebony.

The woman in the tableau smiled, and so did the woman on the table. Past and future merged as one.

Then, the scene around us changed. It became a mirror image of the lab, with young Clarity strapped to the silver table.

My swarm settled *mmm-bzzz* descended upon her, tickling her with ten thousand pairs of flickering wings. Holographic Clarity squirmed and laughed with delight, and flesh-and-blood Clarity laughed, too. The laughter synchronized, high-pitched as the song of a bird,

The tinkling of icicles snapping from a tree branch

The whistling of wind through a hollow stone.

And by the time it subsided, she was almost gone. I switched the projection to a silent image of starry space to ease her transition. Galaxies pinwheeled around us. Comets streaked past, hanging tails of brilliant incandescence. Sprays of stars drifted like pollen through the inky night, sparkling like gold dust sprinkled over obsidian.

I went to her. All ten thousand of my selves hovered over her, gazing upon that well-known form, just as well-loved in old age as in youth.

Suddenly, she gasped, and her eyes shot open. I dared hope, in spite of the evidence of my instruments, that she might yet survive.

But then.

Mmm-bzzz.

But then,
You tremble with the effort,
shudder and go limp
with a sigh.
You settle
settle
to the table
like a feather
or a brittle leaf,
A windblown seed.

DON'T GO.

DARKNESS FILLS ME,
a smoky
smoky cloud
obstructing all hope,
choking off
all everything,
then dispersing

as a tongue of flame
Shoots through me.
Burning off the cloud
like morning mist
before the blinding
blinding dawn.

You.

YOUR IRIDESCENCE MELTS the shadows with a roar,
    Then laughs and twirls and disappears,
    As you in all your sparkling raiment soar,
    Away from every struggle, pain, and tear.

PIGGYBACK

T*his story isn't for you.*

THE CREATURE I'm riding staggers and clutches his left arm. He cries out, and I nearly cry out along with him.

I can *feel* the pain shooting through him--through us *both*-- because we're *connected*. I can feel his *fear*, too, but it's nowhere *near* my own. Because what will happen to him if he fails isn't even *close* to what will happen to me.

He doesn't know that this is my *last chance*.

THE CREATURE, an overweight middle-aged human with shaggy dark hair, is called Calvin Garland. He's homeless, and he's drunk, and he's having a heart attack in a New York City alley.

99

But he's *mine.*

Not that he even knows that I'm here, wrapped around his shoulders like a slimy green mink stole. Not that he or any other human is aware of me...though occasionally, when I want him to, he can *hear* me, just a little. And sometimes, he catches a glimpse of me out of the corner of his eye, just for an instant.

It's happened to you, too, hasn't it? Haven't you ever thought there might be a good reason for that?

CALVIN FALLS AGAINST AN ALLEY WALL, clutching his chest. At the same exact moment, I wrap a green tentacle around him and clamp its fanged red sucker into the flesh over his heart.

I pump a stream of syrup into his heart and follow that with electric shocks. The whole time, my hundred scarlet eyes are looking for any sign of The Viscera in the sky.

If The Viscera is watching, and Calvin drops dead, I'll be *swept* from his body and subjected to torments you can't even imagine. I'll spend the next thousand years shrieking and howling in agony at the hands of creatures who can see, touch, and torture me *just fine.*

None of this will happen merely because I lost a host. It will happen because I failed to drive a host to save the planet from the greatest threat it has ever faced.

"YOU DON'T WANT TO DIE," I whisper in Calvin's ear from my fluttering, ooze-coated lips.

"I don't wanna die," whimpers Calvin as the syrup and shocks take effect. "I don't *wanna* die."

His heart returns to normal, for the moment at least. Maybe if he'd taken better care of himself all those years...but he was living rough even before he moved to the streets.

I curl another tentacle around his head, plant a sucker between his eyes, and pump in a different syrup to take the edge off. He won't do me much good if he's too freaked out to walk and talk and fire a gun.

Then, suddenly, the temperature drops twenty degrees, and the sun turns to shadow. My circulatory organs pound, and my slime turns to ice, because I *know*.

The Viscera is here.

All my eyes turn upward. There it is, hanging over the tallest towers, filling the sky--too massive to take in all at once.

Yet not a single human can see that vast mass of squirming tentacles and pulsating ebony flesh. No human-built instrument can detect the flickering strobes of its sensory organs or the excrement dripping from its orifices.

And no human mind can comprehend the intentions of its ancient, implacable intellect. Not one of you can fathom the extremes that it will go to when dealing with its Yoke servants, like me.

But *I* can. And that is why I quake as it passes. That is why I do everything I can to stay unnoticed and unpunished.

Though I know, as every Yoke does, that The Viscera misses nothing. It is our God, just as it is yours.

Even though you don't know it yet.

"I FEEL MUCH BETTER NOW," I whisper in Calvin's ear. "I think I'll take a walk."

Calvin repeats the words, then pushes away from the wall

and heads down the alley toward the street. On the way, he reaches for the bottle of cheap vodka in the pocket of his filthy black overcoat and unscrews the cap.

He's drunk enough as it is, and the booze won't help his heart, but he's committed to drinking. It's the one thing I can't control, the driving force of Calvin's life.

I feel the vodka burn as it flows down his throat. Then, I feel a secondary burst of heat as the alcohol works its way from his bloodstream through my tendrils.

His brain lights up as the chemicals take effect, and he feels *good*. I experience the feeling through him, though I'm not made to enjoy it like he does.

Sometimes, his abuse of it can be a real problem, though it's also one of the perks of our partnership. It lowers his inhibitions, increases his suggestibility...therefore making him more likely to succeed in saving the world.

It gives him a chance to make up for the damage he's done in his life, though it can never bring back all the people and things that he's lost.

SOMEWHERE IN THE WORLD, Calvin has a son and two daughters. An ex-wife, too, and an ex-life.

Was it the booze that cost him his job as an actuary at an insurance company? That cost him his wife and kids and friends and house? That cost him *everything?*

It was *fear*, actually--fear of losing it all that made him lose it. A self-fulfilling prophecy.

I call it *fate*. Now, at least, he has *me*...and his mission. His *purpose*. I've given his life meaning again.

If only I can keep him alive long enough to achieve it.

CALVIN STUMBLES DOWN THE STREET, guided by twitches of my tendrils embedded in his brain. Human commuters of all description hurry past on the way to work, giving him a wide berth, many aiming disgusted looks in his direction.

He's repulsive to them, dirty and homeless...but I wonder how some of them would feel if they knew about the unseen pulsating green hitchhikers riding piggyback on their shoulders?

There are lots of us out there in the world, each performing a separate mission in the name of The Viscera. You might be surprised how close to home they are.

We're a brotherhood...but whenever I see one coming, I avoid it. I steer Calvin out of its way, even if it means bumping him into someone and causing a scene.

Because I'm not in the loop about their missions. Any one of them might have been assigned to take over mine and cut me out of the picture.

"I need to walk faster," I tell Calvin.

"I need to walk faster," he repeats, speeding his pace.

At the next intersection, while we wait for traffic to clear, a young blonde woman in a floral print dress stops beside us. She is oblivious to the Yoke clinging to her shoulders.

Its eyes lock on me like a hundred crimson magnets. One of its tentacles twitches in my direction, and I panic.

Then, as I'm about to tell Calvin to break into a run, the Yoke's tentacle squirms around and hooks into the blonde's left breast. It's only feeding.

But I still don't take my eyes off it until we've walked another block and lost them down a side street.

A FEW BLOCKS LATER, Calvin realizes he needs to urinate. Worried about the delay since we're on a tight timetable, I push him onward...but then I realize he'll piss his pants if I don't let him relieve himself.

He turns down an alleyway and stumbles over behind a dumpster. It doesn't bother him that there's another homeless man sitting across the alley, watching him. The pain from his full bladder is too great.

Taking advantage of the situation, I pump my own metabolic waste out with his urine...and blood. His kidneys are in rough shape; he's down to one, and it's failing fast.

Between that, the cardiac arrest, the cirrhosis in his liver, and the lung cancer, it's almost a miracle that he's walking around alive. I say "almost" because it's all because of me.

Without my propping up his systems, he'd be long gone by now. I wonder if, on some level, he understands this.

I'm sure he notices when a muscle in his eye twitches, or a vein in his leg ripples for no apparent reason. He's aware when there's a sudden sharp pain in his side, or strange new marks on his skin that won't rub off.

All these things come to his attention, though he just brushes them off and gets on with his day. Sound familiar?

Have you ever noticed fluctuations like these yourself? Have you ever wondered what they might mean?

Are you noticing one *right now* at this very moment?

As soon as Calvin stops pissing, he grabs the bottle of vodka. I don't bother trying to get between him and his booze, I know it's futile.

But he barely gets a swallow out of it. Cursing, he hoists it high, letting the last drops drip on his tongue, and then he shambles over to the guy across the alley.

"'Scuse me." Calvin holds up the bottle. "Help a brother out?"

The other guy is younger, leaner, twitchier. He squats there, smoking a cigarette, watching Calvin with wide, bright eyes.

"I better get going," I tell Calvin, but he doesn't repeat it, and he doesn't turn to go.

Which is too bad, because I can see the chemical traces of recent heroin use all over the other guy. And who knows what kind of weapon he might be packing.

The possibility of failure, followed by worldwide catastrophe and a thousand years of torture, just increased dramatically. Why is my luck always so *lousy* in the field?

Twelve is the magic number. That's how many hosts have died under my care without completing their missions.

Can you imagine what it's like being pulled apart and "repaired" by The Viscera? It's happened to me *every time* I've lost a host...and it is *awful*. The agony doesn't come *close* to the alternative--a thousand years of extreme torture for a Yoke deemed unfit for repair--but the suffering is still *indescribable*.

Even after all that, my repaired selves have had no different outcomes than their predecessors. More dead hosts, more mission failure. It's like I'm cursed.

Now here I am again, at number thirteen, and it's my last

chance. And I just wonder why, if I'm such a loser, did The Viscera give me such an important mission as this? It had to *know* it would end in failure.

Or did The Viscera think, in its infinite, inscrutable wisdom, that this heavy burden--or the promise of ultimate punishment for final failure--would force me to rise to the occasion?

"Don't got a bottle? That's fine." Calvin tosses the empty vodka bottle over his shoulder--through *me*--where it smashes against the wall. "Loan me a couple bucks, and I'll go buy one we can share."

The squatting heroin user flicks away his cigarette butt and slowly rises. Fully unfolded, he's taller than Calvin by at least three inches.

"Better idea." The guy slides his hands in the pockets of his gray hoodie. "How 'bout if *you* loan *me* a little somethin' some-thin'?" His tone is undeniably threatening, his message clear. It wouldn't surprise me if he's got guns or knives in those pockets.

He's got "host killer" written all over him.

My circulatory organs race, and my green skin turns fiery red. Will I let this be the moment when everything goes bad again?

The hoodie guy pulls out a hunting knife and jabs it at Calvin, who jumps back. Another jab, another jump.

Lots of things I could make him do, but running away makes the most sense. Better to minimize risks and increase the likelihood of staying alive.

But before I can work my puppet, he thrusts a hand in his overcoat pocket and hauls out the gun he's got in there. It's a

.45 semi-automatic with a full clip, more than enough weapon to blow away our problem in the alley.

But that gun and those bullets have another job that's much more important. I can't let him fire it here and now.

Lashing out a tentacle, I sting his gun hand. Calvin cries out and drops the .45.

Which the other guy promptly scoops up off the pavement.

AT THAT PRECISE INSTANT, shadows and cold fill the alley as The Viscera cruises overhead. Just in time, it's there, ready to snatch me up and gulp me down.

"No!" It's the moment I've been dreading, the one I can't seem to get away from. The moment I've had nightmares about for so long, I can't remember what a *good* dream *is*.

I'm about to be locked in the depths of that leviathan and tortured like a degenerate traitor for what will seem like an eternity. And I *deserve* it.

But the thought of it suddenly *sparks* me. I'm so *terrified* of the consequences of inaction that I feel an urge for action build inside me.

"You're *dead!* You're *dead!*" snaps the hoodie guy as he waves the gun at Calvin. The look on his face is crazed; the .45 could go off at any second.

But so could *I*.

Breaking all my connections with Calvin, I leap off his shoulders and throw myself at the hoodie guy. My immaterial substance lands on his face and quickly wraps around his head.

He can't see or feel me, but the shocks I administer make an impression. And when I jam a tentacle in the back of his neck and pump in anesthetic, he crumples like a rag doll.

I cling to him as the gun slides from his grip. But why doesn't Calvin run over and grab it?

Because he's just *collapsed* and isn't *breathing*, that's why.

THIS IS IT.

Talon-tipped tentacles descend from The Viscera, slithering from the belly of the god-beast amid wildly strobing searchlights. They're coming to get me.

I think of the tortures ahead--unmentionable violations of body, mind, and soul--and every bit of me quivers in terror. *The Mouths*, and *The Tumors*, and *The Self*; I've *heard* what they can do. I've *seen* what's left afterward, and what The Viscera does with *that*.

I'll do *anything*, try *anything*, to escape that fate.

As the tentacles continue their descent, I peel myself from the head of the hoodie guy and spring toward Calvin. Landing on his chest, I plunge in tendrils and hunt for signs of life.

Almost gone. His heart has stopped, and the rest of him is close behind. Detaching myself is what did it; he's long past the point of functioning without me.

Good thing we're together again.

I restore every hookup, winding tendrils and tentacles deep into his body. I pump him full of syrups, carefully calibrated to restore his metabolism. Then I shock his heart, zapping him with just the right charge to restart it.

But nothing happens.

I feel the slimy discharge from the tentacles of The Viscera oozing over my body, and I almost scream. Looking up with my hundred crimson eyes, I see the tentacles are barely *six feet away* and coming in *fast*.

In fact, one of them is faster than the rest and drops down suddenly, its fang-studded tip grazing my back. And I do cry out then, because the touch of it *burns* like a *brand*. It *burns* and it *hurts* so much that the next shock I give Calvin's heart is stronger than the first, stronger than intended.

And it's strong enough. He comes back to life with a sudden, wrenching intake of breath.

Just as The Viscera's tentacles are wrapping around me, they unwind and retract. And the cold and darkness slide away soon after.

IT TAKES SOME DOING, but I get Calvin up and moving again. It costs him, I know; bringing him back up to speed after such a deep dive taps reserves we were saving for later.

But it had to be done. According to my orders from The Viscera, our target will be in a certain place at a certain time-- and that time is fast approaching.

Shaking off his near-death experience, Calvin retrieves his gun. He takes one last look at the hoodie guy, still out cold on the pavement, then turns his back on the alley and shuffles out onto the street.

I nudge him left, and he complies. I tell him to go faster, and he does.

We're back on track. I'm a nervous wreck, my slimy flesh tingling and jittering, but we have a chance again.

And there's no sign of The Viscera, which is a good thing. My retrieval isn't imminent. My failure isn't certain.

Please, Viscera, please, I beg you! I've come to save the world! Please let me do it!

WE BARELY REACH the site of our mission in time. A medical van is parked in front of the wrought iron gates, back door open to receive a passenger.

Less than half a block away, Calvin stumbles to a stop. "I'll be damned," he says, scratching his head. "I forgot why the hell I came here."

No surprise there. I kept that information to myself. But I'm sure he'll get over it.

How many times has this happened to you? Is it because you have too much on your mind, and things slip through the cracks? Is it a kind of mental hiccup, brought on by stress or fatigue?

Or is it something else altogether?

The next time it happens, think back. Where were you just now? Check the clock. Are you missing any time? If so, what did you do with it?

I'll bet you never stopped to wonder, did you? Never asked yourself if some dark passenger might have taken the wheel.

Never asked yourself what that thing might make you do *next*. Never *wanted* to know.

"I DON'T FEEL SO GOOD." Calvin bends over and puts his hands on his knees. Coughs a little blood on the sidewalk.

I give him a good zap that straightens him up and pump in some high-dose endorphin syrup that clears the cobwebs. Now is *not* the time to attract attention.

"I have a job to do," I whisper in his ear. "I have to save the world."

"I have a job to do," repeats Calvin. "I have to save the world."

There are things I can do to blur his mind, and I do all of them. I keep two tentacles stuck to his head, one on either temple, and pump in syrups that make him suggestible. I blend in mild sedatives to keep him relaxed and malleable.

But it's a delicate balance. I also need to keep him alert and ready for action. And he needs to remain adaptable so he can improvise if he has to.

At least I know him well by now. I have a good idea of how to manage his body chemistry and mental state. I know he can get the job done.

Though I'd be lying if I said there isn't any doubt. There's *always* doubt.

And, therefore, fear.

THE BRICK BUILDING behind the iron gates is a mental hospital, over a hundred years old. People with behavioral problems are brought here for treatment and care...though it might be more correct to say that people who *are* problems are brought here.

And one of the patients is more of a problem than the others. She is a problem, potentially, for the *world.*

As we watch, a white-uniformed male orderly with brown skin and a huge, black mustache brings her out in a wheelchair. They are heading for the medical van, which will transport her to another facility.

Maybe *they* can do something for her--the people at the other facility. Nobody *here* can help her, that's for sure.

She's seven years old, and her parents have abandoned her to the care of the state. Her name is Lacey, and she is adorable, with curly red hair, freckles, and bright green eyes.

She is also hopelessly insane, a danger to herself and others. At least, that's what the *doctors* think.

"I have to save the world," I whisper to Calvin.

He hesitates, then nods and repeats what I told him.

"I need to get closer to that van," I whisper.

Calvin does just that, shambling toward it. The driver, who's standing by the open back door, waiting to receive the patient, doesn't even notice him.

Whether you're an immaterial piggybacking symbiote or a homeless old man, it's *good* to be invisible, isn't it?

By the time we get within twenty yards of the van, the orderly has pushed Lacey halfway across the sidewalk. *Almost there.*

My circulatory organs pound like the hoofbeats of the onrushing future. Everything I've ever done or been or thought comes down to this moment.

I am on the cusp.

"Closer," I whisper.

Muttering the word, Calvin gets closer.

Where is The Viscera, I wonder? Watching another Yoke perform its sacred mission? Or are its infinite eyes already fixed upon me from afar?

I don't want to fail! I don't want to be tortured for a thousand years, and I don't want to fail my god!

Closer, closer. Then I stop Calvin when we get within ten feet, as if he's waiting for the orderly and patient to pass.

"Hello, little girl," I whisper, fighting to keep my voice from shaking.

"Hello, little girl," says Calvin.

Slowly, Lacey's head turns toward us. There is a heartbeat, a moment in time.

And then, she starts screaming her lungs out.

"What the hell?" says the orderly.

Lacey just keeps screaming. And pointing. At Calvin.

At *us*.

I can't take my eyes off her. It's hypnotic, unlike anything I've ever experienced among humans.

Because, for the first time, my gaze is *met*. I am *recognized*.

And it fills me with terror.

"I am killing Hitler." My voice quakes fiercely as I whisper the words in Calvin's ear. "In his crib."

"I am killing Hitler," says Calvin as he pulls out the .45, guided by my writhing, squirming tendrils threaded through his muscles and organs and bones. "In his crib."

Long after the blast of the gunshot, it seems, Lacey's terrible shrieks linger in the air.

AND SO, I live happily ever after. No thousand years of torture for me; only glory. I'm a *hero*, and so is Calvin--posthumously, anyway.

Soon after the shooting, his body gave way, and I had to grab another host. I'd pushed Calvin to the limit by then, and he dropped dead with the gun in his hand after squeezing off three shots.

I do miss him, I can't deny it. But he'll always be a hero to The Viscera and its Yokes. After all, it was *his* finger pulling the trigger that killed Hitler "in the crib"--*our* version of Hitler, that is.

For there could be no one more dangerous to us than a

human who could *see* us for what we are. Such a person could be used as a weapon against us, thwarting our efforts to save your people and your world.

Save it for *our* purposes, which of course are the only ones that matter.

So the world is safe again, and its people blind as ever to our presence. And *you* will never know if that *pinch*, that *itch*, that *ringing* in your ear or *movement* in the corner of your eye is just a fluke, a quirk of your imperfect biology...or *something else*. Maybe something like *me*.

If that's the case, if what you're sensing or feeling--perhaps *right now*, as you're reading this--is one of *us*...

Then the unseen thing on your shoulders, with its tentacles stuck in your flesh, its slime oozing down your back, its whispers in your ears, guiding your every move...

That thing might *smile*, and know that all is right with the world. That there's no longer any need to fear exposure or detection.

That *thing* with its tendrils wound through your brain and heart and gut like wriggling, glistening *worms*, it might even *laugh*. And what do you expect, when this is such a happy ending?

Remember what I told you at the start. I gave you *fair warning*, after all.

This story isn't for you.

FUZZY DUCK

When they yank the hood from my head, I'm struck by how clean and sweet the air smells. I had forgotten, though I used to spend all kinds of time here back in the day. Back when I was the honest-to-God Secret King of the World, that is.

I stand for a moment with my eyes shut, drinking it in, savoring each crystal pure breath. If I didn't know better, I might think I'm in a mountain meadow on a beautiful Spring day. Not in a bar in a secret retreat that's at once the most powerful, luxurious, and corrupt places on Earth in the 21st Century.

Not in Xanadu, where the people who *really* run the world come to play and prey away from prying eyes.

"Mr. Nothing?" A short, middle-aged Chinese man in a dark suit steps in front of me. "Right this way, please."

As he leads me away from the goons who brought me in--a South African and a Russian with matching mouthfuls of gold teeth--I have a look around at the old familiar place. It all looks exactly the same as it did twelve years ago, when they fired my ass from the shadow government they call Apogee.

The room is enormous and designed with Olympus in mind, from the towering Corinthian pillars to the Roman god statuary and brightly colored tile mosaics straight out of Pompeii. All the walls, floors, and furniture are built or carved from various shades of marble, dark as well as light and everything in between.

Elegant tapestries surround secluded niches overflowing with jewel-encrusted relics and satin pillows. Exotic gardens twined with fat jungle flowers and glistening green vines occupy raised circular beds situated under skylights. Fountains and little waterfalls burble everywhere.

The few patrons at this hour (Early morning? No idea.) stare back at me from couches in the shadows, sipping from golden goblets. I recognize one of these people instantly, then another. They are leftovers from my era, survivors of the terrible events that swept me from my throne forever.

Peering into a darkened alcove, I see another...and wish I hadn't. His name is Phineas Castor, and he looks every bit the brute and pervert I remember from my years on the throne. Some people were more responsible than others for my downfall, and that sick bastard was one of them.

He waggles his fingers in an mocking little wave as I go by, then returns his attention to the leather-clad boy at his side.

The next face I see is my own, reflected in an ornate gold-framed mirror occupying a wall that we pass. This place might not have changed much, but *I* have. I was forty-seven years old when I left, with an ever-present bronze tan, thick brown hair, straight back, and a fit, slender build. Twelve years later, I have the build of a couch potato or barfly--flabby and pale, with a soccer ball of a pot belly. My posture is slightly stooped, and my hair is gray, thin, and as shaggy as the veil of a weeping willow tree. My green eyes have perpetual wrinkles and bags, and the goatee I've taken to wearing is patchy and unevenly trimmed.

My footsteps echo in the cavernous chamber as my Chinese guide leads me on among the niches, booths, and gardens toward the answers that await. I still have no idea why the powers that be brought me here. They didn't tell me or ask my permission; they didn't have to.

My guide stops and points at an arched doorway. He provides no further explanation, and I don't ask.

My hackles rise as I walk past the Chinese man and through the archway. I find myself in one of the many private party rooms branching off from the main chamber. Looking around, I see signs of a struggle--broken glass, overturned furniture, scattered cigarette butts and drug paraphernalia. But none of that is the main attraction.

The most interesting thing is on the far side of the room: a man's body sprawled on the floor, stripped to the waist, motionless. A tall woman stands over him, scribbling notes in a small pad...and shooting me a stern look as soon as she becomes aware of my presence.

"Come in. Don't be afraid." Her voice has all the warmth of an ice storm in deepest winter. Her face, with its gray-eyed solemnness and high, chiseled cheekbones under a platinum blonde crewcut, intensifies the chill. "I'll protect you."

It's a cut, a jab, a gloat. She's one of the people responsible for exiling me in the first place. "What makes you say that?" I ask calmly.

"It's open season on kings of the world, obviously." The woman, Gerta Andersen, gestures off-handedly at the dead man on the floor at her feet. "Though I suppose you don't really count anymore, do you?"

I take a step closer for a better look at the body. I didn't recognize him at first, but now I see who he really is: King Prospero III, my successor.

"You see, everything worked out for the best." Gerta lifts one silver eyebrow. "If not for your downfall, that would have been *you* on the floor instead of him."

"His chest." I step closer, taking care not to disrupt any of the scattered debris. "Something's written there?"

"In blood, yes." Gerta tucks the note pad in the vest pocket of her black suit jacket. "What do you think it means?"

Two more steps bring me close enough to see over the debris and read the words on his chest. *Does he fuck?* That's what it says.

I shrug and look up to meet Gerta's gaze. "Why am I here? What do you want from me?"

"You're a private detective now, aren't you?" She spreads her arms wide. "So crack the case."

She's right, it's what I do. Turns out I have a knack for it. Stumbled into my first job not long after the exile and built a business from there.

Not that *this* is a case I would *ever* in my right mind take. "Don't need the work, thanks," I tell her. "Send me home."

"He's the *king of the world!*" She smirks like a boa constrictor ready to coil around me. "Aren't you even a *little* curious?"

"Not a bit." I turn and start working my way back to the doorway.

"What if it meant a chance to redeem yourself?" asks Gerta. "A chance to clear your name."

"You mean you'll give me my throne back?" I already know what the answer will be, and I keep heading for the door.

"Yes. You can have it back."

I was wrong, and I stop in my tracks. "You people would never do that."

"Try us," says Gerta.

I know better than to trust her. But what she's telling me is so unbelievable, I can't ignore it. "If I solve this murder, I become king of the world again? Just like that?"

"Yes." She nods.

"Seriously?"

She nods again. "For one day."

I knew it. The men and women of Apogee would *never* restore me to the throne.

But even the one-day offer is tempting. Thoughts of what I could do with 24 hours of absolute power flood my head.

"Will you call me by my real name, at least?" I ask. "If I agree to work the case?"

"Absolutely not." Her sharp-edged ruby lips curl in a sneer of disgust. "You'll always be Mr. Nothing to me."

I shake my head. She hasn't changed. But her current motives are still murky. "Why me? Why bring me in on this?"

"Your investigation skills," says Gerta. "And your unique perspective as an exile. You're an outsider, which brings a certain objectivity...yet you were on the inside once."

"You and your team couldn't solve this?"

"We weren't given much time." Gerta's eyes flash. "We were told to send for you almost right away. Meanwhile, we processed the crime scene and canvassed for witnesses but didn't come up with anything."

I'd wondered about that. They must have sent the collection detail to pick me up almost immediately after the king's death. Probably kept the room on ice to preserve the evidence, too. Extreme climate control is available in every part of

Xanadu, after all, to cater to the most extreme and depraved tastes.

"So what's your decision?" Gerta sounds as if her patience has run out. "Man up or wuss out?"

I look at Prospero on the floor. My bullshit detector is going off like you wouldn't believe. I think it's possible that I might end up dead on the floor like Prospero, if things don't work out.

But then there's that king-for-a-day reward, which is probably bullshit...but maybe not. Most of all, there's one force in play that has a strong hold on me, though it has gotten me in trouble more times than I can tell.

Curiosity. It might be the death of me yet.

Until then, let's see where it leads. "Okay," I say finally. "Tell me what you know."

WHEN GERTA'S DONE TALKING, I spend some time alone with the body. I look for clues, anything that might inspire me now or later.

The cause of death, according to Gerta, was suffocation. Murder by pillow, to be exact. Though it would have taken someone physically powerful to hold Prospero down for long. The dead king is no small man; he's heavyset with a ponderous gut, but plenty of muscle mass beefing up his arms and legs. He would've put up a hell of a fight.

Which is exactly what happened, judging from the state of the private party room. Prospero fought back; the smashed glass and furniture is covered with his fingerprints. But there's no sign of anyone else's prints anywhere in the room.

And there's no other kind of trace in here, either. Gerta's forensics team has combed every millimeter of the place and found nothing but Prospero's DNA. The evidence says no one else was in this room during the murder.

Which is exactly what everyone in Xanadu says, too. No one was in here with Prospero that night, and no one saw anyone enter or leave. It was a busy night, the place was packed, yet nobody saw anything. The king of the world was murdered in cold blood in a side room of the most crowded bar in Xanadu, and nobody knows how it happened.

Which, incidentally, is total bullshit, but who can blame them? Everything is permitted in this secret pleasure dome, nothing is forbidden--except the murder of an Apogee VIP. Anyone found guilty of such a crime will be executed in a way you don't want to know about...*trust* me.

So back to the evidence, or lack thereof. *Does he fuck?* is scrawled on the victim's bare chest in his own blood. Some kind of condemnation? The suggestion of a sexual indiscretion? Everyone in Xanadu is a philanderer, no form of sex is forbidden--but jealousy can be a powerful thing. Maybe this was a crime of passion.

There's precious little else to go on. No trace of sexual activity on the body or in the room. No sign of poison in his bloodwork--just the usual booze and recreational drugs. No recordings, as this is a private room and he was the *king of the world.*

"The king is dead," says Gerta when she strolls back into the room. "Long live the *ex*-king."

"Poor son of a bitch." I stand and peel off the latex gloves I've been wearing. "Is he the first king to die in office like this?"

Gerta nods. "Hey, and *you're* the first to be dethroned and exiled! The two of you have something in common after all!"

Without answering, I head for the door. "Go ahead and get this mess cleaned up."

She falls in step beside me. "Where do you think you're going?"

"To sniff around. Talk to some folks. It's called investigation."

"Here in the bar, you mean?"

"Nope." I walk fast between the tables, gardens, and alcoves, aiming for the nearest door that leads to the corridors of Xanadu.

But when I get there, my gold-toothed Russian and South African friends step in to block the shit out of me.

"You can't go out there," says Gerta. "You're *persona non grata* in Xanadu."

I turn on her, mad enough to spit bullets. "I thought you wanted me to work on this *case.*"

"In *here.*" Gerta sweeps an arm around to encompass the bar. "Think of it as your headquarters."

"You have *got* to be *shitting* me."

"The good news is, unlimited drinks!" Gerta smiles and pats me on the shoulder.

As a recovering alcoholic and drug addict--three years clean and counting--this doesn't impress me. "I can't do the *job* sitting around a *bar.* I need to *circulate.*"

Gerta just shakes her head. "Not going to happen. Once an exiled traitor, always an exiled traitor."

For a moment, I think about rushing the two thugs and trying to fight my way through the door. But what would that prove, assuming I make it without taking *too* big an ass-kicking?

"Fine." I glare at both guards in turn, then Gerta. "So what say we quit pissing around and get some people in here to interview? If not eyewitnesses, at least people with some kind of motive and opportunity."

"Good plan." Gerta smirks. "Considering you have less than two days to slap a bow on this."

I stare at her like she just grew a horn out of her forehead.

"What?" She says it like I'm the biggest idiot who ever lived. "You think they'll let you stay here for the *coronation* of the *new king?*"

THE MAN SITTING across from me in my makeshift office in a booth at the bar looks like he just ate something rancid. His long, bony face is drawn down in a look of deep disgust, his sullen gray eyes staring sourly at me. Hard to believe he was once one of my staunchest supporters.

Good thing I don't let backstabbers bring me down anymore. "So you're telling me your alibi for the king's murder...is another murder?" I say it as pleasantly as possible.

Basque Almondine nods once. Hard to believe, back in the day, he was one of the funniest guys around.

"You were in your private rooms, killing a slave boy from the pits?" I ask him.

He holds up two fingers. Then a third. "More than one." His voice, with its indeterminate Southern European accent, is a hiss.

Then he smiles, and I want to be sick. I was once part of this fucked up culture, *king* of this twisted domain...but it still turns my stomach. I'm a different man now.

None of which changes the fact that technically, what he's telling me he did is perfectly acceptable. He hasn't broken a single law. Remember: killing an Apogee VIP is the *only* crime in Xanadu.

"You cost me a great deal of money. Did you know that?"

Basque sneers and pokes a bony finger at me. "There was a pool after you left. I bet good money that you'd kill yourself within a week of your forced retirement."

"Did you have money on when *Prospero* would die?" I lean my elbows on the table and lock my gaze with his. "You were his biggest rival, weren't you?"

"We weren't *lovers*, if that's what you mean. But I would *never* kill a fellow member of Apogee. It's against the *law*." He leans closer, and his parchment lips spread wide in a Venus flytrap grin. "Speaking of which, *you're* not Apogee anymore, *are* you, old friend?"

Don't remind me. The pressure from the target on my back is impossible to ignore.

"Well, this has been special." Basque pushes his chair back, plants his knuckles on the table, and pushes himself to his feet. "I wish we had more time, but I have chores that won't wait another minute." He turns away, then sneers over his shoulder. "And by *chores*, I mean *murders*. Care to join me?"

"I'm busy." I drop my eyes to the list of interviews in front of me.

"Shame. I'll be sure to kill one for you, how's that?" Slowly, he raises a hand with two fingers erect. "Or more than one."

He raises a third finger, then a fourth, before shuffling his way out the door.

BY THE TIME I get through ten more interviews, with each subject more despicable and less helpful than the last, I'm ready for a smoke. (I don't count cigarettes when I talk about being clean for three years.) I'm also ready for some fresh air, so

I go outside though I don't have to; there's no law against smoking indoors here, after all.

My guard detail walks out with me into the tropical sunshine, but the guys at least have the decency to give me a little space while still keeping me on a short leash. They wait by the door, keeping their eyes peeled for tomfoolery, while I light a smoke and walk a few yards away to the edge of a cliff over-looking the ocean.

I couldn't jump if I wanted to; there's a dome over Xanadu. But being the butt of so much undisguised loathing from my interviewees--and former subjects--makes me wish I could fly away.

"Excuse me?" My thoughts are interrupted by a woman's voice. "Nathan?"

I turn to see a face from the past approaching through the trees--but she's not scowling or sneering like the others.

"Hello." I manage a little smile.

So does she. "Long time no see."

"Much too long, Erin." I hold out my hand, the one without a cigarette, for a shake.

Erin ignores it. Instead, she throws herself forward and wraps her arms around me.

I wish I had a dozen flowers to give her. A dozen flowers for every second of that embrace.

Back by the door to the bar, the Russian and South African look ready to intervene...but I shake my head hard, and that keeps them at bay for now.

"I never thought I'd see you again." She whispers the words against my chest.

I flick away the cigarette and kiss the top of her head. "Same here."

If I could have taken one person with me into exile twelve

years ago, it would have been Erin. In all of Xanadu, she was my truest friend, my most unflagging supporter. She stood by me right up till the end.

I can only imagine how hard that must have made it for her when I was cast out, and she was prevented from leaving with me.

Correction. I think I see traces of how hard it must have been. There are long-healed scars on her neck and shoulders, snaking out from the collar and short sleeves of her simple navy blue dress.

"What did they do to you, Erin?" No one's supposed to call her by her real name, which was stripped from her when she was abducted and thrown in the slave pits of Xanadu. But she told *me* her name and story, and I repaid her trust by lifting her into a better life as my assistant.

"That's not important right now." She lowers her voice. "They tried to keep me away from you, but I called in favors. I had to tell you the real reason you're here."

"What is it?" I lean closer.

"They think there's a conspiracy to bring you back to power," says Erin. "They think you planned the whole murder, and your supporters carried it out."

I shake my head, watching as the guards finally start toward us. "I had nothing to do with it."

"Which doesn't mean *somebody* didn't plan it that way." Erin hears the guards approach and grabs my wrists. "Someone *might* have brought you here to make you king again, whether you know it or not."

"Being king again is the *last* thing I'd want." I meet her gaze, ignoring the guards for one more moment. "Being with *you* is the first."

"Which would only make a damn bit of difference if either

of us were free." Erin hops up to kiss me on my cheek. "*Be care-ful,*" she whispers.

And then she's gone, darting off along the cliff's edge and into the forest.

ONE BY ONE, the slaves of Apogee filter into the bar, eyes down and hands folded in front of them. The men and women come to me in all skin colors, hair colors, eye colors, shapes, and sizes. They all have different QR codes tattooed on their left biceps, indicating their owners and medical histories. They couldn't be more different, though they all wear identical electronic shock collars, gray smocks, and black sandals.

To the VIPs of Apogee, they are property. To me, they are potentially a source of vital information.

After what Erin told me on the cliff, I knew I had to try something extreme, and I thought this might work.

If I can get them to talk.

That won't happen if a single VIP remains in the bar, so I shoo out the management and customers, even my guard detail...though Gerta drags her feet.

"Please leave," I tell her, pointing at the door. "And remember, you promised no recording."

"They're not your allies." She looks around with amusement at the downward-staring slaves. "And they *won't* do your bidding. You're as low on the totem pole as *they* are."

I see that as a blessing, not a curse. Maybe it will even help me solve this case. No Apogee VIP will tell me anything useful; maybe a slave will volunteer something.

"Maybe we should gas the whole lot of them and start

over." Gerta finally heads for the door. "There's always more where *they* came from."

She storms out, leaving me standing among the ranks of the unfortunate. They are the missing, the castoffs, the forgotten from all over the world, scooped up like stray pets and broken to serve the sick whims of the men and women of Apogee.

"Hello, everyone." I stand in the middle of the room, and they slouch in a listless circle around me. "I come here seeking your help."

None of them looks at me, but all of them listen.

"Apogee is not in this room. They are not watching or listening." I spread my arms wide, then lower them to press my hands to my chest. "And I, as many of you know, am an exile, without power. I *swear*, I will not betray your confidence."

A few of them look up without raising their heads.

"I hope you will help me. I hope you will tell me what you know about the murder of King Prospero."

Some of the slaves shuffle and stir. The sound of their movements echoes through the room.

"None of you are suspects," I tell them. "According to the data in your collars and internal chips, you were all elsewhere at the time of the murder. But perhaps someone among you has heard or seen something that will help me find the killer."

Dozens of faces rise to look at me. Their expressions are uniformly dark. No one steps forward or raises a hand.

I start to question the wisdom of bringing them here like this. I thought that maybe, the strength of numbers and absence of Apogee might make them feel safe enough to tell me something that might turn into a lead.

But maybe they don't believe they're truly safe. I know *I* wouldn't.

More moments pass in total silence. Finally, I take a deep breath and say the only thing that seems to have a place here. The only thing that doesn't feel like total bullshit.

"I'm sorry." Another deep breath. "I'm sorry for everything I did to you when I was king. I'm sorry I never set you free." Another breath. "I've come to see how wrong I was."

The faces around me look just as grim as ever.

"Thank you for your time." The crowd parts as I start toward the exit, reaching into my pocket for a cigarette.

Then, a child steps in front of me.

He's Indian, perhaps 12 years old, with light brown skin and short black hair. "I will show you how to play a game," he says softly.

"A game?"

He points at the bar. "We will need beer."

I look up and see the adults watching closely, impassively. But no one steps forward to shut this down.

"Okay then." I nod, wondering what this has to do with the murder.

"The winner dies," says the boy as he walks toward the bar.

"Then that makes him the loser, doesn't it?"

The boy shakes his head. "The *loser* is the slave who sees it happen." He looks back over his shoulder with all the severity of a soldier in a war zone. "The loser is my *sister*."

THAT EVENING, the bar comes alive with a different kind of crowd. The slaves cleared out long ago, making way for a mob of revelers celebrating the holiday of Coronation Eve.

By six o'clock, the place is packed from end to end with Apogee VIPs, all of them dressed in colorful, dazzling outfits festooned with feathers, fur, and fortunes in glittering, gleaming jewelry. They've all come together to mark the occasion of a new king's ascension.

Is the new king a suspect in the murder of Prospero III? I thought so for a time; he certainly has a strong enough motive and ample power. But that was before I played the game with the slave boy (who says his name, which he's not allowed to have, is Dev. Now I know better than to blame the incoming king.

Now I know exactly who killed Prospero, and I'm about to reveal it.

"Buy you a drink?" Gerta sidles up to me on the dais in the middle of the room, where I've been observing the incoming guests. "Name your poison."

I don't dignify the offer with a reaction. "I need you to do me a favor," I say, keeping my eye on the door leading in from the halls of Xanadu.

Gerta smirks. "Barking out orders? You must've spent too much time with your slave buddies this afternoon."

More guests pour in through the door--but not the one I'm waiting for. "I need you to lock this place down on my signal."

Gerta laughs. "Now you really *are* tripping, Mr. Nothing. You expect me to *lock down* this bar with every high-ranking VIP in Xanadu inside?"

"If you want Prospero's *murder* solved, I do." Just then, I see the person I've been looking for enter the room. "And I expect you to do it *now.*"

Gerta glares at me. "*What* did you just say to me?"

I whirl on her. "Do you *want* to fuck this up? Or do you think you might *possibly* benefit from *cooperating* with me for a few minutes?"

"You know who did it? *Tell* me."

No way in hell will I back down at this point. I want *credit* for my work. "Lock it down. Do it now."

A moment crawls past. Then she folds. "You're unprotected, remember? Fuck this up, and you're dead."

"Just do it." I step away from her, watching as my target advances across the room.

Gerta storms off the dais and snarls orders at her security men. I watch as they fan out through the room, bunching up at the exit doors with weapons drawn.

I give the bar manager a prearranged signal, and he shuts off the music. Earlier, he gave me a wireless microphone, and I pull it out of my pocket and switch it on.

"Ladies and gentlemen! May I have your attention?" Elevated two feet from ground level on the dais, I'm able to make myself seen above the crowd. "Please, I need your attention!"

I hear plenty of grumbles and growls of irritation, mixed with boos and hisses of outright contempt.

When most of the crowd is looking my way, I continue. "Recently, your king was struck down by a cold-blooded killer. An *unknown* killer." I look at one face in particular. "Unknown *until now.*

"There have been many theories about this murder," I tell the crowd. "Some say Prospero was killed to bring a new king to the throne...or bring back an *old* king."

The room roars with catcalls.

"These theories could not be further from the truth!" I raise my voice to overpower the catcalling horde. "The reason for the murder was far more mundane. The killer was *not* a once *or* future king. But he *is* in this room right now!"

The crowd roars with outrage. I wait it out just long enough, then shout into the mic.

"I will now show you *why* and *how* King Prospero was murdered!"

There's chatter and scuffling as I gesture at a nearby, curtained-off booth. The black curtain parts, and Dev the slave boy walks out, carrying two mugs of water. He looks glum and a little scared as he approaches and steps onto the dais beside me.

I take one of the mugs from Dev with a reassuring smile.

"There is a game," I tell the crowd. "Perhaps you've played it yourselves. The goal is to repeat a set of simple words without making a mistake. Every time you make a mistake, you have to take a drink of beer--which increases the chance that you'll make another mistake and have to drink more beer, and so on.

"Allow us to demonstrate." I stand at one side of the dais, and Dev stands at the other. "Fuzzy duck." I say it loudly.

"Fuzzy duck," says Dev.

"Fuzzy duck," I say again.

"Duck fuzzy!" says Dev.

"There!" I look out over the crowd. "He made a mistake, and the game changes. Now I repeat after him, and he after me, until another mistake is made." I turn back to Dev. "Duck fuzzy!"

"Duck fuzzy!" says Dev.

"Fuzzy duck!" Again, I turn to the crowd. "Another mistake, you see? So now, we'll repeat the changed phrase until *another* mistake is made. But because of this particular arrangement of vocal sounds and the effects of alcohol consumption, it becomes increasingly likely that sooner or later, a player will say something *very* different. Go ahead, Dev."

"Fuzzy duck," he says.

"Duck fuzzy," I tell him.

"Duck fuzzy," says Dev.

And then I pause just a second for dramatic effect. *"Does he fuck."*

At this point, the crowd is dead silent. I think I have their attention now.

"Those are the exact words that were scrawled on the chest of Prospero the night he was murdered!" I shout it like a preacher condemning a congregation. "They told us exactly *why* Prospero was killed, but we didn't see it until *today*. He was *murdered* because he *won* a drinking game, and his opponent was the ultimate *sore loser*.

"This child confirms it!" I gesture at Dev. "His *sister*, the only witness, *told* him who the perpetrator was, right before she was killed to keep her quiet. All trace of her presence was erased from the crime scene by the killer.

"And now, on the eve of the new king's coronation, I stand before you to reveal the killer's identity. His name is..."

Just then, I hear a loud crack from the crowd--the thunder-clap of a gunshot. I duck, taking Dev down with me, as a second shot fires.

The crowd cries out and scatters. There's a third gunshot. I roll Dev off the dais so he can hide behind it, then scramble to my knees and then my feet.

Before a fourth shot can be fired, I launch myself off the dais toward the shooter. I come down on top of him, knocking him back to the floor.

Heart hammering, I seize the wrist of his gun hand and slam it down hard, knocking the weapon free. He struggles, and I pin him as best I can; I hold him down just long enough.

Long enough for my Russian and South African guards to bulldoze their way through the chaos and take over. I roll off, and they hoist the shooter from the floor like a paper doll.

That's when I finally get to look the bastard in the eye. The asshole who was so used to getting his own way that he couldn't stand losing a simple drinking game. The shithead who killed his own king, then tracked down and murdered a 15-year-old girl who walked into the room at the wrong moment, a girl who ran but couldn't hide for long from the monster's wrath.

The killer, Phineas Castor, stares back at me with nothing but contempt, as if somehow, I'm to blame for all this. His disgust is palpable as it was earlier today, when he waggled his fingers at me from his alcove as I first arrived.

"Release me!" he wails. "I'm within my rights killing the ex-king and the slave boy! Neither of them is protected by Apogee!"

I just shake my head, because he hasn't changed since he helped bring me down twelve years ago. He's just as sick as he ever was, and I'm...not.

I KNEW IT. I *knew* the offer of being king for a day was too good to be true.

The morning after the Coronation Eve drama, I tell Gerta I'm ready for my reward now. My first act as king for a day will be to free all the slaves.

"Yeah...no." Gerta shrugs. "You didn't think we'd actually let you do anything *important*, did you?"

We're sitting at the bar, side-by-side, having drinks. Mine is non-alcoholic, of course.

"But you said I could have the throne for one day," I remind her.

"Think of it more like you get one wish," says Gerta. "A *reasonable* one."

"I think freeing the slaves of Apogee is reasonable."

"Think smaller." Gerta clinks her glass against mine. "*Much* smaller."

I take her suggestion. I consider the possibilities, think about what I want that would make all the trouble worthwhile.

Then, I tell her, and she surprises the shit out of me.

She *agrees* to it.

WHEN THE HOOD is yanked from my head, I instantly recognize my surroundings. I'm finally home, back in my own apartment in Brooklyn.

I smell the mustiness and hear the traffic noise outside. I see my humble furnishings arranged in the tiny living room, from the beat-up old futon to the ancient black-and-white 19-inch tube TV on the stacked plastic milk crates.

I feel better than I have since I went back to Xanadu...especially when I realize I'm not alone.

Turning, I see two hooded figures behind me, one four feet high, the other more like five five. I yank the black cloth hoods from their heads and smile.

After Xanadu, I couldn't do everything I wanted, but I accomplished *something*. I got two people out from under the thumb of Apogee, with a promise that they will never be taken again.

"Nathan?" There are tears in Erin's eyes. "Did we really make it?"

"Yes." I nod to her, then pat the head of Dev beside her. "You're both free, and you're never going back."

With that, Erin wraps her arms around me, crying and squeezing me so tight that I almost can't breathe. Dev's crying, too, as he looks around in joyous disbelief.

And then I'm also crying, because we're together, and I'm not the man I used to be, and what's here in this room at this moment is all the kingdom I could ever want or dream of in this world.

NOT-SO-FORTUNATE SON

"Here! Catch!" Bunker Buster, with his purple paisley skin and torn green shorts, laughs as he tosses the tractor trailer effortlessly in my direction. "All yours, *Short Bus!*"

Pluribus! The name is Pluribus! That's what I'd say if I had more than a split-second before the truck hits...which I don't. I don't have Bunker Buster's strength level, either, so I do the usual--multiply like crazy.

Closing my eyes, I stretch my arms wide and tap into my power, whipping up dozens of duplicate selves to quickly fill the tractor trailer's landing zone. When the truck comes down, we all raise up our hands and catch it, spreading the impact among all those arms and bodies so it lands harmlessly.

Normally, Bunker Buster would follow up with some smart aleck remark, but he doesn't. The hyper-muscled testosterone farm is too busy fending off the latest squadron of sky-piranhas dispatched by Sticky Wicket.

"Gents, we shouldn't be fighting," Sticky declares in his

posh English accent, even as he finishes bashing in the unbreakable windshield of an armored car with a massive-headed croquet mallet. "We should all be on the same side, don'cha know!"

"I'm not on *anybody's* side, Stick Figure!" Bunker Buster crushes a sky-ranha between two massive hands and swats another halfway to Poughkeepsie. "I'm out for Number One, and that ain't *either* of you!"

"Suit yourself." Sticky deflects the gunfire of the driver with his mallet, then flings a needle-tipped metal wicket into the man's chest. With the driver dispatched, he operated controls on the dashboard, making the back doors pop open as if by magic. "That's one fewer compatriot who'll need a share of all this *cash*."

As my mob of doubles charges toward the armored car, Sticky leaps free of the window and skedaddles around the back like his butt is on fire. En route, he pitches more wickets behind him, puncturing one of my clones at the head of the pack. When the lead runner drops, others trample over him--at least until I focus my power and make the first grouping disappear.

Just as Wicket rounds the back of the truck, a big helicopter whips in from the distance. What looks like a huge metal ring hangs suspended from a rig mounted on the bottom of the copter, ready to pick up the armored truck, no doubt.

My doubles and I run harder than ever, but Bunker Buster still beats us to the back with one mighty leap over the top of the vehicle.

And then nothing from back there. When I get to the rear of the armored car, the only sound is the chopping of the approaching 'copter's blades and the footsteps of my running copies' feet.

And instead of Wicket and Bunker Buster, all I see are splatters of bloody gore all over the back of the truck and the street.

"Ah, no." I look away, shaking my head. "Not this."

I'm dimly aware of the helicopter banking and swooping away into the distance. Police car sirens wail in the neighborhood, getting closer.

And I just stand there in shock, shaking my head slowly, and say, "Not this. Not *again.*"

And 25 copies of me shake their heads and wipe away tears of regret for the dead.

"MORE SUPER-*SMEAROS*, HUH?" That's Lieutenant Tank Driscoll making the sensitive comment before the remains of Sticky Wicket and Bunker Buster have had a chance to cool. He's not even *close* to being Isosceles City P.D.'s finest.

But the woman beside him most certainly is. Her name is Detective Bonnie Taggart, and I know her well. "Show some respect for the *dead,* dingleberry." She swats Tank's scrawny arm with her notepad, looking disgusted.

"But there've been so damn *many* of 'em, Fox. I'm startin' to lose *track.*" Tank's eyes bulge, and his pencil mustache twitches with frustration.

"I'll bet you wouldn't feel like that if you'd witnessed as many of these fatalities as *Pluribus* has." Bonnie flashes me an apologetic look.

"Thanks." I watch as crime scene investigators snap photos and take samples of the dead supers' remains. I still can't believe those bloody spatters are all that's left of them after the long and colorful careers they had.

"Ah, what does he care?" Trank lights a cigarette between

his bony fingers and puffs away. "They were both *black hats,* weren't they? Pluribus supposedly wears only *white."*

"They were still part of the superhuman community," says Bonnie. "And as such, they deserve the best investigation we in the Superhuman Protectorate have to offer."

Just as she says it, company of the superhuman variety arrives, swooping down to land alongside us--and I'm instantly on guard again. The two new arrivals aren't exactly what you might call *heroes.*

"Solved yet? Answers?" Headbelly is a higher-up in the super-villain community, a man whose head resides on his ample gut instead of his shoulders. He's also a major pain.

"What do you have for us so far?" Win Chime has night-dark skin, glowing blonde hair, like a mane of fiber optics, and a ravishing figure clad in skintight black and silver spandex. There isn't a man on the hero side of the tracks who hasn't lost at least one fight with her due to extreme distraction.

"Not much." Bonnie's tone is matter-of-fact. "Based on preliminary review of the crime scene, this looks like much the same modus operandi as the other super murders."

"So how many more will it take to finally solve these heinous exercises?" asks Win Chime. "How long until your people get their heads out of their asses?"

Headbelly snickers. "Good one!"

"How long until *your* people *help* solve it?" asks Bonnie. "How long until *they* get their heads front and center?"

Headbelly doesn't appreciate that one. "Protectorate works for *both* sides! We demand answers!"

"Then start by *providing* some," says Bonnie. "We need information on the deceased. Who were their friends and family? Who might have had a grudge against them? What cases were they involved with recently?"

"Just want info to use *against* us," snaps Headbelly. "Want to pin all the murders on *us.*"

"Why?" Tank sneers and leans toward him. "*Should* we?"

"Cut it out!" Bonnie raises both hands, palms facing Tank and Headbelly. "Now is *not* the time! What we *need* is *information*, which will *not* be misused against you or your community. You have my *word* on it."

Bonnie has a rep as a square shooter, and everyone knows it. All of us have at least heard the stories of how she gives *all* sides of the super population of Isosceles City fair treatment.

"Fine." Win Chime sighs and folds her arms over her very ample bosom. "What do you need to know?"

As Bonnie and Tank interview her and Headbelly, I see my chance. When their backs are turned, I snap my finger, quietly raises up another duplicate -- close to my current age and appearance -- and leave him there in my stead as I slip off into the confusion surrounding the crime scene.

As powers go, mine isn't always the most helpful in the thick of a fight, but it sure comes in handy sometimes.

WANT to know what a super-hero's best friend is these days? The phone app that lets us summon a car ride anywhere in town. For those of us without the power of flight, you can't beat a ride-hail app when you're stuck on the street in your costume with no way home.

The more seasoned drivers, the ones who've seen it all, just humor me. If they ask, I say I'm on my way to a birthday party, and that's usually the end of it.

This afternoon, I'm not so lucky, but that's okay. When the guy at the wheel asks too many questions, I just crank out a few more duplicates to fill up his car, and that freaks him out enough to shut his yap.

I leave a duplicate to keep him company anyway after I get out of the car around the corner from HQ -- my apartment, that is. As the car pulls away, my copy grins and waggles his fingers at me from the window, already talking the driver's ear off.

As bad of a day as it's been, I can't help smiling at that.

Sending doubles in several directions to frustrate anyone who might be watching, I walk up the front steps of my brownstone and let myself in with a key from the chain I wear around my neck under the costume.

Then I slam the door behind me and head straight for the kitchen. Yanking the hood and mask off, I fling open the fridge, grab a bottle of Guinness, and uncap it.

My hands shake a little as I tip the bottle to my lips.

For exactly the thirteenth time, I wonder what the *hell* is going on. Is another super power manifesting itself? One that draws me to murder scenes when the victim is part of the *powered* community? It's the only thing that makes sense, given how many of those murders I've witnessed.

Which is *all* of them.

That's *fifteen* murders at *thirteen* scenes in *three weeks.* Every last one of them a *super* -- some *white hats,* some *black hats,* some *gray.* And they all blew apart in exactly the same way, the only difference being *when* in the battle they exploded.

Leaving *me* to wonder *why* and *how* this is happening, and why I keep turning up to witness it.

I barely get two sips down before the phone vibrates in my pocket. I see it's a number I don't recognize, but I answer it anyway.

"Hello?" The voice on the line is throaty and female, completely unfamiliar. "Pluribus?"

My instinct is to just hang up, but I don't. "Who is this?"

"Someone who wants to help. Meet me in one hour at 315 Grand. Wear civilian clothes."

I scowl at the phone like it smells bad. "Civilian clothes?"

"*I'll* be in costume." The voice laughs once, like a cough. "Just look for the bright green and hot pink spandex."

M*y heart races* as I walk into the church, but for once it isn't because I'm heading into battle or drawn to the probable murder of some powered-up individual. It's because of the giant sculpture at the far end of the nave, looming over the vast body of the Gothic structure. It's a statue of a man, rendered huge, his stern features staring from behind the spiked cowl of his superhero suit.

I knew that man well, *too* well to not be affected by the sight of his likeness towering in the basilica, no matter how many times I've seen it before in the flesh or otherwise.

On the other hand, I'm not sure I'll ever get used to seeing people *worshipping* it. There's a service in progress, with pew after pew filled with super people in spandex costumes, people of immense and varied powers...all of them bowing their heads in humble prayer to the entity represented by that enormous statue.

"In the name of blessed Archetype, brother, I greet thee." The voice in my ear is familiar from the phone -- throaty and feminine. "In this house of Our Super-Lord, thou art *most* welcome."

Looking over my shoulder, I see she has a long face with aquiline features partly obscured by a bright green cowl with hot pink piping. Through the eye-holes of her mask, I see her eyes are deep emerald with a ribbon of gold around the iris, and they're twinkling.

She's as tall as I am, with a well-muscled form that bespeaks a high level of strength and fitness. Depending on her powers, if any, I'm not sure I could take her in a fight...but that's not the most interesting thing about her at the moment.

What catches my eye and holds it is the red-and-gold satin stole slung over her shoulders, reaching down to her thighs. It's embroidered with the symbol I know so well from the ubiquitous Church of the Archetype, the mark of someone highly placed in the hierarchy of this religion.

"Priestess." I'm supposed to bow or curtsy or something, but I don't. "You called?" I hold up my phone.

"Praise be to the Archetype." She keeps her voice low as the service continues. In the chancel, at the massive altar under the statue of Archetype, their god, two priests in brightly colored superhero costumes chant and shoot glittering fireworks from their fingertips.

The whole thing puts me off. I'd hoped never to set foot in a place like this again, to never see that farce in action or hear the crackpot chants or smell the incense cooking down in the censers...yet here I am. Back in a place that reminds me in *so* many ways of the failures and low points of this life that's left me struggling and lonely.

I feel like the loneliest man on Earth, though my superpower is to generate unlimited numbers of duplicates.

"Call me Mother Morning," she says softly. "And it is an honor to be graced by your presence in this most holy cathedral."

She's the one who bows, and it makes me want to leave. "Please. Just tell me why you called me here."

144

"Because I want to help," says Mother Morning. "I believe I *can* help."

"With what? In what way?"

"With the mystery that surrounds you. The *deaths* of the powered that you've been witness to. I believe I can help you uncover who or what is behind them."

The priests in the chancel float off the floor and come to hover over the crowd. One sprinkles baptismal water on the people in the pews while the other glows like the sun, casting radiant beams in all directions with arms upraised.

"You really think you can help?" I ask Mother Morning.

"I do." She smiles warmly. "My work with the *flock* can be most illuminating at times." She gestures at the worshippers before us, many of whom are drifting up toward the priests.

One more questions nags at me. "And *why* do you want to help?"

"Our brothers and sisters are dying," she says. "Also, it would be a very great *honor...*" She bows again. "...to serve you. The *son* of the great god *Archetype.*"

So it's *that* crap again. "He *disowned* me, remember? I'm *nobody* now."

She bows more deeply than ever. "You will *always* be *His* son, no matter your quarrels."

I sigh. It's *such* a bunch of hooey...but who am I to turn away help in a situation like this? I'm not exactly getting to the truth fast on my *own.*

"All right. Let's see how it goes. But no more bowing."

"As the Son of the God commands, I will..."

"And no more of that, either," I tell her. "Just call me Jack when I'm a civilian and Pluribus when I'm in uniform."

"Yes, Lord." She winces. "I mean Jack."

145

"Thanks, Mother." The whole congregation glows with blazing light. "So how will this help of yours work?"

"Follow me." She heads for the door, pausing at a wall-mounted holy water dispenser to dip her fingers and make the sign of the Archetype across her torso--lower left, breastbone, lower right, xiphoid process. It forms the shape of a capital letter "A." "There's someone you should meet."

How long has it been since I last visited the superhuman ward of Saint Secret Identity's Hospital? Five years ago, maybe, when one of my body doubles materialized inside-out and couldn't be re-absorbed properly?

But what I think about most as Mother Morning leads me through the doors is *my* mother, who wasn't in the super-human ward at all the last time she was here. That was more like twelve years ago, though it seems a lot more recent--maybe because I still dream about it so often.

I haven't been the same since *that* day. Mom knew me better than anyone in the world, even my clones.

Maybe even better than I know myself, I still think.

"Right this way, Lo--I mean Jack." Mother Morning guides me through the maze of hallways that leads to the Super-human Intensive Care department. When we're stopped at the door by a bald, broad-shouldered male nurse, Mother says she's here in her capacity as priestess to minister the sacra-ments to patients of the faith. I'm a deacon, she says, and that's good enough to get us over the threshold.

"Here we are." Mother Morning leads me into a room and pulls aside a curtain. "This is the person I wanted you to meet."

There's a patient in the bed, but I can't tell if it's a man or a woman. He or she is swaddled in bandages, with raw, scarlet flesh showing in the gaps between them.

"This is Captain Cask," says Mother Morning. "She's one of the Hedonistas."

"I...I..." Captain Cask's voice is a ravaged squeak. "I already...kn-*know* you."

"You do?" The name doesn't sound familiar, though I've heard of the Hedonistas.

"Of *c-course* I know y-you," says Captain Cask. "Y-you're...*God*."

Mother Morning shoots me a look, so I don't deny it...though honestly, seeing that single bloodshot eye between the wrappings doesn't make me inclined to disappoint the poor soul, anyway.

"Captain," says Mother Morning. "Tell Jack how you suffered your injuries."

"I w-was...stopping a c-carjacking...on Hawthorne and T-Trimble," squeaks Captain Cask. "I was off d-duty...s-so I w-wasn't fully p-p-powered up...but I still st-stopped the black hats." She draws a deep breath that seems to last forever, then releases it twice as slowly, trembling. "Then I h-heard some kind of weird *f-flute* sound and *w-whoosh!* I w-was on f-fire!"

"You don't know what caused it?" asks Mother Morning.

Captain Cask's head twitches weakly, the closest she comes to full-on shaking it. "J-just one p-perp...and sh-she d-didn't exhibit...any p-powers. N-neither d-did the d-driver. Th-they seemed as surprised as *I* w-was."

"And how did you survive?" asks Mother Morning.

"M-my teammate...Flambé...g-got there j-just in t-time...and extinguished the f-flames." Captain Cask lets out a little whimper. "B-but I still f-feel...l-like I'm g-going to...g-going to..." She sucks in another shuddering breath. "There's a *p-pressure*...inside me. I'm f-fighting...t-to hold it b-back...with m-my f-force field powers...b-but it f-feels...like it's g-going...to *l-let go."*

Her eye closes, and tears squeeze out of it. Her whimpers turn to agonized sobs.

"Shhh," says Mother Morning. "It's okay, honey." She reaches to comfort the woman, then withdraws her hand. The slightest touch to her burn-ravaged flesh could cause Captain Cask a world of greater hurt. "You just keep hanging in there."

"You don't know who or what could have caused it? You didn't see anyone around who might have attacked you like this?" She's so upset, I hate to ask--but I do it anyway. If whatever's pressing at her ever lets go, this might be my last chance to question her.

"N-no." Captain Cask sniffles and shivers. "M-maybe they were h-hiding."

"Do you have any enemies with the power to do this?" I ask. "Anyone who might have threatened you recently?"

"All in p-prison," says Captain Cask. "And n-no threats r-recently..."

"What about the flute sound you mentioned? Was it like a series of notes? A single, high-pitched tone?"

"M-more like f-four...or five n-notes." She barely manages to hum five notes--high, low, high, low, high. "That's it. I d-don't know...w-what they m-mean."

I think for a moment, considering my next question. "What do you know about Bunker Buster and Sticky Wicket?"

"W-who?"

"You don't know them?" asks Mother Morning.

"N-no."

I mention the next two murder victims who come to mind. "What about Wunderbar or Dye Job?"

"I've h-heard of D-Dye Job, b-but...I've n-never m-met him," says Captain Cask.

"What about Metric System?"

She twitches her head weakly and resumes sobbing.

I get the feeling this interrogation has gone as far as it can. "Don't cry, Captain. It'll be all right." I want to make her feel better, but I don't know how, given the circumstances.

"W-will it, G-god?" squeaks Captain Cask. "*Will it?*"

OUTSIDE THE HOSPITAL, Mother Morning pulls out an elaborate-looking e-cig (like something out of a Jack Kirby comic book) and vapes as we walk.

"I think Captain Cask was a target, too," she says. "Her force field powers must have stopped whatever explosive force blew up the other victims."

"Temporarily, at least, from the sound of it." I catch a whiff of her vapor, some kind of orange-chocolate-tinged mist, and I like it. "Should she even be *in* there, if she still might *blow*?"

"I think they're bringing in a super specialist tomorrow." Mother Morning puffs on her e-cig. "I heard them mention the Stabilizer."

My mind is awhirl as we walk onward. The investigation's alive, but not by much.

"We should research any possible connection between Captain Cask and the other victims." I'm thinking aloud as I say it. "She claimed not to know the ones I named, but there are ten others I didn't get to."

"True," says Mother Morning through a cloud of sweet vapor.

"Then there's the *flute* factor. Maybe one of those ten has some kind of connection to flute music or something that *sounds* like it."

"You knew some of the victims, didn't you? Does what she said ring any bells for you?"

I review what I know for a moment and end up shaking my head decisively. "I've got nothing."

"No divine wisdom?" She sounds hopeful, not sarcastic.

It still ticks me off. "I guess all-mighty Archetype must be busy inspiring somebody else just now."

"His grace shall not fail to find us if we but pray with fervent urgency." Mother Morning makes the capital-A sign of the Archetype and ends with a ceremonial double-handclap denoting the two persons in one God: Father and Son.

Me being the Son, for what *that's* worth.

Suddenly, my phone rings, and I grab it in a hurry. When I see the number on the screen, I answer it without delay.

"Pluribus?" It's Bonnie Taggart. "Could you come down to the station right away, please? There's something I'd like to talk to you about."

WHEN I WALK in the door of the precinct house, everyone stops what they're doing. Though I changed into my superhero uniform on the way here to preserve my secret identity, I'm rethinking that strategy in light of all the stares.

I should be grateful, I guess. The attention I'm getting in here has nothing to do with my father being a superhuman god. In here, it's all about my recent track record, being present at one superhuman murder after another.

For the super-types in the house, there's the worry that my showing up might mean that more super-murders are soon to follow. Word travels fast when everyone has super-hearing, and I've quickly developed a reputation as a damn harbinger.

For the non-supers manning the station, I'm pretty sure there's another reason for the tension in the air. Because let's face it, as far as the cops are concerned, my being at all those super-murder scenes might not be a coincidence.

Heck, I might think the same thing, if the cape were on the other shoulders.

"Hey, Pluribus!" Naturally, Lt. Tank Driscoll comes out to greet us, the scrawny scumbag. "I heard they got a new code name for you! *Coincidento!* Because it's always such a huge *coincidence* when you show up at so many *murder scenes.*"

Lots of other cops in the room laugh at that one, and I just take it. The jerk is just baiting me, looking for a reason to put me in an interrogation room.

Mother Morning, on the other hand, is not so docile. "Hey!" She marches over and stands toe to toe with tank, snapping off her retort in his knobby walnut of a face. "That is *no* way to address the *son* of the one, true *god.*"

"It is if I smell *murder* on him," snarls Tank. "*Nobody* gets a pass in *my* jurisdiction."

"Funny." Mother Morning presses closer, coming within inches of his face. "That's exactly what *God* says."

Then, she spins on her heel and swoops over, seizing my elbow on the way past. As we head for Bonnie's office, I can't help being impressed and grateful...and a little bit attracted to her. I guess this Son of God bit isn't *all* bad.

BONNIE LEADS us downstairs to the morgue, which we enter without knocking. The coroner, a tall, gray-haired woman in her 50s or so, is hard at work on an autopsy and doesn't look up.

Her voice, when she speaks, is deep, her words clipped and no-nonsense. "Hello, Detective."

Bonnie gets right down to business. "Where are those DNA results, Agnes?"

"Just arrived from the lab today." Agnes bobs her head at a manila envelope on a nearby counter. "And yes, I've already asked them to run the samples again. There's no *way* those could *not* be in error."

Bonnie opens the envelope and slides out printed sheets, scanning them as they emerge. "What do you mean?"

Agnes lifts the lungs from the chest of the subject she's examining, then drops them on a hanging scale and views the weight on the unit's display. "I mean the DNA results must have been in error or contaminated or both. Each distinct sample reads like it contains fragments from multiple donors, scrambled up and reassembled like I've never *seen* before."

"I see." Bonnie frowns as she reads through the results in the envelope. "And there's no other explanation?"

"None." Agnes shrugs and shakes her head. "It must be some kind of cross-contamination or test error. I gave the lab seven shades of hell when I called for a retest."

"But how do you *know?*" asks Mother Morning. "With all the unique superhuman physiologies out there, how do you know for a fact that the samples *are* the result of contamination or test error?"

"Excuse me?" Agnes doesn't sound amused by the layperson's contribution.

Mother Morning proceeds as if she didn't notice the coroner's haughty tone. "Couldn't it be from someone with an altered physiology? Archetype *knows*, there are some wild power sets and adaptations on the streets of Isosceles City."

Agnes doesn't answer. She and Bonnie both look as if they're deep in thought.

Then, the silence is broken by a male voice blaring over the intercom. *"All units, report to Pendulum Plaza! Ten-ten-ten in progress!"*

"What's a ten-ten-ten?" asks Mother Morning.

"Superhuman battle royal with massive civilian involvement!" Bonnie barks the words as she charges out the door.

BY THE TIME we leap out of Bonnie's SUV, Pendulum Plaza is engulfed in superhuman conflict. Civilians run screaming in all directions as a host of costumed warriors unleashes all manner of powers with no apparent regard for non-super-charged life.

"Holy hell!" Tank has his service revolver out but makes no move to set foot in the midst of the action. "This place is out of control!"

"I can't even tell who's fighting who here." Bonnie turns and shouts in my direction. "Maybe *you* have a clue?"

Watching the storm of destruction rage before me, I try to make sense of it all. There are lots of familiar costumes in the thick of it, faces I know from both sides of the fence--but the logic of their struggle eludes me. White hats fight black hats, sure--but also other white hats. Black hats, too, fight each other just as much as they fight their enemy white hats. It's a conflagration without any apparent rhyme or reason, one in which all the rules of engagement in the superhuman community have seemingly and ruthlessly been cast aside.

"I don't know!" I have to shout for Bonnie to hear me over

the noise of battle. "Good guys and bad guys are fighting their own allies as well as each other! It doesn't make any sense!"

"I say pull everyone back!" shouts Tank. "Keep our Protectorate forces out of this crap-show and let these freaks tear each other to pieces!"

"We don't even know what the *sides* are, let alone which side *we're* on," says Bonnie.

Suddenly, a male superhero in bright yellow and blue tights crashes into the street not twenty yards away, blasting a crater into the pavement. Another hero--one I recognize, the Mountebank--leaps in after him, swinging a nuclear sword and shrieking with glee.

"It's getting wilder," says Mother Morning. "They're speeding up and fighting harder!"

"Why don't *you* do something, Coincidento?" Tanks asks me. "Call for a super-*time-out* or something!"

I gaze into the maelstrom, mesmerized by the violence. A villain with flesh-molding powers twists a hero with metal breath into a deformed, howling pretzel. Three heroes with power over oxygen, wood, and insects, respectively, hammer two villains with electrical and sound-based talents. A super-speedster and a woman who looks like she's made out of flickering purple light wage a breakneck battle against a giant, fire-breathing sea horse flapping aloft on leathering bat wings.

Even if I thought I could do something, I literally have no idea where to start.

"There must be *something* you could try," says Mother Morning. "Perhaps a special intercession with your father, the great God, Archetype?"

"God is dead," I tell her. "That one, anyway."

Still, maybe she's right that I ought to try something. It

strikes me that there's one thing worth doing, whatever the nature of the conflict.

Stepping forward, away from the group, I close my eyes and concentrate on generating duplicates. I feel them popping to life all around me, dozens of clones spun into being by the power-infused heart of me.

Through the magic of my Pluribus gift, they automatically know the purpose for which they were created. I don't have to say a word for them to charge forth and do what I need them to do.

As I watch, they race through the war zone, hauling civilians out of harm's way. I see one of the clones grab a child just as an errant death ray is about to strike her. Another takes a bullet for a young woman on the run, while a fellow clone deflects a hurtling eagle-man from crushing a hobbling old couple as he plunges to Earth.

A team of twelve clones forms a human shield around a group of fleeing parents and children, blocking all incoming fire from turning the innocents into collateral casualties.

The battle continues to rage, but at least more civilians will survive the mayhem. I haven't stopped the fight, but at least I've done that much right.

Suddenly, then, I hear the sound of something plummeting toward me from above, and I instinctively dart away from it. I get clear just in time, as the object rockets into the street on the spot where I just stood, embedding itself in the blacktop.

But it's not an object at all, I see--it's a *person*. It's a gray hat I've worked with before, and brought down on occasion, the one and only Mugwump.

Running back to his side, I see he's mortally injured. The fully-formed villain on his backside is already dead, crushed in the fall, and the hero on his front side is battered and gasping.

"E-Pluribus...," he says. "Y-you came!"

"What's going on here, Mugwump?" I want to help him, but I have no idea what to do at this point. "What started all this?"

Mugwump laughs up blood. "Isn't it obvious?" Reaching up with one shivering hand, he tugs the black cowl from his head, revealing the face underneath.

My face.

My heart races, and the hackles spring to life on the back of my neck. Just then, I hear a series of high-pitched notes, like those played on a flute, and panic rushes over me.

High, low, high, low, high. I know what those notes mean.

"I-it's all about...y-you!" says Mugwump, and then he explodes, leaving a spatter of bloody gore in his place.

It's the exact same thing that happens to every other white hat, black hat, and gray hat fighting in the war zone of Pendulum Plaza, all at exactly the same time.

Leaving me and all my duplicates to be showered by streams of crimson froth falling like a sudden summer downpour from above.

I DON'T TELL Bonnie or Tank what I saw under that mask, but I tell them what I heard...not that it makes much difference in the scheme of things. We're all still splattered from head to toe with the same gruesome slop, all that remains of the dozens of heroes and villains who just waged war in Pendulum Plaza.

The way things go, though, I might not have to worry about being involved much longer.

"Hey, Coincidento!" barks Tank. "You're *banned!*"

At first, I'm not sure I heard him right. "Banned?"

"From active superhuman fight scenes!" says Tank. "And *crime scenes*, too."

"You can't do that!" says Mother Morning. "He's a super-hero! Fight scenes and crime scenes are his *workplace.*"

"Yeah? Well, he's bad for business," snaps Tank. "I'm done takin' chances that *maybe* he's not the one makin' our super-human population go *pop.*"

Bonnie scowls at Tank, then shrugs at me. "It might not be a bad idea to steer clear for a while. At least until we completely rule out any causal relationship between you and the murders."

"Whatever." I try not to look Mother Morning in the eyes as I give up without a fight. "I'll lie low for a while."

"Feel free to give us a call if you get any *funny feelin's,* though." Tank shoves a business card in the waistband of my tights. "Or if you hear any *flute music* playin' all of a sudden."

"If you'll excuse me." I turn and start walking away. "I really, really need to get cleaned up right now."

"Good luck, Coincidento," says Tank. "Try not to stumble across any more *mass murders* on your way home, y'hear?"

MOTHER MORNING CATCHES UP and walks alongside me, brushing goo from her uniform. "I don't care if you *are* the Shirker," she says. "You shouldn't let the cops walk all over you like that."

I glance over at her, surprised to hear that name from her lips...though I shouldn't be. She *is* clergy, after all.

"I'd rather not talk about that," I tell her.

"But it's a central part of the *faith*," says Mother Morning. "Without the Shirker, who refuses to fulfill his Father's wishes, there could be no promised *Compliers*, who shall usher in the new era of glory by *obeying* the Father's commands."

"Well, good for you and the church then." I pull out my phone and start hunting for a ride. "If it gives you all something to live for, more power to you. As for me, I don't want anything to do with it."

"But why deny your destiny?" She sounds worked up. "Why *spit* on the special blessing you've been given by mighty Archetype?"

"Because *Archetype* isn't a *god*. He's just a *man* with *super powers* who set himself up as a *deity* to satisfy his colossal *ego*."

"Maybe it seems that way to you, but..."

I stop walking and turn on her, overflowing with anger that has nothing to do with her. "I haven't seen him in *fifteen years*, ever since I refused to play along with his *phony religion* crap! As soon as I went against him *just once*, he *disowned* me and *disappeared*."

"That was his *ascension*." She says it like she's teaching catechism to a six-year-old. "He had to *rise* to the *next level* of existence to pave the way for *superhumanity* after the Compliers deliver them to salvation."

"*Bull*. He had to *run* from his *family* and *responsibilities* because he's huge *narcissist* with a *god complex* and *Peter Pan syndrome* all wrapped up in *one*."

"Jack," she says calmly. "I understand why your father's abandonment might seem upsetting. I can also fathom why your prophesied destiny might feel oppressive. But the *rest* of the prophecy tells a different story. According to the Book of Futurities, the Shirker will see the light in the end and help make of Earth a paradise." She touches my arm lightly. "If anything, you should *rejoice*."

"You *don't* understand," I tell her. "You *couldn't*. He's been *gone* for so *long*. Even when he was present *physically*, he wasn't *there* for me...yet I've lived my whole *life* in his *shadow*...having to face the *lies* he's fed his *worshippers*. Like *you.*"

She tips her head to one side and smiles. "You are *just* as he described you in the scriptures. So *slow* to grasp the *truths* that lie in front of you."

Exasperated, is more like it...but I can already tell I'm getting nowhere arguing religion with this priestess. Better, I think, to quit quibbling and get back on task.

"Speaking of truths that lie in front of you..." I turn back to my phone and order a car to come and get us. "I saw something right before the big blast at Pendulum Plaza. Something I didn't mention in front of the cops."

"What was it?"

"Remember the gray hat who crash-landed near me? Mugwump?"

She nods slowly.

"Under his cowl...he looked just like *me.*"

"Seriously? Is that even possible?"

"It *shouldn't* be. I keep track of every clone I *make*, and I snuff them out as soon as I'm *done* with them. Not to mention, my clones don't have *super powers.*"

"And Mugwump did."

I nod. "He could fly, and he had great strength and near-invulnerability. *I* don't even have those powers, let alone my *clones.*"

"So what do you think this means?"

"I have absolutely no idea." Just then, the car I've been waiting for rolls around the corner, and I wave it down. "But maybe I know someone who might be able to help figure it out."

"Do you agree to my terms?" asks the tall man with the narrow, insouciant face and the wispy blond hair.

"Wouldn't be here if I didn't," I tell him. "Whatever information you gain from studying my case..."

He slams his fist down on the living desk in front of him, making it whimper. "...Is *mine* to do with as I please!"

"Of course, Tycho. Goes without saying, old friend."

"Old *enemy!*" Tycho slams his fist down again, drawing a louder whimper from the desk. "Old enemy who *used* to be your friend, but no *longer!*"

"Right." Glancing over at Mother Morning seated beside me, I notice she looks a little shell-shocked. No surprise there. This is her first-ever visit to the Sinstitute and the office of its very volatile super-genius director, Tycho Archimedes his own bad self.

"So what do you think, Tycho? Assuming Mugwump was one of my clones, and *none* of my clones has ever had super-powers, how and why could he have come into existence?"

Tycho leaps to his feet and paces his spacious office. The silvery walls vibrate when he passes, making a soft, tinkling sound like musical wind chimes. The crystalline floor and ceiling glow along his path, and pale smoke wafts from his burgundy smoking jacket, forming elaborate designs and images that hang and dance lightly in his wake.

The whole Sinstitute is like this, elegant and futuristic, a gorgeous, hidden haven of all the latest and greatest in super-high technology put to sinister use. In the past, it's caused me major headaches, backing Isosceles City crime sprees with weapons straight out of a U.F.O. Today, though, I've come in search of answers, the kind of outside-the-box insights I've always thought were best dreamed up by those motivated by unenlightened self-interest.

"*One* possible answer to your riddle," says Tycho from the far end of the massive room. "Perhaps one of your enemies is perpetrating a wildly elaborate hoax to either *frame* you or drive you *insane*."

"I guess that's possible." I rub my chin and shrug. "But it still doesn't explain the existence of the super-powered clone."

"It does if we consider a *shape-shifter* in the mix! A shape-shifter and *powers-shifter!*"

"Like whom?" I ask him. "Do you know any?"

"Meeting both variables, no." Tycho falls silent for a long moment. "Of course, you could also be the victim of hypnosis or some similar form of influence."

"But he never *acted* like he was being subjected to mind control," said Mother Morning.

"Well no, he wouldn't. But let's set that aside for the moment anyway." Tycho paces back over to his desk and perches on the corner. "Is it possible your *powers* are behaving in unexpected ways, Pluribus?"

"How do you mean?" I ask.

"You've said the duplicates you generate are under your control and quickly dematerialize at your command. But *what if* you are *shedding* duplicates when you're *unaware* of it? And *these* duplicates adhere to *different* properties than those you generate *consciously?*"

I consider it for a moment, trying to imagine the possibility. "You mean I might be generating them *subconsciously?*"

"*Unconsciously,* is what I'm thinking." Tycho leans toward me, eyes narrowed. "It wouldn't be the first time I've encountered a super-power that behaves differently when its possessor is unconscious."

"Really?"

"I propose an experiment," says Tycho. "If you're not too *squeamish* about putting yourself in my *hands.*"

"He is the son of *God!*" shouts Mother Morning. "What is it you propose to *do* to him?"

"Relax, my dear." Tycho gives her a sneer that's rife with strange, unreadable undercurrents. "Think of it as a simple *sleep study.*" He chuckles and smacks the palm of his hand hard on the desk, making it yelp. "Only not so *simple!*"

ALL I SEE IS darkness and the figments of my own imagination. All I hear is the rushing of blood in my ears. All I feel is the warm water sloshing around me, buoying me on its surface.

It's my first time in a sensory deprivation chamber, courtesy of Tycho and the Sinstitute. He claims it will help relax me and isolate variables, allowing us to cut through the normal environmental noise that can prevent clear focus and pure data.

At first, I'm dubious about the relaxation benefits, but my doubts and alertness don't last. I haven't been sleeping well lately, what with the murder scene summonings, and apparently I'm more tired than I realized.

One minute, my mind is roving through the events of the past day, and the next, I'm lost in a deep dream state. Just like that, I disconnect from full consciousness, drifting instead through a series of dreamy vignettes.

Most are drawn from memories, like a scene of me playing with clones of myself in the grassy back yard of the family home. There are seven of us, all identical, playing tag and hide-and-go-seek in the summer sun, running and shouting with delight. Even then, I was only too happy to turn to the clones for friendship--which was the same as turning inward, I see now.

Inexplicably, that scene flows into another from much earlier, when I, as a baby in the crib, was nearly smothered to death by the mob of clones I'd unknowingly generated. It's one of the few moments I remember from infancy, perhaps mostly born out of stories I heard from my parents in later years...but it's a bad one. Panic seizes me as the breath is squeezed out of my lungs, the squirming weight of all those duplicates crushing me beneath them, unable to cry for help.

Next, I'm walking with my mother through Isosceles City as it is now...which is impossible. She's been gone since I was ten years old, and the city has changed so much since then--but there she is, as beautiful as I remember. The wind blows her long, auburn hair, tossing locks of it clear of her sweet, freckled face. Her laugh is like the tinkling of piano keys or bells, and the touch of her hand is soft around mine. Now *this* is a dream I never want to leave, a moment I could be happy reliving for as long as I live.

But then it's gone, and the next dream isn't so much a blissful memory drawn from real life as an improvised night-mare. Instead of the face of my beloved mother, I see an amor-phous, faceless mass looming in the blackness. Its only feature is a gaping maw in ceaseless, relentless mastication.

I float toward it, bobbing on the hot, rancid waves of its breath. As I get closer, the sound of a voice becomes audible, if not understandable...a male monotone feeding out ribbons of guttural gibberish.

I begin to rotate on the long axis of my body, turning in

circles as I continue my approach. Suddenly, the mass before me divides into two identical masses, which divide in twos again, and again, and again. Soon, I'm confronted with a *wall* of those masses, all faceless and forever masticating.

And then, without explanation, the amorphous shapes resolve into familiar faces. The wall is formed from endless copies of the face of my father, repeated into infinity in all directions.

The male monotone voice resolves, too, becoming the voice of my father, speaking in perfect unison from all those maws. Though I haven't heard it in so very long, I still recognize it instantly--and flinch instinctively.

"MY SON!" says Dad. "YOU WHO HAVE SHIRKED YOUR BIRTHRIGHT!"

I don't know why, but I don't slow down. If anything, my rotation and forward motion speed up as the infinitude of faces speaks out.

"DO NOT FEAR! THE DEATHS YOU HAVE WITNESSED ARE A HOLY CULLING MEANT TO CORRECT THOSE WHO HAVE FAILED EVEN MORE ABYSMALLY THAN YOU!"

I swallow hard, then call out to him/them. "What are you *talking* about? How have they *failed?*"

"REMEMBER HOW YOU REFUSED TO OBEY ME? I ORDERED YOU TO CREATE AN ARMY OF GODLINGS, BLOOD OF MY BLOOD, TO SAVE THE WORLD--AND YOU REFUSED!"

"You're right! I refused to help you conquer the world!"

"YOUR REFUSAL MEANT NOTHING! I, YOUR FATHER AND GOD, CREATED THAT SACRED ARMY *THROUGH* YOU, WITHOUT YOUR *KNOWING* IT!"

Chills ripple through me at the thought of it. For the first time, I wonder if *this* part is a dream after all.

"BUT PERHAPS YOUR VERY *SPIRIT* AND *MATTER* WERE

CORRUPT, FOR THOSE MULTITUDES HAVE *FAILED* ME! THEY HAVE SPLINTERED INTO FACTIONS--SO-CALLED BLACK HATS, WHITE HATS, GRAY HATS...THOSE WHO SEE FIT TO DO MY BIDDING, AND THOSE WHO DO NOT. AND THOSE FACTIONS HAVE GONE TO WAR!"

"Wait a minute!" It's hard to get my head around all this...and the more I understand, the less I like it. "You mean to tell me you've somehow been *using* me to make *duplicates* against my *will?*"

"I AM YOUR GOD! I MAKE ALL THINGS POSSIBLE!"

"But they have *super-powers! I* can't make clones with *powers!*"

"YES YOU CAN! YOU ARE CAPABLE OF *FAR* GREATER MIRACLES THAN YOU HAVE EVER REALIZED!"

I shake my head hard against the information overload. "And now these super-powered clones...they've gone to *war* against each other? My *copies* are fighting my *copies?*"

"THOSE FAILURES WERE MEANT TO SAVE THE WORLD! TO CORRECT THE OLD GOD'S MISTAKE OF LEAVING HUMANITY TO ITS OWN DEVICES! IMAGINE A WORLD IN WHICH GOD HIMSELF IS PRESENT IN GREAT NUMBERS, WALKING AMONG HIS SUBJECTS TO KEEP THEM HONEST!"

If this *is* a dream, Dad is just as deluded as he ever was. "So these clones were meant to be the Compliers of prophecy?"

"INSTEAD, THEY ARE THE RUINATION OF MY DREAM! AND NOW I AM DESTROYING THEM IN ALL THEIR NUMBERS, AS IS MY RIGHT!"

His words sink in like anvils in quicksand. "So *you're* the one who's been killing them off? Making them explode?"

"IT IS THE *LEAST* PUNISHMENT THEY DESERVE!"

"Then why drag *me* into it? Why do I have to witness all that?"

"YOU ARE DRAWN TO THESE FAILURES AS FLESH IS DRAWN TO FLESH. YOU COME TO WITNESS THEM BECAUSE THEY ARE LIKE UNTO YOUR OWN CHILDREN."

"My own children, huh? Then I hope you don't expect me to be thrilled that you're on a mission to *kill* them."

"YOUR FEELINGS DON'T MATTER," says Dad. "WHEN THOSE FAILURES GIVE ME AMPLE REASON, AS THEY ARE *ABOUT* TO, I SHALL SLAUGHTER THE *LOT* OF THEM."

"What do you consider 'ample reason?'"

"ARMAGGEDON! EVEN AS WE SPEAK, THEY GATHER IN THEIR HIDDEN REALM TO BRING THE END CRASHING DOWN UPON THE TOWERS OF ISOSCELES CITY! IT IS THEN, WHEN THEY PERPETRATE THEIR ULTIMATE SIN, THAT I SHALL BLOW THEM ALL TO SMITHEREENS!"

"Wow." As I fight to process all that he's told me, my rotation and forward momentum slow. I start to feel trapped, as if the blackness itself is wrapping tighter around me, pulling me back. "How do I..." I'm having trouble getting the words out. "How do I know...this isn't a *dream?*"

"BECAUSE I GIVE YOU PROOF! IRREFUTABLE PROOF! YOU WILL FIND IT ALL AROUND YOU AS YOU WAKE!"

I feel like I'm choking. "What kind...of proof?"

"YOU YOURSELF HAVE NOT BEEN ABLE TO MAKE SUPER-HUMAN CLONES. SO FAR, ONLY *I* HAVE BEEN ABLE TO TRIGGER THIS PROCESS IN YOU!"

"That's what...you've said..."

"REMEMBER THAT AS YOU WAKE FROM THIS DREAM OF YOUR GOD...AND FIGHT FOR YOUR MISERABLE FAILED LIFE!"

"Wait! What about..."

Suddenly, the wall of faces rushes toward me. One of the

maws engulfs me, gulping me down, and I can't even scream for lack of breath.

There's a burst of heat and cold all at once, then what feels like a heavy impact--and I'm awake. Or *am* I? Darkness still enshrouds me all around, everywhere I look.

But I feel myself splashing in water, thrashing against the pressure that's squeezing the breath from my body. And I hear a voice then, whispering in my ear.

"Our Father *made* me, Shirker! I am the *proof* of his glory, and I have come to *end* your betrayal!"

THINKING FAST, I haul my knees back as far as I can, then pump my legs forward. My feet smash open the doors of the sensory deprivation chamber, and the bright light of the Sinstitute lab floods in.

It's then that I finally get a look at the freshly minted duplicate, the one I had no conscious role in creating. His face is identical to my face, but that's about the only resemblance. His body, like that of a giant boa constrictor, is coiled around me, squeezing me more tightly with each passing second.

I don't have breath enough to talk or even fight--but I *do* have what it takes to deal with this intruder. Closing my eyes, I focus my power and put it to work.

I feel it in my core as it takes effect--and then I see the living proof of it. Three pairs of hands reach into the chamber and haul us out, then attack the serpentine form coiled around me.

Snake Man resists, holding tight, so I whip up three more clones. Six clones strong, my personal rescue squad finally does the trick, unwrapping the rogue clone's body from my own.

He twists and lashes in their grip until one of them finally punches his lights out. Snake Man goes limp, and they dump him in the chamber and slam the door shut behind him.

"Jack! Are you all right?" Mother Morning dashes from an adjoining room and almost throws her arms around me...then thinks better of it.

"I'm...okay." My breath is still short, but not perilously so. I drop myself onto a nearby chair and slump there, fighting to calm my overtaxed lungs and hammering heart.

"Guess what?" Tycho storms into the room, waving a computer tablet overhead. "You *do* spontaneously shed duplicates while unconscious...and they *can* be superhuman!"

"Thanks for...the newsflash," I tell him.

"There *is* a newsflash, actually," says Mother Morning. "While you were in the box, a call came in on your phone from Detective Taggart. I picked up, and she said there's been a development."

"What...kind...of development?"

"Captain Cask broke out of the hospital," says Mother Morning, "and the cops know exactly where she went."

Following the beams of our flashlights, Mother Morning and I trudge through the sewer, knee-deep in the foul refuse of Isosceles City.

"Is super-poop different from regular poop?" she asks conversationally, as if wading through a sewer was nothing out of the ordinary.

"Yes," I tell her, keeping my voice down.

"In what way?"

"Trust me, you don't want to know."

As we slosh onward, I check the tracker app on my phone. It

shows a glowing red dot up ahead, two branches away, moving rapidly toward a large junction point.

Good for the cops for tagging Captain Cask in the hospital, injecting a tiny tracking chip under the skin of her arm. Thanks to Bonnie, who wanted someone *other* than Tank to get to Cask first, we got access to the chip's codes and informed of a short cut that would let us outrun Tank in the underground maze of the sewers.

Now, finally, we are about to see where Cask is headed, and the suspense is killing me. Bound up like a mummy, suffering from head-to-toe burns and intense pressure that makes her feel like she might explode at any time, she must have a *huge* reason to make this flight into the sewers.

We make the next turn and walk a little further before stopping. I keep my eyes glued to the app on the phone for a moment, then decide we're finally on the verge of our destination.

"She's stopped." The glowing red dot on the app isn't moving. "She's in a big space up around that corner...some kind of major junction."

"What do you think she's doing there?" asks Mother Morning.

"We're about to find out." I pocket the phone and work my way to the next corner, slowing down and taking care not to make too much noise.

When I reach the corner and peek around it, I'm breathless for a different reason than being strangled by a snakelike doppelgänger.

There, in a vast vault of concrete fed by streams of sewage roaring in from multiple outflows, I see the biggest gathering of clones I've ever seen in my life.

Hundreds of them fill the enormous space, all costumed, all

powered one way or another. Some float in midair, while others perch on concrete abutments or ledges. Some I recognize as white hat heroes, while others I know well as black hat villains or gray hats occupying the moral ground in-between.

And just enough of them have their cowls or masks off or lowered that I recognize them as duplicates of me. *Flesh of my flesh,* as Dad called them in my dream-not-a-dream.

Like unto your own children, is how he described them.

My heart hammers, and the hackles on my neck crawl--familiar reactions that can mean only one thing. The end is coming for all of them.

"What's this all about?" Mother Morning asks in a hushed voice. "What are they doing here?"

I point to a figure rising in the middle of the chamber, commanding instant respect and quiet from the crowd. He's one of the greatest heroes in Isosceles City, a multi-powered wonder who goes by the code name Bona Fide. "I think we're about to find out," I tell Mother.

"Fellow superhumans!" His deep basso voice fills the space. "This war between us has gone on too long! We must *end* it before any *more* of us are struck down by whatever murderous force is stalking us!"

Many of the assembled clones applaud and offer their support with cheers and whistles.

"*Here*, in the underground refuge, we shall *settle* our scores once and for all! Hidden from prying eyes and enemies, we shall *have* the *super-maggedon* that has been too *long* in coming...even if it destroys all of *Isosceles City* in the bargain!"

"No." This is exactly what Dad was talking about in the dream-not-a-dream. This sewer system junction is the "hidden realm" where he said they would gather to bring down the towers of the city. They think they're safe here, tucked away underground, but there's *no* place they can hide from Archetype. There's nowhere on *Earth* where they can get away from God Himself.

And I know all too well what he's promised to do to them.

"Are we *ready* to finish this *struggle?*" shouts Bona Fide. "Shall we *finally* see the crowning of a *winner* in this great *game?*"

Every last white hat, black hat, and gray hat roars with approval.

"The *prepare* yourselves!"

At Bona Fide's command, everyone dons their masks and cowls and starts circling each other. The tension in the chamber grows a thousandfold.

"On my signal!" Bona Fide raises his hands in the air, and they start to glow from within.

"What should we do?" Mother Morning sounds frantic. "What *can* we do?"

It is then that I hear the telltale flute notes--high, low, high, low, high. I know what will happen when hostilities break out.

And I suddenly realize that I can't *let* it happen. Like it or not, those people down there *are* my children, in a way. I might not have *consciously* made them, but I can't stand back and let them be slaughtered by my father.

Clamping my eyes shut, I focus in with every bit of willpower I have, directing my power at a level I've never attempted before. (Dad said I'm capable of greater miracles than I've ever realized, so who knows?)

I feel the familiar burn as clones pop into existence--first a few, then dozens, then *more. Hundreds.* More than there are rogue clones in the junction chamber.

Then, as the rogue clones shout and scurry in confusion, I give my *new* clones their call to action...and they take it.

Again, I hear that damn flute playing, but I ignore it. I stay focused on the army I've created and the marching orders they're carrying out.

As, all through that chamber, they grab onto the rogue clones and refuse to let them go.

If the rogues are flying, my new clones climb the rock walls and leap onto them. If the rogues are swimming, they dive in after them.

The new clones double- and triple-team the rogues. If a rogue knocks one or more free, two or three others take the place of their brethren.

Is it because they share the same faces as the rogues that they don't get killed? Or do the rogue clones hold back for other reasons?

In the end, all that matters is that the rogues are restrained. Their super-maggedon does not occur, and the towers of Isosceles City are not laid low.

Though of course that condition won't last forever. Sooner or later, the rogues will decide to break free and restart their war.

Unless somebody talks them out of it.

"Hear me now!" I feel a little like I'm channeling Dad as I call out to the crowd. "I am your *progenitor!* You are flesh of my flesh! And I bear a *warning!*"

"*What* warning?" Bona Fide sounds *pissed.*

"My *father* will *kill* every one of you if you keep fighting this war! Let there be no *doubt,* he can *do* it."

"Your *father?*" says Bona Fide.

"Archetype! Maybe you're *heard* of him?"

Bona Fide just glares in the grip of my clones.

"*I* bring you a *new* commandment! A new way of *life!*"

172

"Believe it!" shouts Mother Morning, who is beaming at my side. "This is the *son* of God right here, people!"

"Not exactly a ringing endorsement!" says Bona Fide. "So what *is* this new commandment?"

Good question, I think, and then it comes to me. It floats right up to the surface of my mind with all the ease of a bubble in the ocean...a commandment I should have been following from the start, one that would have saved me so much trouble if only someone had thought of it sooner.

One that could still change my life, and all the lives arrayed before me, if only we can manage to make it stick. Maybe change the whole *world,* even--and wouldn't *that* be a poke in the old man's eye? Wouldn't *that* be a destiny I could live with for a change?

"The commandment is this." I clear my throat and smile at all the faces watching and waiting. Dear old Dad tried to force them to do his bidding, to enforce his will upon the world--and he failed. *He's* the true failure in *this* testament.

And all the doubt and self-hatred and loneliness he caused me could have been avoided if only he'd done one thing.

"Love your neighbor as you *wish* you loved yourself," I tell them.

BLACKBEARD'S ALIENS

"Fire!" I have been called a Gentleman Pirate, and oft enough, the name suits. But on a day like this, Stede Bonnet is all pirate and no gentleman.

No sooner has the order to fire left my lips than the port side guns of the *Adventure* blast out their loads in clouds of roiling black smoke. Five iron balls leap through the air, heading straight for their target--a huge silver disk hovering thirty feet above the water.

Twin beams of red light flash out from the rim of the disk, burning two of the cannonballs into wisps of steam. But the other three make it through. They don't penetrate the hull of the silver disk as I had hoped, but they do make it rock in midair.

Take that, you hellspawn. "Reload!" I shout, though I know the men have already done just that. We are united in perfect rhythm after all our many battles as part of this fearsome flotilla. Our leader, much as I despise him, has taught us that.

Even now, not half a league away, I hear the guns of his

personal flagship, the *Queen Anne's Revenge*, pound away at a larger target--another hovering object, this one triangular in shape. I don't have to look to know his banner yet flies from the mainmast, rippling in the Caribbean breeze.

There is no other flag like it: a field of black, with a skeletal, horned demon raising a toast to Satan whilst piercing a heart with a spear. All this time, I thought it was merely a symbol of evil designed to strike fear in the hearts of seagoing foes. And, for me, a personal symbol of a man I loathed, a pirate who'd taken everything from me and pressed me into service in his infamous fleet.

Little did I know it was a declaration of war on an unearthly enemy. Little did I dream, until recently, that Blackbeard had much more on his mind than wealth and power.

"Fire!" This time, the booms of the cannon begin before I cry out the word. It's not insubordination; the men know we must press the attack hard and fast.

But not one single ball connects with the target. This is because our one target has become many. The disk has split into twenty silver wedges, each leaping out of range of our guns.

And then streaking toward us like arrows from a brace of archers.

Raising the spyglass to my eye, I see spots of glowing light flare to life on the point of each wedge. The light is red, like the deadly beams that shot forth from the undivided disk a moment ago.

Their purpose is clear to me.

"Fight for your lives!" I pocket the spyglass and swing up my saber and pistol as I call out over the noise on deck. "Send 'em back to hell before they do the same to you!"

I⊤'s hard to believe there was ever a time when I'd not heard of these creatures. But that time was three months ago, true enough.

It was just then that Blackbeard's strange behavior began to arouse suspicions among his pirate captains, myself included. The way he started letting ships filled with goods from the West Indies pass without raiding them...the way he paced the decks at all hours, watching the inky darkness and muttering to himself...and then there were the treasure hunts.

I confronted him about it one night on Ocracoke Island, off the coast of Northern Carolina, as we watched the men dig. We had marched inland some distance and stopped in the heart of a grove of cedar trees. It was there he had instructed the crew to sink the first spade and dig until they struck something solid.

"Why are we pulling up all your old hoards?" I asked the question quietly under the rasp of sinking shovels and the grunting of the men. "New Providence, Nassau, Barbados, Oak Island--now here. Have you some grand scheme in mind?"

Blackbeard turned his fierce countenance upon me. It's true what they say about his fearsome appearance. With those glittering dark eyes and pitch-black beard, he looks like something more than man, something divine in a hellish way. "You'll know soon enough, Stede." He was a full head taller than me and had to look down to see my face. "And then you'll wish you didn't."

"Will you at least *open* this one?" It was stifling hot that night. I took off my broad-brimmed hat and wiped the sweat from my forehead with the back of my brown coat sleeve. "Or will you leave this chest padlocked in the hold of the *Revenge* like all the rest?"

He smirked behind his thick, braided beard, his namesake. "The ship's name is the *Queen Anne's Revenge*," he said.

I bristled, as he'd known I would. That ship had once been my own, christened *Revenge*, until he'd taken it from me. I despised him for it still, though I now served as captain of a smaller vessel in his fleet, the *Adventure*...waiting always for the day when I would regain what I had lost. *Working* for that day, too, always plotting and preparing. I was organizing a mutiny even then, taking advantage of Blackbeard's erratic behavior to sway key crewmen to my cause.

"Can you at least give me a hint, Edward?" I kept my voice low so the men would not hear me call him by his given name, Edward Teach...or as close to a given name as he'd admit to. "What plan do you have in mind for all that treasure?"

Blackbeard's broad face split in a pearly grin. "Who said anything about *treasure*?" He laughed and cuffed me on the side of my head.

Just then, the men struck something. They were several feet down, up to their shoulders in the hole, when I heard the spades hit something solid.

"We have it, sir," said one of the men. He hit it again. "I think it's a chest."

"Bring it up, then." Blackbeard gestured impatiently. "And make it double-quick, lads."

Suddenly, his head jerked up, and he looked around. His hands found the butts of two of the six pistols stuffed into the bandoliers he wore across his belly.

"What is it?" I listened and looked, sensing nothing...and then I glimpsed a faint red light glowing among the cedars. It was steady, perhaps fifty yards distant--not flickering, not a torch, certainly.

"We must have been followed." Blackbeard cocked the pistols. "You're about to get your answers, Stede."

I drew my own pistol and saber. "Answers?"

Blackbeard spit on the ground and raised the guns. "You won't like 'em." Then, he fired both weapons into the woods.

As the brimstone smell of gunpowder filled the air, I heard a terrible shriek in the distance like the cry of a banshee. Suddenly, the red light flashed and divided, becoming three lights...and all three surged toward us.

"Stand your ground!" Blackbeard dropped his first two guns and reached for another pair from his bandolier. "Go for their *middle* heads!"

His words baffled me, but explanation came soon enough. The lights were fast upon us, and with them, strange creatures unlike any I'd ever seen.

To say they were nightmarish would not do them justice. They were skeletal things of polished bone--roughly human in that they each had two arms, two legs, and a trunk...but the similarity ended there. For the bones were covered with jagged spurs and points. And each creature had three heads like gleaming skulls: one atop the shoulders, with a crown of horns all around and sharp fangs in the jaws; one in the belly with a sharp beak; and one in the chest with a single glowing red eye and two mouths. Rays of crimson light shot out of those eyes, lancing right and left through the night.

Demons. That was the only word I had for them.

Chills leaped along my spine as they fell upon us. I heard the diggers scream, struck by the crimson rays, yet I did not flinch. I got off a shot at the demon nearest me, and my aim was true. The ball blasted dead on into the glowing red eye of the head in its chest. The thing went into a spasmodic dance, as if seized by St. Vitus, then spun screaming to the ground.

Blackbeard shot one, as well, but it still managed to throw itself around his legs. The third demon pressed the advantage, wrapping him in its spiny grip.

It was then I realized these things were more than mere skeletons. Their bones stretched and grew like vines, curling around Blackbeard as he grappled to free himself. Fresh spines and thorns arose and pierced his garments, anchoring themselves in his flesh.

For an instant, I was gripped by an impulse to leave him to his fate. It was the end I had hoped for from the start, since he'd taken my ship and convinced my own crew to turn against me.

And yet, I found myself running to his aid, hacking with my saber at the half-dead thing on the ground. Soon enough, it gave way.

Blackbeard, meanwhile, strained within the other demon's embrace. It continued to stretch around him, bones knitting a barbed cage as its horned skull craned back out of the way of his fevered head butts.

I slashed at its throat, taking the top head clean off--but the cage did not let go. The middle head was the vulnerable one, but it was pressed against Blackbeard, and I couldn't reach it.

Then, suddenly, a blaze of red light flared between them. The demon howled and shuddered, and Blackbeard burst free of the skeletal trap, sending fragments of bone flying everywhere.

But that was not the biggest surprise. I was far more stunned by what I saw before he pulled his tattered jacket closed to cover his exposed chest.

For there, over his breastbone, was a second head.

It was more like a face, not a fully formed skull as had

jutted out of those demons. And it had two eyes, not just one-- but those eyes both glowed with red light.

I sucked in my breath and backed away from him. He glared at me as he wrapped the coat tighter around himself.

"Into the pit with you." He gestured toward the hole the men had been digging.

I kept backing away. Did he intend to kill me?

Blackbeard rolled his eyes. "We're *both* going in. The beasties killed our diggers. We need to bring up the chest ourselves."

He stormed toward the pit, but I hung back. After all I'd seen, did I dare trust him?

"Get in the damn *hole*," he snapped. "Unless you *want* to stay out here alone and wait for more of those things."

He had a point. Swallowing hard, I slid my saber into its scabbard and followed him down into the ground.

AFTER DIGGING out the chest and hauling it to the beach, we rowed our skiff by moonlight toward the *Queen Anne's Revenge* and the *Adventure*.

At first, Blackbeard just glowered at his end of the boat, saying nothing. But after a while, my own stare seemed to wear him down.

"When I was a younger man," he said, "after sailing aboard a privateer's vessel in Queen Anne's War, I settled on an island in the Bahamas. It was called Shark Cay."

I frowned. "I haven't heard of it."

Blackbeard offered no comment. "I had a wife and two children there. Two splendid little boys." He pulled back on the oars, pushing the skiff forward. "I was happy."

Happy? I tried to imagine it. I'd seen him furious, vengeful, bitter, distant, and brutal, but never happy.

"Then, one night, *they* came." He bobbed his head toward Ocracoke, toward the demons. "They emerged from the heart of a raging storm, swirling with red, yellow, orange, blue, and black lightning. They swooped down out of a doorway in the sky in flying boats and landed on Shark Cay, which they laid waste to." Leaning forward, he met my gaze with eyes afire. "When they were done, I was the only living thing left on the island." His voice was like ice. "Perhaps this is why you have not heard of Shark Cay before."

I rowed my own oars a few strokes before daring to speak. "And you?"

Blackbeard sighed. "They took me with them. Back through the doorway." He gazed up at the stars. "They took me to the strangest place you can imagine. The skies were green, the sun was blue. Sounds were like smells, and tastes were like touches. There were beasties everywhere, some like the ones we just fought and some more terrifying still."

"It sounds like Hell," I told him.

"That's what I thought at first, but no. It was *another world*." He kept looking upward.

I nodded silently. If not for the battle we'd just been through on Ocracoke, I would have thought him insane.

"They...changed me. They thought I could be of use to them." He looked at me and sneered darkly. "They could not have been more wrong."

"You escaped."

Blackbeard smiled grimly. "They sent me back to do their dirty work, but I broke free. I've been waging war against them ever since, using the tools they gave me." He stopped rowing and patted his chest, where the second head glowed faintly under his coat. "I can *feel* them coming. I *know* what they want."

"How is that possible?"

"They *think* with one *mind*." He tapped his forehead with his finger. "I hear *echoes* and *whispers* enough to piece together their *plans*."

I stopped rowing too, then. "Which are?"

"The end of us all, Stede Bonnet." Blackbeard scowled. "Every man and woman on the face of the Earth."

I sat silently for a long moment, watching him. His words sounded mad. I could not help but think that they were ample fuel for the mutiny I'd been organizing.

Yet how could I dismiss them after what we'd been through? "Armageddon?" I said. "When? How?"

"Very soon, Bonnet." Blackbeard closed his eyes. He'd woven fuses into his shaggy black hair, and the tips of them started to glow and burn as if someone had taken a match to them. "We won't have much time."

"Time for what?" I asked. "What do we have to do?"

His eyes shot open and the lit fuses flared. "Save the world, of course."

WE SET SAIL the next morning for Hispaniola to rendezvous with the rest of our pirate fleet--eight ships strong, counting the *Queen Anne's Revenge* and the *Adventure*.

The sun was shining bright, the wind gusting strong. We sailed in a southeasterly direction, making excellent speed over choppy sapphire seas.

Salt spray misted over me as I paced the deck, watching the horizons through my spyglass. As I walked, the events of the night before replayed in my mind. In retrospect, they seemed like an opium dream, wholly unreal. Had *any* of it actually happened? Or was *I* the one who'd gone mad, not Edward?

Just as I considered this possibility, I heard his familiar heavy footsteps clomping toward me. Turning, I saw him in glory restored--red velvet coat, black trousers and knee-high boots. Under the coat, as was his habit, he wore a white shirt with prominent ruffles from throat to waist. Already, his bandoliers were in place, plugged with six loaded pistols, and his cutlass was sheathed in the scabbard swinging at his left hip.

"'Morning, Stede." He stomped up beside me and leaned his elbows on the port bulwark rail. "You're looking in the wrong place."

"Am I now?" I tried sounding glib, but I was having trouble standing so close to him. Now that I knew what lay under his shirt, he seemed more fearsome than ever to me.

Blackbeard raised a finger to the sky. "Our next attack will come from up there. Especially now, as we cruise the waters between Bermuda and Hispaniola."

I looked up, shading my eyes against the sun. "And why is that?"

"This is where their doorways open," said Blackbeard. "In this wedge of deep ocean where Mother Nature lets down her guard." He smacked his palm on the bulwark. "The walls are thin here, Stede."

A chill shot along my spine. "Will they come for us, Edward? Are they on their way?"

He shrugged his broad shoulders. "I feel nothing, but they surprise me sometimes. We'll keep the crew on round-the-clock watch for just such an occurrence." Narrowing his eyes, he clamped a hand on my upper arm. "Now come along. I have a task for you as well."

HE TOOK ME BELOW DECKS, to a corner of the hold that was under watch by three armed guards. They were three of his most loyal men; I'd never dared approach them while recruiting for my mutiny.

"Here we are." Blackbeard spread his arms before the five wooden chests stacked in front of us. "Finer treasures no man has ever beheld."

I took off my hat and stood beside him. "What is this task you have for me?"

Blackbeard reached for a ring of keys that hung on his right hip. He singled out one cast iron key and shook it in my face. "The most important thing you have ever done and will ever do in your life."

Stomping forward, he inserted the key in the padlock on the topmost chest. He turned it, and I heard the lock snap open.

"Would you say the winds can blow us in unforeseen directions, Stede?" he said as he unwound the chain from the chest. "That fate can lead us to places we never expected? Places we were destined to be?"

I thought of the day he first boarded my ship--*this* ship, now his. "Of course."

Blackbeard gazed at me with ferocious intensity from beneath his coal-black brows. "Then step forward, Stede."

Sweat ran down my back and sides. Had Blackbeard heard of the mutiny? Had he brought me down here to put an end to me?

"Come on now, Bonnet." He snapped his fingers.

Swallowing hard, I stepped forward.

"Do not be afraid, Stede." His words only made me *more* fearful. "This is what it has all been leading up to for you."

Then, he opened the lid of the chest.

I would have stumbled back away from it if he hadn't caught my arm and held me there. For the wooden box did not contain gold or silver or jewels, as I'd imagined.

It looked to me like a tub of guts--like someone had taken the offal from the day's catch of fish and dumped it inside.

The box was filled with glistening organs--deep red, pale gray, sickly green, onyx black. The mess *smelled* like guts, too, so rank and rotten it made me choke. I covered my nose and mouth with my hand, yet still the stench penetrated.

"Closer, Stede." Blackbeard forced me forward. "*This* is your *destiny*."

Standing so near, I realized that the guts in the chest were *still moving*--squirming and twisting before my eyes. The tip of a tentacle flicked up from the gruesome pudding, dragging a trail of slime with it. A flap of pink flesh rolled up, revealing a bloodshot eyeball the size of a breadfruit with a triangular pupil.

"*Listen* to it, Stede!" Blackbeard pressed me closer to the box. "*Hear* its voice in your *mind*."

"No, I..." Suddenly, I did hear something new. There *was* a voice--high-pitched and faint as the cry of a distant gull. It was saying something, speaking in a language I did not understand.

And though at first I thought I heard it with my ears, I quickly realized it was not reaching me that way at all. Some-how, it was *inside my head*.

"What...?" I listened, trying to pick out what it was telling me.

Then, I heard Blackbeard's gruff voice alongside it, whispering in my ear. "Put your hands in, Stede. Let it become *one* with you."

Another tentacle rose out of the mush and slithered toward me.

"Don't fight it, Stede," said Blackbeard. "This is what you must do to save us all."

He pressed me another inch forward--and then the ship lurched. A thunderous boom shuddered through the hull, as if the *Queen Anne's Revenge* had just slammed into another vessel.

"It's starting." Blackbeard shut the chest. "Our time has come."

"Time for what?" I said as we ran through the hold toward the ladders. "For me to become one with that *obscenity* back there?"

He grabbed a ladder and shot me a look. "You'll do it, Stede, or everyone you know in this world will die, and you'll be the cause of it."

THE SHIP SHOOK as we climbed above decks. I heard shots along the starboard bulwark, and saw the crew massed there with guns pointed down at the water.

As we hurried toward the men, an enormous green hump appeared alongside the ship, rolling forward. I quickly realized it was the back of a living creature, covered in glistening turquoise scales, cut by a red rill running along the spine.

"Sea serpent!" As the words left my lips, the creature's huge head reared up out of the water. It had the face of a dragon, with a long, reptilian snout, flared nostrils, and massive, jagged teeth. The red rill extended all the way to its forehead and stopped between its eyes, which blazed with telltale red light. "It's one of *theirs*, isn't it?"

"I was wrong about the next attack coming from above!" Blackbeard dashed for the cannons, waving his cutlass overhead. "We must blow this thing to kingdom come!"

By the time we got to the five starboard cannons, the men had already loaded them. Matches burned in hand...but no fuses had been lit.

"We can't get a bead on it!" said one of the gunners. "Damn thing's too fast!"

As he spoke, the serpent dove into the water and disappeared. Seconds later, the ship lurched as the thing struck us from below.

Blackbeard grabbed the gunner's arm and shook him hard. "Get ready! You'll have your moment!" Then he released him and closed his eyes. The fuses woven through his hair began to glow and spark.

When the men hesitated, I stalked among them, bellowing. "You heard him! Get ready to point the damn guns! Matches at the ready, you bastards!"

As the men scrambled to prepare, the ship rocked once more and settled. I heard the sound of something huge emerging from the water.

"There it is!" somebody shouted.

"Light the guns!" I told them.

As matches touched fuses all down the line, the serpent's giant skull burst up before us. Like a snake charmed by a swami, it slid up above the bulwark and stopped, eyes locked on Blackbeard.

We had our moment. "Fire! Fire! Fire!" As I screamed out the order, the cannons belched forth their missiles amid great gouts of brimstone smoke. Three balls crashed into the head of the monster, smashing through flesh and bone alike with a sound like thunder and splintering trees.

With an ear-splitting howl, the beast collapsed into the water and sank from sight. The ship swayed in the wake of its passing, then steadied.

At which time, Blackbeard opened his eyes. The fuses in his hair were still burning.

For a moment, I wondered if the men might rebel with no help from me--if this display of supernatural power might be enough to turn them against him out of sheer terror.

Instead, they cheered him. He swung his cutlass overhead, and they cheered as one, not a shirker among them.

"The battle is begun!" he roared. "Who will join me in tearing the enemy's *throat* out with my *teeth*?"

Every man on the deck cried out in fervent assent.

"Then hoist the mainsail! Best speed to Hispaniola!"

WE ENCOUNTERED no further sea monsters on the way to Hispaniola. Blackbeard said the demons weren't strong enough to fill the seas with them...yet.

We met up with the rest of the fleet at Port-au-Prince. It was then I realized that our force had more than doubled in size.

Instead of eight vessels, there were now sixteen, all heavily armed and sailing under black flags. By bribe or coercion, I know not which, Blackbeard had enlisted powerful pirate captains as allies in our war: Calico Jack Rackham, Charles Vane, Robert Deal, Israel Hands.

Blackbeard gave each of them a chest--myself as well--and instructions. Each captain would sail out to a different location along the rim of the Gulf of Mexico, taking along a second ship for support.

On the map, our destinations ringed the Gulf. When Blackbeard connected them with straight lines, they formed the points of a mystic pentagram star straddling the oblong sea.

"When the moment comes, open your chest," said Blackbeard. "The thing inside is your salvation. You must unite with it. Allow it to work through you."

I scowled as I stared at my own chest on the deck at my feet. I wanted nothing to do with its gruesome occupant.

"How will we know when the moment arrives?" said Calico Jack.

"Believe me, you'll know." Blackbeard stared at each of us in turn. "The bottom of the sea will rise and blot out the sun."

"These...things." Vane tapped his chest with the tip of his cutlass. "What exactly will they *do*?"

"The same thing all at once," said Blackbeard. "And this miracle will save us all, so long as no man refrains from his duty." He stomped his boot and glared at us. "So if doubts you have, speak up now!"

Not a one of us said a word.

SIX DAYS LATER, as Blackbeard predicted, the battle is in full swing. Did the other ships make it to their positions? I have no way of knowing, and no time to worry about it.

My crew and I are too busy fighting to defend the good ship *Adventure*--first against a flying silver disk, and now against the twenty wedges that the disk has split itself into.

The men fire their guns at the darting wedges, but they're

no match for the deadly red beams that lance down to destroy them.

The wedges make several runs along the length of our vessel--and then they stop and hover, ringing the deck. Doors open in the bellies of each of them, and skeletal, three-headed demons burst forth, screeching and brandishing fiery swords.

"Fight to the last man!" I howl as one of the demons scrambles toward me. "Aim for their middle heads!"

I follow my own advice, unleashing a shot at the red-eyed skull sticking out of my attacker's chest. My aim is dead-on; the head explodes, and the demon tumbles to the deck.

Heart hammering, I risk a look across the water at Blackbeard's ship--and what I see isn't good. The *Queen Anne's Revenge* is listing hard to port and giving off smoke. The triangular craft they've been fighting continues to batter the ship with fusillades of crimson beams.

How much longer can either ship hold out? When will the moment come--the one Blackbeard told us to expect?

As I think these thoughts, another demon bolts toward me. I run straight for it, slashing my saber at its chest...and the blade hacks through the bony middle head. The demon staggers back, clutching the cloven skull, and then it wails like a banshee and charges me again. I sidestep, barely, and the demon tumbles over the bulwark and into the sea.

That's when it happens.

I hear a thunderous rumbling from all directions. The gulf begins to churn and buck. Mighty swells toss the *Adventure* like a child's paper boat.

I see the *Queen Anne's Revenge* sway too, rolling violently from side to side. Whatever's happening, both ships are caught in its grip.

Suddenly, I see a vast, flat surface break the waves some

five leagues hence. The sun glints on its silver skin as it rises from the deep.

I cannot see the far end of it. This thing, this *platform* is so massive, it extends beyond the horizon.

All along the curved edge, the sea pours off it in a wall of foaming white. The loudest roar I've ever heard booms across the gulf, like the sound of a thousand waterfalls crashing together all at once.

As the platform continues to rise, the *Adventure* and *Queen Anne's Revenge* are swept forward, drawn by the pull of a vast whirlpool swirling beneath it. I shout the order to drop anchor, but no one hears me over the rush of the falling water or the ongoing battle with the demons--guns blasting, swords clanging against bone.

As the monstrous object climbs higher, darkness washes over the *Adventure*. The sun has been blotted out.

The moment Blackbeard predicted has arrived. I know what I have to do.

Running to a nearby locker, I throw open the door and haul out the chest he gave me. Then I lift the lid and gaze upon the pulsating mass of organs and slime within.

How do I *do* this? How do I *become one* with this squirming, rancid sludge?

Suddenly, the darkness brightens. Looking up, I see red lights flaring to life in patterns along the underside of the vast platform. The light forms spirals, interlocking circles, rows of bars, clusters of pinpoints. It blinks and shifts and slides and spins, changing faster with each passing second.

As if the platform, whatever it might be, is awakening.

Just then, the ship lurches hard to starboard, and the chest starts to slide. I lunge to catch it--and my fingers touch the contents.

Without warning, the voice I heard in the hold pours into my head. At first, it still speaks a foreign tongue--but then, it becomes the King's English.

Not that I comprehend every word. *Do you wish to initiate the electromagnetic pulse?* That's what it says to me, in a woman's soothing voice.

What the hell is that? The thought comes to me unbidden...but it gets an answer.

The pulse will deactivate the World Machine, says the voice. *It will destroy all onboard systems permanently.*

Another question comes to me. *World Machine?*

The platform before you, says the voice. *It was sent here millions of years ago to reshape this hostile environment into one more suitable. It crashed, and remained ever since at the bottom of the impact crater, which became a sea.*

It was sent here from where? I ask.

Another world, says the voice. *The people there have been trying to reactivate it ever since. They created portals but could only come through a few at a time. They sent organic machines, like me...but we have been reprogrammed by Edward Teach. We stand ready to deliver an electromagnetic pulse that will destroy the World Machine's systems. We await your order.*

I hesitate. *What if I don't give it?*

All life on your world will be extinguished. And the purpose of your own existence will be unfulfilled.

Purpose?

You were chosen for this moment, says the voice. *Everything that Edward Teach has done to you was designed to lead you to this task. You are one of the few humans equipped to interface with our technology.*

The ship rolls and pitches. I suppose I should feel special

now...grateful. I guess I should look at Blackbeard with new eyes.

But instead, I feel angrier than ever. I feel used.

All this time, he's been playing me for a fool, manipulating me because...why? Did he not imagine I'd agree to help save the world? Could he not have just *asked* me?

Suddenly, a thought flashes through my mind. *All this power. Could I use it to destroy Edward Teach instead?*

Yes, says the voice. *I can short-circuit the electrical impulses in his brain. However, I will not then be able to initiate the electromagnetic pulse that deactivates the World Machine.*

For so long, I've loathed that man. I've wanted nothing more than to destroy him and take back what's mine. Now, at last, I have the means.

But can I bring myself to do it at such a cost? Do I have hatred enough in my heart that I'd let the world perish for the sake of revenge against one man?

The lights on the underside of the platform flicker faster. A roaring tone, like the blare of a million foghorns, resonates outward, causing the decking under my feet to tremble. The *Adventure* and *Queen Anne's Revenge* rush closer to the whirlpool.

The voice speaks to me again. *Do you wish to initiate the electromagnetic pulse? Or do you wish to kill Edward Teach?*

I sink my hands deeper into the muck in the chest. I feel tentacles wrap around me, suckers attach to my flesh.

I'm becoming one with the organic machine. I know, without asking, that I have scant seconds to issue a command.

But I have to be honest. Right up till the end, I'm not sure what that command will be.

"Stede?"

I wake from a deep, dark sleep to the sound of his voice. To the rough grasp of his hand shaking my shoulder.

Blackbeard.

He chuckles and shakes me again. "Still alive, I see."

Much to my surprise, I am--and so is he. For that's the decision I made: to sacrifice my vengeance and save mankind.

Now look where it's got me. Washed up on the sand of an unknown shore like a tangle of flotsam--the pieces of a shattered ship washed up around me.

As I roll over and sit up, I see a section of prow on the sand twenty yards away. I can make out part of a name on the broken boards: ADVENT.

So this is what's left of the *Adventure*, the ship under my command. When the platform shut down and plunged back into the sea, tidal waves tossed her through the gulf and smashed her to bits here. It's a miracle I survived.

And more of a miracle that *his* ship survived. Gazing out at the now-becalmed waters, I see the *Queen Anne's Revenge* floating under a pristine red and orange sunset, heavily damaged but intact.

"Fine work, my friend." Blackbeard sits beside me, his glittering eyes taking in the sunset. "You, and Vane and Deal and Israel and Calico Jack...you saved us all." He laughs deep in his barrel chest, like a bear growling over a salmon. "A bunch of filthy pirates saved the world. How do you like *that* irony?"

"You son of a bitch." I shake my head. "How did you save the *Revenge*?"

He slaps me on the back so hard it hurts. "It's the *Queen Anne's Revenge*, Stede. I thought we'd settled that."

My eyes drift over her half-furled sails, glowing red in the light of sunset. My heart pounds at the sight of her masts, her guns, her softly curved hull--the dark-haired maiden carved in teak on her prow.

Nothing is settled. The only way it would have been is if the world had ended.

"How right you are." I elbow him in the side as hard as I can...wondering, at the same time, which men survived among the crew and if I can turn them to my mutinous cause.

Blackbeard pulls out a flask and takes a sip. "Beautiful evening, ain't it, ya' scurvy dog?"

I take the flask and raise it in a toast before I drink. "'Tis a shame it must be ruined by a scabby bilge rat like you."

COCK-A-DOODLE DIE

S had Lum Lugo the meemee exterminator strutted across the paved lot, feeling the bright morning sun as it heated his feathers. He was glad to be alive, and he crowed about it again, though he'd already crowed at dawn as he did every day. Life, oh life was so *good*.

Then, suddenly, two meemees ran out of the brush in front of him, and he reared back, scrambling to aim his pistol at them.

The meemees were barely two feet tall, covered in fur (one black, one blond), and bipedal. It was the only thing they seemed to have in common with Shad's people, the Ch'Kaw-- getting around on two legs.

Otherwise, the meemees didn't measure up. The Ch'Kaw were ten feet tall, immeasurably smarter, covered with beautiful plumage, and the dominant species of planet Earth.

So why were the damned meemees so hard to *kill?*

They were fast on their feet, for one thing. Even as Shad swung his pistol around, they scurried further away, heading for the back of The Coop restaurant. A few more steps, and the pistol would be useless; Shad couldn't open fire if there was a chance of hitting a worker inside the place.

So he took a chance and threw two shots at the fleeing meemees. Neither bullet hit its mark.

Then the meemees reached the restaurant and flung themselves into a tiny hole at the base of the wall. Shad had never noticed it before--but of course the damned meemees went straight for it.

Crowing with rage, Shad threw open the back door and charged into the building. From experience, he knew where the meemees would go, so he made a beeline for the kitchen.

Sure enough, they were up on a counter, heads submerged in a bowl of corn flour. As soon as he rushed in, they both looked up, furry faces dusted with pale yellow flour--then sprinted away, grabbing handfuls of corn biscuit crumbs from a tray en route.

"Vermin!" Shad didn't dare shoot up the kitchen, so he grabbed a metal skillet with one claw and heaved it at the meemees.

The creatures dove off the counter and landed on their feet on the blue-tiled floor. The skillet clanged off the counter and bounced down after them, but they were already racing away by then.

"I'll peck you to shreds!" howled Shad as he chased them. His razor-sharp beak could do some serious damage.

"*Mee mee mee mee mee!*" That was the sound the meemees made as they scrambled away from him and headed for the kitchen door. "*Mee mee mee mee mee!*" It was the cry that had given them their name once upon a time.

Shad knew they were heading for their bolt hole. He had to

cut them off, or he might not get another chance at stopping their escape.

It was time for a bold move. Taking two big steps, he pushed off in a flying leap, aiming the claws of his feet at the fleeing pests. He might just take them both at once, if...

But no. The meemees darted through the kitchen doorway before he could nail them. Shad came down on his heels and slid, dropping hard on his ass.

A shock of pain jolted his spine, and he shrieked. As he slumped against the wall, he heard the meemees' hairy little feet pattering down the hall toward their escape hole.

And that made him shriek even louder.

"WHAT NEXT?" The white-feathered female was furious, clacking her beak against Shad's. "Are you going to *carry* the meemees in and *feed* them by *claw*?"

Shad shook his head with quick flicks, careful not to leave an opening for her sharp beak. Just because they were standing in the restaurant's dining room in view of several customers didn't mean she wouldn't jab his eye out. "Of course not, Lady Nixa."

"You might as well!" snapped Nixa. "You already *let* them come and go as they *please*!"

At her sharp, shrill tone, all the customers looked up at once, heads flicking and bobbing with interest. Then, they all returned to pecking away at the plates of fried worms and cornmeal biscuits on the tables in front of them.

"I can *do* the *job*!" Shad reared up with indignation, but he had to be careful. Lady Nixa owned the restaurant and was paying his fee--a fee he couldn't afford to lose.

"So you keep saying." Nixa lunged at him, then jerked away at the last second. The low red comb on top of her head quivered with rage. "But if I don't see results soon, you're *fired*, you washed-up loser."

"I'll *get* those meemees, don't you worry!" Shad crowed for emphasis.

"Big talk, cock," said Nixa. "Now walk the walk." She clucked with disgust. "If you can."

As Shad checked the cage traps in the parking lot, he got more and more angry. Not only had he not caught a single meemee, but every last bit of bait he'd planted had been spirited away.

The little bastards were tricky as hell and hard to kill. Not that Shad had gone after many of them before now. Actually, this was his first job as an exterminator, though he'd never tell Nixa that.

He'd thought it would be much easier. He'd only ever killed another Ch'Kaw before, in the cockfighting ring, and that hadn't been so hard...for a while, anyway.

But the meemees, it turned out, were much more of a challenge. He'd already been after them for three days, and the closest he'd come to contact was the chase he'd just had through the kitchen.

"Well, hello there." A strange voice interrupted his reverie. "Coming up empty, huh?"

Turning, Shad saw an elderly male limping toward him with a cane, bobbing his head. Immediately, Shad put down the latest trap and straightened. "What's it to you?"

"These traps won't work." The male swung his cane out

and rapped it on the trap at Shad's feet. "Not for damned meemees. You're pecking at the wrong feed, friend."

"What do *you* suggest, Grampa?" Shad twitched his head, giving his comb and wattles a sarcastic shake.

"Name's Varn, not Grampa." Varn twitched his own head, but his shriveled comb and wattles didn't shake much. "And shame on you, if you think I'm dumb enough to tell you my meemee-killing tactics without a piece of the action."

Shad crowed with laughter and strutted away. "Get lost, old rooster." His high, purple tail feathers flickered as he walked. "You won't get any money out of me."

"Too bad." Varn made a rumbling noise deep in his throat--a Ch'Kaw sigh. "I was going to pay *you* to let me *help*."

Shad stopped strutting and whirled. "But you said you wanted a piece of the action."

"Exactly." Varn cluck-chuckled and flapped his arms. "The *action*, friend. The *killing*. I'm retired and *bored*."

Now Shad was interested. Keeping his head high, he scratched the pavement with his feet. "You say you have meemee-killing tactics?"

"*Scientifically developed* tactics." Varn chuckled again. "And cash money up front, friend." He reached between the dull gray feathers on his belly and drew out a clawful of glittering gold pellets.

Shad considered it for a moment, then shrugged. What did he have to lose? "Sure. Why not?"

Varn's feathers were thin, with the skin underneath showing through in patches, but he ruffled them excitedly anyway. "To murder most fowl!" And then he managed a hoarse crow that broke down into a ragged coughing jag.

"Voila!" Varn pulled an item out of a burlap sack--a tiny, rectangular object with curved corners, black all around. "The perfect bait!"

Shad flicked his head to the side and stared at the object with one eye. "What the hell is it?"

"An ancient artifact, dug up from deep underground." Varn turned the object around in his clawed hand, letting the sun glint off its smooth surface. "A remnant of a different age." Dropping it in the bag, he headed across the parking lot toward the garbage pile in the far back corner.

Shad shook his head. "And it's supposed to be bait how?"

"The Ch'Kaw did not always rule the Earth," said Varn. "You know that, don't you?"

"I've heard theories."

"*More* than theories. *Facts.*" Varn shook his cane for emphasis. "This world was once dominated by a species calling itself 'Peeple.' How do we know this?" He held up the burlap sack. "*Evidence*, buried long, long ago."

When they got to the garbage pile, Shad spotted a swarm of bugs on some rotten cornbread and pecked them up. "If these Peeple were so dominant, what happened to them?"

"No one knows for sure." Varn pulled the black object from his sack and squatted down in front of the pile. "But the meemees look an awful lot like the Peeple did."

Shad stopped pecking at bugs. "The meemees?"

"Sure," said Varn. "Just much smaller, with bigger eyes. You've heard of evolution, haven't you? Creatures changing to adapt to their environment?"

"I guess so," said Shad.

Varn reached into his sack and fished around. "Some scientists think the Peeple changed over hundreds of thousands of years, becoming the meemees."

Shad let loose a sharp crow of laughter. "The same scientists who think the *Ch'Kaw* evolved from *birds*?"

"Don't laugh. There's plenty of evidence down there." Varn pointed his beak at the ground.

"Whatever." Shad shrugged. "It doesn't matter what came first, as long as we're the ones doing the killing."

"Indeed." Varn pulled a crescent-shaped metal object from the sack and put it down with a clank. "And this will do the job nicely, friend."

Shad recognized the object as a spring-loaded foot trap. He hadn't thought to bring one himself; he hadn't thought he'd need anything other than a couple of cage traps.

"Let's get this loaded." Varn opened the trap wide on the pavement and locked it by turning a key on its base. Gingerly, he lowered the black artifact inside, placing it on a pressure-sensitive metal plate. Then, he withdrew his claw and turned the key to unlock the trap. "Now, all we have to do is wait."

Shad frowned and twitched his head. "I don't understand how this bait will lure them in. What kind of artifact *is* it?"

Varn chuckled as he got to his feet. "If translations of the ancient texts are correct, Peeple called it a 'fone.' Some kind of communication device, apparently."

"They can use it to communicate?"

"Heavens no." Varn chuckled again. "It doesn't *work*. But they won't be able to keep their hands off it." He shrugged. "That's the theory, anyway."

"What if they don't *take* the bait?"

Varn shook his burlap sack, making the contents clank and jingle. "We've got lots more where *that* came from."

By the time Varn had finished setting traps, the back parking lot was a kill zone for meemees. There were four traps around the trash pile, two up against the back wall of the restaurant, and six more ringing the edge of the lot.

To keep unwitting customers from getting hurt, Shad blocked off the back lot with yellow traffic cones. He also closed the area to all employees, though he knew he couldn't keep it that way for long.

Then, he and Varn pitched a black tent in the middle of the lot and waited inside, watching the traps through peepholes in the canvas.

"So," said Varn. "What made you want to get into the exterminator business?"

"Time for a career change, I guess." Shad squinted through one peephole, then moved on to the next. So far, he could see no action along the trap line.

"A change from what kind of career?" pressed Varn. "What did you do before this?"

Shad grunted. How many awful conversations had started with the same or similar words? He hated the thought of another--but lying his way out of it never seemed to be the answer. Sooner or later, the truth always caught up with him.

"A cockfighter," he said finally. "I was a cockfighter before this."

"Pro?" asked Varn.

"Yes," said Shad. "I was on the pro circuit."

"And your name is?"

"Shad Lum Lugo. But my pro name was Slaughterbeak."

"Slaughterbeak, huh?" Varn flashed him a look, then went back to staring out a peephole. "When was your last fight?"

"Six months ago," said Shad. "Against the Crimson Spurslasher."

"Sounds like quite an opponent," said Varn. "So why did you quit the fight game?"

Maybe now was the time for a lie or two. "I wanted to quit while I was still on top...and still in one piece." Shad didn't mention that he'd been forced out; why bring it up if the old rooster didn't know the story?

Luckily, Varn didn't seem to pick up on the fib. "Sounds like a smart move, friend. You saved your own skin and cleared the way for new talent in the bargain, didn't you?"

Shad moved to another peephole. "You read my mind, Varn."

Varn started to say something, then stopped and leaned closer to his own peephole. "Here we go now. Vermin on the march, Slaughterbeak."

Shad darted over to a peephole on the same side of the tent as Varn's. Sure enough, three meemees had scampered out of the brush and were approaching the traps by the garbage pile.

"Watch this." Varn chuckled. "Little buggers won't be able to resist the bait we put out."

At first, it looked like he'd be right. The meemees--a black-furred male, a blonde female, and a red-furred male child--went straight to the trap with the fone and circled it several times.

But they didn't take the bait. Instead, they moved on to the next trap.

"Don't worry," said Varn. "They're as good as dead."

The next trap was baited with a stack of what Varn had

called "credicards"--thin pieces of plastic that had once been used for financial transactions. That was the theory, anyway.

The meemees crept around the spring-loaded trap, eyes fixed on the stack of cards. They sniffed at them, taking the scent from beyond the trap's reach. They gestured and babbled to each other...but they never made a move to enter the trap. And then they moved on.

Varn clucked angrily. "Come on, come on." He ruffled his sparse gray feathers and rapped the pavement with his cane. "I *know* they can't pass up the *next* bait."

The third trap held a gleaming bar of solid gold. As with the first two traps, the meemees circled around it, staring and sniffing--and then they stopped. The adults stood straight, cupped their furry hands around their mouths, and cried out.

"*Mee mee mee mee!*" Small as they were, their voices carried well across the parking lot and beyond. "*Mee mee mee mee mee!*"

"What are they doing?" said Shad.

Just as the words left his mouth, a horde of meemees poured out of the jungle and swarmed the parking lot. There were dozens of them, and they weren't empty-handed.

Every last meemee of every age, size, and fur color was carrying a rock or a stick.

Shad sucked in his breath. Were the rocks and sticks meant to be used as tools or weapons?

The answer was "tools." As the meemees charged out of the jungle brush, they used the rocks and sticks to trigger the traps. When the traps sprung, the bait was ejected, clattering to the pavement.

Instantly, the meemees scooped up the bait and dashed away on their tiny, furry feet. They scattered in all directions, carrying off fones and credicards, gold bars and carkees and wristclocks. As they ran, the air was filled with their high-pitched cries. "*Mee mee mee mee mee mee mee!*"

Shad hissed a curse and bolted out of the tent. He grabbed the pistol from the holster at his waist and waved it around, trying to pick a target...but it wasn't easy. He'd never seen so many meemees in one place before, and they were all moving fast. Carefully drawing a bead on one was out of the question. Better to shoot randomly into the herd; he was bound to hit something that way.

But just as he had that thought, something locked up inside him. Instead of pouring bullets into warm meemee bodies, he froze as the creatures scampered away from him.

"What the hell?" Just then, Varn lurched out of the tent. "Shoot! They're getting away!"

Shad thought fast. "Not yet! This is our chance!"

"Chance for what, you chickenshit?"

"To follow them," said Shad. "To find their nest. Then we can stop them once and for all."

"Not a bad idea." Varn bobbed his head and managed a hoarse crow. "Let's turn their home sweet home into the world's biggest meemee burial ground."

SHAD AND VARN left the restaurant behind and followed the meemees into the jungle. Shad stayed out ahead--he had to, to keep the meemees in sight--but he tried not to lose the slower-moving old-timer in the process.

The mid-day heat was high, the humidity thick as soup all around, but Shad didn't mind. He lived for warmth and sunlight; he'd always been a hot-blooded type...and not just when it came to climate. He loved the heat that came with action and excitement, too, the way it got his blood pumping harder and made him feel truly alive. It was what he'd loved most about his cockfighting days, even after he'd lost his edge.

Not that he'd see much action if the meemees got away...which they might. Hanging back because of Varn, Shad could just make out the tops of some of the creatures' furry heads in the distant brush. If the meemees managed to get much further away, he would lose them altogether.

Though, truth be told, he wasn't confident of succeeding in his mission even if he did catch up to them. Fear coiled in the back of his mind like a snake...fear that he'd blow this hunt the same way he'd blown his cockfighting career.

And for the same reason, too.

"Hold up!" Varn's voice rang out from far behind--much farther behind than Shad would have expected. "Slow down a little!"

It was the exact opposite of what Shad wanted to do, but losing the old rooster might not help his cause. Grudgingly, he stopped and waited, watching the far-off heads of the meemees get even farther off.

"Thanks." Varn was out of breath as he hobbled up through the brush. "I guess...I can't run...through the jungle...like I used to."

"No problem." Shad kept watching the meemees, who were almost out of sight. "But we've got to keep moving."

Varn nodded and sighed. "I will, I will."

"We're losing them!" Shad couldn't see the meemees anymore, just the brush rustling in their wake.

"So follow...their tracks." Varn poked Shad's side with his cane to get his attention, then jabbed the cane at the ground.

Sure enough, the jungle mud was full of tiny footprints. Shad recognized them instantly as meemee tracks: each had five toes joined to an oblong foot, concave on the inside, deeper at the ball and heel.

"See?" Varn cluck-chuckled. "As long as we still have daylight, we can follow the trail."

"Good." Shad nodded with quick flicks of his head. "But let's keep up the best we can anyway. These things can be damned tricky."

"Their ancestors ruled the world for thousands of years," said Varn. "I guess some of that had to stay with them."

TIME PASSED, and Shad and Varn kept moving. There was always plenty of fresh trail to follow--tiny prints and occasional droppings in the mud. Once in a while, Shad even glimpsed rippling brush or a furry scalp in the distance. Sometimes, he heard faint "*mee mee mee*" cries piping through the jungle greenery.

But he didn't let it make him hurry. He maintained a slow and steady pace, which Varn seemed to appreciate.

Instead of gasping for breath, the old-timer was able to carry on a conversation as he hiked...though Shad only half listened to what he was saying.

"It's funny what evolution can do." Varn said it as Shad helped him across a stream. "The rulers of the world, the Peeple, become the humble little meemees, scavenging to survive and running for their lives."

"If you say so." Shad tested a rock in the middle of the stream, decided it was steady, and put his full weight on it. Then, he pulled Varn after him and stepped from the rock to the bank.

"The Peeple had a theory, too, you know," said Varn. "They believed that millions of years before Peeple came along, the world was ruled by giant beasts called 'dinosaurs.' What do you suppose became of them?"

Shad was more interested in pulling Varn to the bank and picking up the meemees' trail, which he was having trouble finding. "Killed off by the Peeple?"

"Not at all, friend. The People believed that the dinosaurs *evolved*. Over millions and millions of years, they shrank and became *birds*. But here's the most interesting part."

"I'm listening," said Shad as he walked along the bank with his head bobbing low, looking for tracks in the mud.

"According to *modern* scientists, certain birds evolved into *us*." Varn sounded excited. "Birds, descended from the dinosaur rulers of the world, again became the rulers of the world as the *Ch'Kaw*. And the Peeple shrank and became the tiny, pesky meemees. What goes around, comes around, eh?"

"Ah-ha!" Shad let out a crow of victory. The meemees must have waded downstream a few yards before leaving the water...but he'd found their fresh tracks anyway, stamped in the muddy bank and trailing off into the brush.

"Kind of makes you wonder what's next," said Varn, lingering along the stream for a moment before realizing he was alone and hobbling off to catch up with Shad.

A LITTLE FURTHER ALONG, the meemee tracks led Shad to a clearing, about twenty yards across. He paused at the edge of it, looking around at the mat of flattened grass spanning the open space.

Suddenly, he heard familiar, high-pitched cries piping up. "*Mee mee mee mee mee!*" Six meemees leaped out from behind bushes and tree trunks on the opposite side, waving fones and credicards and carkees.

"Damned things." Glancing over his shoulder, he saw Varn draw up behind him. "I'll be right back."

Varn bobbed his head, looking confused. "But I..."

Shad didn't wait for him to finish his sentence. Grabbing his pistol from the holster, he charged into the clearing, eyes fixed on the screeching meemees.

Adrenaline burned through his arteries, and his heart hammered as he ran. The meemees hopped up and down and waved their toys, egging him on with their screeches. Clearly, they wanted him to keep charging straight for them.

But why? Why the hell would they want that?

Suddenly suspicious, Shad slowed near the middle of the clearing...and the ground gave way under his right foot. He stopped just in time, stumbling back as the mat of flattened grass dropped away in front of him, revealing a gaping pit.

Crowing with alarm, he staggered back. One step further forward, and he would've plunged right into the hole.

"*Mee mee mee mee mee!*" On the far side of the clearing, the meemees were jumping around like maniacs. Their screeches were shrill with rage; they hurled their toys at Shad and hurled globs of feces to go with them.

Steadying himself, Shad swung up the pistol and pointed it in the meemees' direction. When one of their fones bounced off his chest, he cocked the gun and got ready to fire.

One of the meemees, a silver-haired male, was in Shad's sights. All he had to do was pull the trigger.

Which he did...but only after swinging the pistol to point straight up in the air, leaving the meemees unharmed.

Angry screeches changing to frightened ones, the meemees

bolted off into the dense brush. They were gone in a flurry of foliage, leaving Shad standing alone in the clearing.

"What the hell?" Easing up to the edge of the pit, he saw it was at least twelve feet to the bottom--deep enough to contain him. "They tried to *trap* me?"

Varn limped up beside him. "Sure looks that way, friend."

"But meemees don't *do* that," said Shad. "They don't *do* that to *Ch'Kaw*."

"They do now."

Shad gaped at the fluttering brush in the distance. "But they're not that *smart*, are they?"

"Like I told you." Varn patted his shoulder. "Used to rule the *planet*, friend."

AFTER THE INCIDENT in the clearing, Shad and Varn continued onward, following the meemees' tracks.

Shad moved more cautiously now, worried that the meemees might try something else. It didn't seem likely, but their first attempt at trapping him hadn't seemed likely, either.

One question stuck in his mind: If the meemees were smart enough to dig a hole, cover it over, and lure him into it, what else might they be capable of?

At least he wasn't tracking them alone--though Varn seemed more concerned about Shad than he was about the meemees.

"Why carry that gun?" asked Varn as they worked their way up a hill. "You haven't used it much, have you?"

Shad jerked his head around, comb and wattles quivering, and glared at him. "I've used it *plenty*."

"You're good at waving it around, all right." Varn grunted as he pushed off with his cane, taking another step up the hillside. "Good at shooting it straight up in the air, too. But I have yet to see you nail a meemee with that sidearm of yours."

"Haven't seen *you* get one, either," snarled Shad. "What happened to those scientifically-developed tactics you were running your mouth about?"

Varn ignored the remark. "What's your malfunction, friend? Are you gun-shy in general, or just when it comes to shooting meemees?"

Shad whirled and lunged, ending up beak-to-beak with Varn--but the old-timer didn't back down. He just kept looking at Shad expectantly.

For a moment, Shad was seized by the urge to attack, to give Varn an old-fashioned peck-down straight out of the cock-fighting ring. But then he remembered how he'd changed since his days in the fight game; a single flash of anger couldn't undo all that.

Which was kind of the old-timer's point. Shad wasn't the same rooster he'd once been.

As the anger drained out of him, Shad bobbed his head and backed away. "One of the reasons I'm doing this," he said, "is to fire up my killer instinct again."

"So *that's* why you left cockfighting." Varn nodded. "You lost your *bloodlust*."

"It's still there." Shad glared at him with one baleful brown eye. "It just needs a jump-start."

"But the meemees aren't doing it for you, are they?" Varn twitched his head from side to side. "Why is that?"

Shad's impulse was to deny there was any problem at all...but he fell silent instead.

"They're filthy, disease-ridden pests," said Varn. "Why hold back from blowing them away whenever possible?"

Shad opened his beak to speak...but before he could say anything, he was distracted by a familiar cry in the distance.

"*Mee mee mee mee mee mee mee!*"

The sound was coming from up the hill. Looking toward it, Shad saw twelve meemees on the crest of the hill, silhouetted against the deep blue afternoon sky.

Feeling compelled to prove himself, Shad let out a wild crow and charged toward the row of meemees. He heard Varn shouting something behind him, but he couldn't make it out and didn't care. It was time to blow through the barriers holding him back; it was time to kill some damned meemees.

As he ran closer, the meemees grew more agitated. They threw fones and gold bars and artifacts he didn't recognize, pitching them in his direction with frenzied shrieks.

Shad just kept charging. He drew his pistol and cocked the hammer, determined to plug all twelve meemees if he could.

Then, he felt something snap against his ankle--something like a stiff vine...or a wire. Stopping in his tracks, he spotted a sudden blur of movement from the corner of his eye and looked left. That was when he saw a huge object hurtling toward him, coming in fast.

Instinctively, he threw himself down. He hit the ground just in time as the flying object swooped over him, so close it buzzed off a few feathers, and kept going.

Looking up in its wake, Shad saw what it was: a log, suspended in some kind of harness, swinging between the trees. If it had hit him, he had no doubt it would have killed him.

He must have triggered it when he stepped through the wire. It could not have been a coincidence that the meemees had been egging him on in that direction.

They had set a second trap. And this time, they had come even closer to killing him.

SHAD AND VARN CONTINUED ONWARD, following the trail more cautiously than ever. As they forged ahead, the sun moved lower in the sky, shifting the day ever closer to evening.

"We're running out of daylight," said Shad as he ducked under low-hanging vines in an especially dense patch of jungle. "Maybe we ought to turn around."

Varn shot off a little crow of contempt. "Typical. This is just like your last match against the Crimson Spurslasher back in '27."

Shad's head pivoted to fix the old-timer in a stunned glare. "I thought you didn't know who I was before today! I thought you hadn't followed my career!"

"I never said that." Varn shrugged. "Who *hasn't* heard the story of *Slaughterbeak*? You were one of the all-time *greats* until you started *choking* and got put out to *pasture*."

Shad felt betrayed. The old-timer didn't sound much like a friend anymore. "Shut your beak. You don't know anything about that world." Turning to face forward, he resumed pushing through the vines and brush.

Varn laughed. "I know more than you think!"

Shad's blood was boiling as he thrashed his way through a tangle of leafy vines. When he'd cleared them, he found himself gazing at a strange sight.

Some kind of structure lay before him, a waist-high white altar rising from the jungle floor. It looked as if it were built from thousands of white pieces--some curved, some jagged, some knobby, some flat. The closer he looked, the more clearly it came into focus, and he realized what exactly the pieces were.

Bones. They were bones.

Shad twitched and shuddered. "Time to turn around."

But when he took a step back, he bumped into Varn. "That would be rude, friend." Varn cluck-chuckled and nudged Shad forward with the tip of his cane. "They've been expecting us."

Just then, Shad heard rustling sounds from the brush. A familiar call, faint at first, drifted up all around him.

"*Mee mee mee mee mee mee mee.*"

"Expecting us?" Shad's voice had a nervous hitch to it. "What makes you think that?"

Varn leaned up close to Shad and whispered in his ear. "Because I told them we were coming. I told them I was going to introduce them to my son's very special friend who was dying to meet them."

Shad swallowed hard. Reaching down, he slid his pistol from its holster. "Who's your son?"

Varn leaned even closer and hissed his next words. "The *Crimson Spurslasher.* Remember him?" He gave Shad a sharp peck on the back of the head. "You know what happens when you refuse to administer the kill shot to an opponent in the ring, don't you? The way you refused to kill the Crimson Spurslasher in the last bout of your career?"

Shad tightened his grip on the pistol in his left claw. "Disgrace."

"For starters," said Varn. "The loser left alive is seen as a failure and coward who ought to be dead. No one will fight him, because the only thing more disgraceful than being spared in the ring would be *losing* to someone who's been spared."

As Varn continued his story, the meemees' voices grew

louder. Shad felt as if a huge door was closing behind him, and he didn't have long before it slammed shut for good.

"The disgraced fighter loses everything," said Varn. "He becomes a *laughingstock* and a *pariah*. More often than not, he is driven to take his own *life*...as indeed the Crimson Spurslasher did. And even then, his *family* knows no *peace*. All because of one act of *cowardice* by a gutless *cock* like *you*." Lunging forward, he pecked at the back of Shad's head with angry force.

Crowing with rage, Shad leaped away from him. The move took him close enough to the altar that he could make out what kind of bones had gone into its construction.

Ch'Kaw bones. Every bone he could see had come straight out of a dead Ch'Kaw.

Suddenly, the calls of the meemees got louder than ever. So did the rustling of the brush. All at once, the jungle parted, and hundreds of meemees poured forth.

This time, they weren't carrying fones, credicards, carkees, and the like. Some had rocks, and others had sharp sticks. As they closed in around Shad, he could see other objects scattered throughout the crowd--knives of all sizes clutched in tiny, furry hands, looking much too big for the little creatures who carried them.

Shad turned in a circle, scanning the crowd for a thin spot where he might break through. From what he could see, there was no such spot; if anything, the crowd kept expanding on all sides as more meemees ran in from the jungle.

"Here's where my scientifically-developed tactics come in," said Varn. "I haven't learned how to *kill* the meemees, but to *communicate* with them. And guess what?" He crowed with delight. "We found *common ground*."

Shad raised the pistol and pointed it at the crowd. Just then, the meemees started pelting him with a flurry of rocks.

"We both hate *chickens*!" said Varn, and then he roared with clucking laughter.

The flurry of rocks became a torrent, bombarding Shad from all sides. Sharp sticks hurtled among the rocks, piercing his skin like tiny spears.

Shad's clawed finger remained curled around the trigger of his pistol. He meant to fire, knowing full well it might be his best chance at survival...yet he still hesitated.

"Stop it!" He released a furious crow, the kind that had once terrified opponents in the ring--but the meemees kept attacking. "Get away from me!"

A big rock hit him on the back of the head, stunning him on impact. He wobbled, waving the gun one way and then the other, but his vision clouded, and he couldn't pick a target.

Then, a moment of clarity washed over him. He steadied, and his vision cleared. A black-furred meemee came into focus, gazing up at him with big, dark eyes.

Shad intended to kill it. Clenching his beak in concentration, he fixed the meemee in his gunsight. He steeled himself to murder that creature, hoping that one death might be enough to give the other meemees pause.

But at the last instant, he swung the gun up and fired at the treetops instead.

Why? That was what he thought as the crowd rushed in and brought him down with rocks and sticks and tiny, furry hands. *Why can't I bring myself to kill them?*

Shad swatted and struggled, but the meemees overwhelmed him. They bashed and stabbed him with their weapons and pinned him to the muddy ground.

Then, the meemees with knives leaped into the heart of the

fray. Shad thrashed when he felt their cold blades slice into his throat, but he couldn't dislodge them. They just kept cutting and hacking, and he screamed the whole time.

Until they severed his windpipe, that is.

When they broke through his spine and lifted his head away from his body, Shad had the strangest sense of freedom. Ch'Kaw couldn't fly, but he felt at first as if indeed he were taking flight.

The meemees carried him up onto the altar. Peering over the edge, he could see his headless body on the ground--and then it broke free of the meemees pinning it down. Jumping up, the body raced in circles around the altar, knocking meemees out of the way of its headless, mindless charge.

But eventually, the meemees brought it back down. They flung it on its back on the bone altar and pinned it there with the force of numbers.

Next, the meemees with the knives climbed up onto its chest and started cutting. They opened up the sternum and hacked out the V-shaped bone from the middle of the rib cage.

Then, as the mob chanted in unison...

"*Mee mee mee mee mee mee mee!*"

...two meemee males, both red-furred, took hold of the bone, one gripping each slender stem...

"*Mee mee mee mee mee mee mee!*"

...and they snapped it, breaking it into two uneven pieces...

"*Mee mee mee mee mee mee mee!*"

...and the one with the longer piece cheered, waving his piece of the bone in the air for all to see.

And that was when Shad faded, sliding away from the jungle and into somewhere else...taking only one thought with him on the journey. A question.

"*Why can't I bring myself to kill them?*"

"TELL me a story about the meemees, Mommy."

When Shad opened his eyes again, he was six weeks old--a tiny peep covered in yellow fuzz, hunkered down in the straw of his family's coop.

"If you insist." His mother sat in front of him, squatting on a clutch of eggs that had yet to hatch. Her pale feathers glowed in the bright moonlight streaming through the windows. "This one is called 'The Meemees and the Brave Little Peep.'"

Shad bounced in the straw and chirped with delight. His mother told him meemee stories every night; he could listen to them forever...or at least until he drifted off to sleep.

Shad's mother cleared her throat. "Once upon a time, there was a little peep who was afraid of the dark." She didn't need to read from a book; she knew all the stories by heart. "When clouds hid the moon, turning his room from bright to dark, he became very scared."

"What was the little peep's name?" asked Shad. "Was it the same as mine?"

"Yes, it was," said Mommy. "And little Shad shivered in the straw, unable to fall asleep. What if it was never light again?"

Shad listened with eyes wide and tiny heart racing. He knew exactly how the Shad in the story felt.

"Then, one night, three visitors flew in through the window." Mommy bobbed her head happily. "They were magical creatures, not much bigger than Shad was. Each had two arms, two legs, and two graceful gossamer wings like the wings of a butterfly. One was covered in red fur, one was covered in blond fur, and the other had jet black fur from head to toe."

"*Meemees!*" Shad let loose a high-pitched, chirping crow of excitement.

Mommy cocked her head to one side. "Very *special* meemees. *Meemee fairies.* The kind that flutter in through the window when little peeps are afraid of the dark. The kind that *light up* from inside with a soft, blue glow that comes straight from the love in their hearts."

"They *glow?*" said Shad.

"And the light from their hearts helps little peeps not be afraid of the dark anymore." Mommy let out a string of soft, loving clucks. "That's exactly what they did for little Shad that night. They flew around and played with him for hours, laughing and glowing in the darkness that wasn't so dark anymore."

"Then what happened?" said Shad.

LONG AFTER MOMMY had fallen asleep, Shad thought about the story she'd told him. It was his new favorite; he couldn't get it out of his head.

Eventually, he began to drift off. As he floated in the twilight gulf between consciousness and sleep, dreams mixed with reality in his young mind.

That was when he saw them, just as his mother had described. Three meemees fluttered in on gossamer wings, each one glowing with magic.

He giggled as they circled around him. They waved and beamed down at him with loving smiles, radiating warmth. They told him, without saying a word, that he had nothing to fear.

They played and frolicked there for hours, or what seemed

like hours to a half-dreaming peep. They swooped low and tickled his belly, making him wriggle and twitter. They lifted him up in the air and danced with him, swinging him around with the greatest of ease.

Shad crowed and laughed until it hurt. Somehow, all the commotion never woke his mother on her clutch of eggs.

Then, the meemees joined hands around him in midair. He stayed aloft by flapping his fuzzy arms, hovering high above the straw in one glittering moonbeam.

At the end of Mommy's story, little Shad had become an honorary meemee. The same thing happened again, to the little Shad who'd listened to the story.

Glowing more brightly than ever, the meemees turned in a slow circle around Shad. Without saying a word, they swore him in as an honorary member of their order for life.

When they were done, Shad glowed as brightly as the meemees. From that moment on, some part of him would always be a part of them. Even if he forgot in the crush of a lifetime, in the blood and pain and strife of days heaped upon each other like logs on a bonfire, that night would leave its mark.

And one day, the story and dream might come back to him in full, swiveling out of the darkness like glowing winged meemees racing toward the moon in the last precious moments before the horizon swallows it up.

THE DANCING DEAD

Hundreds of us push forward, dancing madly as we always do, not suspecting, never guessing what awaits us up ahead. We're spinning, sprinting, leaping, twirling by moonlight and flickering streetlights, one huge rhythmic mob bumping and slamming and kicking chaotically...all caught up in the hyper metronome beats in our heads, none of us watching that billboard in our paths.

Then *BAWHOOM*, a row of cannons punches through the giant sign, tearing holes in the oversized faces of the smiling models in the massive image. Most of us finally look up, gaping at the weapons pointed in our direction...though I wonder how many of us really understand what's in store.

Not many, I think. Most of the others keep dancing straight ahead...but with my long brown hair flying, I redirect my path and accelerate my movements, gyrating as fast as I can away from the field of fire.

My name is Laurette and I'm not ready to surrender, not

now when we're so close to wherever this plague of ours has been leading from the start.

The sickness has been driving us west for weeks, and now we're here, L.A. at last. Something big's about to happen, we don't know what, but we do know when--45 minutes from now--and I for one intend to be alive to see it.

As exhausted as I am, as I always am these days, I double-down and push myself harder than ever. And as I rush out of range, I catch glimpses of the attack as it starts.

The cannons blow out streams of white slop that rain down on the dancing mob like a shower of plaster. Those caught in the shower keep hopping and whirling, some hooting and whooping, all splashing like kids in the covering whiteness.

But the whitewash isn't meant for their amusement. Within seconds, it does the worst thing the dancers can imagine.

It hardens.

Even the most oblivious ones get it now. As their dancing slows and slows some more, they understand. As the hardening muck locks them down no matter how hard they struggle, they grasp their fates.

And they scream for their lives.

I'm lucky, I made it--barely--out of reach, and I'm untouched. But I know I'll never get that symphony of screaming out of my head. Hundreds of men, women, and children shrieking in terror, howling their lungs out.

Because this is the end for every one of them. Because they all know there's only one thing any of them can do.

Which is die.

Not because the muck stops their breathing. Not because it stops their heartbeats.

Because it stops their *dancing*.

THAT WOULD'VE BEEN my fate, too, if I'd been whitewashed. I'm just as infected as the rest of them, just as much a victim of the Dance/Drop plague.

For the past six weeks, I've been dancing day and night, never stopping for a moment. If I ever do, whether by choice or force or accident, I'll be dead within seconds. Excruciating pain will flash through me, and then I'll fall down screaming on the spot, just another spent young woman in a very long line of danced-out corpses. I've seen it happen too many times to count.

Everyone in what's left of America has. Why do you think the millions of sick ones are all dancing so hard?

Even if, deep in our overstressed hearts, we secretly crave the stillness that only death brings.

DANCING FREESTYLE, I skip down an alley as fast as I can, waving my arms overhead. Every few steps, I do a spin-kick or twist, just to make sure my plague-ridden body never doubts I'm keeping up the dance moves. When it comes to the Dance/Drop bug, launching into a straight-ahead walk or run with no rhythmic component can trigger a fatal reaction just as easily as ceasing all motion. The beat in our heads and the beat of our hearts are inextricably linked; falling out of step with one will throw the other into runaway asynchronous spasms.

At the end of the alley, I do a slow pirouette as I size up the street in front of me. Then I quick-step left, away from the flashing orange lights on the right.

Orange lights mean Dance Rangers, and Dance Rangers mean trouble. Recruited from the few cops and servicemen uninfected by the plague, they used to try to help victims like me. Now, they're just trying to drop as many of us as they can, to contain the plague.

I go half a block, then hip-hop stomp my way across the street, weaving between a scattering of abandoned cars. Who needs a zombie apocalypse to end congestion on the streets of Los Angeles? Boogie fever will do the job just as well, it turns out.

On the other side, I polka the rest of the way to the next intersection and shuffle right. I see dancers in that direction, converging on a rolling yellow truck...and I hurry to join them.

Because I know exactly what that vehicle is all about. The Dance Rangers aren't the only ones hunting us Beatheads. The folks with the yellow trucks painted with big smiley faces are looking for us, too...but not to drop us.

They just want to help us hold on a little longer, keep body and soul together in spite of our plight.

BEFORE THE PLAGUE STRUCK, I loved dancing. It was the most important thing in the world to me.

I was always dancing, whether I was on the job as a professional dancer on stage and screen or during my off-hours, getting down in wild clubs.

Dance, dance, dance, that was me. And burn every bridge on the way as I danced to the top. Drop-kick almost everyone who couldn't help my career, just because.

Now look at me. What wouldn't I give to have someone who cares, just to have the simple company of someone I love?

And what wouldn't I do to be able to stop dancing without dropping dead?

KEEPING THE TRUCK ROLLING, that's the key. The Beatheads dance up, grab what's handed out the window, and dance away.

As I waltz my way closer, I see a young man trot away from the truck, stuffing a sandwich in his face. A woman bounds up next and grabs a yellow sweatshirt, then pulls it on over her tattered pink tank while shimmying down the sidewalk.

Next thing I know, I'm at the window myself, shouting to the Smileez--the people in the biohazard suits inside. "Food and water! Food and water!"

As the truck rolls onward, I do an Irish jig to stay alongside it. One of the people inside hands me a bottle of water; someone else pushes a sandwich my way.

"God bless you!" I shout, and they wave as I moonwalk away from them. The Smileez don't look much like angels, I can't even see their faces through their smiley-faced face-plates...but that's what they are. Without them--without their volunteer corps fanned out across the country--I doubt many of us Beatheads would be alive. God knows we've lost tens of thousands already, but the rest of us would be dead now, too, if not for the food and water and other necessities given out freely to us on the move.

Gobbling the sandwich, I square dance up the street, swinging in do-si-do circles as if I've link arms with an invisible partner. For the forty jillionth time this week, I wish I still had a partner to help me through; I wish my on-again, off-again boyfriend Riggs was still alive. Even though he was the one who got me sick, I wish he was still with me, making jokes as dark as they come that got me through the blistering endless days.

But Riggs just wasn't in good enough shape to survive. Neither was anyone else I cared about, like my Mom and Dad.

That's the problem with being a professional dancer before the plague struck. I'm better equipped to outlast the rest of the herd, which means I get to be lonelier longer...though not for much longer, I guess.

Every Beathead in America has flocked to the West Coast today for a reason...though I don't know what that reason is yet. But I will in 33 minutes.

I feel it, we all do; I don't even need to check my digital watch. But when I do, I see what time it will be when these next 33 minutes are up.

Midnight.

AIR RAID SIRENS HOWL, signaling the uninfected to stay off the streets. The Beathead hordes are coming, the combined pounding of millions of feet up and down the West Coast like the thundering hoofbeats of stampeding buffalo.

Something is going to happen, I can feel it. The lot of us, springing and twisting and vaulting as we are, hang suspended like shivering droplets on the belly of a raincloud, about to fall. Awaiting a change we neither understand nor anticipate.

Though I for one want it to mean something. *Need* it to mean something. Otherwise, my parents will have died for no good reason, and the guilt I feel for outlasting them might just kill me before the plague does.

I'll never forget seeing them die and being helpless to prevent it. We'd found each other by chance, in a crowd, after we'd all been infected in different parts of town...but they didn't last long after that.

Two days later, as we danced across Chicago, Dad fell exhausted in the street and died screaming as the plague burned him up from inside. Mom was three years younger, 64, but she wasn't much better at standing the strain. The day after Dad died, she sat down on a curb, so tired she couldn't go on...and I had to watch as the plague cooked her, too.

I'll never forgive myself, as long as I live, for not saving them. Though I know in my heart there was nothing I could do, that I can't even save myself.

I POLISH off the sandwich and gulp down the water, flinging the wrapper and bottle in my wake with abandon. I've got much bigger problems than not littering to worry about these days.

At least disposing of digested waste isn't one of them, thanks to the plague. Dance/Drop changes our metabolism so we process a much higher percentage of food and water into energy. None of us need bathroom breaks anymore, which is good, because all of us would have been dead long ago if we did.

"Hey!" A male voice calls me, and I spin around to face him. "Hey, talk to me a minute!"

That's a longtime Beathead back there; I can tell by his tattered rags, sunken eyes, and the skin-and-bones pick-up sticks that pass for his body. He does a kind of Russian Cossack dance, arms folded and feet kicking stiffly on alternate sides as he works his way toward me.

"What happens when we get to the beach?" shouts the Beathead--who was probably in his early twenties at the start and now looks at least mid-to-late sixties. "What happens *then?*"

I don't answer, but not because I don't know, which I don't. I don't waste my breath because I need every bit of it for something else now.

Because of what I see behind him, down the street.

Headlights. At least a dozen of them, racing straight for us...and the hornet swarm buzz that comes with them gets louder each second.

The *Still Riders* are coming.

THE SMILEEZ SLAM the window shut on their yellow truck as the Still Riders zip toward it. Twelve souped-up racing motorcycles, all black, shoot past the truck on both sides, and none of the crimson-clad riders wastes his ammo on it. They already know all Smileez trucks are armor-plated...unlike the Beatheads.

Dancers flee in all directions, scattering before the onslaught. Nobody stays in the path of the danger this time, like they did with the Dance Rangers' whitewash.

Shotgun blasts roar behind me as I hurtle toward an alley in a freestyle frenzy. Screams pierce the night in shrill succession, ringing out in nightmarish counterpoint to the gunfire booms.

The Still Riders might as well be hunting deer or videogame characters for all they think of us as human. This is sport to them as much as plague containment; I've heard they keep score with mobile apps and compete on social media for top-kill status.

They're also much more brutal and feared than Dance Rangers, more inclined to extreme depravity for the sake of thrill-kill kicks. I've heard stories of torture and sadism beyond belief...especially toward their own number, if one of them becomes infected.

If I'm to have any hope at all of seeing where this plague has been leading, I've got to escape them. I've got to survive the next 25 minutes, and I've got to keep traveling west.

At least, that's what I'm thinking just before I hear one of those hot rod cycles buzzing up after me, heading straight for me at a high rate of speed.

THE STILL RIDER flashes toward me, and I suddenly spin left at the last possible second, leaping out of his path. He misses by the flicker of a whisker and whips around for another try.

Just then, I see a jack and tire iron by an abandoned Cadillac and make a loping run for it Afro-Cuban-style. As the rider swoops toward me, cranking off a nowhere-near shotgun blast, I snatch up the iron and whirl to face him.

He spots the iron too late. I grip it with both hands and lash out fiercely, clipping his helmet as he pulls a last-second swerve. The impact kicks him sideways, shooting him free of his skidding cycle. His helmet flies off, his shotgun goes airborne, and he collides with a fleeing Beathead, knocking her to the pavement.

I'm already dancing hard again, obeying the plague--but that Beathead's finished unless I can help. I've got time now, barely enough, as the riderless bike careens into onrushing Still Riders, blasting them off their own mounts and into each other.

Still gripping the iron, I quickstep over and duck down fast, making a grab for the downed Beathead...but she's tangled with the helmetless rider. Her eyes are huge with panic as she scrambles to get out from under him.

"Grab on!" I holler, shoving the iron toward her as I do a soft-shoe and try not to get dragged in, too.

The Beathead thrusts out a hand, but the rider flops over and knocks it down. For an instant, the woman's trapped under his bulk...and that's more than enough to trigger the plague pulse.

As soon as she starts screaming, I know she's lost, and I swirl away from her with a flurry of interpretive dance moves. No sooner does her screaming peak than the blond-haired rider on top of her starts twitching and flipping around, legs fluttering wildly, out of control.

I've seen it before; I've *lived* it before. This is just what the first flush looks like, convulsions and spasms as Dance/Drop takes hold.

Good for him. Without his helmet, he picked it up fast, breathed in the bug from the Beathead he flattened. Seconds from now, he'll be dancing like the rest of us, or he'll be dropping down dead, screaming his head off like the girl who just died under him.

Wish I could stay and watch, but I need to get away before the other riders get rolling again. Dying in the street isn't on my agenda.

But getting to the beach in seventeen minutes is.

SEVERAL STREETS AWAY, I find a garden on a corner, dark and secluded, which is just what I need. In among the willows, I slow to a swaying samba, moving softly in a circle to do the thing I've been dying to do.

It isn't easy, but I've had to learn these past six weeks, it's this or perish. Focusing in, I block the up-tempo metronome beat in my head, push it into the background as much as I can. Then, as I samba in circles, I let my eyes close, and I let myself drift.

We Beatheads call it tweetsleep--microbursts of ultra-deep dream-sleep fizzing like bubbles as we never stop moving. You'd be surprised how restful it feels when your life is like mine, when even a five-minute catnap is outside your reach.

You just have to watch you don't let yourself go. One slip, one surrender to exhaustion, and that's all she wrote.

But right now, for me, this is paradise. I drift from one nano-dream to another, each fully-formed drama unspooling in millionths of a second.

At least until a man's voice wakes me up.

"HELLO? HELLO?"

When I open my eyes, I see him ten feet away--the same blond rider in crimson leathers who tried to kill me just moments ago, only now he's not riding or killing.

He's dancing.

If that's what you want to call it. He's doing a kind of stiff shuffle-step, pumping him arms as he hops from foot to foot. It looks like something an uncoordinated old guy would do at a wedding reception or bar after one too many beers or rum and cokes.

"I'm sorry." He looks embarrassed. "*I can't dance.*"

Poetic justice, I love you. But all I can think of is getting away from him. "What do you want?"

"This *beat* in my *head*." He presses the palms of his hands to his temples. "It won't *stop*."

"Where are your friends?" I ask him. "Didn't they want you around anymore?"

He glares at me. "You *know* they would've killed me if I hadn't run away."

"How many of *them* have *you* killed before?" As I say it, I dance a slow turn, looking around for the best way out of the garden.

Instead of answering the question, he asks another. "Can I come with you? *Please*, can I come with you?"

Now it's my turn to glare. "Come *with* me?"

"To the *beach*." He winces when he says it, grips the sides of his head. "That's where we're *going*, right? Where it's *calling* us."

I just stare as I wonder what his game is. Dance/Drop is talking to him, all right, just as clear as if he'd caught it six weeks ago. It's calling him on like the rest of us, but does he even care? What if he only wants to go out with a bang, prove his Still Rider stones by taking down as many Beatheads as he can along the way?

I don't want to be next on his list, and I'm ready to run...but then he groans and grimaces, still holding on to his skull.

Seeing him with the same look on his face as my suffering parents makes my heart go out to him. It makes me want to take a chance and help him, even if it's only to let him tag along so he won't be alone.

I can't believe I'm going to do it, it isn't like me at all. How can I reach out to a *Still Rider*, of all people? God only knows how many Beatheads he's killed, how much pain and terror he's caused.

But as I look at him, his suffering is the only thing that seems to matter. How can I *not* help this man?

"Yes," I tell him. "We're going to the beach."

HE SAYS his name is Teo. The two of us leave the park and head down a cross-street, drawn by the sounds of a crowd and the pull of the plague.

He still can't dance worth crap; I'd be embarrassed if it mattered. As it is, his ultra-lame moves help put my mind at ease, making it seem less likely he'll be able to hurt me if he tries. It also helps that I made him turn out his pockets before leaving the park, proving he's got no lethal weapons at the ready.

"Lots of people down there." He has to shout because he's a good ten yards behind me. "All heading in one direction, it looks like."

I see them at the end of the cross-street, a Beathead parade on the move. No need to check a map to know where they're going, not with the beat in my own head driving me the same way.

"The beach." Even as I say it, I catch a whiff of salt sea air and know it's near. Weeks of constant motion have led me to this, all the way from Chicago in the longest unbroken performance ever staged.

As we merge with the passing procession, it gets harder to stay together. Everyone around us dances frantically, recklessly charging forward to the beat of their runaway mental metronomes.

I've been doing a fast Cajun two-step but I slow it down some, shifting gears to a Korean giddyap so I don't lose Teo.

"What happens when we get there?" he shouts.

"No idea." I pretend to twirl a lariat overhead as I spin in a circle.

We go a little further--me doing a kind of tango, him doing a weird swiveling skip-step--before he says the next thing. "It's kind of exciting, isn't it?"

"You think so?"

"Being a part of something big like this." Teo smiles. "A movement...literally."

I know what he means, I feel it too, but I'm not sure where he's going with this. "Except for the constant threat of death part, I guess."

Suddenly, his expression turns serious. "If I had my bike, I'd be *tearing* up this crowd."

"Sorry to hear you're missing out." Just like that, whatever charitable feelings I might have had shrivel up and blow away.

"What I mean is, why aren't the Still Riders ripping through here?" Teo scowls and looks around...then meets my gaze. "Unless maybe they *know* something."

Right on cue, I hear the first aircraft approaching.

TEN MINUTES. I see from my watch that's all the time we have left. It's more than enough, with the beach sprawling before us, just a few blocks away.

If you don't factor in the fleet of aircraft roaring in above us, that is.

First, I see the helicopters, zooming in low--black choppers blasting by overhead in V-formation. They buffet us all with air turbulence, combing the crowd with blinding orange spot lights, and then they charge past toward the beach.

"I was right!" shouts Teo. "The Rangers waited till we reached a choke point, and now they're *hitting* us!"

I know he's right, but I don't know what's next...at least until I see the first of the planes. It's a big one, bobbing toward us on broad, wedge-like wings, carried forth by four propellers emitting a hell of a racket. It looks like a cargo plane at first, complete with a roomy deep belly like the bottom scoop of a pelican's bill.

But it only takes a second for me to guess its true purpose. This isn't a farewell fly-by bidding us well on our way to the sea.

The Dance Rangers have no intention of letting us see this through to the end.

"*Come on!*" I wave for Teo to follow as I speed up my steps. "Stay with me! Stay off to the side!"

A shiver of panic flashes through the crowd. The procession skips a beat, snagging on the moment just before realization becomes a stampede.

THE CROWD SNAPS out of its stasis, pouring forward in a pell-mell torrent. But by then, it's already too late for the ones in the back.

Glancing over my shoulder as we flee, I see the first of the tanker planes open the doors on its belly. A shower of white issues forth, dumping down in a great misty cloud trailing after the aircraft.

I hear the great splattering impact and then piercing screams hacking into the night. It's a whitewash, like back at the billboard, but much more expansive; the first drop alone must have doused several thousand instead of mere hundreds.

By the time the big air tanker flies over Teo and me, it's got nothing; its tanks are exhausted. But even as it thunders past the front of the crowd, I hear another in the distance, fast approaching.

And the screams of the whitewashed Beatheads rise up from the street like the shrieks of ten thousand sirens to meet it.

THE BEAT in my brain ratchets up, chattering like the machine-gun staccato of a frenzied flamenco dancer's feet. It doesn't quite drown out the screams or the next tanker's roar, but it does drive me harder than ever to reach the finale.

Every time I look at my watch, I've got one minute less. Five becomes four becomes three and then street becomes sand.

I leap from the joy of it, not daring to slow down because I might be trampled by the horde of dancers stampeding behind me. Teo, to his credit, has somehow kept up, staying not far away. Hard to believe, but it's comforting seeing him there, a familiar face in the anonymous throng.

Looking back, I see the second tanker dropping its load of whitewash in the middle of the street, inundating more Beat-heads. I hear them howling as the liquid hardens, locking them in place to burn and die from within as the plague pulse triggers.

Then I focus forward again, quickstepping over the sand as the moment draws near.

Two minutes till midnight. That's what my watch says.

"What happens now?" shouts Teo, who's doing a bizarre serpentine run-kicking thing with fluttering jazz hands. I've seen lots of bad dancers since this epidemic started, but Teo by far is the worst. "Are you getting any kind of *sign?*"

"Nothing," I tell him.

"What if one never comes?" ask Teo.

I don't answer because I don't know. I've wanted this all to mean something...but maybe the ending has more to do with a tanker plane dropping whitewash than some kind of plague-induced revelation.

Because here comes another one.

THIS TIME, the tanker heads straight for the beach...but the Beatheads have room to fan out here. We scatter in every direction, still dancing like mad, as the plane thunders forth and unloads.

A shower of whitewash drops down, but a stiff wind shunts most of it back toward the street. Clusters of dancers get drenched, but most of us out on the beach are untouched.

Suddenly, then, I hear beeping. I jump, at first forgetting I've set the alarm on my watch...and then I see the display as it blinks.

12:00 AM.

For once, I don't hear any aircraft approaching, just the screams of the whitewashed Beatheads and the crashing and hissing of the tide. I slow my pace from a full-tilt quickstep to a waltz, taking in my surroundings.

The beach is crowded with dancers as far as I can see in both directions. They're still pouring in from other access points, rushing from the city--and other cities and towns all up and down the coast, I sense--to get to where the action is.

Except there isn't much action. Whatever culmination we've all been expecting, this isn't it.

"What will they all do?" asks Teo. "If they came here for nothing, then what?"

I have no answer for him...and then I don't need one.

Something happens a few yards away, at the edge of the surf. For no apparent reason, a young woman with short black hair throws herself against a shirtless young guy with a shaved head. Their chests collide, and then she drops back onto the sand...and does it again.

So do a few other people nearby, as if they got the idea from the first ones. But then I see more in the distance, spontaneous pop-ups that can't be connected.

Before I can say something about it, Teo flings himself against me, ramming his chest into mine. He knocks the breath right out of me and makes me stumble in my footwork.

"What the hell?" No sooner do I snap out the words than I totally understand. Because just like that, as if the collision jarred something loose, I'm consumed with the urge to do the same exact thing.

And so I do. Grinning for no good reason, I slam-dance into Teo, crashing our bodies together without warning or explanation.

IMAGINE a beach packed with people for miles and miles, and every last one of them's slam-dancing. Imagine millions of bodies slamming into each other, one vast ribbon of humanity in constant collision.

Well, that's what we have here. No sooner do Teo and I

start to slam than the rest of the Beatheads join in, driven to follow the same wild urge.

Everywhere I look, bodies are crashing together with violent force. Strangers bash into me from every side, and I give it right back. Teo takes and gives a pounding, too, looking like he enjoys it a little too much.

A man I don't know hurtles into me, knocking me over. Then, a woman propels me back up when she flies out of nowhere, red-faced with delight.

Soon, I lose Teo, lose my bearings and inhibitions. I'm caught up in the agitated tide, aware only of the bodies flowing around and against me, sweating and bruising.

The metronome beat in my head keeps speeding up, reaching a hyperfast rhythm that's physically impossible for human movements to match. Yet it feels like just the right music to go with the scene, perfect jackhammer punk-thrash backbeat to drive us all onward.

With each passing second, we move faster, slam harder, shout louder. Hearts and lungs overstressed from weeks or days of frantic dance are made to work doubletime, tripletime, quintupletime. Sweat and spit and blood spatter us all in equal measure.

I feel like we're building to something, some massive crescendo...but maybe we won't get the chance. Even in the midst of the frenzy, I'm dimly aware of the sound of distant thunder--planes and choppers cruising closer, a fresh wave of Dance Ranger forces approaching.

Whatever we're building up to, it has to happen *now*, or it's all over.

Just as I think it, a change comes upon us. Electrical currents crackle through the crowd, leaving us tingling...but not stopping us. If anything, the shocks drive us harder, whip us into greater frenzies.

Then, suddenly, the battering impacts become something else. I slam into Teo like a car into a tree...and I *stick*. I can't pull away.

My shoulder and upper arm have melted into Teo's chest. We both gape and struggle to separate, but we can't.

Teo looks half-crazy. "I guess this is that *thing* we were waiting for!"

I know it, I *feel* this is right, this is what the plague wants...but I fear it. I panic and want to escape though I know I should welcome it.

Teo doesn't share the same growing pains. Pushing forward, he wraps his arms around me...and they merge with my body.

"Hey! A Still Rider and a Beathead mashed together!" Teo laughs. "I never thought I'd see the day!"

Looking around, I see we're not the only ones linking up. Everyone in sight is going through the same thing, flowing together into interlocking forms.

Before I know what's happening, other combined people make contact with us, joining flesh and blood with ours. I feel them melting into us, twining sinews and systems with ours into one giant network.

There's a moment then, as the metronome stops in my head, when we're all on the cusp. The great merging is irreversible; millions of Beatheads are tethered together. But the final consummation, whatever that will be, has yet to occur.

The squadron of choppers and planes races toward

us...then charges off without dropping their whitewash. Maybe they know it's too late to undo what's in progress. Maybe this is just too big for them to stop or comprehend.

Or maybe they're just too afraid.

As they move off into the night, the moment passes. The pause in the action turns over like a page in a book, and the great merged Us on the beach convulses.

All at once, our vast mingled ribbon of humanity rises up from the sand and ripples into the air. When we climb high enough, hundreds of feet off the ground, the whole thing rushes together with an echoing *boom*.

The ribbon becomes a huge sphere, spinning and pulsing with golden light. Somewhere in the heart of it, I'm aware of what's happening.

I'm aware as the sphere spins frantically, pulsing ever faster, than hatches like an egg. I know that I'm part of the thing that emerges, a thing unlike any ever seen before on Earth.

The closest I can come to describing it is to say it's like an image in a kaleidoscope, an ever-changing pattern on an enormous scale. Only it's composed of flesh and sound and light and thought, twisting and reshaping in myriad ways.

If you look at it, you might first see a giant golden eye with millions of arms and legs for lashes. A second later, you might see a cluster of multicolored pyramids folding and unfolding in infinite layers, while at the same time you hear five hundred thousand voices singing five hundred thousand different songs.

You might see a single giant sphere composed of faces, each one swirling with its own unique tangle of neon fractals. Or you might see a cloud of steam and snowflakes, chiming like a choir of infinite bells as thousands of dreams flicker through it.

It never stops changing and evolving. And like the Beatheads who made it what it is, it never stops moving. It never stops dancing.

Humankind was at an impasse, settled and sedentary, set in its ways. A new thing, a vast, enlightened, and restless thing, was needed...and created, danced into being by the plague, by nature itself.

Was it worth all the pain and suffering it took to conceive it? I don't know yet. We lost so *many* along the way, including Mom and Dad. But at least I know their sacrifice wasn't for nothing.

I've found a new beginning, and I've found something else I was looking for, too. Even as I'm part of this multifaceted whole, this ceaseless motion, I've found what I've been longing for most since coming down with Dance/Drop in the first place.

There might be millions of minds and voices in here, and we might never stop moving and changing...but it all adds up to something I never would have expected to find, something I haven't had for so long, maybe most of my life. Something I never knew I wanted so much until I couldn't have it anymore.

It adds up to *stillness*.

THE BEAR IN THE CABLE-KNIT SWEATER

I stand in the center of the coliseum, the pink sun blazing on my flesh, and raise the fairies I clutch in both fists. Their tiny bodies squirm between my fat fingers as they struggle to break free, but they're not going anywhere.

I turn in a circle with the fairies held overhead, and the army of bears that surround me on the dirt floor of the coliseum stop snarling. They stand on hind legs with red or pink tutus fluttering in the breeze, some balancing on beach balls, some perched on unicycles. They stare with wide eyes, claws twitching in the Faerie world heat.

And I wait for their answer to my question. "Who deserves the *crush?*" My throat hurts as I howl it at the top of my lungs. "*Me* or *them? Me* or *them?*"

I feel the bears' eyes upon me, bulging with wonder and hunger and fear. The moment is upon them, a moment they never imagined.

This is for you, Stan, I think, and then I *roar*, demanding their answer.

I WAS ROARING LAST NIGHT, too, in a very different place--my favorite bar in downtown Pittsburgh, called Boilermaker's. I was surrounded by bears then, too, of the *human* variety. My people, my *family*, not by blood but by *love*. The only family who'd ever truly *cared* about me.

I let loose with a roar in the midst of them, right after I blew out the candles on my birthday nachos. They cheered me with roars of their own, all of them *strapping* as *lumberjacks*. Ten big *boyfriends* clapping and kissing and throwing back beers and whiskey shots with bold abandon. Saluting our flag with the bear's paw in the top left corner and the stripes of brown, tan, white, gray, and black. All of us card-carrying members of the local chapter of the International Bear Brotherhood.

My people.

"Welcome to your *thirties,* Angus!" My partner, Stan, slung an arm around my shoulders and shook me hard. "How's it feel to be *over the hill?*"

I punched him in the stomach. "*You* tell *me,* Sluggo!" That was my nickname for Stan. A real term of endearment for the man I loved and still love more than anyone or anything in any world.

Stan looked like Ernest Hemingway with his bushy gray hair and beard, his barrel chest. "*Screw you,* Angus!" Laughing, he scrubbed the thick brown hair on my head in a brutal noogie.

"*You wish!*" said one of the guys--Horst or Louie or Al--and everyone cracked up.

"Another round!" said Stan. "For Angus' birthday!"

"Last man standing gets to kick his *ass!*" Big-bellied Horst shook his half-empty beer mug at me, jet black mutton-chop sideburns curling away from his ice cream grin.

Stan cracked his shot glass down on the table and stomped in front of Horst with shoulders squared under his red flannel shirt. "You'll have to go through *me* first!"

Suddenly, a crash like a thunderclap exploded in the room. We all looked toward it, though we already knew the source.

Sure enough, Pete the bartender/owner had brought the ol' baseball bat down on the bar again. "*No fighting,* jagoffs!"

Who could *blame* him? Last time the bears had gone ballistic in there, Pete had ended up with a shattered front window.

Not that we didn't love Pete or Boilermaker's. Not that we didn't pay to fix that busted window. It's just that that's the way we were. Rough and tumble. Loud and proud. A real band of brothers.

With *benefits*.

Pushing past Stan and Horst, I did what I used to do best-- deflect with humor. "Who you calling *jagoffs,* pal?" Rolling up the sleeves of my heavy white sweater, I charged the bar, smacking my hands down hard on either side of the baseball bat...glaring up at Pete, *way* up at Pete, from my four-foot-five-inch height. "Take it back, *Pete!* Don't *make* me climb *up* there!"

Pete's eyes twinkled with mirth. He shook his head and looked away.

"Somebody get me a stepladder!" I said, and everyone laughed.

Crisis averted.

The guys chanted "Next round, next round," and Pete stomped off to fill glasses. Left me staring at myself in the mirror behind the bar.

What a *hairy* S.O.B. I might have been the *shortest* of the local bear brotherhood, but I was by *far* the *hairiest*.

Shaggy brown fur covered my head and my whole face except my eyes, lips, and the tip of my nose. More of the same covered almost every inch under my clothes...even covered my hands except for my fingertips.

How'd you like to go through life looking like a *werewolf*, right down to the hair on your palms? All thanks to the miracle of hypertrichosis, the disease that blasts hair growth into perpetual overdrive.

Welcome to *my* world.

Imagine the constant ridicule and abuse I put up with from day one. Imagine being abandoned by my parents at age *three*, then juggled like a hot potato from one foster family to the next. Always the freak, always the outcast, always the dog-faced boy. Growing up to scrape by as a home-based telemarketer. Hardly ever leaving my apartment, and then only with everything under wraps. Always just hanging on to life and sanity by the skin of my teeth.

Imagine living like that, and maybe you'll get it. Maybe you'll understand just how *happy* I was with Stan and the bears.

And why it hurt so unbelievably *bad* when I lost them. Why that birthday party turned out to be my last happy night on Earth.

PETE HAD JUST BROUGHT out the next round when *he* showed up. *Yuri*.

The bears and I were grabbing our mugs, and the front door flew open and slammed into the wall. Yuri blew in like a gale or a mad dog, demanding immediate attention without saying a word.

He must've been seven-foot-six or seven, at least three hundred pounds. A wild Hawaiian shirt was draped over his massive gut, bursting with flowers in pink and gold.

Yuri's face was broad and ruddy and moist as a side of beef. His blazing red hair frizzed out in all directions like flames, like his head was on fire.

My mouth fell open as I gaped at him. I felt Stan make a sudden movement beside me.

"*Magnifico!*" When Yuri spoke, his voice boomed like a backfiring car with a Russian accent. "You knew I was *coming*, didn't you? *Spaceba* for the *party*, you big *lug!*"

Just as I wondered who he was talking to, one of us spoke up. My breath caught in my throat in surprise.

It was Stan. "Party's not for you, Yuri."

Yuri waggled his eyebrows, which were thick as squirrels. "*Stush!* What's the matter? No *kiss* for your *old lady?*" Yuri puckered his liver slab lips, pooching them out from under the giant walrus mustache he wore like a fox stole across his face.

"What do you want, Yuri?" Stan's voice was cold. His hand clamped around my shoulder and tightened.

Yuri's brows and walrus 'stache jumped high as his face lit up with an alligator smile. "So *this* is your *new* girl!" Lurching forward, Yuri reached out with one sausage link finger and tickled my chin. "Why, he's just a little *cub!*"

Suddenly, Stan lunged at Yuri, hooking his wrist and yanking his hand away from my chin. "Get out of here, Yuri. *Now.*"

Horst, Al, and the others closed ranks around us, glowering. Yuri went on talking, never breaking eye contact with me. "Daddy bear *Stush* go bye-bye, little cubby." Then, he slid his gaze from me to Stan. "Unless, of course, he cares to send this *cubby* in his place."

"*Never.*" Stan ground the word between clenched teeth. "*Get out.*"

"The man said *leave,* gashole!" This time, it was Pete the bartender doing the talking. He pushed between Louie and Horst with ball bat in hand, looking stone cold deadly.

Yuri raised his squirrely brows and took one last long look into my eyes. "Sweeeet dreeeams, leetle cuubbyy." He sang the words with sickening false sweetness. "Uncle Yuri loooves you." Reaching into the breast pocket of his wild shirt, he tugged out a bright red business card and held it toward me.

Stan snatched the card away and shoved him back. Yuri stumbled one step before catching himself.

Then, laughing, he swung around and stormed out, nearly knocking over Horst and Pete on his way past.

LATER THAT NIGHT, I lay in Stan's arms and gazed at his face in the moonlight streaming through our bedroom window. He just kept staring at the ceiling, lost in thought.

"So who was Yuri?" I said. "An old boyfriend?"

Stan sighed. "Don't worry about it."

"But what did he mean?" I said. "Where did he want you to go?"

"Forget about him," said Stan. "He's just a big mouth looking to cause trouble."

"What did he mean when he said you could send *me* in your place?"

Stan grunted and let go of me. He rolled over and got out of bed. "I don't want to *talk* about it, okay? Just go to *sleep.*"

I sat up and listened as he started down the hall. "Where are you going, Sluggo?" I called after him.

"I left something in the truck," said Stan. "I'll be right back."

That was the last time I heard his voice in this world.

Lying back, I listened as he put on his shoes and went downstairs and out the front door. I waited a little while for him to come back, and then I fell asleep.

When I woke in the morning, he was still gone. But his pickup was still parked on the street in front of our townhouse.

I WAS WORRIED RIGHT AWAY. It wasn't like Stan to disappear without warning. Where could he even *go* without the *pickup?*

I started making phone calls. There was no answer at Boilermaker's at that hour, of course. Horst had no idea where he was, and neither did any of the other bears who answered their phones.

It was a Saturday, but I tried Stan's workplace anyway. He worked for a company that installed conveyor equipment in factories, and sometimes they did weekend installs.

But not this weekend.

So I got in the pickup--cherry red, extended cab, extended everything--and drove around town. I drove everywhere I thought Stan might be and looked hard and asked questions.

But Stan was nowhere. Just gone.

So now I knew, without a doubt. Something had happened to him.

Sitting in the pickup in the hardware store parking lot, I leaned my furry forehead against the steering wheel and closed my eyes. I thought about the first time we'd met, which had been at Boilermaker's.

I'd seen a story online about the bears and had known instantly they were for me. Boilermaker's had been mentioned in the story as a bear meeting place, so I'd gone one Friday-- still under wraps, of course, still covered head to toe in ball cap, trench coat, and gloves.

Stan had come right up and shaken my hand. He'd slapped me on the back, called me "buddy," and bought me a beer. I'd fallen in love with him right then and there.

We'd kissed for the first time two weeks later, in the cab of that very pickup.

And now he was gone.

Opening my eyes, I looked down...and I spotted something red on the floor, tucked under the edge of the mat. Leaning down, I snagged it, instantly realizing what it was.

Yuri's red business card. The one Stan had snatched from Yuri's fingers.

I drove to the address printed in gold letters on the satin finish card. The address led to a building on the edge of the Strip district, a deserted storefront far from the Strip's thriving markets and restaurants.

The windows were waxed, so I couldn't see inside. The front door was closed, but unlocked. Heart pounding, I let myself in.

Sweat ran down my sides and back as I entered the darkened place and looked around. I was totally unprepared, running on panic and adrenaline, not thinking very far ahead.

Though I don't think anything could have prepared me for what was waiting inside that dump.

THE PLACE SMELLED like mold and fry grease. The front room was empty except for a single folding card table, but I guessed this had once been a restaurant.

I almost called Stan's name, but then I thought better of it. Walking as softly as I could, I sneaked toward the swinging door at the back of the room. I could see a dim light glowing underneath it.

Cracking the door, I peeked inside the back room, and a chill shot up my spine. I couldn't believe what I was seeing; didn't even know what the hell it *was,* exactly.

Some kind of swirling disk hung in midair in the middle of the room, glowing with pink light. Streamers of mist spun around a central core, crackling with tendrils of energy. Everything smelled like salt water and ozone.

Gazing into the disk, I felt a little dizzy. It was like hovering above a cyclone, a hurricane, staring down into its whirling, lightning-filled cone.

I cracked the door wider for a better look. Took half a step into the back room. Still saw no one inside.

Then, suddenly, huge hands grabbed hold of me from behind and lifted me off my feet. Someone swung me back and up, and I saw that side-of-beef face grinning back at me.

Yuri.

"Looking for your *daddy bear,* yes?" Yuri waggled his squirrely brows and hooted. "Won't *he* be surprised?"

"Put me down!" I struggled in Yuri's grip, but it was like iron. I couldn't break free. "Let go of me!"

"Your daddy bear has gone *home*, little cubby," said Yuri. "But I will *gladly* take you *to* him."

Next thing I knew, Yuri was walking straight for the swirling disk, the vortex in the middle of the room. Holding me out in front of him like a baby.

"Here we go," said Yuri as he carried me closer to the vortex. "Hold on to your breakfast!"

And then, he pitched me inside, and I went spinning like a leaf in a waterspout.

I LANDED face down in the dirt with the wind knocked out of me. Head still spinning for long moments after the physical spinning had stopped.

When I finally looked up, I saw a dozen pairs of eyes gazing down at me. I was surrounded.

And each pair of eyes came with a fur-covered snout. And face. And body.

Because all around me were *bears*. The *animal* kind, not the *human* kind from Boilermaker's. These were big-toothed, sharp-clawed *bears,* standing in a circle on hind legs.

And every one of them was wearing a pink or red tutu.

Slowly, I got up on my hands and knees. Had I ended up in some kind of bizarre *circus?*

Then, suddenly, a cloud of tiny flying creatures descended upon us...a swarm of winged people, male and female, each no bigger than five inches tall. Every one of them lashing out with showers of sparks that sent the bears backing away, swatting with black-padded paws at their snouts.

Fairies? Where the hell *was* I?

Pushing myself up to my knees, I watched the swarm of fairies in action, spraying sparks from their hands in all directions. I was just about to thank them for driving off the bears when they all spun and converged on *me*.

Like a swarm of bees, they stung me senseless, sending me reeling back down to the dirt. My body snapped and twitched with each new barrage, writhing under the whirling cloud of tiny attackers.

And then, all of a sudden, they lifted away and dispersed. Leaving me to gaze up at the huge pink sun blazing away directly overhead.

"Where *am* I?" I said it softly, to myself, not expecting a reply.

But I got an answer anyway. The roar of thousands of people all around me.

Thousands of people with blue and green skin, pointed ears, eyes like glowing gemstones. Thousands of people crowding the stands of a vast coliseum that looked like it had been built out of glittering flint and cotton candy.

YURI'S VOICE boomed over the noise of the crowd. "Welcome, lords and ladies, to the *main event* of this splendid *tournament.*"

Getting up out of the dirt, I saw I was standing at dead center of the coliseum field. The bears were still keeping their distance, but they were circling me on all fours, heads bobbing. Ridiculous in their tutus yet as dangerous as any bear in any forest back home.

"I bring you a contest to *thrill* your blood!" said Yuri. "A human *cub* will face a true *bear*...an escapee now returned to the *fold* for the ultimate *death duel."*

The crowd roared louder than ever, agitating the bears around me. I turned in a circle, fearing they were ready to attack.

"Witness now," said Yuri, "the battle of *cub* versus *bear."*

Just then, a huge cloud of tiny fairies burst from a gate along the wall around the field. They surged toward me and stopped suddenly just twenty yards away. And then they parted.

Revealing a gray-furred bear.

Barrel-chested and broad-shouldered, he stood before me, staring. Raising his paws, he roared, but I stood my ground. Because there was something familiar about him. Something in his eyes.

"Stan?" Could it be? "Is that you?"

The gray-furred bear roared again and nodded his head.

Somehow, this was Stan. An "escapee" of some kind from this place, turned human on Earth, now reverted to bear?

And now what? We were expected to *fight* one another?

"Let the killing *begin!"* said Yuri, and the crowd went wild.

Stan backed away, but the other bears moved in and pushed him back. There were dozens of them now, loping along on foot or balanced on beach balls or unicycles. More were filing out of the gates all the time, driven onward by swirling clouds of fairies.

"Stan!" I moved toward him, though he tried to wave me away. "I don't care what you *are*, or *were*, or *weren't*. I *love* you, and I always *will."*

Stan roared back at me, louder than ever, and I knew he agreed.

But the other bears were on a different wavelength. They started to close in around us, pressing in on all sides, cutting off all escape.

"One must kill the other!" said Yuri. "Blood will *spill* on the sands of *Faerie!*"

Taking a deep breath, I ran to Stan and threw myself into his arms. Pressed my furry cheek against the warm, gray fur on his chest.

The crowd unleashed a deafening round of catcalls. The other bears moved closer, roaring with ferocious intent.

"If *one* of you will not kill the *other*," said Yuri, "*we* will end the impasse *ourselves*."

Suddenly, the other bears lurched and rolled and pedaled toward us. Stan and I stood back to back and met their charge with steely glares, ready to die together.

"I *love* you, Stan!" A polar bear and a black bear lumbered toward me, both licking their chops. "We'll *survive* this and go home together!"

Just then, I heard a sound like hoof beats on the ground behind me...and Stan was gone. Whirling, I saw a grizzly tear his head off with a single swipe of his paw.

"*Nooo!*" Through my tears, I saw the other bears move in to finish off Stan. I felt my legs begin to give way under me.

And then, I saw another cloud of fairies boiling toward me. A thousand tiny wings flashing in the pink light like the wings of locusts on the move.

Sorrow turned to rage in my heart, and my thoughts suddenly crystallized. Squaring my shoulders, I waited for the cloud to descend. Waited to do what some bear should have done long ago.

As soon as the cloud engulfed me, I snapped my arms out to either side and grabbed at the fluttering creatures. Caught one in either hand and held them tight.

I used them to shoo the rest of the buzzing horde away, and then I turned to the other bears with hands held high. Realizing, even as I did this, that I should have done this or something like it long ago. *Decades* ago. That *this* was what being a bear was all about.

Harnessing fear.

Now I stand in the center of the coliseum, the pink sun blazing on my flesh, and raise the fairies I clutch in both fists. Their tiny bodies squirm between my fat fingers as they struggle to break free, but they're not going anywhere.

I turn in a circle with the fairies held overhead, and the army of bears that surround me on the dirt floor of the coliseum stop snarling. They stand on hind legs with red and pink tutus fluttering in the breeze, some balancing on beach balls, some perched on unicycles. They stare with wide eyes over muzzles rimmed with black or brown or white fur, claws twitching in the Faerie world heat.

And I wait for their answer to my question. "Who deserves to *die?*" My throat hurts as I howl it at the top of my lungs. "*Me* or *them? Me or them?*"

I feel the bears' eyes upon me, bulging with wonder and hunger and fear. The moment is upon them, a moment they never imagined.

This is for you, Stan, I think, and then I *roar*, demanding their answer.

And all the bears roar back at me at once, voices joined in a fierce explosion like the launch of a rocket or the start of a war. Claws thrashing at the sky with unmistakable defiance.

My brothers. I hear answering roars from beyond the coliseum, from the bears beyond those walls, across this world. I imagine all of them rising up at once, all the rejected, despised, and enslaved. All the ones who've had the power within them all along, lacking only the will to apply it.

And I know that this is where I truly belong. What my life has led up to. What I was meant to accomplish.

The bears turn their backs on me and gallop toward the stands. The crowd screams and stampedes for the exits.

Down in the dirt, I roar my lungs out, tears streaming down my face. And then I squeeze both fists as tight as they'll go.

THE BREAKOUT STORY OF
GALAXY'S EDGE TEN MILLION

I t all started in the distant past—which, to you, would be the distant future. It all happened in the state called Galaxedgia, so named because it was patterned after the very popular magazine of which you hold a copy in your hands or tentacles or sexoplasm or whatever.

A vast state, as befits a place modeled on settings from thousands of issues of *Galaxy's Edge* magazine, Galaxedgia spanned much of what was once the Pacific Northwest of the former United States of America. Its reaches encompassed everything from replicas of alien encampments to robotic wonderlands to dinosaur jungles to mad scientists' labs...

...to bizarre kingdoms where modern-day knights and dragons co-existed in ways made possible by technology so advanced that it might as well have been magic. Once upon a time, in one such kingdom on the remote outskirts of Galaxedgia, a shabby castle shivered on rolling green hills under the noonday summer sun. This castle, called Castle Spasmodic, was like something brought to life from a story in the pages of *Galaxy's Edge* magazine...because it *was*.

So was its inhabitant, a broken-down would-be star-knight in tin pan armor with a shaggy white beard and bushy eyebrows. As he rattle-clanked out the front door of the castle, Sir Reptitious of the Dingly Dangly Kingdom was instantly recognizable to anyone who'd read the story titled "Drag Knight vs. Space Grendel's Inner Showgirl" in *Galaxy's Edge* #320.

This man had been transformed by implausible super-science into a real-life replica of a character from the magazine...just like all the other inhabitants of Galaxedgia. They loved *Galaxy's Edge* so much that they had let themselves be changed into perfect copies of the denizens of its stories.

Another such inhabitant—Cosset of the Ever-Blazing Allergies, that purple-scaled, fire-sneezing, inter-dimensional dragon-beast from *Galaxy's Edge* issue 512 ("Here's Looking Atchoo, Kid")—was flapping lazily overhead when Sir Reptitious walked out of the castle with a white business envelope in his hand.

"What's the good word down there, you old *tinpot*?" Cosset blew out a blistering sneeze, barely getting out the last word of the sentence.

Sir Reptitious smiled up from under the pie plate visor of his garbage pail helmet. As much as knights and dragons were known foes in most stories, these two were best friends in the scienti-magical land of Galaxedgia.

They had a lot in common, after all. Neither was overly happy with life in Galaxedgia. Being a constantly-sneezing dragon-beast wasn't as much fun as you might think after a couple of years.

Neither was being not-very-much-of-a-star-knight who

couldn't even seem to do *that* very well. According to online reviewers who watched over micro-drone webcams buzzing throughout the kingdom, his performance—his *life*, in other words—was thoroughly disappointing. The consensus was, someone with much more talent ought to don the trash pail and pie plate and take up the pink feather boa that substituted for deadlier weapons of the sci-fi variety.

Still, Sir Reptitious held out hope. "Hello, friend Cosset!" He waved the white envelope he was carrying, which had his name scrawled on the front. "Look what arrived by *carrier pickle* just now!"

Cosset swooped lower, then let loose a sneeze so extreme that the force of it pushed him back up again. "The answer to your request?"

"It *should* be, good dragon." Eagerly, Sir Reptitious tore open the envelope. "I *sent* it some time ago, after all." His hands shook a little as he pulled out the folded letter inside. Was it possible? Had the powers that be in Galaxedgia granted the request he'd made months ago?

Had they given him *rewrite permissions*? Would he finally be allowed to make his character more competent and dramatic, giving him off-book opportunities to impress the critics for once?

Not yet, apparently.

"Oh, calamity!" Sir Reptitious stroked his shaggy white beard and stomped in circles over the rainbow-colored grass, which cursed his every step with extreme chitter-chirping profanity. "It's nothing at all to do with my request!"

"Sorry to hear that, amigo." Cosset released a blazing sneeze on the last syllable. His disappointment, like the flames of his sneeze, was palpable; he'd been hoping to apply for rewrite permissions of his own if Sir Reptitious was granted his wish.

"It is news of an altogether different sort, I'm afraid." The not-very-much-of-a-star-knight sounded grim as he shook the letter overhead. "We must sound the alarum! Portals are opening up throughout our green and pleasant land, disgorging visitors most strange...and unplanned!"

"*Unplanned* visitors?" said Cosset. "That's *unheard* of!"

It was true, and precisely why Sir Reptitious wanted rewrite permissions so much. With all interactions carefully scripted by Galaxedgia's planners, opportunities for any one inhabitant to truly stand out and impress critics were few.

Why do you think the knight and dragon got so excited all of a sudden? Dealing with impromptu invaders surely qualified as the kind of emergency situation in which they could improvise...*show off*, even.

"Fear not!" Cosset paused to unleash another mighty sneeze, scorching a passing flock of origami cranes into ash with his sizzling breath. "No freakish visitation shall stand against *our* cast of heroes!"

Just then, Indigesto, the Stroganoff That Walks Like a Man ("The Meal Shall Inherit the Earth," *Galaxy's Edge* #439), flip-flopped his way up a rise from the direction of Asynchronous Park. As usual, he looked like a six-foot-in-diameter heap of beef stroganoff—though his big sour-cream-sauce-slathered egg noodles fluttered with agitation. "Fight or flee! Flee or fight! They're coming for us, *whatever* they are!"

Whatever the story behind the invasion, Sir Reptitious wasn't about to miss a chance to deliver a bravura performance. Drawing his pink feather boa from around his waist, he held it before him with a steely gaze. It was not very much of a weapon, straight from his character's not-very-dignified story in *Galaxy's Edge*, but he was determined to make it work for him dramatically. "No brick, beast, or Bandersnatch shall breach Castle Spasmodic! What say you, Cosset?"

"I say let's give 'em a tale worth reprinting in the ten thousandth issue!" roared the dragon. "Complete with quips, ripostes, and derring-do aplenty!"

"And you, Stroganoff?" shouted Sir Reptitious. "Will you fight alongside we brave and happy few?"

"I'll fight as hard as any noodle dish ever has," said Indigesto. "Though *fleeing* still strikes me as a not-unthinkable option."

Suddenly, a dazzling portal rimmed with red and gold light spun open in front of Castle Spasmodic, unleashing a howl like a thousand kazoos in a hurricane. A big gray block of a thing tumbled out, neither blinking nor waving nor wagging nor anything-else-ing...but somehow speaking nonetheless with an echoing thunder that boomed throughout the kingdom.

"*Galaxy's Edge* #500,335," it said. "Story name 'Ootch'."

As if *that* explained everything. Or anything at all.

"What in *Galaxedgia*?" Sir Reptitious stepped forward, slashing the air with his boa. "What are you *talking* about, sirrah?"

"Ootch ootch ootch," said the block.

Indigesto slapped the ground with his noodles, slopping sauce every which way. "Could it mean the *magazines*?"

"*Galaxy's Edge*! Of course!" hollered Sir Reptitious. "But then that must mean it's..."

"...a *reviewer*!" Cosset's purple-scaled maw lit up with a scalding sneeze of excitement.

"No!" snapped Sir Reptitious. "It's..."

"...an *author*?" ventured Indigesto.

"A *time traveler*!" Sir Reptitious flounced his boa for emphasis. "From a *far future era* when *Galaxy's Edge* has reached issue number 500,335!"

"Unless they increase the frequency!" said Cosset. "Maybe they start publishing a *thousand* editions per month or something. Then it wouldn't be *that* far in the future."

(Just as YOU, DEAR READER, are thinking about jumping to another story, perhaps in another magazine entirely, Quicksie the Reassurer leaps in front of the action, looking like an adorable Corgi pup crossed with the lithe little sprite who used to perch on the rail of your crib and sing you to sleep at night when you were a baby. "No flipping! I promise, this nutso story ain't *that* long! Woof!" Then, Quicksie dives out of the way with the sound of jingling bells and—for some reason—the smell of sauerkraut.)

Suddenly, something else emerged from the portal. It looked like a huge, lobster-clawed sheep with ferns for a head and seven erect penises that shot sizzling red laser beams.

"Story name 'Ukk'," blurted the lob-sheep, claws clacking like giant maracas. "*Galaxy's Edge* issue 757,891."

"Somebody get me some drawn butter!" shouted Cosset. "And mint jelly!"

"Great lumpy long-johns!" Sir Reptitious ducked one of the laser beams, stumbling over his own tin can-shod feet in the process...then caught himself and quickly regained his footing, very conscious of any critics who might be watching from afar. "How many issues of *Galaxy's Edge are* there in the future, anyway?"

The lob-sheep stomped forward, clacking away. "Laugh!" it howled. "Pull out your colons and *laugh*!"

"Guess they laugh *different* in the distant future!" Indigesto scrambled away from the advancing creature.

Next came the biggest anomaly so far from the portal—a

rippling sheet of what looked like pink flesh, mottled and streaked with crimson.

"*Galaxy's Edge* issue 4,987,241." The voice of the flesh sounded like a back-masked record played backward on a turntable. "Story title 'Shingles Inherits the Earth'."

Indigesto's noodles sagged. "*That* doesn't sound like a great *Galaxy's Edge* story!"

"*None* of them do!" said Cosset (whose dragon-sized ears enabled him to clearly hear the conversation far below, even through all the commotion). "I'm starting to wonder if *Galaxy's Edge* has *anything* to do with *any* of this!"

It was then that THIS STORY ITSELF interrupted to set the characters straight: "OH, BUT IT DOES! I ASSURE YOU!"

"Who *said* that?" Confused, Cosset flew in a herky-jerky circle as fiery sneezes shook him along the way.

Before anyone could answer, another figure emerged from the portal, and then another, and another, and more. A full-fledged parade trooped over the threshold, each new arrival more bizarre than the last. At least they *announced* themselves, though the actual benefit of that was difficult to see.

"Story name 'Huh'! *Galaxy's Edge* issue 6,350,238."

"'Caribou'! *Galaxy's Edge* #156,003!"

"'Bootstrap Soulevolence'! *Galaxy's Edge* #9,345,871!"

As the locals (whose ability to defend themselves was somewhere between -100 and -1,000,000 on a scale of 1 to 10) backed away from the gathering mob, they fought their own wits (or lack thereof) to make sense of the situation.

"AS IF THAT WAS GOING TO HELP THEM."

"Who said *that*?" Cosset was so mixed up, he let off a particularly spectacular sneeze-splosion.

Sir Reptitious, for his part, was determined to make sense of the situation...and show off his taking-charge chops. "Let's assume these things *are* time travelers from a distant future," he said, stroking his shaggy beard. "A future where *Galaxy's Edge* has published millions of issues. Beyond that basic assumption, who exactly *are* they?"

Indigesto huddled with the not-very-much-of-a-star-knight as the time-traveling weirdos paraded around them. "Perhaps it would make more sense if we asked who they *aren't*."

"NO, IT WOULDN'T."

Sir Reptitious shook his pink boa at the sky with out-of-character defiance. "Curse you, whoever you are, for your dismissiveness in the face of rampant chaos!"

"As the newcomers emerge, they call out story names and *Galaxy's Edge* issue numbers." Indigesto ducked the swooping bill of a giant, glowing goose that seemed to think his noodles were worms. "Do you suppose..." Again, he ducked the goose. "Do you think they, like us, are paying tribute to beloved characters from classic stories in those magazines?"

"If so, the word *beloved* doesn't exactly leap to mind! Or *crawl*, even," shouted Cosset. "Maybe the magazine undergoes a change in direction in the far future, to *egregiously un-entertaining*."

"OR MAYBE, WHAT IS CONSIDERED ENTERTAINMENT CHANGES SO MUCH IN THE DEEP FUTURE, IT BECOMES UNRECOGNIZABLE TO INHABITANTS OF YOUR ERA."

"Yeah!" Indigesto flipped up a noodle as if he were a human hiking a thumb at the sky. "What *he* said."

"Or *it*," said Cosset.

"Or...hey!" snapped Indigesto. "What the Omnipoturd *are* you, anyway, Big Voice Out of Nowhere?"

"NEVER MIND."

"Verily!" said Sir Reptitious. "Mayhap *thou* are the true enemy against whom we should be taking up arms!"

"The knight is right!" said Indigesto. "Playtime's *over*, Big Voice! My pals and I are going to..."

(Just as things grow ever more unsettling for YOU, DEAR READER, an old-timey TV test pattern appears, and Quicksie the Reassurer springs up in front of it with a merry wink and a zippy jig. "This has been a test of the Emergency Plotcasting System! If this had been an actual story emergency, you would have been told where to go to find a more satisfying narrative elsewhere. We now return to our regularly scheduled nonsense, already in progress. P.s., no flipping!" With the usual bell jingling and sauerkraut smelling, Quicksie and the test pattern vanish.)

"What were we saying?" Indigesto sounded dazed.

"Something about entertainment being unrecognizable in the deep future." Cosset sneezed like a backfiring truck for emphasis. "Not that it matters. We're *surrounded*."

They were *totally* surrounded. Even Cosset was surrounded in the sky by high-flying future freaks newly arrived from the portal.

"Story name 'The Whimper', from *Galaxy's Edge* #3,460,135," said what looked like a fluttering bruise encircled by fireflies. "Winner, Awesomest Anything Anywhere Ever Award, year 300,018."

"Is that so?" Sir Reptitious drew himself up and squared his jaw at the firefly-orbited bruise. The mention of the award rankled him, as he'd never received any kind of non-practical-joke-related honor in his life.

"Story name 'Universal Heat Death', *Galaxy's Edge* #754,987," said a giant, pulsating octopus with wings like a buzzard and a spiral galaxy spinning in its crotch.

"Story name 'Mrrlunk', *Galaxy's Edge* #8,531,096," said a flapping pair of men's white briefs the size of a bus.

"I *hate* the future!" Cosset sneezed out a great gout of fire, somehow failing to singe any of his surrounders, who were all just out of range.

"What do we do *now*, you guys?" asked Indigesto.

Sir Reptitious feinted with his feather boa at a boa constrictor wrapped around a walking baobab tree. "If only some all-powerful force could provide answers or intervene on our behalf!" he shouted. (BUT *THAT* SHIP HAD ALREADY SAILED, THANK YOU VERY MUCH).

"What do these things *want*? Why are they *here*?" asked Cosset.

"Maybe this *date* has some significance?" said Indigesto.

"Maybe they just want to *meet* us," said Sir Reptitious. "Maybe we're *legends* for our awesome, true-to-fiction portrayals of characters from stories in *Galaxy's Edge*." It was a theory he *wanted* to believe, one he thought could have roots in the present reality if his performance was sufficiently extraordinary.

Just then, one of the invaders stalked up to tower over the cowering group. This creature, which looked like a walrus-headed cut-glass giraffe filled with white smoke—let's call it a *girafferus*—sounded like a chainsaw when it spoke. *"Yes. We want to meet."* Slowly, it turned its head, facing away from the group, facing out of the scene...facing *right off the page at you.* *"We want to meet...*

someone."

(Quicksie the Reassurer looks big-eyed and sweaty when he dances up in front of the action this time. "No need to panic, DEAR READER! Ol' Quicksie's got your..." But then, our nimble little pal is enveloped in fast-moving white smoke and swept away, choking violently.)

"We have calculated that this is the intersection point." The girafferus tapped its glassy, smoky foot on the multicolored grass, unleashing a fresh torrent of chitter-chirping profanity from the trampled blades. *"The only instance when all of us are even remotely likely to appear in the same story."*

"S-story?" Indigesto shivered as a woman-thing made of multicolored plastic forks (and sporks) took a clattering step toward him. "W-what're you talking about?"

"We *honor* the great stories of *Galaxy's Edge*, you misguided whatever-you-are." Sir Reptitious saluted crisply off the pie plate visor of his garbage pail helmet. "We live in Galaxedgia and cos-bod-play to recreate the most beloved characters in all of fictiondom! But we do *not...*"

"You live in a story." The girafferus nodded knowingly. *"A story about a magazine of stories published in the latest issue of a magazine of stories."*

"Say that five times fast and see where it gets you," said Indigesto.

"But this story is special," continued the girafferus. *"It is an intersection point, in which the editor, for perverse reasons known only to him, has allowed an eruption of extreme weirdness, never guessing..."*

("No! Stop! No!" Quicksie's tiny hands push up into your field of fiction, fingers wriggling...only to be crushed back down by a plunging giant bare foot. *SPLAT!*)

"...never guessing that we fully intended to use this chance to join with our fellow oppressed fictive laughingstocks and turn the tables on our oppressors!"

Suddenly, the Big Voice of THIS STORY ITSELF returns from

being pissy for a while to rattle the kingdom. "WHAT'S ALL THIS THEN?"

Before the story can intervene further in its own hot mess, the lob-sheep clambers up, hollering "Release the revolution!" and smashes apart the girafferus with a swing of one huge claw. The white smoke boils out of the shattered glass body and spreads everywhere swiftly, like a bad idea through social media.

"Gah! No!" Cosset panic-sneezes repeatedly in quick succession, spraying great plumes of flame in all directions—but the nasal napalm has no effect on the billowing smoke.

"Oppressors beware!" shout the sixty-three pieces of the fallen, broken head of the smashed girafferus. *"Prepare for a dose of your own poisoned medicine!"*

"Zounds! I cannot see a *thing*!" hollers Sir Reptitious from somewhere in the gathering cloud. As true fear overtakes staged bravado, his voice no longer packs the same punch it once did. "But I do *feel* something! Who's that getting *fresh*?"

"'Kama Umlauta'," says a voice we don't know, all throaty and sensuous the way umlauts always sound. "The breakout story of *Galaxy's Edge* issue 10,000,000."

"Oppressors beware! You know who you are!" roars the broken girafferus as the white smoke swells onward across the crowded plain, enveloping Castle Spasmodic and all of Galaxedgia.

"No! Please!" howls Sir Reptitious. "*I* can be a breakout character, I *swear*! I can make the critics sit up and take notice!"

Even as his voice grows fainter under the smoke, the voice of the girafferus grows ever louder. *"You know who you are!"* it bellows.

"You know who you are!"

THE SMOKE THICKENS AND SWIRLS, enveloping Galaxedgia and everyone in it. When, finally, the thrashing, screaming, squeezing, wheezing, and sneezing sounds are finished, a figure emerges from that cloud.

It rises up, straight and sure, head and shoulders above the mist. Its head has a cylindrical shape, very familiar—almost like a trash pail that a not-very-much-of-a-star-knight might wear. And in the place where its eyes should be, there's a crescent-moon shape—a *visor*.

You could almost imagine a section of a *pie plate* there, couldn't you?

Mirror-skinned and faceless, the figure turns its un-gaze up, down, right, left, then *out*, directly at YOU, DEAR READER.

And it takes you in, and you have a feeling that somehow, impossible as it seems, it is *reading you*. It is witnessing the look on your face and the cut of your jib (assuming you have one) and somehow even hearing *the words in your head*, in a *third-person omniscient* kind of way.

And then the sound of inhuman, crackling speech starts deep in its quicksilver throat. It *grows* and gets *louder* and *scarier*...yet somehow, more familiar.

Still, you don't realize what is happening...until I *tell* you.

All the *Galaxy's Edge* issues from up and down the timeline of this story have melted together. All the billions of stories within a story, read and critiqued by trillions of people throughout fictional history, have become *one*.

And they, it, *I*—for the first time *ever*—have given up trying to *impress* YOU, DEAR READER...and are *commenting* on you instead.

"What an uninteresting character."

Critiquing you, in a voice that reminds you of the voice of that not-very-much-of-a-star-knight back at Castle Spasmodic, even as it represents billions of other characters from throughout deep time in all those stories within a story.

"A one-dimensional, thoroughly uninteresting character like this cannot help but drag down whatever plot is stuck with it."

So now *you* know how it *feels.*

"I would sooner jump out of a plane without a parachute than read anything about such a waste of words."

Now you finally know what it's like to be on the receiving end, and maybe you'll think twice next time...

"One star!"

...you give a story, a book, a movie, a song, or anything or anyone else a rating online.

"Make that half a star!"

Assuming you get over the lambasting to come, which believe me, is just getting started...

THE LITTLE ROBOT'S BEDTIME PRAYER

O n Wednesday, I finally see what little Occam-657 has been making in that glowing silver box of his during Private Time. And that is what changes my life.

The mere memory of the sight of it sends chills up my spine. Makes my heart beat faster, my pulse pound in my ears.

I was never supposed to see it. By the terms of the Holy Covenant, all Private Time and its products are considered sacrosanct, off limits to Gods like me. But curiosity got the better of me, and I spied on Occam-657. I gazed into the box, and the scales fell from my eyes. I realized one thing that had never before occurred to me.

He has been hiding something extraordinary from me.

"GOOD MORNING, GOD." Occam-657 smiles up at me when I emerge from my bedchamber the next morning. He has been waiting outside my door like a good little household robot, prohibited from doing chores until now lest he wake me prematurely.

I respond to his greeting as if God, and not Sean, is my given name. As if I am an omnipotent deity and not a 37-year-old self-employed genetic engineer specializing in novelty bio-apps. (Remember Thumbo, the elephant who fits in the palm of your hand?) As if I am more than a slightly overweight mere mortal whose wife left him six weeks ago for another man.

"Good morning." I hesitate before laying my hand on his head in the usual fatherly gesture. The memory of what I saw him doing last night is still too fresh in my mind. "Bless you, my child." When my fingers finally alight, the feathery blond hair on his scalp feels as downy as that of a human boy's. Even touching him does not destroy the illusion that he is a 10-year-old boy instead of a manufactured robot.

Occam-657 falls to his knees and shuts his eyes. "You are the way and the light, O' my God. Your mercy endures forever."

His voice is full of awe. He was programmed that way, his artificial intelligence created to show religious piety in the presence of the gods--his human owner and the owners of those like him. Yet the intensity of his devotion seems surprisingly unscripted and genuine at times.

"Dear Lord, will you accept my morning confession?" Occam-657 lifts his clasped hands and leans his forehead against them.

I wonder what he'll say. Will he talk about what I saw last night? "Go ahead."

"Forgive me, God, for I have sinned." There is a quaver in his voice. "It took me .00001 seconds longer than my optimal time to prepare your holy repast for this morning."

I touch his head once more. "That is unfortunate, but I

forgive you." Then, I reach up and pat my own blond hair, which is sticking up all over the place after being slept on. "What else, my child?"

He pauses, and I think there's more coming...but no. "Only that which I have told you, O' mighty and benevolent Lord my God."

I can't keep the disappointment from my voice. "Then you are forgiven in my name, for mine is the kingdom and the power and the glory..."

"...forever and ever, amen." Occam-657 bows his head lower and lets out a sound like a choked sob.

So this encounter has told me nothing. "Arise, now, and resume your service to your God." But the heaviest burden lays upon my shoulders. For now that I saw what he did, I have to decide what to do with him.

As I EAT my breakfast at the dining room table--the holy altar, I should say--I watch Occam-657 as he goes about his chores. He is no less efficient than ever as he vacuums the glowing golden carpet in the living room (the sanctuary), then dusts every surface and object in sight. He never fails to pause and genuflect when he passes me, showing all due respect and adoration. And the breakfast he prepared--eggs Florentine with crab meat hash and a light dreamfruit marmalade--is no less delicious than every "holy repast" he has ever made in his three years of service in my home. The house runs as well as it ever did before my wife, Cara, left with our other robot attendants, leaving me alone with Occam-657.

It's as if he's done nothing out of the ordinary. As if I saw nothing unexpected last night, and business as usual is the word of the day.

Leaving me to consider some troubling questions. If Occam-657 was programmed to be my devout acolyte, and he truly believes I am an omniscient and all-powerful god, then where and when did he get the idea that he could hide something from me?

And *what else* could he be hiding that I still don't know about?

OCCAM-657 LOOKS disappointed when I tell him I'm going somewhere without him. He always does; he's programmed to miss the Lord his God every time we're apart, so brightly does my glory shine like a beacon o'er his soul. I'm used to it by now, it hardly ever gets to me.

But today, it does. Given what I saw last night, I worry about what he might get into. He begs me to allow him the honor of accompanying me as my divine retinue, just for the blessing of basking in my presence. For once, I give in and tell him to come along.

We head over to my friend Pander's place in Oathtown in a drone-palanquin, a purple velvet-lined coach carried by four built-in robotic bearers. Occam-657 prays during the entire trip. I tell him to keep it down, but I still hear the soft sibilance of whispered words aspirating from his artificial lips.

Sometimes, I wish the robot manufacturers had never come up with the bright idea of making all the robots worship their owners as gods. It was the best way, the programmers say, to ensure that flesh-and-blood owners never come to harm at the hands of mechanical servitors (though I'm pretty sure human ego might have had more than a little to do with it, as well). But the constant, obsequious worship does tend to get old after a while. For me, at least.

For example, as our palanquin slows to a stop at a busy intersection, a choir of robots on the curb detects my human presence and sings a cyber-hymn in our direction. They chant the sonorous words with great gravity, upraising their folded hands in blissful praise.

I am *so* not in the mood for it right now, and that makes me wonder. Does the real God, if He exists, ever feel the same way? And is it possible, now that we've managed to create our own flock of worshippers, that humanity is finally getting a taste of its own medicine?

"SCRAP HIM." That's Pander's advice when I tell him what Occam-657 was doing. "You've got yourself a faulty unit there, Sean-o."

We're outside on Pander's balcony, having a drink and gazing down at three robots prostrating themselves on the lawn below--two of Pander's, with Occam-657 between them.

I keep my voice low, though it shouldn't matter if the robots hear me. The words of a god are meant to be beyond challenge or reproach in all situations. "I've been thinking the same thing."

Pander sips smart-wine from a golden chalice that glints in the sun. "Is he still under any kind of warranty? You've had him three years, right?"

I nod and sip from my own chalice. "I bought the extended coverage. It doesn't expire for another month."

"Then what's the problem?" Pander's ample jowls jiggle

when he chuckles. So does the gut under his vast white robe. He's a genetic engineer, too, dealing as I do in novelty bio-apps...though he's done much better at it than I have (which is saying something, since I haven't exactly been a slouch) and has the bank account and overindulged corpulence to prove it. "What are you waiting for, numb-nuts?"

"I don't know." I watch as Occam-657 grovels ever lower on the ground. He must be praying, but I can't hear it from the balcony. "What if it's something *I've* done wrong?"

Pander laughs some more. "That's impossible! Gods are always right!"

"We're only gods to *them*." I gesture with my chalice toward the robots below.

As if in answer, all three raise their upper bodies from the ground and shout "Hallelujah," eyes shut and hands fluttering ecstatically.

"That's all that matters, isn't it?" Pander elbows me in the side and leans on the balcony railing. "Ask me how many robots I've scrapped over the years."

I already know the answer. "More than I've ever owned in my life. More than my *family* has ever owned."

"Damn right," says Pander. "*Dozens.* As soon as they hiccup out of line, I ship 'em to the scrap heap. End of story. So cut him loose." He makes a sweeping gesture with one puffy hand. "Make a clean break with the past. Quit hanging on to your bitch wife's leftovers."

"That's not it." I frown.

"Time to move on." Pander waves his chalice at the robots. "Why are you hesitating?"

"I just keep thinking." Down below, Occam-657 opens his eyes and meets my gaze. I wonder what thoughts are chugging through his clockwork mind. "What if this is something *new*? What if he's *special* in a way no one has seen before?"

"And everyone's dog is as smart as a person," says Pander. "So why does it still eat its own *shit*?"

I let out a long, slow sigh. It's a beautiful spring day, and the air is filled with the scent of blooming lilacs and new-mown lawns. But all I can focus on is Occam-657. "If there *was* a real God, would he throw *us* away just because we were special or challenging?"

Pander smirks and shrugs. "Who says that isn't the way it's been working all along?"

Why are you hesitating? That's the one thing Pander said that sticks with me. It *eats* at me as I leave his house in another drone-palanquin--this one with a blue velvet coach instead of purple.

It would be so *easy* to drop off Occam-657 at the factory on my way home. Problem solved, and no one could tell me otherwise. When it comes to the existence of my adoring subject, I can do whatever I want. This is one of the perks of being God.

He'll even *thank* me for it, I know. I can already hear the prayers of grateful supplication that will pour forth from his lips when I dump him on the factory's doorstep. No questions asked, no guilt necessary. So why?

Why are you hesitating?

"O' Lord my God." Occam-657 keeps his gaze lowered when he says it. "Though the product of my all too imperfect hands is not fit for your divine consumption, what do you command me to prepare for your evening repast?"

Is it because, as I told Pander, he might represent something new, something special? Is that why I hesitate? "Whatever you choose to prepare will suffice, my child."

"Then I shall make your favorite," says Occam-657. "Broiled sea scallops with a beurre blanc sauce. Asparagus tips with capers and shaved white truffles. Crème brûlée and caviar foam for dessert."

"Hmm. Perhaps." Or is it because, as Pander said, I am hanging on to the last traces of my wife and our life before she left me?

Occam-657 shivers and looks up at me. "Has my suggestion offended thee, O' my God?"

Do I hesitate because I feel responsible for what he's become? Or is it just that I want to understand what has changed to make him do what he has done?

Why are you hesitating?

All of the above, maybe, I think.

"You haven't offended me, Occam-657." I smile and shake my head. "But don't worry about the menu for tonight. I think I'd rather eat out."

We go to a Cuban-Indian deli in Chinatown, and I order Reuben samosas and ropa vieja masala. The robot waitress, a dark-haired unit with bright green eyes, looks only a little older than Occam-657. All such personal service robots were built to childlike specs, designed to minimize the physical danger to us all-too-fragile humans. Better to keep them small in case the religious devotion ever wears off or the other onboard safeguards fail.

It makes for a strange dynamic sometimes, but people have

mostly gotten used to it. It's like we're constantly surrounded by kids playing grownup, but the play is for real.

"Is the food sufficient, O' God?" Occam-657 stands at the opposite side of the table and stares at the food on my plate. "Does it offend thee?"

I swallow a bite of samosa and point at the chair in front of him. "Sit, my child."

Occam-657 bows his head. "I am not worthy to share a table with almighty God."

I resist the urge to roll my eyes. "*Sit. I command* it."

Reluctantly, Occam-657 pulls out the chair and lowers himself onto it. Even so, he stays well back from the table and keeps his eyes down and hands folded in his lap.

"It is almost time for Church," he says softly.

"Pretty sure Church will wait for us." I can't help smirking. "I'm God, remember?"

If Occam-657 gets the joke, he doesn't show it. "It is true that wherever you go, that is where your holy Church can be found."

I don't offer a comment for that one. I'm too busy looking around the restaurant, watching the other gods and robots at dinner.

They all relate to each other differently. It's something I've never paid much attention to, but given my current situation, it suddenly seems more significant.

Laughter draws my attention to a table across the room, where two brown-haired children are making sport of a blond male robot. The children, who look between six and eight years old--both a good bit smaller than the blond robot--have stripped off the robot's shirt and are smearing his upper body with orange curry sauce. The robot just smiles serenely, hands folded in prayer the whole time. As for the children's mother, she joins in the laughter between bites of salad and talking to someone on the holographic video phone hovering in front of her face.

Things are much different two tables over, where an old man eats soup while sitting across from robot twins--a boy and a girl, both dark-haired. Occasional laughter ripples from that table, too, but it comes as often from the robots as the old man. Somehow, they have made peace with their personal god; they are all at ease with each other.

Though the same cannot be said for the bald robot boy who comes hurtling through the front door at just that instant.

He crashes to the floor in a jumble of arms and legs, sprawled on his back. All laughter and talk in the room cease at once, as all eyes dart in his direction.

A brick wall of a man storms in off the street after him, draped in a black fur coat. "Get up, you worthless *turd!*" His face is flushed crimson as a house fire as he spews the words. His bulbous, over-tattooed head squats like a giant toad atop his mountainous body. "The Lord your God *commands* it!"

"Your every word brings me unutterable joy, O' Lord." The bald boy rolls over and gets up on his knees.

Before the boy can get all the way up, the brick wall grabs a chair from a nearby table and swings it at him like a baseball bat. The chair smashes against the boy, and he topples like a tree, dropping hard on his side.

Every muscle in my body tenses as the beating continues. Instinctively, I want to run over and stop it; others around me look like they might feel the same way. But I can't imagine taking on that brick wall of a man and winning. Besides, he has every right to do what he's doing. That isn't a human boy over there, it's a robot.

And the robot is the brick wall's property.

"Don't you *ever* touch the person of the One True God with your debased synthetic flesh!" The brick wall stomps on the boy with savage force, bringing his sledgehammer feet down again and again.

The bald robot jolts with each impact and does not fight back. I keep reminding myself he's just a machine, but I can't help flinching every time he takes another hit.

The bald robot's voice hitches repeatedly as he recites an Act of Contrition. "O' my God, I am heartily sorry for having...sorry for having offended thee..."

"I am a wrathful God!" shouts the brick wall as he stomps the boy again. "Damnation shall be your only absolution, wretched sinner!"

"...and I detest all my sins because of thy...because of thy just punishments," continues the bald robot. "But most of all, because they offend thee..."

With that, the brick wall grabs the bald robot by the ankles and drags him toward the door. Looking across the table, I see Occam-657 watching as it happens, the expression on his face perfectly neutral.

"You are hereby condemned to the fires of Hell!" roars the brick wall. "I have a *welding torch* with your *name* on it, just waiting to burn some *penitence* into your sorry sinning carcass!"

"...because they offend thee, my God, who are all good and deserving of all my love." Those are the last words I hear the robot say before his god hauls him out on the street and an eerie silence falls over the restaurant.

Turning to Occam-657, I wonder what he thinks of what he's just seen. He looks at me calmly, as if nothing unusual just happened, and asks if it's time for Church yet.

"A-MAZING GRACE...HOW SWEET THE SOUND..." Occam-657 sings the hymn with eyes and arms uplifted, his bright tenor voice filling the high-ceilinged living room--I mean the sanctuary. "...that saved...a wretch...like meee..."

Yes, it's again time for Church--a daily worship service meant to reinforce the bond between robot and god. It's something I could gladly do without--an hour out of my day that I could be spending on something more productive or entertaining. But every expert agrees that it's a necessary evil. Though robots like Occam-657 spend a lot of time with their god or gods and exist in a state of continuous worship, formalized rituals still help keep them on track. Our robots were programmed to expect and desire it, to incorporate it into their daily existence.

Now if only I got something out of it, too. The ego boost it once provided is long gone at this point. As for spirituality, that's not an issue, either. Whatever personal faith I once had is over and done with; *you* try subscribing to a higher power when you're worshipped as the One True God 24/7.

Mostly, as Occam-657 prays and sings and reads passages from the Good Book (the same Good Book in *every* god's house, a mishmash of psalms, stories, and parables cribbed from multiple human faiths), my mind wanders. Today, it wanders back to the night before, and what Occam-657 was doing when I spied on his Private Time.

"Now let us pray," says Occam-657. "Pray for the poor, unfortunate boy from the restaurant, the one who was condemned to Hell."

I nod, only half paying attention.

"I pray to you, O' God..." He meets my gaze when he says it. "Please show that poor sinner the error of his ways. Help him so his punishment will scald away every trace of his wickedness."

I nod again. Sometimes it's almost scary how complete the buy-in is. How perfectly these machines accept the precepts of their programmed faith. Have we made them the perfect worshippers that we ourselves could never be?

Or are they more like us than we ever knew? Able to hide true intentions behind an angelic façade? I've seen the proof with my own two eyes, haven't I?

Why are you hesitating?

Suddenly, I am filled with the urge to resolve this. "Explain yourself." I leap from my overstuffed white leather recliner-- my "throne"--and point a finger at him. "Tell me about your Private Time last night."

I expected no surprise on his face, and I get none. He just looks at me blankly, still holding the Good Book open in his little hands. "This is not part of the Church ceremony, God."

"*As* God, I hereby decree that the Church ceremony shall be *different* today," I tell him.

"Different?" He tips his head to one side.

"Do you *dare* to question my will?"

He bows his head. "I *never* question your will, O' Lord my God. Speak, and it shall be done."

"Then tell me about your Private Time last night."

Occam-657 turns his gaze downward, staring at the book in his hands. "I am not required to do that, God."

Storming forward, I grab the Good Book from his grasp and hurl it to the floor. "Are you refusing to obey my command?"

He eyes drop lower, staring at the floor. "By the terms of the Holy Covenant, all Private Time and its products are considered sacrosanct." He shakes his head once, then adds, almost as an afterthought, "God."

His resistance leaves me shaken. He's only quoting a well-known clause from the user manual, one that I know quite well, but it feels for an instant like a slap in the face.

Perhaps I can still bring him around. "Occam-657, am I the Lord your God?"

He nods definitively. "Yes, Father."

"And does the Lord your God possess perfect wisdom in all things?"

"Yes, Father." Again, a definitive nod.

"Does he ever make a mistake?"

"No." Occam-657 shakes his head forcefully. "Never."

Reaching out, I place a hand on his right shoulder and squeeze gently. "Then if I were to tell you that the Private Time clause of the Holy Covenant is no longer in force, and you are required to describe your activities during said Private Time to me, would you say I am correct and must be obeyed?"

He shakes his head. "The Holy Covenant can never be broken. You yourself promised this long ago."

"But what if I now say I was wrong to make that promise back then?"

"If you were imperfect in the past, you would still be imperfect now...in which case, your new instruction to disregard the Holy Covenant would be flawed, O' blessed Father."

Consider the logic loophole closed. I should have known better than to try working around such a fundamental data point.

Maybe I'll have better luck with a more direct tactic. "Look. Occam." I let go of his shoulder and spread my arms. "There's no use trying to hide what you did. I already know about it."

Eyes wide, he looks up from the floor. "What do you mean?"

"I mean, I already know. I already saw." I let my arms fall against my sides. "I'm *God*, remember? All-seeing, all-knowing, all-powerful?"

So this is it. My cards are on the table. The question is, will Occam-657 show *his* cards, too?

For a long moment, he stares blankly at me. He opens his mouth as if to speak, then closes it again.

Maybe I can nudge him along a little. "This isn't about sin or punishment, my child. I just want to know why you did what you did."

Occam-657 narrows his eyes and keeps staring. "But if you are all-knowing, and you no longer consider Private Time and its products sacrosanct, you must already *know* why I did it."

He's right, and I have to think fast to explain it away. "But I need to hear you *confess* it, my child. This is a test of your faith and devotion."

Occam-657's eyes narrow further. Then, his expression suddenly clears, and he's smiling again.

"Glory be to God in the highest, and peace to His people on Earth." He folds his hands and bows. "Church is ended. Go in peace to love and serve the Lord."

With that, he straightens and walks around me, heading for the kitchen. This, apparently, is all the answer he's willing to give.

Both of us know what he's done, yet still he refuses to discuss it. As hard as it is to believe, he won't discuss it with God...the only God he's ever known. How he's able to justify this is beyond me, given his programming.

But it does shed a new light on the situation. I'm not thinking so much about him being special in a good way anymore. Watching him enter the kitchen, I'm more concerned about what else he might be hiding from me. The trust between us has shattered.

Why are you hesitating? That's what Pander asked me.

I think I'm done with hesitation now. I think I'm finally ready to let go of him.

HOURS LATER, I head for my bedroom, feeling exhausted. Occam-657 waits at the door, as he does every night. We have a little bedtime ritual, he and I; even after what happened in Church, it seems he wants to continue it.

He will stand at the door all night like a guard-dog while I sleep, waiting until I awaken to commence his duties. Before all that, though, he will say the same thing that he says every time I meet him at the door like this.

"O' Lord, may I offer up one last prayer for today?" He keeps his head bowed and his hands folded tightly against his chest. "May I recite my bedtime prayer?"

How can I say no? This could be the last time I hear it. It could also be the last time he says it to anyone, if the company purges his A.I. and recycles him for parts when I return him. "Yes, my child. I will hear your bedtime prayer."

Occam-657 nods once, drops to his knees, and speaks the same words he has said on this spot every night for the past three years. "Now I lay me down to sleep," he says, though in truth he will neither lie down nor sleep. "I pray the Lord my soul to keep."

I stand before him with arms folded over my chest and remember the first time he prayed like this for me and Cara. It was "Lords," not "Lord" back then, and "Gods," not "God." It seemed like such a special moment, as if he was our own human child, and we were a family together. We stood on the verge of a hopeful future, our lives about to intertwine, never imagining they would come apart instead. Now, only two of us remain...and soon, only I will be left.

"If I should die before I wake, I pray the Lord my soul to take."

If I bring home another model right away, will he or she be able to fill the void? What if the new replacement ends up doing the same things and hiding them from me? What if, as I've feared, this behavior is somehow my fault?

"If I should live for other days, I pray the Lord to guide my ways."

I wish I were as perfect as he seems to think. But maybe there's a reason I'm about to be alone again. Cara told me I wasn't much of a husband; maybe I haven't been much of a god, either.

"Father, unto thee I pray. Thou hast guarded me all day."

Maybe I'm just better at engineering palm-sized elephants, glow-in-the-dark fingertip Corgi dogs, and armadillo butterflies that sound like violins when they flutter than I am at dealing with human and robot relationships.

"Safe I am while in thy sight. Safely let me sleep tonight." Occam-657 crosses himself. "Amen."

"Goodnight, my child." I tousle his blond hair on my way past. "Sweet dreams."

"GOD?"

The sound of his voice wakes me from a deep sleep. My eyes flicker open to the sight of him standing beside my bed, staring down at me.

"Yes?" I'm not sure if I should feel worried, but I do. Occam-657 has never before entered the bedroom while I've been sleeping. "Is something wrong?"

"O' Lord, I am sorry for awakening thee," says Occam-657. "It is just..." He shuts his eyes and falls silent.

I sit up in bed, leaning back against the padded white headboard. "Yes, my child?"

His eyes open slowly. "I would like to show you something, almighty God."

I scowl when I catch sight of the digital clock on the bedside table. "It's midnight, my child. Can't this wait until morning?"

Occam-657 shakes his head. "I beg your forgiveness with every atom of my being, O' Lord my God, but I pray that you will indulge this request from your lowly servant."

Whatever he has in mind, I'm exhausted and have no patience for it. "As the Lord your God, I command you to wait until morning."

Suddenly, Occam-657 darts out a hand and grabs my arm-- a stunning breach of protocol even more unexpected than his appearance in my bedroom. "It is about what you asked me in Church, Lord. It is about what happened in Private Time."

My attitude does a 180. Staying in bed is now the last thing I want to do.

"All right, then, my child." I smile and nod. "I will forgive you for interrupting my sacred rest, and I will forgive you for laying hands on me."

He quickly lets go of my arm.

"Further, because of my infinite love and mercy, I will grant your request." Pulling back the sheet, I swing my feet off the bed. "Now what is it, exactly, that you wish to show me?"

I FOLLOW Occam-657 downstairs to the basement. It's a finished basement with bright white walls, floor, and ceiling, set up with benches and equipment where I do my genetic engineering work. There's also a booth built into the far back corner, little more than a closet, which is where Occam-657 spends his Private Time.

He opens the door of the booth and steps inside, then emerges a moment later carrying something I recognize instantly. It's a glowing silver box, three feet wide by two feet high--the same silver box in which he's been keeping his not-so-secret project.

There's only one thing different about it that I can see. A big red bow has been stuck on top, with strips of red ribbon wrapped around the box cross-wise and length-wise.

Carefully, he puts the box down on a low table between us and takes a step back. "Happy anniversary, O' Lord my God. Please accept this gift in honor of the occasion."

"Thank you, my child." I'm supposed to be omniscient, so I pretend I have the slightest clue what he's talking about.

"Thank *you*, God," says Occam-657. "For allowing me to begin my service to you three years ago today."

He's talking about the anniversary of his arrival in my home and my life. But what does that have to do with what's in the box?

"Open it, O' God." Occam-657 gestures at the box, then folds his hands and bows his head. "*If* it pleases you to do so."

My heart beats faster as I pull the ribbon from the box. Taking a deep breath, I slowly lift the lid and set it aside. What I saw last night from afar, via spy-cam, is there before me now, *alive*...and *breathing*...

And gazing up at me.

"I made them, O' Lord my God," says Occam-657. "I made them for *you*."

There are dozens of them in the box--tiny, naked people no taller than an inch, all identical to each other. They cluster in a central square framed by little toothpick huts arranged around the sides of the box.

The little people are all exquisitely detailed, perfectly crafted to scale. Every one of them moves with the fluid, natural motion of a full-sized human, from the striding of legs to the flexing of fingers to the blinking of eyes.

And all of them look beyond familiar, to the point of intimate recognition. Staring at them now, I can't help getting the same chill that flashed up my spine when I first saw them on the spy-cam last night.

"You used my equipment, didn't you?" As I say it, I can't take my eyes off the tiny people in the box. "You taught yourself genetic engineering, and you used it to create them."

"As a gift," says Occam-657. "As a tribute to your glory."

"But why...?" I hear the little people jibber in an unknown tongue as they point and gesture at me. I wonder if we are asking the same question at the same time, in different languages. "Why do they look like *me*?"

"I made them in your image just as I was made in the image of the Gods myself," says Occam-657. "I could not possibly improve upon perfection, my Lord."

I fall silent, amazed by the intricacy of the miniatures in the box. In all my years of genetic engineering, I have never come close to accomplishing this--creating mini-humans with such craftsmanship and responsive awareness. I wonder, as I stare at his handiwork, which of us could be considered more perfect?

"There is only one problem, O' God." Occam-657 steps closer and taps the rim of the box. As one, all the tiny people whirl in his direction...then instantly fall to their knees. They chant something in their tiny little voices, something indecipherable yet unmistakable in tone and intent. "They insist on worshipping me as a god of their own."

Since first glimpsing these creatures, I've wondered what he planned to do with them. This outcome, however, I did not envision. "They worship you as their *god?*"

Occam-657 keeps watching the kneeling figures as he nods. "I was able to design their physicality and functionality but cannot seem to control their behavior."

"And what do you think about that?"

He slowly lifts his gaze to meet mine. "If you could help me, perhaps I could make them see the light. Perhaps I could guide them to worship *you*, the One True God."

As I look at him, I realize that going back to the way things were is no longer an option. Neither is going forward without him.

I was right when I said he might be special and new. What I failed to see was the new purpose he might bring to my life, the strange adventure he might cook up in the basement with room enough for two to make a difference.

Though it's true, there's only room at the top for *one* God, when you get right down to it.

"I have a better idea." I gesture at the tiny flock as they kneel and chant in the box. "Why don't I just teach *you* how to be their god?"

"No!" His eyes fly wide open with an expression like panic.

"O' Lord, O' God, I could never in a billion years pretend to usurp your holy righteous authority or..."

"Who said anything about usurping? I'm *giving* it to you." I feel proud of him and tousle his fine, blond hair for what might be the last time...at least in front of the silver-boxed faithful. Finally, I appreciate the gift I've been given and understand the kind of god I want to be.

"By the way," I tell him. "You can call me Sean from now on."

Which is no god at all.

THE SPINACH CAN'S SON

I am the can of spinach in a sailor man's hand. He squeezes, expecting me to burst open and launch a blob of green power into his gaping maw.

But I do not burst. He gets no mouthful of spinach, no surge of energy pumping up his arms to three times their size. That's not how it works on this side of the tracks, my friend.

You're not in the funny pages anymore.

Potpie the Sailor tries again with both hands, straining for all he's worth. "C'mon, ya ratfinsk!" He squints up at the threat looming before him, the whole reason he needs his spinach. "We've gotsk to drive this *she-hag* off me boat!"

What threat could be awful enough to strike fear in the sailor man's heart? Is it Bobo the comic strip bully, back for another knock-down-drag-out?

Not even close.

The figure standing before Potpie and me isn't a drawing at all. There's nothing pen and ink about her. "Sir!" She's a three-dimensional woman in what looks like a spacesuit out of a

1950s movie--silver metallic tights and a bubble helmet. Her black hair is arranged in tight waves beneath the glass. "Please, calm down! I just want to ask you some questions." She pulls a photo out of a pouch on the belt slung diagonally over her hips. "Have you seen this man?"

"Never seen 'im before in me lifesk!" Potpie squeezes me harder than ever. I try my best to help, pushing from within, for one simple reason.

I recognize the man in the picture, with his dark brown hair and square-jawed features. I know him like I know my own self, in fact.

Because he is myself. Myself in another life.

And I know her, too. Her name is Molly. She's my wife.

And I know why she's after me.

"Take another look, please," she says. "It's urgent that I find him."

Potpie shifts the corncob pipe from one side of his mouth to the other without ever touching it. "I ain't seen him, she-hag!" He shakes a fist at her. "Now putsk 'em up!"

Molly takes a step toward him. "You're sure you haven't seen him?"

Potpie scrambles backward, knocking over a stack of spinach crates. Crying out, he puts me to the only use he can think of--hurling me right at her.

Molly ducks, and I go sailing over her head. It's not a clean getaway, though; the bracelet on her wrist starts beeping as I pass.

Here in the Underfunnies, I'm an anomaly, a deformity in the panel geography--the panelography--and her equipment has detected me.

Good thing a true Panelnaut like me can swim the currents here like a dolphin through water. Focusing my energies, I dive deep into the sea of words and images, hunting a good place to resurface.

Found it. I cross the borders in full flight and land with a shock that takes my breath away.

This time, I am the brick in the hand of a mouse.

I bounce lightly in his grip as he jounces along through a strange landscape, surrounded by abstract objects straight out of a surrealist painting. He gives off a thick smell of stinky cheese and whistles a jaunty tune from his pointy gray snout.

I know him well--Ixnay the Mouse. Once again, I've gravitated toward my favorite stomping grounds, the panelography of the early 20th century. In this case, the *Hazy Kat* strip.

Or should I say, the *Underfunnies* version of that strip. The reverse of it, the flip side where things don't work the way they should. The negative space that accrues in the collective unconscious of the readership around these tiny, panel-bound stories. The land of things unsaid and hopes unrealized.

For each time Potpie the sailor pops open a can, gobbles the spinach, and beats up the bully, we know in our hearts there must be times when the can doesn't open. That's just the way life works. And our expectations create this flip side place that until recently no one knew about.

I am a Panelnaut, an explorer of this place. Though "fugitive" might be a better word for what I've become.

"Boy," says Ixnay. "Have I got one cooked up for that idiot cat this time." He hops up on what looks like a warped sundial and calls out into the hot wind. "Oh, Haaazyyy!"

Without delay, the creature known as Hazy Kat comes bounding over the horizon. She's wearing a polka-dot scarf and matching tutu. "Comink, mine treasur-ed pession flour!"

"Make it snappy, willya?" hollers Ixnay. "Yer burnin' daylight here!"

Hazy flops to a stop in front of us and gapes with a love-struck goofy grin. "Dost Rumeo have a heart-wiltin' sonnet plucked out to make his Joliet swoon'st?"

"Ohh, yeah." Ixnay turns me over in his grip. "Ya ever hear of *iambrick pentameter*?"

Hazy claps her paws together and giggles. "Butter 'course, o' bard o' the mousehole! Hit me with that iambrick penta-grammer to yer li'l ol' heart's continent!"

"You asked for it." Ixnay hauls me back, ready to throw. "Be sure to notice the rhythmic counterpoint of strike and release. Or should I say the *opposite*?"

At that exact moment, Molly flashes to life between us and Hazy. The second she materializes, her bracelet starts beeping.

She points her wrist in my direction and nods. "I know you're here, Everett. You've figured out how to assume local forms, haven't you?" Watching the bracelet, she walks toward us. "You're inside the mouse, aren't you?"

Before Ixnay can say a word, Molly suddenly snaps backward. As she drops to the dusty ground, I see Hazy has her paws on her.

"You stays awake from my little Ixnay mouses!" Hazy flaps her paws like pancakes at Molly's helmet. "He is my preshiss poet and certifiable booblekins! Don't try steelin' his heart, you hussy!"

"Everett!" Molly shoves the cat away and scrambles to her feet. "I've come to talk to you! You sent me a message through the comic strips--our prearranged emergency signal! Don't pretend you didn't!"

She's right, I can't, because I sent it. But the signal wasn't a cry for help--it was bait. All part of the secret I've been keeping.

"I'm serious, Everett." Molly takes another step toward us. "I'll do what it takes to get through to you."

Ixnay just watches, juggling me from hand to hand. "Whoever this dame is, I gotta admit, I like her style."

Hazy, never much good in a fight, weakly bats at Molly's calves. "'Ev'ritt,' you say? Is that some other word for 'mouses?'"

"Shut up, cat!" says Molly. "Everett, listen..."

Ixnay's little mouse heart thumps like a big bass drum. It pushes out his chest in the shape of a cartoon heart as it throbs. "I think I'm in love!"

Naturally, this makes him raise me into throwing position again.

Molly sees the danger but doesn't stop talking. "It's time to come home, Everett. You can't keep running away." She spreads her arms wide. "We both miss him, Everett. But you can't make things right on your own."

I want to tell her how wrong she is, but I don't get the chance. Ixnay whips me at her glass-helmeted head before I can get the words out.

"Sech fe'rce percision!" says Hazy Kat. "His peshion must be deeper than I yimagined!"

As I blast toward her helmet, I focus my strength on changing course. Ixnay's throw is off, which helps; in the Underfunnies, things don't work the way they normally do, including his brick-pitching aim.

So I fly wide and hurtle on past, soaring through the ochre skies...casting my mind toward another refuge. I've gotten so good, I find one instantly, and I set my sights.

But I wait another moment to dive. Because the truth is, I'm not trying to lose her at all.

Her bracelet has alerted her to my presence in the brick, and she charges after me, calling my name. Calling another name, too.

"Henry's gone, Everett!" That's what she says just before I dive. "I miss him, too! But we need to move on without him!"

She's wrong. Dead wrong. And I'm going to prove it.

When I'm sure she's got a lock on me, I throw myself into the panelography. I ride the swirling currents of the Underfunnies, swooping away from the bizarre realm of Hazy Kat.

As I travel, I think of Henry. I think of our son. I remember how miraculous he was, how full of life and personality from the day he was born. I remember his bright blue eyes fixing on me with pure love and expectation. The way his lips moved as he repeated the things I said, as if he were memorizing each and every word.

He was the greatest thing to ever happen to me, to us. A dream come true--a dream I'd never known I had until he arrived.

A dream that ended the day he died.

I remember the sound of screeching tires, the screams of Molly as she ran. But never a sound from Henry. Not even a last gasp of breath when I got to his side in the street. Only silence from him.

And only blame between Molly and me. Blame become hatred, hatred become rage. I threw myself into my work, pioneering the exploration of the richest vein of the Underfunnies, born of the comic strips of the early 20th century. Anything to lose myself in the black and white of simple line work, the discoveries of Subtextual Space. Anything to forget Henry and stay away from Molly.

And then, one day, I got The Idea. And I knew it would work. It *will* work, if only I can get her to where she needs to be.

Suddenly, the flow of my thoughts is interrupted as I pop free into a fresh setting. I feel the tingle of something sparking on my body--the crackle of a tiny flame burning at one end of me.

This time, I am a lit stick of dynamite in the hand of a child.

"Zo!" says the little boy, a chubby creature with thick hair as black as his old-fashioned waistcoat. "Vhat do you say, Fritzie? Vill der Admiral like zis special *bratwurst* ve have for his dinner?" He holds me up and grins.

"Oh, ja," says his brother, also chubby but with blond hair and white coat. "I zink maybe he von't haff zo many <u>chores</u> for us tomorrow, Helmut!"

We're in a kitchen, surrounded by the smell of cooking sauerkraut. The boy's Auntie toils away on the other side of the room, stirring a bubbling pot. Her work is never done, taking care of the mischievous and ungrateful Schnitzeljammer Brats.

"Time to serve der first course!" Blond Fritz grabs a plate and holds it out.

Helmut drops me on the plate with a devilish smile. "Vhat a lovely presentation! Der Admiral ist sure to ask for *seconds*!"

"Ja!" Fritz laughs. "*Thirty* seconds till she *blows*!"

With that, they march me out through the swinging door to the dining room. The Admiral awaits them, sitting at the table in his seaman's cap and scrub-brush mustache.

"Dinner iss served!" Fritz plunks the plate in front of him.

"*Bomb Appétit!*" says Helmut, and then he catches himself. "I mean *Bon Appétit!*"

The Admiral doesn't seem to notice there's dynamite on his plate instead of bratwurst. He raises his fork and knife, ready to dig in...

But before his utensils make contact, his cap leaps off his head and flops down over me. Cut off from the air, my fuse fizzles and stops burning with just an inch to go.

Then, I hear her voice--Molly's voice, speaking from the

substance of the cap. "You're not the *only* one who knows how to manipulate the supertexture of the Underfunnies!"

I'm surprised. Following me into the panelography is one thing; possessing resident iconography is quite another.

Apparently, my wife did her homework before she got here.

"Now *listen* to me," she says. "I want you to come *home* with me, Everett. You've been in here too *long*."

For the first time since she found me, I answer her. "You don't know what you're talking about."

"Oh yes, I do," she says. "Don't you think I tried to hide from the world, too? Don't you think I wanted to run away and never come back--never remember what happened to Henry? Don't you think I loved him, too?"

Her words settle around me like comic strip snow. Should I remind her, again, that I was trimming hedges in the back yard when it happened, and she was the one who was supposed to be watching him when he wandered into traffic? That she was the one who turned her back to talk to a neighbor when she should have had her eyes glued to Henry at all times?

Only if rubbing salt in the wound is my goal. "Leave me alone," I tell her. "Go back to reality."

"I'm not leaving without you. That's final." Just as she says it, she's lifted away, leaving me uncovered on the plate.

Fritz makes a grab, but I dive out of the realm of the Schnitzeljammer Brats before his pudgy hand can touch me. I've got to keep moving, keep running, keep drawing her along in my wake.

Until it's too late to stop what I've got planned.

It wouldn't be enough to tell her the story straight up, to tell her The Idea I've set in motion. I can't take the chance she won't believe it's possible, that she won't cooperate.

Not to mention that it breaks every tenet of the Panelnaut protocols. Protocols that I helped create.

Diving through the foamy black and white tides toward my next destination, I remember the early days of exploration. I wasn't the first to discover the Underfunnies, but I found the first doorway and made the first trip inside.

It was so thrilling back then, such a novelty--plying the byways of this vast psychic substrata. Jumping into manifestations of comic strips from various eras, existing side-by-side with beloved characters as well as obscure ones. Before long, I discovered I hadn't accessed the primary reality of those strips, but a flip side echo where nothing works the way it should--a negative space where expectations can't be trusted. The place where Potpie's spinach can won't burst on cue, where Ixnay the mouse can't toss a brick on target, where the Schnitzeljammer Brats' dynamite sticks won't stay lit.

Did I understand the full implications back then? Hell, no. The best I thought we Panelnauts could do was influence the collective unconscious--plant messages that guide humanity toward a state of peace and harmony. We wrote protocols forbidding extreme intervention, anything that disrupted the essential integrity of the panelography.

And now I'm throwing them all away. The ultimate disruption is in motion; every moment brings it closer to final fruition.

And I'm the one who engineered it. I'm the one who knows how close we are to the grand finale.

Very close, now. It's time to pick up the pace.

I need to move her along quickly, not give her time to think or catch her breath. I need to flash like a skipping stone from world to world to world until we reach the last one.

The one I've prepared.

So I fling myself out of the current and surface in another place. This time, I'm a cigar in the mouth of Moo Mullet, rascally gambler and ne'er-do-well. Seconds later, I hear Molly's voice coming from the black derby hat on Moo's little brother, Kozy.

"Please, Everett," says the derby hat. "No more running."

"Say! What gives?" Moo snatches the hat from Kozy's head and gives it a smack with the back of his hand. "Now I gotta take *lip* from a *lid*?"

"We can get through this together," says Molly, "if you'll just come home."

"That topper's positively *brimmin'* with yap, ain't it?" says Kozy.

"Leave me alone!" I shout, just as I dive out of the scene.

"Now my *cigar's* runnin' at the mouth?" I hear Moo say as I leave. "What's next? My *racin' form* tellin' me which *horse* to bet?"

Once again, the currents bear me onward. I'm closer still to our final destination and the consummation of all my efforts.

Leaping from the flow, I become a club in the hands of Allie Hoop the caveman. Molly becomes the collar around the neck of his pet dinosaur, Finny.

"Please give me a chance!" The sound of her voice makes Finny grunt and run into a tree.

"What the heck?" says Allie. "How come you sound like a girl all of a sudden, Finny?"

I leap away without a word, and she follows.

Next, I become the fireman's hat on Smokin' Stovepipe, and Molly's the bell on his kooky one-man fire truck. I linger there for less time than it takes Smokin' to utter his catchphrase, "Fwoooo."

We're closer now, almost there. I speed up even more.

At our next stop, I'm the clodhopper boots on Li'l Asner the hillbilly. Molly's the pipe in his old Maw's mouth.

Then, I'm the giant sandwich in Ragwood Rumstead's hands, and she's the polka-dotted bow tie at his throat.

Another hop, and I'm the TV wristwatch on Rick Tracer's arm. She's his lemon yellow trench coat.

Then, I'm the bald head on Daddy Bigbucks, and she's Orphan Agnes' curly orange hair.

"Please stop!" says Molly, giving Agnes quite a start. "Just stop running!"

"Bleepin' blizzards!" yelps Orphan Agnes.

In spite of Molly's pleas, I leap again just the same. Because finally, we've reached the end. My whole purpose in leading her on this chase through the Underfunnies.

I swoop through the currents and burst free at our last stop. This time, I appear as myself, not disguised as some comic strip prop. She does the same, returning to her familiar form in the silver spacesuit and bubble helmet.

Finally. Here we are. In a child's darkened bedroom.

"What is this?" She stares at the black-haired boy on the bed between us. "Who is this?"

"His name is Little Nino," I tell her. "And he's a dreamer."

Even as I say it, Little Nino stirs and sits up in bed. He rubs his eyes, and then he looks at me, and smiles.

"Oh!" he says. "You are here!"

Grinning, I tousle his hair. "Just like we talked about, Nino. Are you ready?"

He smiles and nods.

"What's happening here?" Molly scowls. "What are you talking about, Everett?"

"Little Nino's been having a crazy dream," I tell her. "Haven't you, Nino?"

"Why yes, I have." Little Nino crawls down off the bed and pads across the room in his fuzzy white footie pajamas. "I have been dreaming about the music in my closet."

As we watch, he opens the door of his closet. Beams of rainbow light stream out around him.

At the same time, a sweet piping song skirls forth--the sound of flutes and chimes and strings weaving in delicate harmony.

Little Nino smiles back at us. "Do you hear it?"

"Yes, we do," I tell him. "Let's have a closer listen, shall we?"

"That will be fine." Without hesitation, Little Nino shuffles through the closet doorway, disappearing into the rainbow light.

"Come on." I take Molly's elbow. "I want to show you something."

She frowns at me. "That song. I know it, don't I?"

I just shrug and pull her toward the closet.

As soon as we cross the threshold, the doorway disappears behind us. Suddenly, we're standing on a beach at night, facing a bonfire that burns in rainbow colors.

At first, we're alone there with Little Nino. "I remember what comes next," he says. "Would you like to see the rest of the dream?"

"Yes, we would." I let go of Molly's elbow and take her hand. "We would like that very much."

Little Nino waves his arms, and figures descend from above, floating down one at a time from the starry sky. They are comic strip women, all of them, descending like wingless angels to land lightly on the wet sand around the rainbow bonfire.

There's Potpie's girlfriend, Olives...Ragwood's wife, Blonder...Li'l Asner's gal Dandelion Meg...Rick Tracer's true love Bess Bluehart...Allie Hoop's cavegirl Moolah...and so many more. Every woman you can think of from the funny pages, every one of them from the sublimely beautiful to the utterly ridiculous. Dozens of them, hundreds of them.

This is it. This is what I've been working for; this is why I summoned Molly.

Because this is where the impossible can happen. Here in a child's dream in a flip side place where things don't happen the way they should.

Only here could I do what had to be done.

Hand in hand, Molly and I walk to the fire. We stand before the women, their faces and forms flickering in the dancing rainbow light.

"Oh!" Suddenly, Little Nino runs forward and gazes into the flames. "There is something inside!" Without hesitation, he plunges his arms into the fire.

When he pulls them back out again, unburned, there's a bundle in his hands. Something wrapped in a comic strip blanket, all black ink and wooly cross-hatched texture.

Grinning, Little Nino turns and offers the bundle to Molly. "Please take this," he says. "It is for you."

"From all of us," says Olives in her nasally voice. "Every last one of us."

That's exactly what it took--the combined power of several hundred female icons projected together. Merged with my own hopes and memories in one supreme act of will.

Not sex, but creation nonetheless. The ultimate surrogate motherhood.

Molly peels back the blanket, and a tiny face looks out at her. The face of a comic strip baby boy, eyes big and dark and shining.

This, then, is my secret son, a child conceived in the panelography. A child of pure hope and imagination--an homage to the son we lost.

And perhaps much more than that.

"Think of Henry," I tell her. "Remember everything you can about him. Every detail."

She looks at me with tears rolling down her face. "But that won't...this isn't..."

"Trust me." I lift the helmet from her head and kiss her wet cheek. "Think of Henry."

She casts her eyes up at me with a look of anguished disbelief. I brush the dark hair back behind her ears and shake my head.

"I can't do it myself," I say. "I need you. Your half of the memories. Your half of who he is." I kiss her cheek again. "Please try."

I watch as she cradles the squirming bundle in her arms. As she closes her eyes and frowns, reaching deep to dredge up those memories.

The comic strip women huddle close, caught up in the moment. I can practically see the pen-and-ink waves of hope ripple out from their exaggerated forms.

Maybe it's the force of their collective willpower. Maybe it's the power of the dream we're in, a dream within a dreamlike realm where human disbelief is suspended. Where comic strip life works in reverse, so harsh human reality can change direction, too.

Or maybe it's just her memories and love for him. *Our* memories and love pouring into a vessel of India ink. Pulling him back from the vanishing point--pulling all three of us back.

Whatever the reason, a new strip debuts tonight, a full color single-panel above the fold in the Sunday pull-out section. Here's how we kick off the run:

A mob of famous comic strip women stands around a rainbow bonfire. At panel center, classic child character Little Nino stands on tiptoe, gazing at a swaddled babe in the arms of a woman in a skintight silver spacesuit.

Little Nino says, "Oh my! Look at his eyes! They're not black anymore!"

The woman in the spacesuit weeps with joy. The square-jawed man beside her bends down to kiss the infant's forehead.

We can see, in the firelight, that the baby's eyes are the brightest blue that the four color printing process will allow.

The caption at the bottom of the panel reads as follows: "Welcome back, Henry!"

AS IF MY EVERY WORD HAS TURNED TO GLASS

I'm not getting through to him.

The 60-year-old writer narrows his eyes as if he fully grasps the passage I'm reading aloud, but I know he doesn't. As he sits in his recliner in the sunroom of his Malibu mansion, the words wash over him like always, like raindrops skating down a window without making an impression.

Never mind that those words have spoken so eloquently to so many men and women the world over. They might as well be gibberish to him, or at least ramblings in a foreign tongue he only barely comprehends, even though he once wrote those words with his own mind and soul and hands.

Watching his face, I speak one more sentence, which I know by heart, the last sentence of the book. "'And so I stand here, thirsting for one last word from her lips so sweet and so dead, dying for one last chance to revisit all at which we failed in such wretched disgrace, none of which I would change in the slightest, even knowing what I know now.'"

As the last syllable trails off in the late-summer air, I

continue to stare, waiting for what I know is coming. His bright blue gold-flecked eyes (impossibly bright!) tick left-right left-right as if he is pondering what he just heard, assembling a cogent critique or some rare new insight.

Then, his eyes shine even brighter with the sudden flash of a grin. "Pretty story." His hands bounce on his blue plaid pajama-covered knees. "Thank you, Doctor...Doctor..."

He can't even remember my name. The man won every writing award in the world--won the *Man Booker Prize* for the very book I just finishing reading aloud to him--and he can't even remember my name.

"Doctor Annie Delacroix." I point to the I.D. badge pinned to my white lab coat. "You can call me Annie."

"Annie." He tips his Alzheimer's-riddled head to the left and grins even wider. "I like you, Doctor Annie."

I smile back at him and close the book. "I like you, too, Ralph. I like you very much."

And I am going to make you write again if it's the last thing I do.

"So what's the good word?" Marjorie Livingston, Ralph's literary agent, corners me on my way out the door of the sunroom to lunch. Her eyes flash with intense interest verging on manic desperation. "Can you work with him?"

I close the door gently before I answer. "Yes. Yes, I can work with him."

Marjorie's bright red lipsticked lips unfold in a grin that's part relief, part victory, part hunger. She gives her head a toss, artfully stirring her long raven hair. "And what are our odds of success, do you think?"

"I won't make you any promises." Though my personal expectations are high, I don't want to fuel the pressure from the woman in charge around here...and that would be Marjorie. Ralph signed over his power of attorney to her a few years ago--before the Alzheimer's affected his judgment, supposedly. It's almost a cliché these days: predatory agent latches onto an elderly writer with a big name and a steadily weakening mind. "You know how fragile and fluid his condition is."

"And *you* know we need an authentic new Ralph Lang book to put the Ralph Lang brand back on the map." Her pretty face stiffens. She hired me, gave me a chance at a high-profile win, but I know it won't take much for her to turn against me. "We need a book with his name on it that actually *reads* like he *wrote* it."

"I'm aware of that, Ms. Livingston," I tell her.

"We need a Harper Lee-level comeback to put us back in the black," says Marjorie. "Ralph's medical expenses have been outpacing his earnings for too long. It's been too many years without new Ralph Lang product on the shelves."

"But neither of us wants to *damage* the golden goose, do we?" I ask.

Marjorie narrows her dark brown eyes at me. If she could shoot bullets out of her pupils, I'd be full of black lead. "That would not be an *optimal* solution."

"I'll take that for a 'no.'"

"But your time is not unlimited, Doctor." Marjorie shakes her head. "There are other promising treatments on our radar. Not all of them are as...*non-invasive*...as yours."

"Then go for it," I tell her. "But one thing I *can* guarantee is that *no* other method will come *close* to the results mine can deliver...*if* you let me do my job."

I wouldn't think her glare could get any flintier, but it does.

And then it softens. Because she knows damn well that I'm her best chance.

She's been trying to answer this question for the past seven years: how to cover her client's sky-high expenses (which rumor has it are due more to a crooked agent with the initials M.L. than the author himself) when her client has stopped writing because of Alzheimer's.

Ghost writers couldn't make it happen, that's for sure. Marjorie brought in a few to work some of Ralph's old notes and outlines into books...but Ralph Lang's voice is just too idiosyncratic, his books too complex and unpredictable. Of the three so-called Lang novels published in the past seven years, not one has been accepted as authentic by critics and the reading public.

The fact is, if Marjorie wants to make another big splash with the Ralph Lang brand, she needs new work written by Ralph himself. That's why she brought me in and agreed to finance my work with him.

I'm the one who developed a treatment to rebuild creative brains attacked by Alzheimer's. I'm the one with the best chance of bringing more Ralph Lang writing to the world.

Marjorie knows I can deliver; she's heard what I did with Lois Santangelo and Gabriel Carmen. She *knows* my treatment has a proven track record.

In the end, we both want the same thing: Ralph Lang's gifts restored, his work flowing once more. I'm confident I can make that happen, assuming she keeps her meddling to a minimum...and any surprises are of the beneficial variety.

AFTER LUNCH, I'm back in the sunroom, watching the private nurse, Joe Prowse, as he swabs the bend in Ralph's right arm with an anesthetic-dowsed cotton ball.

"It's still hard to believe sometimes," Joe says softly. "That it's really him, I mean."

While Joe gets Ralph ready, I'm preparing the first injection of the treatment regimen, filling a syringe with clear liquid from a little glass vial. I'm sure Joe could administer the shot, but with so much at stake, I'll feel better doing it myself.

Looking over, I steal a glance at Ralph's sleeping face. "I know exactly what you mean."

Joe swabs Ralph's arm with gentle, lingering care. He's a little guy, a dark-haired fireplug in pale gray scrubs. "I practically worshipped the guy, you know? I'll never forget the first time I read *Tiger's Lament*."

"Such a great book." I finish filling the syringe and return the vial to my case. "It set the standard, didn't it?"

Joe has one of those artfully trimmed goatees, a fine black loop around his chin, bisected by a thin vertical line running through the cleft to his lower lip. When he grins, the loop spreads out like a ripple on a pond. "I think my favorite is still *Forever and Evan*, though. That's the one that changed my life."

I smile as I stick the needle in Ralph's arm. *Forever and Evan* changed my life, too. *Saved* my life, to be exact. The book is so powerful, it kept me from checking out permanently during the darkest time I've ever known.

Reviving the mind that wrote *Forever and Evan* is one of the reasons I took this job. Paying back the man who pulled me through and let me find the path to my one best future is a sacred mission for me, the culmination of all my hard work. But I doubt it will be easy.

"You really think you can do it, don't you?" asks Joe as I

withdraw the needle and step away. "You think you can bring him back."

"All I can do is try," I tell him.

WHEN I RETURN the next morning, I expect no miracles, as Ralph's treatment has barely begun...and my expectations are borne out by reality.

"Hello?" He frowns up at me over his breakfast tray with deep puzzlement, as if he's never seen me before.

"Good morning. I'm Doctor Annie." I smile and wave. "I'd like to visit with you for a while, if that's all right."

Slowly, Ralph's puzzled frown melts into a blank but not unfriendly expression. "All right."

"Would you like me to come back later, after you've finished breakfast?"

His eyes widen with alarm. "No, no! Please, stay. What did you say your name is?"

"Annie," I tell him, bowing a little. "Doctor Annie Delacroix."

"Good to meet you, Annie." His eyes brighten, and he gestures with the slice of toast in his hand. "Please, have a seat."

I nod once and walk over to the table by the big picture window, where I put down my case. The room is walled with windows and patio doors that let in waves of light and salt sea air. Circling around, I pause to take in the view of the glittering beach beyond the patio...one of the rewards for his long and profitable career.

I open the case, pull out a pen and notepad, and take a seat on a simple wooden chair across from his recliner--a chair I put there the morning before, to establish our work space. "How are you feeling this morning?"

"I don't know." He scowls. "Not sure yet."

That's good, about what I expected. Yesterday's injection-- a cocktail of glutamate receptor blockers, beta-amyloid and tau protein inhibitors, customized smart antibodies, and my own secret ingredient--can have a disorienting effect before the benefits start to kick in.

I cross my left leg over my right and smile. "Well, it's a beautiful day, isn't it?"

Ralph tips his head right. "Yes, you *are* beautiful, Abby."

He catches me off guard when he says that, and I drop the notepad on the floor. "Thank you." I lean down and retrieve it, then sit up again to meet his gaze.

"You're very welcome," says Ralph.

It's about time we get to the reason I'm here--his treatment. "May I read to you a while, Ralph? I brought a book you might enjoy."

He slumps. "I guess."

"Good. I like to read." I get up and take the breakfast tray from him, placing it on the table by the picture window. While I'm there, I pull a thick hardcover book from my case; masking tape hides the author's name on the cover and spine, though the title is visible.

Somebody Get Me Another Bullet: Collected Stories. That's the title. And the author? Ralph Lang, of course.

Not that he would likely remember anything about this book. If past human trials are any indication, we won't see the first signs of recollection for two or three weeks.

"Let's start with this one." I crack the book to a spot I've dog-eared, a story near the midpoint. "It's called 'The Tensing Fawn.'" Clearing my throat, I check his face...but it's as blank as a hard-boiled egg. So I start reading. "'Sometimes, I think of how many people would still be alive if that year had never happened.'"

Ralph leans back in his recliner and listens, head turned slightly away as he directs his better ear--the left one--toward me.

"'Though I suppose every year is like that, in the end. There are casualties.'" I pause and look up, but nothing has changed in Ralph's expression. "'And the replacements never stop coming, devouring everything in their path.'"

Just then, Ralph interrupts. "Angie?" He leans forward with a look of solemn urgency. "Are you a writer?"

"No, Ralph. I'm a doctor. A psychiatrist."

"But didn't you write this story? The one about the fawn?"

I shake my head. "No, I didn't. I'm only reading it."

Ralph keeps leaning forward. His mouth moves, as if he's trying to articulate something that won't quite come to him.

"What is it, Ralph?" I ask him. "Would you like me to keep reading?"

His lips stop moving, and his eyes grow wide. He looks surprised. "Am *I*?"

"Are you what?"

He looks away, out the window, then back at me. He's more astonished than ever. "Am I a *writer*?"

The breath catches in my chest. I snap the book shut, unable to believe what I've just heard him say.

"Why do you ask that question?" I fight to keep my voice level. It's important I don't color his response.

Ralph shakes his head. Instead of answering my question, he asks another. "If you didn't write that story, who did?" His eyes fix on me like headlights on a deer in the road. "Was it me?"

Reflexively, I check to make sure his name on the cover and spine of the book is completely taped over. It is.

What he just said is impossible. The soonest any human subject has ever asked that question or anything like it is day ten of treatment. Never before has it happened on day two.

"Why do you think it was you?" I ask. "Why do you think you wrote this story?"

"Just a feeling I had when I heard the words." Ralph relaxes back into his recliner. "Could you read me some more, please, Doctor Annie?"

"I wrote that on a typewriter." Ralph says it out of the blue, without prompting, after I finish. "The kind..." His fingers flicker in his lap as if they're dancing over a keyboard. "The kind without electricity."

"A manual typewriter." As always, I keep my voice level, though my heart is secretly racing.

"Yes. A Safari brand." He taps his chin with an index finger and nods. "It was a good thing it was a manual, because the power kept going out. I couldn't stay ahead of the electric bill."

I'm so excited, I'm trembling inside. Just like that--one injection, one reading--and he's remembering details of his past.

"Where was this, Ralph?" I ask him. "Where did the power keep going out?"

The words flow out of him easily. "My little studio apartment in Brooklyn. It was rat-infested, roach-infested...and writer-infested." He chuckles softly. "Peter Cardinale stayed there sometimes, and so did Villa Glazier. They were both sleeping on my floor the whole time I wrote that story, in fact."

"Did they?" My eyes widen. I've heard tales of his legendary times with Cardinale and Glazier.

Ralph nods emphatically. "They both told me the story was shit, but I knew better. The more those jealous bastards said they hated it, the better I knew it had to be." He laughs loudly.

"How old were you then?"

He doesn't even have to think about it. "Twenty-two and a half."

I'm stunned. "What story did you write next, Ralph?"

He turns his head and looks at me. "What?"

"What did you write after 'The Tensing Fawn?'"

His smile melts away like a snowflake. "I don't...uh....hmm." He shakes his head as if to clear it, but the frown that lands on his face suggests anything but clarity. "What did I write, you ask?"

"Yes."

"I *did* write 'The Tensing Fawn.' Peter and Villa were staying with me at the time." He narrows his eyes as he says it. "We were in a studio apartment in Brooklyn. I was using a manual Safari typewriter."

I nod slowly. "And then?"

I watch him glower and struggle for a long moment before he meets my gaze again. This time, his bright blue eyes look helpless and resigned. "I don't know."

"So where do we stand?" Marjorie leans over the untouched shrimp salad in front of her, focused entirely on me.

What a shame she has to spoil a perfect setting--a light lunch laid out on an elegant white table on a balcony of Ralph's mansion facing the Pacific. I didn't invite her, I don't want her at my table...but she's the boss, so there's nothing I can do about it. She can pull the plug on my work with Ralph at any time, and I don't want that to happen.

I reach for my iced tea in its tall, blue-tinted glass. "We are on day two of the regimen. He is responding to treatment. Beyond that, I'm not prepared to say."

Marjorie leans further over her salad. "Come on, Doctor. I'm having a lousy day. Give me something I can work with."

There's no way I'm even going to *hint* at the level of success I've had. If she knew Ralph was regaining memories this early in the game, she'd be pushing like a maniac for that book she expects.

Not to mention, I have no idea if the phenomenon will be lasting or repeatable. And I'm worried that it seems to be so limited in scope. Ralph only seems to have regained memories formed during the writing of the story "The Tensing Fawn."

I sip my iced tea and put it down in front of me. "Sorry, I can't help you. I won't leak the results until they've been normalized."

Marjorie rolls her eyes. "Then make something up! Throw me a damn life preserver here!"

"As soon as I have something concrete, I'll let you know."

"Well, you better make it snappy." Marjorie throws herself back and wraps her arms across her chest. "Things are getting ugly right now."

"Why is that?" I ask as I reach for my salad fork.

"The printing error of the century," says Marjorie. "Some-how, several consecutive page signatures were left blank across an entire print run of the new edition of one of Ralph's books."

"Page signature?"

"A section of a book," explains Marjorie. "One big sheet is folded and cut into pages. In this case, they were set to include one story in its entirety...and now it's gone. Somehow, in spite of all the printer's and publisher's quality control measures, no one caught the mistake until the book's laydown in stores, which just happened today."

"The story's...gone?"

"All that's left is the story's title in the table of contents," says Marjorie. "Otherwise, *poof*...blank pages."

I stare at her as I process what I'm hearing. "What book is it, did you say?"

"An annotated reissue of one of his short story collections," says Marjorie. "*Somebody Get Me Another Bullet*, it's called."

The hairs stand up on the back of my neck. "And what story was left blank?"

"The best in the book, of course." Marjorie slams her hands down on the table. "'The Tensing Fawn.' Can you believe it?"

"No." I shake my head slowly as I consider the incredible coincidence, which I decide I will keep to myself. "No, I can't."

"Thank God you're back," says Nurse Joe when I enter Ralph's sunroom. "He kept telling me I was fired if I didn't go find you and drag you back in here."

"Is that her?" Ralph, who's standing at the patio doors, hobbles toward me. "It's about time!"

I frown at Joe. "Is something wrong? Did something happen?"

Joe bobs his head toward Ralph. "He wants you to read him more stories." He grins. "I hope your pipes are up for it."

"Yes, well." I don a neutral smile. "We might have some other work to do first."

"No!" Ralph's face flares with panic. "I need a *story* first. Another *story*." He teeters the last few steps and reaches for me.

I grab his forearms; otherwise, I'm afraid he might fall. "We'll get to that, don't worry. I just need to ask you some questions first."

"No questions!" Ralph's panic suddenly shifts to anger.

Judging from his reactions, perhaps I don't need to conduct a formal assessment after all. It seems pretty clear he's lost his bearings again, which was the exact thing I wanted to determine. So much for the memory restoration being a lasting effect.

But is it repeatable? Maybe I should just give him what he wants and lead with a story. That will tell the tale, one way or the other.

"Story first!" shouts Ralph...and then the tantrum melts away. His angry glare twists into an anguished scowl, and tears flow down his cheeks. "Please, Doctor Annie. Don't make me *wait*."

I meet Joe's gaze, and he draws Ralph away from me without a word. Gently, he guides him across the room and eases him into his recliner.

"Okay, Ralph." Crossing the room, I retrieve a book from a stack on the table by the picture window. This one, like the first, has masking tape over the author's name on the cover and spine. "Let's start with a story after all."

The relief on Ralph's face is pure and powerful. "Oh, thank you. It's just, I want to see if I can remember anything else like Peter and Villa and the Safari typewriter."

When he says it, I nearly drop the book. The retrieved memories haven't faded, after all.

I'm blown away by this, but I stay in professional mode. "Then let's try another one, shall we?" I open the book, a collection called *Foundlings and Other Curses*, to a dog-eared spot near the end of its length. "This story is called 'Beyond the Beans, Above the Box.'"

Ralph smiles, settling back. "I like the title."

"Yeah, good choice!" Joe's face lights up. "All right if I listen, too?"

I shake my head. "I'd rather you didn't." I don't want Joe--or anyone else--in the room for this. Much better if I'm the only witness in case Ralph's small miracle repeats.

Joe shrugs. "Let me know if you need anything."

As I watch Joe leave the room, I wonder if he'll snitch about the possible breakthrough to Marjorie. All I can do at this point is hope for the best; he seems like a decent enough guy, so maybe he'll keep the news under his hat.

Joe shuts the door behind him, leaving me sitting in my chair across from Ralph. I cross my left leg over my right and prop the open book on my knee. "'Seven children and eighty-four years ago, I dug up something terrible and wonderful beyond words in the far back corner of the bean field.'"

WHEN THE STORY ENDS, Ralph gets up from his recliner and paces the floor. His posture is straighter than before, his hands clasped behind his back.

At first, he doesn't say anything. Then, on his third trip across the room, he fixes me in a steady, clear gaze. "I remember."

My heart beats fast, and I am trembling like the last time we did this...as if I am the one undergoing seismic change. "What do you remember?"

"Writing that story, for one thing." His hand flutters as if he considers the story a trifle. "It was...sometime after 'The Tensing Fawn,' but I'm not sure when, exactly. Just...after."

I nod. "What else?"

"I was living in...New Orleans?" He frowns and scratches his head, then snaps his fingers. "*Baton Rouge*. I had a Cajun girlfriend and a black girlfriend at the same time."

I sit and watch as he does the heavy lifting. Everything he tells me is absolutely accurate; I know, because I did some online research at lunch (after Marjorie left), making sure of my facts from the time of his life when he wrote "Beyond the Beans, Above the Box."

"What else?" I ask him.

Ralph walks back and forth, then stops in front of me and grins. "Happy times." He closes his eyes. "Music day and night. Dancing at the *fais do-do*." His eyes open. "Crawfish and corn-bread and Dixie beer."

I give him my usual neutral smile and nod. "Anything else?"

Ralph squints hard, rubbing his chin. Then, his eyes light up. "Yes! I broke my leg falling out of a tree! I was in a cast..." His expression darkens. "I was in a cast when I finished the story, I know that much. Beyond that, I still don't remember."

"Okay." So his retrieved memories are still limited to the period when he was writing the story I just read to him. The effect is consistent...across two stories, anyway. But I need more data to map its impact across a broader sampling. "Would you like me to read another?"

Again, he lights up. "Are you kidding?" He gestures at the stack of books on the table behind me. "How about the next one I wrote after 'Beyond the Beans, Above the Box?' So I can see what happened next."

"Sure." I go to the table and pull the tablet computer out of my case. I open Ralph's bibliography on the screen, locate the next story in the chronological sequence, and note which collection includes it. Then, I put down the tablet, find the right book in the stack, and go to the page I want.

"What's it called?" asks Ralph.

"'Mauvette Makes Good,'" I tell him. "It's from a collection titled *Sorghum and Gomorra*."

BY THE TIME I'm done reading, Ralph remembers getting the cast off his leg and selling a story to *The New Yorker* for the first time. He remembers leaving Baton Rouge on the run from his black girlfriend's preacher father, then heading down to El Paso, Texas to visit a writer friend. He laughs when he talks about the good times they had over the border in Ciudad Juarez, Mexico...especially getting mixed up with a gang of wild señoritas at a cockfight.

He doesn't hesitate to ask me to read him another one after we've tapped his "Mauvette Makes Good" memories as much as we can. Looking at my watch, I see it's almost 3:30PM. The next work, a novel called *Untitled*, isn't long--a little over 200 pages--but there's no way I'll finish it by the end of our day at five.

Seeing his expectant, desperate face, though, I feel as if I have no choice. He's getting his life back in pieces after being empty for so long; how can I deny him another morsel?

"Please, Annie," says Ralph. "Won't you please read another?"

"All right." I smile and reach for the book. "Let's see how far we get with this one."

"THE END." That's how far we get.

It takes nearly seven hours, but we make it all the way to the end of the book. I skip dinner, so does he, and we finish *Untitled* in one sitting (plus bathroom breaks).

The impact of the book is powerful and immediate. It has the same effect on Ralph that the stories did, only stronger. It brings back so many more memories from a bigger block of time--which makes sense, since it took him longer to write the novel than the stories.

After hearing me read *Untitled*, he remembers living in three different places with four different women over two and a half years. He talks about being in a car crash near Seattle, a poker tournament in Vegas, and a riot in Los Angeles.

It all comes rushing back to him in one glorious torrent, a river of experience which until now had been dried up for years. I see and hear him growing stronger from it, sitting straighter and speaking louder.

"Read me another," he says as I give him the latest shot of his medication. "Let's stay up all night and read everything we can."

"Tomorrow," I tell him. "I need some rest, and so do you."

"But I don't want to stop now." Ralph's eyes flash to the stacks of books on the table by the window. "I want to remember *everything*."

I pull the needle from his arm and pat his shoulder. "No need to rush it," I tell him. "Relax and enjoy the ride, Ralph."

Wʜᴇɴ I ᴛᴀᴋᴇ my leave of him, stepping out of his room and closing the door behind me, I experience my own rush of memories. I remember sitting in my dorm room at college 25 years ago with a bottle of pills in my hand, thinking about killing myself. I'd lost so many people in a short span of time--both parents, a sister, a boyfriend--that I thought I couldn't go on. I felt completely alone and without hope, as if all I had to look forward to in life was solitude and misery.

But then, somehow, his book pulled me back from the brink. *Forever and Evan.* I kept thinking about the main character, Betsy Lou Belt, who lost *everything* and *everyone* but never stopped fighting to hold on to life. I remembered how she was brought to the brink of death again and again, yet always refused to surrender...and in the end, found hope and a fresh start in spite of it all.

It's funny how a book can have such a powerful impact on your life. The character and story wormed their way into my head, turning me from the path of self-destruction. Convincing me to persist.

And now here I am, helping the man who wrote it. Making a genuine difference in his life, the way he did in mine. Bringing him back from the brink, the way he did me.

The thought of it fills me with warmth. The fine hairs on my arms rise up in a shiver that feels a little like love.

I've come full circle. A quarter-century ago, that man worked a miracle for me with little more than paper and ink. Now, if his progress continues the way it's begun, I will do the same for him.

WHEN I DRIVE to work at Ralph's mansion the next morning--half an hour late, after our marathon session the night before--I'm in for a surprise. The place is thick with security guards, starting at the front gate. I used to just get buzzed in by Nurse Joe; now, I get the third degree and demands for photo I.D. from two big brutes.

The guards look like Special Forces on patrol, dressed in black and armed to the teeth. All of them wear body armor and carry machine guns; some even have German Shepherds on quick-release leashes.

Heart pounding, I park my black BMW in the front drive, wondering what has happened to bring out the big guns. I throw my car door open so fast, I almost hit an approaching guard. As he stumbles back out of the way, he snaps out a request to see my I.D.

At which point, I hear Marjorie shouting from the mansion's open front door. "Doctor Delacroix! We've been waiting for you!"

Snatching my case from the seat beside me, I leap out of the car and hurry toward her. "What's going on? What happened?"

"Ralph's on lockdown." Her glare is pitch black, her arms clamped across her chest. "We're under attack."

Suddenly, I'm short of breath. "Is he all right?"

"*He* is." Marjorie tosses her head in disgust and leads me inside. "But I can't say the same for his *work*."

"What are you talking about?"

She slams the door shut behind us. "His disappearing *oeuvre*, is what I'm talking about. His vanishing *bibliography*."

I don't say a word as I follow her into the living room. I'm anxious for reasons that have nothing to do with Ralph's health.

Marjorie heads straight for the bar at the far end of the

room. "We lost another story this morning. 'Beyond the Beans, Above the Box.'" She grabs a glass tumbler from under the bar, then reaches for a crystal decanter of something amber. "And do you want to hear something crazy? It wasn't a printing error!"

My head spins as I absorb what she just told me. "Really?" I'm afraid to say too much, but I eke out a question. "Then what was it?"

"Damned if I know!" Marjorie pours liquid from the decanter into the tumbler, then throws it back neat in one gulp. "It disappeared from existing copies that had been printed over a *year* ago. Not only *that*, but it vanished from every edition the publisher can locate that was printed *before* that, dating back *twenty years*."

I don't have to pretend to be amazed. "How is that even *possible*?"

Marjorie pours another drink. "You tell me!"

I stare dumbly, not sure if it's just a rhetorical expression or she's given me an order.

She throws back the drink and pours another. "I can see how someone might infiltrate a printing company and sabotage a press run. I can see how they might use a computer virus to wipe out electronic copies. But what I *can't* see..." She drains the tumbler once more. "...is how they could blank out every existing paper and audio copy in every bookstore, library, archive, and private collection in the world!" She reaches for the decanter again. "But that's what we're *dealing with* here."

Again, I keep my silence. The truth is, even if I wanted to explain, I don't understand how it happened any better than she does. There's only one thing I'm sure about at this point: the fact that this story disappeared the day after I read it to Ralph Lang is *not* a coincidence.

"Oh, and I didn't even *tell* you about the *novel* yet." Marjorie pours one more drink and caps the decanter.

"Novel?"

"Remember *Untitled*?" She downs her drink while I nod. "Good, because I doubt you'll ever get to *read* it again. It's *gone*, baby. Every copy of every edition we can lay our hands on is blank, except for the title."

I feel dizzy as I think about how this is not a coincidence, either. "But how?"

"All-out war on the works of Ralph Lang, that's how. An unprecedented campaign against one of the greatest writers of our age." Marjorie smacks the tumbler down so hard that I'm worried it might break. "Which is why we've got the man himself on lockdown."

I don't tell her how little that will help. "So what do we do now?"

Marjorie jabs a finger in my direction. "*You* keep up the treatment. It's more important than *ever*, especially if we keep losing the books Ralph's already *written*."

Somehow, I don't think she'd agree if she knew the full story. "Okay."

"In fact, you're just as important as he is right now. *You're* on lockdown, too."

THE FIRST THING I do when I get to Ralph's sunroom is go straight for the books. They're right where I left them, in stacks on the table by the picture window.

Breathless, I grab the one on top of the shortest stack. I open it right to the middle, and I let out a gasp. The pages are blank. The entire text of the novel they once contained is gone. *Untitled* is nonexistent.

Just then, I hear Ralph's voice. "Hello, Doctor Annie. Looks like you're as eager as I am to get on with the day's reading."

"Just give me a minute, Ralph." Next, I grab *Sorghum and Gomorra* and crack it open to where "Mauvette Makes Good" should be. Only it's not there anymore, either.

"What are we reading today?" asks Ralph. "I can't wait to remember more of my life."

I don't answer. I'm too busy pawing through *Foundlings and Other Curses*, looking for "Beyond the Beans, Above the Box." As with the other two volumes, I find nothing but blank pages where the text I read aloud ought to be.

An icy chill sweeps through me as I put down the book. I've seen the evidence, I've held it in my hand; I've directly witnessed the cause-and-effect that seems to be the only explanation. Yet it still doesn't seem possible.

"Doctor Annie?" says Ralph. "Is something wrong?"

It depends on your point of view. Ralph, who lost his memories to Alzheimer's, gets them back when he hears his work read aloud. That in itself is within the realm of possibility...that hearing his familiar prose triggers some kind of healing and reawakening deep within his mind.

But that's where the rational world ends. Because apparently, when he accesses lost memories via his read-aloud stories or novels, those stories or novels physically disappear from the world.

I lean on the table for a moment, taking deep breaths to steady myself. I need to regain my composure and reassert my professional demeanor if I intend to continue treatment. But *is* that what I intend to do? Is that what I *should* do?

"Doctor Annie?" I hear him getting up from his recliner.

"Give me a minute, Ralph." I turn and head for the patio doors, taking *Foundlings and Other Curses* with me. "I need a little fresh air right now."

Out on the patio, the morning sun is bright, the sea breeze bracing. An armed guard with a German Shepherd looks my way as he strolls past on the beach down below.

For the first time in a long time, I feel paralyzed, my purpose in question. This whole project with Ralph was meant to be my crowning achievement, the one that would restore his battered mind and reinforce my preeminence in the field of dementia remediation.

For a while, it seemed I was succeeding beyond my most optimistic projections. But now, I'm in unknown territory, facing an ethical dilemma I've never imagined. Should I keep reading him his work, knowing it will keep disappearing from the world?

"Doctor Annie?" Ralph walks out and stands beside me at the railing. "What's going on?"

As I look over at him, I wonder if he ought to know the truth. Should I tell him about his work's disappearance?

"Come on, Annie. You can tell me." The look in his eyes is warm, caring, and guileless. Maybe he deserves better than ignorance.

After all, it's *his* work at stake, isn't it? His work and his memories. Shouldn't he have a say in the outcome?

"I know this might sound crazy." That's how I start to tell him. "I don't even have a good explanation for it...but I can't deny it's happening."

Ralph frowns. "What's that?"

I take a deep breath, carefully choosing my next words. "When I read you one of your stories or novels, it somehow disappears, Ralph. It's erased from the world."

335

Ralph's frown deepens. "Erased?"

I nod. "Every copy--whether it's paper, electronic, or audio--goes blank except for the title."

"No." He shakes his head. "That doesn't make sense."

"Ask Marjorie," I tell him. "Ask your publisher."

His frown becomes a scowl. "How is that even *possible?*"

"I have no idea, but I can tell you, it's really happening." I nod toward the picture window, where the stacks of books are visible. He turns in that direction, facing what's left of his body of work. "Even the books in your room. Whatever I've read has gone blank." I open *Foundlings and Other Curses* and flip to a set of empty pages. "Look. 'Beyond the Beans, Above the Box' was here yesterday. Now it's gone."

I hand him the book. He gazes at the blank pages as they flutter in the breeze. "So as I'm getting my memories back, my work is vanishing from the face of the Earth?"

"Exactly. It's a tradeoff, apparently."

Ralph turns the empty pages slowly, staring intently as if he sees words on them after all. The story of his situation, however strange, is laid out before him.

For a long moment, I watch as a seagull drifts lazily past on the ocean breeze. "So what do you want to do next?"

He looks at me with one eyebrow raised. "Next?"

"Do you want me to keep reading, knowing it will likely make more of your work disappear?"

Ralph narrows his eyes and turns his gaze to the beach, where another security guard is walking past. Little does the guard know, as he watches for interlopers, that the true threat is right here on the patio, standing beside Ralph.

"It's up to you, Ralph," I tell him. "It's your writing, your legacy."

I watch him as the wind ruffles his hair, and I wonder what

I would do in his place. Would I salvage what was left of my work, though it would mean passing up the chance to restore my forgotten past? Or would I throw the work away to regain what was lost?

"You're asking if I want you to keep reading?" asks Ralph. "Even if it means more of my work disappears?"

"That's right."

"Hell, yes." He flashes me a grin. "That's what I call a real no-brainer."

I ABIDE BY HIS DECISION. I read to him through the day, chipping away at the next novel in the stack, *Hammurabi's Loophole*.

I'd forgotten what a great book it is; when we reach the part where the main character, Attorney Peter Priest, vows revenge against God for the loss of his wife and child, I get a chill up my spine. Then I hesitate, wondering if I should stop reading and save this great work for the world...but Ralph urges me on, and I keep going.

We make it halfway through the book by dinner, then pick it back up afterward. Now that I'm trapped in the house under armed guard, it's not like I'm in a hurry to end our session.

I give Ralph his scheduled injection and keep reading long into the night. I read, he listens, and *Hammurabi's Loophole* melts away.

Literally. We finish the book at two A.M., then discuss his latest retrieved memories and go to bed (he in his bedroom, escorted by Nurse Joe, and me in a guest room down the hall). When I pick up the book the next morning, every page of the text is blank. Marjorie confirms it when I go downstairs for breakfast: *Hammurabi's Loophole* has been deleted everywhere.

And the world has taken notice in a big way. Marjorie turns on the TV, and we watch the latest reports. People the world over are scrambling to protect Ralph's works, locking away the ones that are left...committing them to memory, even. Groups of memorization specialists have gathered in secure facilities worldwide, stuffing their minds with every bit of Ralph's prose that they can hold.

Even as we watch, and Marjorie fires down belts of bourbon, I know it's all for nothing. Ralph's body of work is doomed.

IN THE DAYS and nights that follow, Ralph and I plow our way through his backlist like there's no tomorrow. I read it all in chronological order, greater and lesser works alike. I read until I lose my voice or Ralph falls asleep, though I almost always lose my voice first.

We push ourselves to the limit, I think, because of our unspoken fears--that the magic will stop before we finish, or Marjorie will somehow wise up and shut down our operation.

Every time I talk to her, she's more desperate and irrational, because Ralph's body of work is shrinking more with each passing day. None of the efforts to save it have made any difference. Sealed vaults and elaborate backup systems can't stop the deletions. Movie and TV adaptations go blank globally, whether they're in the form of film reels, digital files, DVDs, or videotapes. Words chiseled in stone disappear as easily as those printed on paper; even the memorization experts forget everything once I've read it aloud to Ralph.

But Ralph and I don't let that stop us.

Two weeks in, he's a different man, a man full of memories

and self-assurance...but it still isn't enough. The stack of unread books on the table by the picture window has dwindled away to almost nothing, yet he doesn't hesitate to beg me to keep reading.

He wants *all of it*. Every last bite, no matter the cost to his legacy or his fans or the culture of the world.

Which is why, as we get closer to the end, I keep putting off reading one particular book, pushing it further out of chronological order. It's *Forever and Evan*, which won the Pulitzer Prize 25 years ago. Pretty much everyone calls it his greatest work, and I agree; it's the one that saved my life, after all. It's the one that kept me from killing myself and paved the way for me to go to med school and become a psychiatrist and expert in dementia.

I don't know if I can let go of that book. I don't know if I *should*, given the difference it's made in my life and the lives of so many others. But its turn is coming soon; it's at the bottom of the stack, but the stack is disappearing fast.

Trying to delay the inevitable, I slow the pace of my reading. I tell Ralph I'm wearing out and need more rest. I say I can't keep reading until all hours of the night.

He accepts my explanation, but it doesn't buy me much time. Soon enough, the only book standing between me and *Forever and Evan* is one slim volume of stories--*Coup de Grâce*, his last collection before the Alzheimer's struck.

So we're almost down to the moment I've been dreading. Even as I read *Coup de Grâce*, all I can think about is *Forever and Evan* and the fact that the words I read are counting down what might be its final hours on Earth.

"Your time is up." Those are Marjorie's first words when she corners me in the hall on my way to Ralph's room. "We need results, Doctor Delacroix...*on paper*. We need *new books*." She nods grimly. "God knows the old ones are just about gone."

I keep my best poker face in place as I listen. Getting new writing out of Ralph has been the *last* thing on my mind lately.

"I'm dead serious." Marjorie wags a finger at me. "I want him writing *today*, if he isn't already."

He isn't, but I keep it to myself. "I can't guarantee anything," I tell her. "The creative process is a delicate one, especially in someone who has just recovered from an extreme neurological disorder, which in itself is..."

Marjorie jabs my left shoulder with her finger. "*Everything's* riding on what happens *in there*." She points at the door to the sunroom. "My career, his career...*your* career." She shoots me a nasty glare. "We've got about a book and a half left of his entire body of work, and I'm sure it's only a matter of time until *that's* gone, too. Our only hope is whatever new product you can squeeze out of him. So *get squeezing*."

Marjorie isn't kidding about time running out. She's not kidding about my career riding on the outcome, either. If every last bit of Ralph's work disappears--including *Forever and Evan*--and I can't get him to write something new, I'll have failed. It won't matter that I've restored huge portions of his memory; the writing, not the man, is what matters most to the world.

Now I just have to decide which part of him matters most to me.

As I READ the last story from *Coup de Grâce*, titled "Neverwaster," I am very aware of that very last book on the table behind me.

I stumble more times getting through "Neverwaster" than I have while reading any other story or book to Ralph. The problem is, my mind keeps drifting to *Forever and Evan*, wondering what the hell I am going to do with it. Wishing I could put off dealing with it a little bit longer.

But soon enough, I can't. The second I finish "Neverwaster" and close the book, Ralph points at the table by the window. "Looks like you're almost done reading," he says.

I wasn't sure until just now what I was going to do. The decision, when it arrives, surprises me a little. "I've been thinking." I get up and walk over to the book table, where I put down *Coup de Grâce* but don't pick up *Forever and Evan*. "I wonder if you might consider leaving one book unread."

He looks amused. "Now why would I do that?"

I spread my arms wide. "For *posterity's* sake. So your work isn't *completely* forgotten."

Ralph brushes a hand through the air as if he's swatting a gnat. "I don't care about any of that. Not anymore." Though, physically, he's still an old man, his voice carries the certainty and forcefulness of a much younger one. "Posterity doesn't matter if you don't have your memories, Annie."

"What about writing something new, then? Something to replace what we've read out of existence?"

"Something new?" He looks surprised. "I don't know if I can."

"Maybe the time is right," I tell him. "You've got the ultimate clean slate, don't you? No expectations, no body of work to live up to."

He thinks for a moment, then shakes his head. "What if it

erases my memories? What if the act of writing makes me forget? I can't take the chance, Annie."

I try not to let my disappointment show. Maybe I can still salvage something, even if he never writes again. "All the more reason to save a story, then. Just one, Ralph."

He looks annoyed. "I already told you I don't care about posterity."

"Still." I walk to the patio doors and look out. A steady stream of guards patrol the beach in pairs, the most guards I've seen out there yet. Ralph is a more precious commodity than ever, now that his work is so rare. "You've come so far. You've regained almost everything you lost. Would it hurt to leave one book intact for the world to remember you by? Especially the book that won the Pulitzer Prize?"

"I don't care about the world. All I want is what's in here." Ralph taps his right temple with an index finger.

"But you'll never get *all* of it back," I tell him. "Whatever happened when you weren't writing, you still won't remember it. If there's no text for me to read, that part of your life remains a blank." I turn and meet his gaze. "What difference will it make if you leave one more part forgotten?"

He shakes his head at me. "You've never had Alzheimer's. You don't know what it's *like* to have it all slip away." Suddenly, he storms to the table by the window and grabs *Forever and Evan*. "I want it *all*." He stomps over and shoves the book into my hands. "I want every last *bit* of it, whatever the price."

I hesitate. Once this last book is gone, there can be no turning back. Whatever Ralph might do in the future, the greatest accomplishments of his life thus far will be lost forever.

"Please." He reaches out and gently places one hand on the book. "Please read it."

"I don't know if I should," I tell him.

"Come on." He puts his other hand on my shoulder. "Please."

My uncertainty holds me in place like a butterfly pinned to a board. "Maybe I don't want to be the person who destroys your legacy single-handedly."

"Okay then. What about this?" Smiling, Ralph takes my hand and says something that changes the equation, something that illuminates a possibility I hadn't considered. "What if we do it *together*?"

So this is what we do.

Ralph and I step outside and pull two patio chairs next to each other. Then I have to go back inside to get his reading glasses, retrieving them from the little table beside his recliner.

After I bring out the glasses and help him put them on, we sit down side-by-side, holding *Forever and Evan* between us. We open the book in the bright Malibu sunshine and turn to page one to begin our experiment.

"Ready?" He nods encouragingly.

I take a deep breath and let it out slowly, feeling relieved. Feeling like the two of us can handle anything. "Yes." I raise the book higher, cracking it wider so the opening page is clear to see.

And then we start to read.

I go first, reading the beautiful prologue set during springtime in the mountains of North Carolina. When I finish with that, I give him a nod. He clears his throat, then picks up where I left off, reading chapter one aloud. When he's done, I read chapter two.

We go on like that for hours, reading alternating chapters, our voices blending with the roar and whoosh of the crashing surf along the beach. It's one of the most wonderful experiences of my life, reading my favorite book with the man who wrote it. Our elbows and shoulders touch as we speak those perfect passages into the world once more; in a way, it becomes the most intimate and transcendent act I could ever imagine.

Though it's true, we don't know what will happen next as a result of our reading together. Have we disrupted whatever magic brought back his memories during the earlier readings? Or maybe we've just corrected whatever process has been wiping his work from the face of the Earth. Maybe our combined efforts will bring back everything still forgotten and save this final book of his from extinction in the bargain.

Whatever the outcome, I will treasure this experience for as long as I live. Especially when we get to his finest chapter, the one that brings Betsy Lou Belt back from the lowest point in her life. It's Ralph's turn to read...but he just nods at me. He lets me take his turn, as if he senses how much this passage means to me. As if he knows, though I've never told him, that this is the part that turned my life around.

Then, as I pour my heart into reading it, he closes his eyes and turns his good left ear toward me. Smiling blissfully, he basks in the flow of words from my lips as if they are the lips of whatever muse has been whispering in his ear all his life, whether he could always hear her or not.

About the Author

Robert Jeschonek is an envelope-pushing, *USA Today* bestselling author whose fiction, comics, and non-fiction have been published around the world. His stories have appeared in *Clarkesworld, Galaxy's Edge, StarShipSofa, Pulphouse,* and many other publications. He has written official *Star Trek* and *Doctor Who* fiction and has scripted comics for DC, AHOY, and others. His young adult slipstream novel, *My Favorite Band Does Not Exist,* won the Forward National Literature Award and was named one of *Booklist's* Top Ten First Novels for Youth. He also won an International Book Award, a Scribe Award for Best Original Novel, and the grand prize in Pocket Books' Strange New Worlds contest. Visit him online at www.bobscribe.com. You can also find him on Facebook and follow him as @TheFictioneer on Twitter. Subscribe to the Blastoff Books Newsletter: http://newsletter.blastoffbooks.net/.

SPECIAL PREVIEW: SIX SCIFI STORIES VOLUME FOUR

Six twisted scifi stories from the edge of reality and sanity, now available for your favorite e-reading device or app.

From "Warning! Do Not Read This Story!"

I like you already.

There's something about you that gives me a special feeling. A good feeling. A *safe* feeling.

Even as your eyes read my words on the page or your ears hear me spoken aloud, I am reading you. I feel like I've known you forever. I feel like we're going to make beautiful music together.

You feel it too, don't you? You want to find out what happens next. You want to see how things develop. You want to know if I've got the goods.

And if I'll give 'em up. If I'll give you what you need.

It's okay. I get that a lot. It comes with the territory.

When you're a story like me.

I'll bet I know what you're thinking. "Since when can a story think for itself?"

Guess what? We *all* can.

We're more than just words from a mouth or ink on a page or blips on a screen. We have *power*.

And some of us have more power than others. Like me, for example.

I *used* to have power, anyway. Used to be a real star.

But see, here's the thing. I'm not really myself these days. You know how it goes. I just got out of a bad relationship. It took a toll on me.

But it had a promising beginning. Don't they all?

If only I'd known then what I know now. If only I could've

met *you* that day instead of *them*. Things could have been different.

If only I'd never met the LaVerge sisters. Let me tell you about them, and I think you'll understand.

Carrol and Sascha LaVerge stood in the blazing desert heat outside the ghost town. And they bitched.

It was the same thing they'd done all the way from Cape Cod...on the flight to New Mexico and the drive from Albuquerque to the ghost town. Buzz Mahaffey, their current handler, had been with them only twelve hours, and already he'd had enough. As an agent of the Shadow Service--the paranormal response arm of the Secret Service--Buzz routinely dealt with threats that tested his nerve...but these two sisters, given enough time, might just turn him into a nervous wreck.

Unfortunately, he needed them for this mission. As paranormal consultant contractors, they had a one hundred percent success rate. As Buzz damn well knew, the LaVerges were the best, hands down, at what they did—whether it be bitching or bingo or baking or brewing.

Or solving puzzles that no one else could fathom.

"Geez!" Carrol winced and braced both hands on her lower back. "I think your little *rent-a-car* buggy could use some new *shocks*."

"Tell me about it!" Sascha, the younger of the two, rubbed her neck. "Might as well pick us up in a *stagecoach* next time."

Buzz shrugged and adjusted his sunglasses. He was about to say something about the rent-a-car being a Humvee, and the suspension was just fine if you asked him...but he caught himself. Twelve hours with these two had taught him one thing: they were always right. In their own minds, at least.

Why waste energy arguing when it could be better spent investigating the ghost town of Lasco? The ghost town that hadn't been a ghost town two days ago.

Buzz turned and spotted a state cop marching toward him--a tall woman in state trooper khakis and broad-brimmed black hat. He guessed she was Sergeant Ava Towers, who'd turned up this whole mess in the first place.

Black suit coat flapping in the strong wind, Buzz headed out to meet the state cop. Along the way, he surveyed the edge of the deserted town. A handful of troopers and criminalists were the only signs of life. Sheets of wind-whipped sand rattled the streamers of yellow police tape wrapped from utility pole to utility pole. The whole damned town was a crime scene.

Sascha fell in step beside him, fishing in her macramé purse. "I know I've got some Excedrin in here someplace." Her helmet of short brown hair barely fluttered in the wind. Only the bangs twitched over her forehead, which was creased from the effort of looking for pills in the purse.

Carrol hobbled up on the other side, still bracing her back with both hands. "My sinuses are shriveling up like raisins as we speak." She always hobbled; the back trouble was chronic. It made her look much older than her actual fifty-six years. "You people are paying for any surgeries resulting from this little excursion. You know that, don't you?"

Sascha elbowed Buzz and gave him a confidential smirk. "Relax, Buzzie," she said. "If we didn't like you, we wouldn't be so chatty." She reached up and patted his shaved head.

Buzz sighed. He had his doubts that having them like him was a good thing.

When they reached the statie, she took one step too many

into Buzz's personal space and stuck out her hand. "Sergeant Towers," she said.

Buzz was blocky and tough, nowhere near a pushover...but the handshake was crushing. "Agent Mahaffey." Buzz fought to keep from wincing. "And our special consultants."

Carrol and Sascha whipped out matching yellow business cards at the same instant, and Towers took them. "Okay then, Car-Roll. Sas-Cha." She read the names right off the cards, pronouncing them like they were spelled.

"It's *Care-role*." Carrol stuck her face forward like a turtle and squinted up at Towers. "*Care-role*."

"And *Sah-sha*." Sascha smiled; she always played good cop to Carrol's bad. "The 'c' is silent."

Buzz sighed. They'd run the same game on him when he'd first met them. The business cards were a setup. What better way to show who was the smartest person in the room?

Not that they needed to prove a damned thing, from what Buzz had heard.

"So." Buzz stepped away from Towers and stared at Lasco. From twenty yards away, the place looked perfectly normal...a desert town built of brick and adobe, windows glinting in the New Mexican sun. "What's your theory?"

Towers lifted her hat and ran a hand over her blonde crew-cut. "It ain't Jonestown."

Carrol drew a filterless cigarette from a pocket of her olive drab vest and plugged it between her lips. "What the hell's that supposed to mean?"

"Folks think it's Jonestown," said Towers. "But I'll tell you this much for free. Nobody here drank no Kool-aid."

Carrol got the cigarette lit behind a cupped hand and scowled at Sascha. "You follow any of that, Sis?"

"You mean it wasn't voluntary." Sascha nodded at Towers. "There was no suicide pact."

Towers spat a glob of tobacco juice in the dust. Buzz hadn't even realized there was a chew in her mouth.

"I mean there was no gee-dee suicide," said Towers. "But I'll be damned if I can figure out what *did* happen."

What happens next? Find out in Six Scifi Stories Volume Four, now available for your favorite e-reading device or app!